MW01384101

A POTENTIAL INTERNATIONAL BESTSELLER

ECHOES
FROM FAR

A NOVEL

BY ASHOK MALHOTRA

A sequel to The Golden Sparrow,
the story is set in the early years following the Independence of India,
and chronicles its ambition to acquire political,
scientific and technological prowess.

Printed by

Createspace,
An Amazon.com company

ECHOES FROM FAR;
Copyright © 2014 by Ashok Malhotra
ISBN: 1499717342
ISBN 13: 9781499717341
Library of Congress Control Number: 2014913702
CreateSpace Independent Publishing Platform
North Charleston, South Carolina

This may be a work of fiction, but in the realm of imagination...
everything is real.

ASHOK MALHOTRA

TABLE OF CONTENTS

ACKNOWLEDGEMENTS
AND MUSINGS

My sincere thanks to all my friends and relatives; for without their help, guidance and good wishes, this book would not have been possible. And, as Barry Padolsky reminded me, the responsibility for any faults in the book rests on my shoulders.

THANK YOU my friends:

Tom Sinclair for putting the idea of a novel in my mind; Yodha Singh for showing me the path to novel writing; Barry Padolsky for reading the early draft and words of encouragement and requesting Boyce Richardson O.C. to read it; Boyce Richardson O.C. for taking the time to read the first 60 pages and writing the encouraging letter which fillped me to keep writing; Ramesh Sabharwal for periodic review of the manuscript; Paul Johannsen for the much admired Author's photograph; Emilio Granata, my neighbour of 40 years, for reading the drafts late into the night; Desikan for reading the manuscript and encouragement; Tina Bradshaw for insight and help in proofreading and formatting; Professor O.P. Kohli for reading the manuscript and words of encouragement; Asmat and Nancy Malik for refreshing some of my memories of Lahore; Asha Chopra for reading the manuscript and offering insightful comments; Jaideep Singh, the host of the TV programme, *Aaj Kal*–the Mirror of Our Times, on Vision TV, for the interview about my first novel, *The Golden Sparrow*; Baljit Nagpal for hosting my interview on his radio programme, *Aap Ki Farmaish*, on Radio Carleton, Ottawa; Chandrakanth Arya, the Chief Editor of The Ottawa Star, for the article in The Ottawa Star; Ellen O'Connor, the Editor of The

Ottawa Star, for writing the widely admired article about The Golden Sparrow; and David Whynot for designing and maintaining the websites for The Golden Sparrow and ECHOES FROM FAR.

THANK YOU my family:

Bipin Aurora for reading the drafts twice, in-depth comments and words of wisdom; Rajiv Aurora for facilitating the process;

Malhotras: Anil, Stephanie, Rick and Louise for constant help and encouragement; Rabinder for editorial advice; Subhash and Romina for strategic advice and Rajender for critical appreciation of various incidents in the book.

My grandchildren arrived at different times during the planning and writing of the book; it is their inspiration that kept me going.

Last but not least, but above all, my best friend and my wife, Anjou, for sitting by me evening after evening after evening.... for thousands of hours, reading one page at a time—hot off the screen—day in and day out over a period of some 5 years, while the Indian TV channels, such as NDTV and Zee, playing on the Asian Television Network were immersing my body and soul in the Spirit of India.

IN MEMORY of:

My father, Late Professor Narinder Nath Malhotra, Vice-Principal and Professor of English literature at S.N. Das Gupta College, Lahore and New Delhi; and my mother, Late Mrs. Shakuntala Malhotra, who was a teacher at *Mahila Maha Vidyalay*, Lahore, in the 1940's before the partition. Inspiration for the characters of Surinder Mehra and Kamla Mehra is based on their lives.

Dedication:

This book is dedicated to the the 550 million Citizens of India, who, during April and May, 2014, despite the 40° C heat, stood in lines for hours to cast their vote to select the government of the people, by the people, for the people. Lest we forget!

THE BACK STORY

"Sometimes I feel that I have always existed.
I do not have any memory of not existing"

I am Vikram Mehra

I want to tell you what happened in the first book, **The Golden Sparrow**, before you start reading this book, **ECHOES FROM FAR**.

Meet the Mehra family of Lahore—then in undivided India, now in Pakistan—circa 1940. Surinder, the second of the four sons, is a professor of English literature and teaches at a private coaching college. Unknown to him, he has the Sixth Sense and is able to guess the university examination papers. His uncanny ability, his command of the English language, his tall and handsome looks make him a star in the business of private education—so much so that, among the students, he is lovingly known as *Shakespearewala*. He gets married to Kamla, and they have a son, Vikram. Yes, that is me. As I grow up, I start calling my father, Surinder as Daddyji, and my mother, Kamla as Mummyji.

The World War II has started. The Japanese are closing in on Burma. Mummyji's brother, Daulat Ram, is a prominent businessman of Lahore. He represents foreign companies in India. The British Intelligence suspects that the Japanese have sympathizers in India. David Rankin, the police commissioner of Lahore, has recruited Daulat Ram to spy on the local community.

Surinder is in great demand as a tutor and works hard day and night to take advantage of the high tide and accumulate a fortune. However, destiny has something else in store for him. In early 1943, his health starts to deteriorate. Mummyji's brother, Daulat Ram, takes him to his own doctor for examination.

He is diagnosed with TB and is advised by his doctor to go to a hill station, as the air around the pine trees is known to be curative. They are devastated to hear of the diagnosis, as it is considered a death sentence. They decide to go to Srinagar, about 500 kilometers north of Lahore, to recuperate.

One day, while travelling by bus from Srinagar to Verinag Ashram, they meet a Canadian couple, Adolf Hoffer and his wife Jane; they start a conversation and become friends. Adolf works in civilian support of the Canadian Army units in Burma during World War II and is also going to the same Ashram. As Surinder learns that the Canadian man's name is Adolf, he finds it uncanny. During the short journey through the mountains, they all doze off. Adolf Hitler appears in Surinder's dream looking for the *Brahamastra*—the flaming weapon noted in the Hindu scriptures to be able to annihilate cities.

A decade or so before the time Surinder and Adolf Hoffer are visiting the Verinag Ashram; the Nautiyal family—one of India's wealthiest business families—has started a research project at the Ashram to study the ancient Hindu scriptures and their connection to modern scientific discoveries and especially communications—particularly communication by thought transmission. The ultimate objective of the research project is the development of techniques that will give India the power that will deter future raiders from subjugating the country—as the British did, and before them, the Moghuls had done.

At Verinag, Surinder and Kamla meet Swami Ravi Anand—both a Cambridge trained physicist and a scholar of Hindu scriptures—who is spearheading the research activities at the Ashram. Surinder requests him for a palm reading. The Swami tells him that he will have two sons, he will have a long life and he will pass his last days overseas. This tells Surinder that he is not going to die of TB; he miraculously starts to feel better.

And then, one day, about two years later, on his way to work on August 6, 1945, he picks up the morning newspaper and reads: US DROPS ATOMIC BOMB ON HIROSHIMA. Surinder's dream comes back to life. He reads as much as he can about the Atom Bomb. He finds out that the American scientist, famously referred to as the father of the Atom bomb, Robert Oppenheimer, was a scholar of Sanskrit and Bhagavad Gita, the Hindu holy book, and the first words he spoke at the time of the test explosion was a *Sloka* or a verse from the Bhagavad Gita. Is there a connection between atomic physics and the Hindu scriptures? This question begins to haunt Surinder. He writes to Swami Ravi Anand of Verinag. The reply confirms his suspicion.

In March 1947, Lord Mountbatten, the Governor General of India, declares that India would be granted self-rule and Independence on August 15, 1947, and that the country would be partitioned into India as a secular state and Pakistan as an Islamic state. As soon as the news gets out, riots break out between Hindus and Sikhs on one side and Muslims on the other.

Eventually, Surinder's family, being Hindus, move to India as refugees—part of a mass exodus that results in over one million lives lost and over 10 million people displaced. With Daulat Ram being well known to Kevin Bond, Surinder gets a job with a British firm, Bond & Sons, in New Delhi.

One day, to his surprise, Surinder receives a letter from Adolf Hoffer, who informs him of his name change from Adolf to Max. Surinder writes back to him. As a result of regular exchange of letters, Surinder finds out that Max and he have the same birth date, and that Max too had the same dream about Adolf Hitler in the same bus at the same time.

As a result of the riots and displacement of large population, thousands of children become orphans. Surinder and Kamla adopt an orphaned infant girl, Suneeta. One day, a Muslim couple turns up and claims that the baby girl they had adopted is, in fact, their daughter. The Mehra family is devastated.

In 1949, Surinder receives a letter from Max Hoffer informing him that he is in India as part of the Canadian Contingent of the United Nations Military Observer Group in Kashmir. He is based very close to the Verinag Ashram and visits with the Swami on a regular basis. He writes in detail about the progress that has been made, in the research activities at the Ashram, related to Communication by Thought, a procedure named *Mindeffect*. He even gives him a detailed description of the procedure for affecting the thoughts of another person.

One day, Daddyji and Mummyji receive a letter from the Ministry of Rehabilitation asking them to appear at a hearing about the matter of the adoption of their adopted daughter, Suneeta. They go to attend the hearing. The Muslim couple, Munnavar and Salma, the claimants, is also present. What follows at the hearing is a conquest of human spirit over fear and despair. Munnavar and Salma mysteriously withdraw their claim for baby Suneeta.

When asked, what made them withdraw their claim?

They reply, " *Allah.*"

Daddyji and Mummyji go home happy, but the matter does not end there. Mummyji claims that it was she who was responsible for affecting Munnavar's and Salma's mind by the powers she gained by fasting, praying and making offerings to the Gods.

Daddyji, however, has a different take on the happenings. He claims that it is he who practiced *Mindeffect* upon Munnavar and Salma, the procedure his friend Max Hoffer had described to him in his last letter, to change their mind.

The story continues........

I

NAUGHTY SECRETS
Delhi: 1951

A white Morris car stops in front of a bungalow on Hailey Lane, New Delhi. As Kevin Bond gets out of his car to enter David Rankin's house, he notices two Indians sitting on the ground at the edge of a drainage ditch across the street smoking *Beedies* and talking to each other. He glances at them, checks the crease of his white trousers, caresses his moustache and walks towards the entrance. He opens the squeaky steel-grilled front gate, walks in and closes it behind him.

As he is about to ring the bell, David opens the door and says, "Kevin, thanks for coming by; I really appreciate it."

David Rankin, the India Liaison Officer of the well known British conglomerate, Madison Industries, has invited Kevin Bond of Bond & Sons for a curry lunch on Sunday afternoon. David's wife, Joan, is out for the day with other ladies of the British High Commission visiting their favorite charities.

David gestures to Kevin to have a seat. It is a warm afternoon. A ceiling fan is going round and round in a monotonous tone.

After they both sit down, David asks, "Can I get you something to drink?"

Kevin replies, "A cold Bitter would be good now."

David gets up, brings two bottles and hands over one to Kevin, who says, "Thank God, they still allow us to import this."

David replies, "For your information, it was bought at your store, the Imperial Stores, at Connaught Place."

"Thanks for the business," Kevin says, and they both laugh and he continues, "David, tell me; how do you find your new job as compared to your job as the Commissioner of Police of Lahore."

"Before the partition of India, we were the rulers; now we have to follow the rules, and that is not easy."

After they finish their beer, David calls for the maid servant in his broken Hindi-Urdu, "*Sally, Khana lagao.*" Meaning: Sally, serve Lunch.

Sally, assisted by a boy servant, places two sets of plates, silverware and two white cloth napkins on the dining table.

Sally is in her mid thirties and has been hand picked by David's wife, Joan, to be the cook. She had brought her from one of the many refugee camps that were set up after the partition of India. Sally's husband had been killed during the communal riots that broke out at the time of the partition of India. Her real name was Sulakshna and difficult to pronounce, so they nicknamed her Sally. She is dark but attractive and tall with a full bosom and a narrow waist. She stays in the servant quarters behind the house.

Today, she is wearing beige cotton *Shalwar and Kameeze* with a dark brown *Chunni* and a round shining red *Bindi* on her forehead. Her long hair is braided into two *choties* hanging in the front.

As they are both having their lunch, she brings in freshly cooked *chapattis* for them. When she bends to serve *chapattis*, her *Chunni* keeps slipping exposing her bosom. And, as she walks around to place *Chapattis* on David's plate, she touches David's shoulder. The way David looks at her and the interaction between the two is not lost on Kevin. He can notice some electricity between David and Sally, and he whispers, "David old chap, no wonder you are looking younger every day." And he winks at him.

"My dear chap, it is nothing of the sort you are thinking. You have a naughty mind."

After lunch, Sally and the boy servant pick up the dishes and move to the kitchen. David and Kevin move to the drawing room and carry on the conversation.

"So Kevin, how is business with all the import and foreign exchange restrictions?" David asks trying to steer the conversation to the subject he ultimately wants to bring up.

"Well, we have to improvise, if you know what I mean."

"Not really," David replies.

"We have found some innovative ways of getting around the foreign exchange regulations." Kevin says trying to keep his cards close to his chest, realizing that David Rankin is an ex-policeman.

David keeping up the line of conversation asks, "How do you see things in the long-term? By that I mean in the next five to ten years."

Kevin replies, "It is hard to say. I think the import business will die, but we see us getting into the export business."

David says with surprise, "Export business? What on earth would you export from India; they hardly make anything here?"

"Well, I am talking about export of handicrafts, shoes and, more importantly, export of services."

"What do you mean by export of services?" David Rankin asks.

"Well, a lot of development projects are getting underway and that will require import of machinery and other goods. You know, British firms and firms from other countries are looking for established firms with India-wide network of offices and distribution centers; we can provide that."

David Rankin is quiet, deep in thought, scratching his chin and thinking how to ask the next question, and then he takes the plunge. "Kevin, if you don't mind my asking; are you getting any inquiries from arms suppliers—you know, the companies who make guns and ammunitions?"

Kevin, not sure how much he should disclose, says cautiously, "Well, we have received some inquiries, and we have decided to represent some of them as their local agents. It is a very lucrative business, you know."

"Are you dealing with any British firms?" David asks.

Kevin is a bit hesitant at first but, then, reluctantly nods his head and says softly, "Yes." And at that very moment, he notices Sally standing in the doorway to the kitchen behind the curtain as if trying to eavesdrop. Kevin looks at David and signals towards the door with his eyes.

David, knowing why she is standing behind the curtain waiting, says, "She is reliable; don't worry. Moreover, she has no idea what we are talking about."

Kevin says mischievously, "I hope she is not waiting for me to leave; if you want I can leave right now."

"Come on Kevin, don't be silly; there is nothing of the sort... Oh, yes, there is one more thing I wanted to ask; have you ever been contacted by the Soviets, or have you heard any buzz about any arms deal between Soviet Union and India?" David asks feeling finally relieved at having raised the subject he had invited Kevin to talk about."

Kevin replies, "Oh, heavens, no, I have had no dealings with them. But why do you ask?"

David seeing the opportunity to get right into the subject says, "Well, the Soviets have been a thorn in our side ever since the end of World War II. You must have heard of the Gouzanko Affair in September 1945, when a Soviet cypher clerk defected in Ottawa, Canada, with the proof that the Soviet Union had a network of spies in Britain, Canada and the United States. That is when the Cold War started, and we have all been distrustful of them ever since."

"I have never heard of this; I have read about the term 'cold war' but always thought it was a new brand of beer that I should stock in my stores.... No... no... I am just joking. David, I am not really that interested in politics, but why are you asking me all this?" Kevin says feeling uncomfortable with the subject and thinking: *Is David with the British Intelligence Agency MI5?*

David continues, "Kevin, we believe that the Soviets have designs to increase their influence in India, and India places a lot of importance on Indo-Soviet relations. Do you know who India's, first ever, ambassador to the Soviet Union is?"

Kevin looks at him blankly and nods his head sideways.

David continues, "Mrs. Vijaya Lakshmi Pundit, the Indian Prime Minister's sister. That tells us India places a high degree of importance on the relationship."

"David, as I told you I am not into politics, but I sense that you are trying to tell me something; what is it? We have been friends for a long time; you can count on me."

David says, "I appreciate the sentiment. I don't want to impose, but we need your help. We want to have information about Soviet activities in India such as trade, cultural exchanges and arms sales. We want to know everything that goes on between the two countries. I know people in the Indian government who are not in favour of Indo-Soviet relations; they will provide us the information. As the Liaison Officer of Madison Industries, I personally do not want to be seen to be involved in any intelligence activities. Moreover, as you know, Madison Industries wants to be in the good books of the Government of India; they have their eyes on the big supply contracts. They do not want to be seen to be meddling in politics. Our understanding with the Delhi Intelligence Bureau is that I am to be in an advisory role only. We are looking for a conduit; are you willing to be one? If you help us, we will make it worth your while. You will see a lot of business flow your way. You will have every arm supplier in the world as your client, as long as you can keep the Soviets out of this business... and it will be good for Britannia at the same time." David looks at Kevin for a reaction having just appealed to his sense of patriotism for Britain.

"Well, now that you bring Britannia in the picture, you don't leave me any choice but to cooperate. But, David, I don't want to do anything that will be bad for *Bharat Mata,* either. You know Mother India is as dear to me as Britannia," Kevin says with a smile and asks. "How may I serve your Majesty? Oh, and by the way David, you are not with MI5, are you?"

David laughs and replies, "Oh, no… not at all. I am not connected with any government agency. If you are agreeable to helping me, then let us meet here next week same day, same time."

Kevin gets up to leave, and they both walk out into the front yard. David says, "You see those two men," pointing across the road, "they have been assigned to me by the Delhi Intelligence Bureau for my protection–having been with the police service for 20 years–but, basically, to keep an eye on me. Your visit will be duly reported. So, be discreet."

• •

David goes in and bolts the door. The sun is shining outside. The two bottles of Bitter are beginning to cause a stir in the middle of his body. His brain is responding accordingly. He pulls the curtains closed. He can hear Sally working in the kitchen from the sounds of washing of plates and utensils. His heart begins to race. He moves towards the kitchen. As he enters the kitchen, he sees her sitting down on her haunches, with her back towards him, washing the dishes and utensils; her *Chunni* is lying on the side. He looks to see if the boy servant has left. He can't see him around. He is feeling warm. He had never thought of her that way till, one day, she walked by him touching him with her bosom and looking back and smiling as if she was challenging him. In the past few weeks, it had happened many times. When he had mentioned that he had invited Kevin for lunch, she had offered that she would come down and serve lunch.

His heart and mind are racing. Should he or should he not. The water tap is running, and she is still washing the dishes. And then, she turns the tap off and stands up, turns around and bends to pick up the plates. Her bosom is half exposed. David has lost his control. He walks towards her. And, as she is getting up, he holds her by her shoulders and pulls her close; taking her in full embrace. She responds by putting her arms around him. As they are locked in a passionate embrace, the doorbell rings. They suddenly separate, and he moves away and turns around. And as he starts to walk away towards the front door, she holds his hand and pulls him towards her. There is another passionate embrace, and he pulls away and goes to the front door.

His wife Joan is at the door. She looks at him and says, "David, you look flushed. Are you all right?"

He replies, "Kevin just left. I think we had one too many."

• •

David and Kevin meet again a week later.

After lunch is over, David hands over a piece of paper to Kevin.

Kevin takes a look at the paper and says, "David, I can't make any sense of what is written here; these are all numbers."

David replies, "Well, you know, we, the cloak and dagger people, have a language of our own. Just subtract the numeral *one* from each number; the resulting number will give you the number of the alphabet. You can do that in your office, but let me give you the names verbally." And he whispers the information in his ear.

Kevin Bond asks, "David, how is this all going to work?"

David Rankin replies, "Kevin, the objective is to make the arms and ammunition supplied by the British companies more attractive to the Indians than those offered by the Soviets and to find out what they are up to."

Kevin Bond again asks, "And how is that going to be accomplished?"

David replies, "We have assets within the Defense Ministry who will tell you the terms and conditions for the Russian arms sales or any other bilateral activity between the two countries. These are the names I just gave you. Once you have this information, you write it up in a discrete manner and send it by ordinary post to Post Office Box 371; GPO, New Delhi."

Kevin Bond asks, "All right David, let us assume, for example, that the terms provided by the Russians are so good that the British companies cannot match them. What happens in that case?"

David Rankin replies, "You need not bother about that. It will be looked after by the higher authorities."

While David and Kevin are talking, Sally is standing near the door that leads from the kitchen to the dining area; most of the conversation is loud enough for her to hear. David can see her, but Kevin cannot. David is eager for Kevin to leave; he only has one hour before his wife, Joan, returns.

Kevin gets up to leave and says, "After all, you had to seek the assistance of the old East India Company to do your work. Do put in a good word for me to His Majesty's Government, will you."

Kevin's company, Bond & Sons, claims to be the descendent of the East India Company that came to trade in India in 1600 as traders and, eventually, came to rule large parts India with their private armies.

Kevin Bond drives away.

David Rankin walks in, bolts the door, closes the window curtains and walks towards the kitchen. He walks through the door to the kitchen, excitedly, anticipating that Sally will be sitting on the floor washing utensils. He is disappointed. Sally is no where to be found. He looks around and concludes that she must have gone to her room in the servant quarters. He turns around to walk back into the dining area when Sally, who had been hiding behind the door, wraps her arms around him from behind and says to his utter surprise, "Surprise!"

David turns around and wraps his strong arms around her. As they are exploring each other's bodies, David gently guides her to the bedroom. And as he lifts her up and is about to lay her down on the bed, she says, "David sahib, don't do that mistake, Joan *Memsahib* will find out."

David pauses and looks at her questioningly, and she says, "Body smell and perfume." David realizes that she is right and puts her down. She looks at him, pointing to the drawing room carpet.

The doorbell rings, and she runs towards the kitchen and out through the back door to the servant Quarters. David walks to the front door and, before he reaches there, the door opens and his wife, Joan, walks in.

She takes a look at him. David looks very nervous with sweat on his forehead. Joan asks, "Hello David, are you all right, dear?

"Yes, I am perfectly all right, dear," David replies.

Joan touches his forehead and says, "David, you have been looking flushed, lately. You must go to see Dr. Buckley for a check up. This can be a sign of high blood pressure, you know."

2

MERCHANTS OF ARMS

At the end of a long day, as Daddyji comes down the stairs from his office at Bond & Sons in Connaught Place, he is approached by a short stocky bald man chewing *Paan*. The man asks, "Can I speak to you for a few minutes?" Daddyji stops, looks at him and waits for him to say something.

The man clears his throat and says, "Surinder ji, I have a business proposition that will be of great interest to you. I know you have just built a new house; the extra money will come in handy."

Daddyji is curious and says, "May I ask, who do you represent?"

The man replies "Please forgive me; let me introduce myself. My name is Ashim Majumdar. Surinder ji, you are working for and helping people who ruled over us for two centuries. I would like to invite you to work with us, your fellow countrymen."

Daddyji is puzzled and asks again, "What business are you in?"

The man replies, "I have been in the same business that you and your employers are trying to get into, the arms trade. Our contacts tell us that you are doing a good job of making connections with powerful people in the government. Come and work with us. Why do you want to work with the British?"

As the man is talking, he is also looking sideways towards one of the round pillars of the colonnade of Connaught Place. Daddyji can also see him from the corner of his eye; an *Engrez,* a white man, with dark glasses is standing and looking towards them. The *Engrez* realizes that Daddyji has seen him. He slowly walks over and introduces himself in a thick European accent, "I am Alexander. Pleased to meet you. Ashim talks very highly of you."

Now Daddyji is getting a little concerned. He senses something sinister in the *Engrez* man's tone of voice. He turns around and starts to move towards the entrance to the staircase to his office. He wants to go back into his office to get away from the strangers.

Ashim moves ahead of him, blocking his way, and says, "Surinder ji, you are playing with fire. The business of arms trade is a very dangerous business. You are stepping into our territory. Stay away if you want to stay healthy, or work for us." And both the men slowly walk away leaving Daddyji in a state of shock.

Daddyji slowly walks up the stairs to the office, enters the front door and sits down on the sofa in the reception area. There are a few staff members still in the office. Daddyji gets up to see if Kevin Bond, his boss, is still in or not. The door to Bond's office is closed but there is the sound of him talking to somebody. After a while, the door opens, a staff member comes out, and Daddyji immediately knocks at the door, and asks, "Mr. Bond, I would like to speak to you? It is very urgent."

"Come in Surinder. You seem very worried. Is something the matter?"

Daddyji closes the door behind him and slumps down on the chair. He tells Kevin Bond all that transpired downstairs right in front of the office building.

Kevin Bond says, "I am flabbergasted. I would never have thought of such a thing happening. Now, to think of it… Oh, I will go and see David Rankin tomorrow. I never imagined that we will be up against international arms merchants."

Daddyji gets up and goes home.

By the time he reaches home, he has a splitting headache. As he enters the house, he calls, "Kamla, can you please get me a Saridon tablet; my head is going to burst," and he goes to his bedroom and lies down.

Mummyji is working in the kitchen and, as soon as she hears the words 'splitting headache'; she comes running to the bedroom.

"What happened? "She says.

Daddyji tells her everything that happened with him at the office.

She says, "Listen ji, I have told you so many times to resign from this job and join Nautiyal Industries. They offered you the job six months ago, but you wanted to experience how the arms business works; well, now you know that in the arms business you can lose your life. You know, all members of Nautiyal family are such decent people. Ever since they have taken over the Galaxy orphanage, things are going so smoothly. Although I am just a manager of the Galaxy, they treat me with such respect. Mrs. Nautiyal sometimes even asks me when you are going to join Nautiyal Industries. It is one of India's largest companies. They have coal mines, cement plants, cloth mills and anything else you can think of. Believe me; you will be very happy with them."

By the time she is finished speaking, Daddyji is fast asleep.

• •

The next day, Kevin Bond stops by at David Rankin's house on way to his office. He knocks at the door. The door is opened by David's wife, Joan.

As soon as she sees Kevin Bond, she is a bit taken aback and says, "Good morning, Kevin, what brings you here so early in the morning?" She goes inside the house and calls, "David, you have a guest… Sorry to leave you like this, Kevin. I have an early appointment." Saying this, she goes out of the front gate of the house.

David comes out of the house and asks Kevin to join him on the lawn chairs in the front yard.

Kevin says, "If you don't mind, can we go inside and talk?"

David Rankin gets up and leads him indoors. As they settle down and begin to talk, David Rankin calls out in his broken Anglicized Hindi, "*Sheroo, doo cup Chai Lao.*" And then he looks at Kevin Bond, "To what do I owe this honour of an early morning visit?"

As Kevin starts to tell the story, David stops him by placing a finger on his lips, and says, "Let us go for a walk," They both get up and walk out of the house towards a nearby park with the two Indians walking behind them at a safe distance. Kevin Bond tells him what Daddyji had told him. Both men are silent for a good five minutes.

In the end, Kevin Bond breaks the silence, "David, we need your help if we are to continue in the arms business. I never thought it to be a dangerous business."

David is still quiet. After a minute or so, he starts to speak carefully measuring his words, "Kevin, I hate to tell you this, but we cannot help you. The only thing I can tell you is that there is a lot of competition in arms trade. The Russians, the French, the Swedes and others are all lining up to sell arms, and they all want local influential people to represent them. You should have realized that arms are a dangerous commodity involving big money in sales, profits and commissions. That, by its very nature, attracts danger. If you want to get out, I will not stop you."

They stroll back to David Rankin's house. Along the way they are both in deep thought. No words are spoken. As they reach David Rankin's house, he invites Kevin Bond to come in for a cup of tea. When they enter the house, they see two cups on the centre table. David Rankin realizes that the tea has gone cold and he again calls, "*Sheroo, Chai cold.*"

Sheroo comes in and picks up the cups of tea. Kevin is looking around and asks, "David old chap, where is that lady servant of yours who served us last time?"

David Rankin does not appear comfortable, but in the end says, "Well, she has left us."

Sheroo brings two hot cups of tea. After sipping tea and some small talk, David Rankin says, "Kevin, I should tell you something." And after a pause he continues, "One morning when we called for Sally, there was no answer from her Quarter. When we went in, we found that she had taken off during the night. Obviously, we found it suspicious. After due investigation, we came to the conclusion that, most likely, she was a plant by some entity; who, we do not know yet. It could be the Russians, or it could be the Indians. I think she heard everything we talked about last time we met. So, just as well that you abort your venture into arms trade."

Kevin Bond says, "Surely, It could not have been Indians. You are helping them out, are you not?"

David Rankin replies, "In this game of cloak and dagger, you cannot tell who is who. First my driver left and now Sally disappeared, both under suspicious circumstances. I want you to know that I may not be with Madison Industries for too long. You know, what bothers me is that I fell for the oldest trick in the spy trade—seduction. I think I am getting old; it is time for retirement, old chap."

"So what are you going to do?" Kevin asks.

David replies, "I think we will go back to Britain. But... you know, Kevin, having lived in India for the last 30 years; I feel that I belong here. That is why I accepted the job with Madison Industries, hoping that I would continue staying in India and at the same time keep in touch with goings on in the old country. But, I think, we will move back to Britain and see how things go."

Kevin says, "Happens to the best of us, David. You served His Majesty's Government for over 30 years with distinction. You have nothing to be ashamed of."

With these words, Kevin Bond gets up, shakes hands with David Rankin and goes to his office.

• •

The same morning, when Daddyji reaches his office, he sits down at his desk and writes out a brief letter tendering his resignation without giving any reasons. He gets up and walks towards Kevin Bond's office. As he starts to knock at the door, Kevin Bond opens the door as he is just coming out of his office and says, "Oh Surinder, I was just coming to see you. Come in, please." After both of them are seated, Kevin Bond starts to speak before Daddyji can say anything.

"I went to see David Rankin this morning to find out if he can help us. It turns out that he is having his own problems and cannot do anything for us. I have been thinking about it all night. I have finally come to the conclusion that we should get out of the business of arms trade. I will write to all the companies we have been considering working for and that will be it. You can inform your contacts in the government about this."

Daddyji has the letter of resignation in his hand and does not know what to do. He decides to hold on to the letter for a day or so. As he gets up from his chair to go out of the office, Kevin Bond says, "Surinder, I am having dinner with Hari Nautiyal tonight at the Imperial. He rang me up and said that he wants to meet me about an important matter. I wonder what the Chairman of one of the leading business houses of India wants to talk to me about."

• •

In the evening at about 8:30 P.M., when Kevin Bond reaches the Imperial Hotel, Hari Nautiyal and his son, Veer, are already in the lobby talking to some people. As soon as they notice Kevin Bond, they walk towards him and greet him warmly. They all walk into the dining room, where a table has been set aside for them in a quiet corner. Kevin Bond and Hari Nautiyal order Scotch with water, and Veer orders orange juice.

To this Kevin Bond comments, "Come on, Veer, you must join us with a cheerful drink."

He replies, "I don't drink alcohol in the presence of my father."

Kevin Bond comments, "Come on, Veer, we are in new India now. You should drop the old taboos. What do you say, Hari? Should we order a *Chotta Peg* for Veer?"

Hari replies, "We have these long standing traditions in our family. Let us maintain them. It helps orderly functioning of the family."

As they are waiting for the drinks to arrive, Hari Nautiyal says, "Kevin, you must have heard that a number of British companies in India are selling their businesses to Indian businessmen. Have you ever thought of it?"

Kevin Bond replies, "Well, we have thought about it but not too seriously. However, if the policies of Government of India continue in the direction they are moving—by that I mean import restrictions and emphasis on indigenous production—we may have to think more seriously. As you know, most of our business depends on importing goods from Britain and selling them in India. And if that stops, there isn't much of a business for us to do here. All we will have left are a few warehouse buildings and stores."

Hari says, "If you ever decide to sell, Nautiyal Industries would be very interested in being the buyer."

Hari Nautiyal, being a shrewd businessman, is hoping to pick up assets of departing British businesses at fire-sale prices.

It appears that Hari Nautiyal has planted a seed in Kevin Bond's head. As Kevin Bond is driving home, the seed is beginning to sprout.

He is thinking: *I have been noticing that conducting business in India is becoming more cumbersome. There are new regulations being introduced everyday. More and more permits are required to conduct business. He decides to talk to his brothers and strike while the iron is hot. He knows that, with cash proceeds from the sale of all their assets in India, they can start new businesses in Britain. After the war, there is a lot of development taking place in Britain that has opened new opportunities.*

As soon as he reaches home, he books trunk calls to his three brothers in Bombay, Calcutta and Madras. After a great deal of discussion, they unanimously decide to pursue the offer from Hari Nautiyal.

• •

Next morning, when Daddyji reaches his office, he goes and sits at his desk waiting for Kevin Bond to arrive. He is uneasy and fidgety; he is not able to concentrate on the files on his desk. He has decided to tender his resignation. As soon as he sees Kevin Bond, he gets up and walks towards his office. But, as he is nearing the office, he sees Shelly, the receptionist, walk into Kevin Bond's office and close the door behind her. Daddyji stands outside hoping for her to come out so that he can go in. After a while, there is the usual sound of giggling. Daddyji is thinking: *The bugger is having fun, while I am sweating it out.*

He considers sliding his resignation letter under the door but decides otherwise.

In the meantime, an office clerk, Chobayji, is walking by as he is chewing *Paan.* He says, "Surinder ji, Bond sahib is doing his morning constitutional. At his age, it is very good for his health."

Daddyji gives him a look, and Chobayji moves on with a smile.

Daddyji goes back to his desk and gets busy with his work. Just before lunch, he finds Kevin Bond's office door open. He goes and knocks at the door. Kevin Bond looks up and says, "Surinder, please come in." Daddyji enters the office, closes the door behind him and takes a seat. Kevin Bond looks up and says, "I have been meaning to talk to you about my conversation with Hari Nautiyal last night. I must say, I was surprised at what he had to say. He has offered to buy Bond & Sons."

At first, Daddyji has a blank look on his face. He does not really understand what Kevin Bond has said. After a brief pause he asks, "You mean he wants to own your company?

Kevin Bond replies, "Yes."

Daddyji has his letter of resignation in his hands. He tactfully slides it in his shirt pocket. He feels as if a load has been taken off his head. Although he had decided to leave Bond & Sons, and he already had a job offer with Nautiyal Industries, he felt guilty just walking out for no apparent reason; now he does not have to, if Nautiyal Industries is going to buy Bond & Sons.

As Daddyji is savoring his sense of relief, Kevin Bond says, "Surinder, you seem lost."

Daddyji says, "Mr. Bond, what will you do if you sell your company?"

He replies, "We will all go back to England. We thought the Independence of India would not be complete without the East India Company making its final exit; after all, Bond & Sons are the descendants of the East India Company." And he laughs and continues, "Last night, my brothers and I decided to sell our assets to Nautiyal Industries, provided we can make suitable financial arrangements." Realizing that Daddyji is the one who had come to see him first, he says, "Oh, pardon me, Surinder, did you want to see me about something?"

Daddyji replies, "Oh yes, I did, but my question has been answered."

He gets up and goes out to lunch at *Kake Da Hotel.* Afterwards, he decides to go for a round of the inner circle of Connaught Place. He walks leisurely through the colonnade verandah looking at the shops and enjoying the breeze. As he is looking at the shop window of Janki Dass & Sons, somebody taps at his shoulder. He looks back, startled. It is Veer Nautiyal.

Veer says, "Looking to buy a new suit, Surinder?"

Daddyji replies, "No, just dreaming of buying one. Veer, is it true that Nautiyal Industries wants to buy the assets of Bond & Sons? Kevin Bond told me this morning."

Veer replies, "Yes, only if we can buy at a price attractive to us… Surinder, when are you planning to join us?"

Daddyji replies, "I think it will be better for me to continue until you finalize the purchase of Bond & Sons."

Veer says, "Yes, that makes sense."

Within two weeks of the dinner at the Imperial Hotel, Bond & Sons passes into the hands of Nautiyal Industries. Hari Nautiyal, a *Kutter* nationalist, is beside himself having become the owner of one of the British icons in India. Bond & Sons is where all upper class pseudo–British Indians and expatriates buy their luxuries. He has no intention of changing the name of Bond & Sons. It is part of the agreement that he has the option to keep the name or change it as he wishes. He realizes that, with import restrictions, he will not be able to import many of the luxury items that Bond & Sons had become famous for, but he plans to use the Bond & Sons Brand as an import substitute company.

• •

Daddyji's office is moved from the Bond & Sons office, near Odeon cinema, to the Head office of Nautiyal Industries at Scindia House. It is right across from the Imperial Hotel on the Queensway. This is his first day at this office. He has joined the company as the executive director of the Civics division—a new division set up to further the altruistic and political aspirations of Nautiyal family. As he is setting up his office, he sees something that shocks him. Ashim Majumdar, the man who had threatened him with dire consequences if he did not quit the arms business, is standing and talking to Veer Nautiyal. Daddyji is nonplussed. He sits down on his chair and takes a deep breath.

He is thinking: *Is Ashim Majumdar just a casual visitor to the office? Is he here to threaten Veer Nautiyal? Is he an employee of Nautiyal Industries?*

As he is lost in his thoughts, Veer and Ashim walk towards Daddyji's office. There is a knock at the door. Daddyji wakes up from his reverie. He gets up from his chair in deference to Veer Nautiyal, who is the Managing Director of the company.

Veer introduces Ashim, "Surinder, meet Major Sidharth Khosla. He is our chief of security."

Daddyji is confused and says, "But when he met me, he told me that his name is Ashim Majumdar."

Veer says, "Let me clarify the circumstances. When we found out that Bond & Sons is planning to become an agent for arms suppliers, we wanted to stop that. You know my father and his nationalistic fervor. He did not want an established British company to represent British arms suppliers in India. In fact, my father believes that India should not be buying armaments from Britain at all because that would be like buying a gun from somebody who just robbed you. So we came up with a scheme to terrify Kevin Bond, through you, about the perils of getting into arms trade. We succeeded. We did not think it was going to be this easy. We had to play a few other tricks, but it is better that you don't know about them." And Veer puts his arm around Daddyji's shoulder and continues, "Surinder, my friend, we live in a dangerous world. We have to play all kinds tricks to survive. Sorry to have put you through so much anxiety."

After they leave, Daddyji sits down on his chair and is thinking:

The Nautiyal family drives a British made Jaguar car, they send their children to boarding schools established by the British, they sing English nursery rhymes, they speak the English language, eat English confectioneries, and they behave as if they are more British than the British, but they don't like the British people. Bloody hypocrites!

As Daddyji is finished with his thoughts, Hari Nautiyal, the Chairman of the Company, walks into his office. Daddyji gets up again from his chair in deference. Hari Nautiyal says, "Surinder, welcome to Nautiyal Industries. I hope our association will last a life time. What do you think of our acquisition of Bond & Sons?"

Daddyji replies, "That is quiet a coup on your part; it is like buying the East India Company. Well, they have a very good brand name. I think we should be able to grow it, albeit in a different direction."

Hari Nautiyal says, "You know Surinder, this is just the start. I am looking to buy a newspaper. If one wants to have influence, one has to own a Newspaper. I have my sights on Delhi Herald, currently owned by a British firm, Hamilton Robinson."

"Mr. Nautiyal, I have a different point of view about this matter," Daddyji says.

Hari Nautiyal asks, "Oh, what is it?"

"If you don't mind, can we please wait till I present the strategic plan for the Civics Division?" Daddyji replies.

"All right," Hari Nautiyal says, pointing to the road across from his office, "Surinder, I have heard that they are going to change the name of this road from Queensway to *Janpath*; many other roads and places with British names will also be changed to Indian names. I am glad that the job of erasing the British legacy has started in earnest."

Daddyji says "Mr. Nautiyal, just by changing the names of the roads, we cannot erase the British legacy; the British culture is intertwined with Indian culture. Are we also going to get rid of the Indian Civil Service, the Army, the Navy, the Air force, the Public Schools, the Convent schools? Are we going to stop playing badminton, hockey and cricket? And look at our top leaders; most of them were educated in Britain. On the contrary, instead of erasing the British legacy, let us establish the Indian legacy by excelling in the sciences, the letters and the sports. Let us show the British and the world that we can do better without the British and better than them."

Hari Nautiyal stands spellbound for a while and then asks, "Surinder, what do you have in mind? How do we accomplish, what you are suggesting?"

"Mr. Nautiyal, how about beating the English cricket team in a Test match, for a start."

Hari Nautiyal purses his lips, while in thought, and then walks away without saying anything.

Daddyji thinks that he may have said too much and annoyed his boss. As he is thinking and looking at the scene down below at the Queensway, Hari Nautiyal walks back in. Daddyji turns around and looks at him in anticipation.

Hari Nautiyal walks close to Daddyji, holds his both shoulders and says, "Surinder, I think you have a point. But why cricket?"

"Mr. Nautiyal, cricket has entered our consciousness; and not only ours but of the people of all the past or present British colonies. Just look; all the cricketing nations are the British colonies. Cricket was introduced in India during the British rule, while we were fighting them to attain independence. During that time, we were desperate to overpower the British in any field we could. And we took up cricket. We see winning in cricket akin to wrestling the British down to the ground—what better balm for India's soul than beating the English cricket team in Test Cricket."

Hari Nautiyal smiles, shakes Daddyji's hand and says, "Let us go get them, Tiger."

3
STRATEGIC INITIATIVES
1951

Our servant, Chottu, is up early and is out cleaning the BSA motorcycle getting it ready to carry Daddyji to his office. Today, he has a meeting with the Chairman of Nautiyal Industries, his employer. Being the executive director of the Civics Division of the company, Daddyji is going to present the Strategic Plan for the division. As I am still getting ready for the last day of my Grade 4, I hear the motorcycle kick started and leave. Usually, Daddyji warms it up for a few minutes, but, today, he seems to be in a rush. As I look out, he is already at the end of the street riding in his favourite white shirt and trousers, with his shirt inflated behind him like a sail.

As he reaches his office, he parks his motorcycle in the courtyard of Scindia House near Connaught Place and goes up to the third floor where his office is located.

At precisely 9:30 A.M., Hari Nautiyal, accompanied by his son, Veer, walks into the boardroom. Daddyji and ten other executives of the company stand up as a mark of respect for the bosses. After an exchange of morning pleasantries, they get down to business.

First, Hari Nautiyal explains his Vision for the Civics Division. He says, "The raison d'etre of the Civics Division is to spend the money that our other two Divisions—manufacturing and distribution—earn for the benefit of our countrymen. We will divide the Civics Division into three departments: Health, Education and Strategic Initiatives. The Health department will open dispensaries and small hospitals for the needy. The Education department will open schools and colleges for those who are not able to afford education, or who do not have facilities near where they live. The most interesting department is the Strategic Initiatives. This will include: lobbying the politicians to see our point of view; supporting research in our ancient scriptures in order to leverage the knowledge, therein, for the benefit of our country and the world and any other initiatives which will improve the human condition in our country and the world at large. For example, you all know how we out-smarted Bond & Sons, deterring them from entering the arms business and, in the process, acquired them; this is an example of what we mean by strategic initiatives." And he laughs and carries on, "Surinder, I think we should institute some initiatives to get the better of the British in rather a friendly manner. Don't get me wrong, I have nothing against the British; I like them, but I did not like to be ruled by them. Keep in mind that we should not spend too much time on the British, for the British *Raj* is over; this is the dawning of the American *Raj*. Surinder, you should try and cultivate good relations with the Americans; the next century belongs to them."

After the conclusion of the Vision speech by Hari Nautiyal, Daddyji gets ready to make his presentation. He gets up from his chair and walks over to the blackboard. As soon as he picks up the chalk, he is energized. He chalks down the salient points of his presentation. It reminds him of his days in Lahore where he was a professor of English literature; he starts to speak with enthusiasm. Before getting into the details of his Strategic Plan, he recites a quote from Shakespeare's Julius Caesar and writes it down on the blackboard.

"The fault dear Brutus is not in our stars,
But in ourselves, that we are underlings."

Hari Nautiyal smiles and nods his head in appreciation of the sentiment expressed in the quote and says, "Surinder, your brother-in-law, Daulat Ram told me that your students used to, affectionately, call you *Shakespearewala*. One thing we have to admit that there is a lot of wisdom in English literature."

"That is correct. …Those were the days…," Daddyji says with a shy smile and continues his presentation, "Well, we have nobody to blame but ourselves for the predicament that India finds itself in. Mr. Nautiyal, I present a Three Point Plan for transforming India from being an Underling to a Leader.

"*One*: I propose that we start two news magazines to be published twice a year, to start with. I remember you telling me that you would like to own a Newspaper.

Well, why not start one from scratch; in that case you won't have to suffer the idiosyncrasies of the existing editors. As a newspaper owner, we will have the ability to shape public opinion; in addition to distributing news, we will be the news through our editorials. I propose the names of the two news magazines: LESTWEFORGET in English and *Yaadrahe* in Hindi—the same names, Mr. Nautiyal, which you had selected. The objective of these magazines will be to uplift the morale and the confidence of our people by publishing articles that make us feel good about ourselves. People of India have been subjugated for so long that they feel like underlings."

"*Two*: I propose that we re-discover the Spiritual Capital of India; it lies buried in the Vedas and other Hindu scriptures. To that end, Mr. Nautiyal, I commend your family's vision in setting up the Verinag Ashram devoted exclusively to conducting research in Hindu scriptures. I have had the pleasure of meeting Swami Ravi Anand, who runs the Ashram, during my trip to Verinag in 1943. I had been diagnosed with TB at that time and had been told that I have a short time to live. He read my palm and declared that I would have a long healthy life and would have two sons and a daughter. I believed in him, and thus far his predictions have been right on target. During the same trip, I also met a Canadian, Max Hoffer. He works for the Government of Canada. Since then, we have become pen friends."

As soon as Hari Nautiyal hears Max Hoffer's name he says, "I know him; he was with us on the Burma front with the Canadian Army during World War II. The American, Indian, Canadian and the British armies were jointly fighting the Japanese."

"Yes, Mr. Nautiyal, I know; he wrote to me about you in one of his letters. Oh, and just for your information, now-a-days, he is in Kashmir with the United Nations Peace Keeping Mission." And he continues, "Swamiji and I have exchanged letters, off and on, since 1945 and, more recently, after taking over my responsibilities as Director of the Civics Division of Nautiyal Industries. We have drawn up a five year plan to develop *Divya Drishti*–the ability to communicate at long distance using our brain waves–and also to develop meditation techniques to enhance human potential. Swamiji wrote to me that Max Hoffer has visited Verinag Ashram a few times in connection with our *Divya Drishti* Program. Mr. Nautiyal, once we achieve our goals the world will beat a path to our door to learn these techniques. I can assure you that this program will help regain our lost glory, and India will again begin to be known as the *Golden Sparrow*."

After the completion of this oration, Daddyji pauses for effect and looks around; his audience is spell bound. And then he says, "Gentlemen, I promise you that the third point of my plan will not be as philosophical as the first two." He goes on to the third point of his plan.

"*Three*: The third point is about cricket. Now you might wonder why cricket, and how can cricket uplift the self worth of the people of India. Gentlemen, in our sub-conscious mind, we identify cricket with our ex-colonial masters, the British. And nothing will uplift our spirits more than beating them at their own game. The plan is to beat the English cricket team in a Test match. The English cricket team, the MCC, is coming to India later this year; the first match is starting on November 2nd. India has not won even one Test match against England since 1932—when the Test matches started. If we can beat them in even one Test match this time, it will be a great morale booster for India. I suggest that we provide support to Cricket in India in order to uplift the game. J.C. Mukherjee has just been elected, beating Anthony De Mello, as the President of the Board of Control for Cricket in India, the BCCI.

Before Daddyji could finish, Hari Nautiyal suddenly asks in a state of shock, "Anthony lost to whom?"

Daddyji repeats, "J.C. Mukherjee, the President of the Cricket Association of Bengal."

Hari Nautiyal asks, "When did this happen?

Daddyji replies, "Just a few days back."

Hari Nautiyal says, "I have met Anthony several times at the Roshanara Club."

Daddyji says, "I will contact the BCCI and Delhi and District Cricket Association to find out how we can help. We should strive to raise Indian Cricket to the same level in the world as Indian Hockey. From 1928 to 1948, India has won Gold medal in Hockey at all the Olympic Games. One day, Indian Cricket can rise to the same heights. Mr. Nautiyal, India's pride has been bruised for centuries; therefore, excelling in sports will raise the self-image and self-confidence of the people of India and enhance the image of the country as a whole and internationally."

Daddyji presents a detailed action plan and budgets and hands over a copy to Hari Nautiyal. He briefly looks through the sheaf of papers and says, "I will issue an order approving the, initial, twenty five thousand rupee expenditure. Let us meet in month's time to review the progress and decide on the next steps."

4
GOLDEN SPARROW WON
Delhi: 1951-1952

When Daddyji comes home in the evening, my friend, Suraj, and I are standing near the front gate talking and playing catch with a tennis ball. He drives his motorcycle into the front yard, pulls it up on the stand and walks towards us and says, "Boys, you should take up cricket; you are old enough now."

I say, "Daddyji, there is no playground nearby, and there are not enough boys in the locality."

"Vikram, look at all the empty land all over the place," he says pointing to the empty plot beside our house, "you boys can clean it up a bit, make a cricket pitch and start playing. You will see how boys from nearby localities will come over and want to play with you. I will buy you two bats, two balls and wickets. And I will make another promise; I will take both of you to watch one of the five days of a cricket Test match between India and England. It is starting on 2nd of November. Howzat?" He says it exactly as the players in a cricket match shout when making an appeal to the umpire.

Both of us look at Daddyji with awe. Suraj asks, "Uncleji, did you play cricket when you were in school?"

"Yes, I did. And I promise that I will play with you also."

As we are talking, our neighbour, Dinesh Jain, who had been standing outside his house, walks over to where we are all standing and says, " Surinder ji, I overheard you talking about cricket. I am mad about cricket; I have played cricket in college. You know the Karol Bagh cricket team practices not too far from here."

Daddyji says, "Oh, I did not know that. How far is it?"

"It is just three streets away, in Block 5, on the empty land that is designated for a school. We can walk there."

When we arrive at the cricket ground, the cricket practice is in full swing. Boys in white shirts and trousers are bowling one after the other at the batsman, and the fielders are running around to catch the balls. Dinesh Jain stops near an elderly man and says, "Dr. Batra, how is the practice going?"

Dr. Batra seems like a jovial fellow and says, "Which one; the medical practice or the cricket practice."

Daddyji steps ahead and introduces himself, "I am Surinder Mehra. I am with Nautiyal Industries; you must have heard of them."

"Yes, of course, I have; who hasn't? I am Dr. Batra; I am the sole sponsor of this cricket team, with some help from a few generous people like Dinesh Jain."

"We have set aside some funds for promoting the game of cricket. If we can help in any way, please let me know." And Daddyji hands over his business card to him.

Dr. Batra places the card in his shirt pocket and says, "We are in need of matting; it is really very hard to keep the playing surface in good shape. There are too many small stones in the ground; when the ball hits one of them, it bounces unevenly and the players get hurt. Matting will cover the uneven ground surface and make the bounce more predictable. So if you can help us with procuring matting, the players will really appreciate it."

Daddyji replies, "If you can get me two or three quotations for the required matting, I will see what we can do." And then he turns to me and Suraj and tells Dr. Batra, "Just a little while back, I was trying to convince these two boys to start playing cricket."

Dr. Batra says holding both of us by our shoulders, "My young friends, we can give you some coaching before you start. We are about to conclude today's session, and, after that, we can give you some coaching in bowling and batting."

Both Suraj and I look at each other and say in unison, "Sir, thank you."

I have played street cricket before with worn out tennis balls but never with a real cricket ball on a real pitch. This is the first time. The wickets on the other side seem so far away and the ball much heavier. I am standing with the ball in my right hand, my heart thumping hard and practically in my mouth.

As I am getting ready to take a run at the wickets on the other end of the pitch, Dr. Batra says, "Vikram, don't worry about the speed at which you throw the ball; make sure the ball is directed at the stumps."

I start my run and, as I am running and gaining speed, my concern is: Will I even be able to get the ball to the other end. As the ball is released from my hand, it feels like eternity, and then there is the sweet sound of the leather ball hitting the timber stumps—every bowler's dream. There is clapping all around, and I feel as if I have taken a wicket in a Test match. Suraj and I spend almost half an hour being coached by Dr. Batra and others.

At the conclusion of the training session, the conversation between Daddyji and Dr. Batra turns to the forthcoming cricket Test match series between India and England.

Daddyji asks, "Dr. Batra, what do you think are India's chances of beating England?"

"I think we have a very good team. We did very well against the West Indies in the 1948-49 Test match series. I would be very surprised if we don't take a Test match or two from England."

When we are walking home, both Suraj and I are running and practicing our bowling action and pretending that we are bowling in a real game of cricket. Both Daddyji and our neighbour are walking beside us talking and laughing at us. Our neighbour says, "I think these boys are now hooked to cricket. Surinder ji, we may have created the next generation of Indian Test cricketers today."

As we walk into the house, I am still practicing my bowling action and nearly hit Mummyji as she is coming out of the front door. She gets hold of me and says, "Vikramyoustupidboy, what are you doing?"

"Mummyji I am practicing to bowl like Phadkar, the famous Indian cricketer. You will see, one day, I am going to become a Test cricketer."

"Come, Vikram and Suraj, sit down and have a glass of milk first. You have to be strong before you can become a Test cricketer; they drink six glasses of milk everyday."

When we are sitting on the dining table sipping milk, Suraj asks, "Uncleji, how is your motorcycle running? I am sure you will be buying a car soon to go with your new house."

Who would not be flattered by talk like this; Daddyji is no different.

He says, "Remember, Suraj, I promised you I will give you a ride on the motorcycle one day. Well, today is the day. Let me take you along; I have to buy some fruit."

Suraj replies, "I would love to but only on one condition."
Daddyji asks, "What condition?"
"You will have to buy fruit at our shop." Suraj replies.
"I did not know your family has a fruit shop; Vikram never told me."

Daddyji kick starts the motorcycle; Suraj sits behind him, and they are gone.

When they reach Suraj's father's fruit shop, his father is standing there attending to the customers. As he hears the sound of a motorcycle, he looks around, and he is surprised to see his son seated behind Daddyji. Suraj leads him to where his father is standing. Suraj's father is wearing typical Punjabi clothes—white *kurta* and *paijama* crumpled and soiled at the edges. He is short and stocky with a partially bald head. Daddyji and Suraj's father shake hands. The shop is essentially on the foot path with a very small *Khokha,* a rudimentary room made of wood, just big enough to store the goods at night in case it rains.

"Mehra sahib," Suraj's father says to Daddyji, "We may not have met in person, but I know all about you. Suraj talks about you and your family very fondly."

Daddyji looks at Suraj, smiles and says, "Suraj has very unique qualities. We all like him very much. Rajpal sahib, I was going out to buy some fruit, and Suraj told me that you have a fruit shop. So here we are."

As Daddyji starts to look at the selection of fruits, Mr. Rajpal starts to give him a running commentary. Picking up each fruit in his hand, he says, "See this bunch of grapes, these are from Chaman; these pomegranates are from Kandahar, and these apples are from Kashmir."

Different fruits are in their respective wooden packing boxes arranged on a wooden platform. Daddyji picks up each piece of fruit, looks at it and takes in its fragrance to assess whether the piece is just ripe, over ripe or under-ripe. As he is moving from box to box, he keeps selecting what he likes and hands it over to Mr. Rajpal to put it in paper bags made of old newspapers. After he is finished with his selection, he asks Mr. Rajpal, "How much...?"

Mr. Rajpal says, "I don't accept payment from near and dear."

Daddyji replies, "Rajpal sahib, if you do not accept payment from me this time, I cannot come again."

Mr. Rajpal reluctantly agrees to a payment. As Daddyji is placing the paper bags full of fruits in the carrier of the motorcycle, a car stops and blows the horn three times to announce the arrival of somebody important. The driver gets out and opens the rear door. A dignified lady, wearing a light blue sari with a deep blue blouse, and loaded with shining gold ornaments, gets out of the car. As soon as Suraj sees her, he runs towards her with his hands folded and says, "*Namaste* Sheelu *Massiji.*"

She looks at him with a fake smile on her face, and, while re-arranging the end of her sari, she walks towards his father with the driver in tow. She is Suraj's mother's sister. The fact that she is married to a prominent Jeweler of Delhi is evident from the way her heavy gold earrings are stretching her pierced earlobes.

Again, trying to keep the end of her sari from slipping off her shoulder, and touching her heavy gold necklace to make sure it is still there, she addresses Mr. Rajpal, "He has asked me to tell you to send the best fruit for tonight's party." She does not even tell Mr. Rajpal what or how much fruit is required. As soon as she is finished saying the few words, she goes back to her car. As she is entering the rear compartment of the car, she tells Suraj who is just standing beside the car holding the car door for her, "Suraj *beta,* can you bring the fruit to our house." As Suraj is about to say something, the car door is slammed shut, and she drives away.

Suraj picks up one pomegranate from a wooden box and, using the cricket bowling action, pretends to throw it towards the car to express his frustration.

His father notices it and says, "Well bowled, sir. Since when have you become interested in cricket? "

Daddyji is surprised to hear Mr. Rajpal's comments and says, "Vikram and Suraj got cricket coaching today. They have decided to start playing cricket."

Mr. Rajpal says, "In Rawalpindi I used to play cricket also."

Daddyji places the paper bags of fruits in the side carrier of the motorcycle and says, "Suraj, let us go now."

Suraj replies, "No Uncleji, I will stay back now. I will have to help my father."

Daddyji thanks Mr. Rajpal and kick-starts his motorcycle and drives away.

Mr. Rajpal packs the required fruits, ordered by his sister-in-law, in paper bags and places the paper bags in three wooden crates. He calls the man who regularly transports his goods. The man brings his hand-drawn cart and loads the wooden crates on to the cart. Mr. Rajpal asks Suraj to accompany the cart to his *Massi's* house. Suraj abides by his father's wish without fuss, but inside he is fuming because he knows that his *Massi* could have easily taken the fruits with her in the car.

As he is walking beside the cart, he is repeating the cricket bowling action with an apple in his hand as if he is bowling in a real cricket game. And every now and then says: Well bowled, sir–the traditional cricket saying. He feels perspiration flowing down his back making his shirt wet. Suraj notices that the man pulling the cart has no such problem because he is not wearing a shirt; the perspiration dries out as it forms. And, as Suraj is walking, he becomes very interested in the cart-puller. He notices how easily he pulls the cart; bending slightly forward and putting his one foot ahead of the other with a purpose. And then he realizes that the cart-puller is not even wearing any shoes. Suraj always thought that he himself belonged to a poor family, but today he realizes that there are even poorer people around. He is having a hard time keeping up with the cart-puller. What is motivating him to do this work? He is wondering. The answer comes to him very easily: Money............ It suddenly dawns on him that one must have money. A House, motorcycle or a car, they all cost money. He must grow up to have lots of money. More money than his *Massi*; more money than anybody......... he wants to be rich............ at all costs............ every thing costs ...even getting rich has a cost. In his eleven years of life, he has seen that you need money to make money. His father had to borrow from his *Massi's* husband to start his fruit shop. What a demeaning day that was. He still remembers how his father had to mumble in front of his *Massi's* husband with cap in hand. He starts to walk faster trying to keep up with the cart-puller. His brain is boiling with thoughts brewing inside: *I want to be rich with lots of money at any cost.* Rich at any cost becomes the motto of his life. At the ripe old of eleven, Suraj decides to work hard and do anything else that is required to become richer than his *Massi,* come hell or high water. Little does he realize that there is plenty of Hell in India, but there is a shortage of water!

He awakes from his reverie and finds that he has reached Ajmal Khan Park and his Massi's house. He goes in the verandah and knocks at the door. His Massi opens the door. Suraj says to her, "*Massiji,* I have brought the fruits."

"Bring it in," she says. Suraj waves at the cart puller to bring in the crates.

"No, no, I do not want him coming into the house. Suraj, *beta,* you bring the fruits in, good boy!" Suraj picks up one crate and starts to go inside the house.

As soon she sees him coming in with his dirty shoes, she says, "Suraj, *beta,* take off your shoes. We have just cleaned the floors."

Suraj sits down on the floor, unties his shoe laces, kicks his shoes off and carries the crates into the house. When the last crate is in, he looks at his Massi.

She is looking at him, and, as he starts to walk away, she says, "Suraj, you are a good boy. Have some water before you go back."

He looks at her briefly and walks away with his shoes in hands. As he is walking on the road with the cart-puller beside him, he places his shoes on the cart and practices the cricket bowling action with bare feet all the way back home. As his feet feel the heat of the melting asphalt pavement, his resolve to become rich becomes frozen in his mind; never to melt again.

• •

When I reach my school next morning, I see Suraj, with a worn out tennis ball in hand, walking with a limp outside the classroom waiting for the prayer meeting to start.

"What happened to your feet," I ask.

He replies, "I was practicing bowling last evening all the way from our fruit shop to my Massi's house and back. Vikram, I want to become a Test cricket bowler. I want to be rich." And he bowls the ball to me. I miss it, and it is caught by our Physical Training Instructor, Joginder Singh, who happens to be passing by.

He catches it and bowls the ball back with a stylish swing of hands and says, "Well bowled, sir."

Both Suraj and I are taken aback, for we were expecting a tongue lashing from him for playing ball within the school premises, but he says, "I see you boys are interested in cricket; why don't you come for the selection trials for the school junior cricket team after school today?"

As the school ends, Suraj and I rush to the school playground. When we reach there, we find a lineup of about twenty boys—all older than Suraj and me. We are told that the junior team is up to grade 8; we are in grade 5. Nevertheless, we also join the line-up. The first trial is for bowling. One by one the boys are asked to bowl three balls, and if the PTI is satisfied with the performance the boy is asked to ball three more balls. When Suraj's and my turn comes, the coaching by Dr. Batra proves useful—so much so that we are both selected for the team.

When we are walking home after the trials, Suraj says, "Vikram, I think I have taken the first step towards fulfilling my dream."

"Oh, and what is that?" I ask.

He looks at me as if I am stupid and says, "I told you in the morning; I want to be a Test cricket bowler and batsman. Just imagine: My name will be in newspapers; people will be lining up for my autographs; I will make lots of money, and I will be rich. And then I will show my *Massi* what the price of bananas is."

"What has the price of bananas got to do with cricket?" I ask.
"You know all the fruit she buys at our shop, she does not pay a paisa for it. When I am rich and famous, we will move our shop to Connaught Place; and then I will make her pay." He says looking at a distance—as if he knows that what he is saying is far into the future.

Daily cricket practice after school has become a routine. Suraj's enthusiasm begins to rub on me. I also start dreaming of becoming a test cricketer. Daily practice at school, supplemented by coaching at the Karol Bagh Cricket Club, earns us a place in the school junior cricket team.

• •

As I am getting ready to go to school, Daddyji is getting ready to go to see the first of the five Test matches between India and England to be played at the Feroz Shah Kotla cricket ground. As he is putting his shoes on, he says, "I hope the match starts on time; it is so foggy outside," and he opens the newspaper to look at the weather and says, "It is supposed to be a sunny day today. Oh, Vikram, tell Suraj to be here on Sunday at 8:30 A.M.; I have tickets for both of you."

Daddyji starts his motorcycle and departs to see the cricket match, and, shortly thereafter, I go to school.

At the end of the day, I am in a rush to get home from school to find out the match score. As soon as I hear the sound of Daddyji's motorcycle, I run outside; I am eager to find the score on the first day of the Test match. I open the front gate of our house, and he drives right in. The engine of the motorcycle is just shutting down when I go and stand next to him and ask, "Daddyji... Daddyji... what was the score today?"

He pulls up the motorcycle on the stand and says, "Vikram, England were all out for 203 runs."

While Daddyji is talking to me, our neighbour, the cricket lover, comes over and says, "Surinder ji, I think India could win this time; oh, what a performance by our bowlers! Shinde took six wickets; the English team is not going to able to stand up to him."

Daddyji looks at him and asks, "Did you go to see the match?"

"No, no, I was listening to the commentary on the radio at Gupta Stores," he says.

．．

It is, finally, Sunday, November 4, Day 3 of the five day Test match. The taxi drops us off near the main entrance to the pavilion of the Feroz Shah Kotla cricket ground. Daddyji is wearing the press identity card on his coat, so he is waved in, but when the gatekeeper sees Suraj and me, he looks at Daddyji. He takes out two tickets and hands them over to the gatekeeper, and we walk into the pavilion. Both Suraj and I are feeling nervous with all the elders moving in and out; we are the only two boys. We walk behind Daddyji looking around and feeling self-conscious as he finds his way to the grounds. As we are about to walk into the ground area in front of the pavilion, Daddyji meets the president of the Delhi and District Cricket Association. He looks at Suraj and me with a smile, and before he can say anything, Daddyji says, "Mr. Chabra, these are two budding cricketers; who knows they may one day play for India."

Mr. Chabra shakes hands with Daddyji and says, "Mr. Mehra, Dr. Batra told me about the matting that Nautiyal Industries has donated to the Karol Bagh Cricket Club; we are thankful for that. Please convey our thanks to Mr. Nautiyal; I will send him a letter of thanks also."

We move onto the grounds in front of the pavilion. It is sunny but a bit cool. Some people are standing and talking to each other, while others are sitting and are being served by waiters wearing white uniforms. Due to all the excitement and nervousness, my mouth is dry, and I am feeling thirsty. As Daddyji is looking around trying to find a suitable place for us to sit, he notices Uncle Daulat Ram, wearing a navy blue blazer and white shirt and trousers, sitting comfortably in an arm chair talking to another man sitting beside him. We walk towards him; he notices us, walks towards us and shakes hands with Daddyji.

He says, "Surinder, I was expecting to see you, but seeing *Vadha Cuckoo* is a surprise." He still calls me by my childhood nick name; now being a cricket bowler, I am embarrassed when some people address me using my childhood nick name.

Daddyji replies, "Vikram and his friend, Suraj, are crazy about cricket, and they also play in their school's junior cricket team. I had promised them that if they do well in the tournaments, I will take them to the Test match. So here we are."

Uncle Daulat Ram says, "Boys, see those benches near the entrance to the pavilion, you can sit there; you will see all the players coming in and out of the pavilion from that door."

Suraj and I go and sit on the bench near the entrance to the pavilion. Soon the English cricket team walks out of the pavilion. I have goose bumps as I see the players we had only heard of and seen in pictures in the newspapers walking, in person, right beside me. Suraj looks to his left and up and just keeps looking, for this is the first time he has seen an Englishman.

After the players walk past and away towards the field, Suraj says, "Vikram, *yaar,* they are white like milk and red like apples. Do they use cream and powder on their faces to look white? I wish I was white like them."

And then there is a round of applause as the two Indian batsmen, Vijay Hazare and Vijay Merchant, walk out of the pavilion. Both Suraj and I look at them in awe; the players that we were dreaming of emulating are walking right beside us.

After the match starts, some members of the English cricket team take the empty chairs on the other side of the door to the pavilion not too far from where we are seated. Instead of watching the game, Suraj keeps turning his head to look at them. We are able to hear them talk, but we are not able to understand what they are saying, Suraj turns to me and whispers, "Vikram, they are all talking in such a stylish manner; I wish I could talk like them."

As we are appreciating the looks and speaking style of the English team, there is a loud roar from the crowd. We both stand up. Vijay Merchant has hit a boundary on the first ball of the day. Thereafter, all day, the spectators are jumping up and down on their seats clapping and shouting support to the Indian batsmen. Merchant and Hazare are hitting the English bowling to smithereens. The day ends with India scoring 418 for the loss of six wickets; Vijay Merchant scores 154 and Vijay Hazare is 164, but he is not out.

When we are driving back home in a taxi, Suraj says, "Uncleji, I think India will beat England, don't you think?"

"Suraj, it all depends on how England plays tomorrow."

"Daddyji, I have heard how Shinde and Mankad bowl; they spin the ball up in the air and it seems that the ball hangs in the air for a while, and the batsman is kept wondering where the ball will drop. I think I am going to try that in the practice tomorrow. What do you think, Suraj?"

Suraj is looking at a distance; he is in a different world; I know that he is imagining playing in a Test match in the distant future.

• •

Next day, when I reach school, Suraj is hanging around the classroom waiting for the prayers to start; he is looking away from me, which is very unusual. "Hey Suraj, how did you like watching the test match yesterday?" I ask.

He looks at me with a sheepish smile, but he is looking somewhat different. For a while I am not able to figure out why? And then I realize that his colour is looking fairer; I notice that he appears to have applied something white on his face.

I ask, "Suraj *yaar*, what is this white powder on your face?"

He replies, "Does it not look nice? It is called *Fair Face*; I bought it at the general store near my house. You know, Vikram, it says on the packet that your skin will become white like milk and red like apples. Just read this."

He takes out the cardboard box with a glass bottle in it. Sure enough, it guarantees white complexion. It also says in Hindi: Use it for six months and find a good husband..."

I hand over the bottle back to him and say, "Suraj, this is for girls who are dark and want a fair complexion so that they can find a husband."

He replies, "But, I am also dark. You know, Vikram, ever since I have seen those English players, I want to have a fair complexion. Look at you; you have a fair complexion; not as white as the English players, but it is good. Were your ancestors English by any chance?"

"I don't think so, but Daddyji was a professor of English when we used to live in Lahore."

Suraj smiles and say, "I think that is the reason for your fair complexion."

I shrug my shoulders, the school bell rings, and we walk to the prayer ground.

• •

When we are going back home after cricket practice in school, we are walking and practicing the cricket bowling action at the same time. Suraj says, swinging his arms like a spin bowler, "Mankad bowls like this. You see he lets the ball go like this."

And I take a run like a fast bowler and say, "Phadkar bowls like this."

"I wonder what happened in the Test match today," Suraj says bowling another spin ball like Mankad.

"When Daddyji comes home in the evening, we will find out." Then I realize and continue, "Suraj, you know, Gupta General Store, near our house, has a radio, and he always has the running commentary on whenever there is a cricket Test match. We can go there and find out the score."

When we reach Gupta General Store, people are clapping and crowding around the radio which is sitting on the front show case of the store. "What is the score?" I ask one of the neighbourhood boys.

He replies, "England is 309 for 6; today is the last day; we have not been able to get them out; the match is going to end in a draw, where nobody wins."

Two hours later when Daddyji reaches home, I run to him. "Daddyji what happened?"

"Oh, India lost a golden chance to win the Test match. We had a lead of 200 runs after the first innings; England played for full two days, and we could not get them out. Well, there are four more matches to go."

• •

About two months later.

Our neighbour, Dinesh Jain, walks in when we are all seated in the front verandah of the house and discussing the fact that India has lost the fourth Test match and drawn the other three. Daddyji is feeling despondent having made cricket as one of the cornerstones of his strategy of boosting India's prestige.

"Come in Dinesh, have a seat," Daddyji says, getting up to greet him and directs him towards an empty chair. Mummyji gets up and goes in, for she knows that some serious discussion of the fifth and final Test match is about to take place.

Dinesh Jain takes his seat, lights a cigarette, takes a deep puff and exhales blowing rings of smoke high up to the ceiling of the verandah and says, "Surinder ji, if something is not done, Indian cricket will go up in smoke like this."

Daddyji is intrigued by the drama and the metaphor—being a professor of literature. He looks up, and Dinesh blows another puff up towards the ceiling.

"What do you have in mind?" Daddyji asks.

"It is now or never; I think we have to take help from our divine masters. I went to see my Guruji and asked him for some *Upaya*, or means, to make the Indian cricket team win."

Daddyji, instinctively, pulls his chair closer to Dinesh Jain and asks, "What do you mean?"

"Well, my Guruji recommends that we should hold a *Kamyakarma Yagya* starting a day before the start of the Test match and ending a day after the conclusion of the match."

"Are you serious?" Daddyji asks suspecting that Dinesh Jain is putting him on.

"This is what Guruji has told me and, in any case, what have we got to lose?—apart from the cost. You know, holding a *Yagya* is a well accepted Hindu ritual; if it is believed to work in other instances; why not in a cricket match?"

Daddyji, not finding anything wrong with the logic, asks, "What do you want from me?"

Dinesh Jain says, "This is a very expensive *Yagya* to hold. In addition to the cost of four priests, several pounds of *Ghee* and other oblations are required to be offered into the fire. As you told me the other day that Nautiyal Industries has a plan to support cricket, I was wondering if they will be agreeable to footing the cost of the *Yagya?*"

Daddyji is quiet for a while and, after some thought, says, "Well, I will talk to people in the office and let you know."

Next day, as Daddyji is parking his motorcycle in the parking lot of his office, his boss, Hari Nautiyal, is getting out of his car. Daddyji waits for him and they walk to the office building. When they are climbing the stairs, Hari Nautiyal asks, "Surinder, what do you think is going to happen in the fifth Test match?"

Daddyji replies, "Well, anything can happen; India is capable of winning. I think England were lucky in the first Test match. With a little bit of luck, India could have won."

And then he relates what Dinesh Jain had told him the previous night. Hari Nautiyal stops in his tracks and say, "He has got to be joking."

"No, Mr. Nautiyal, he seems to have worked out all the details."

"Come to my office; let us think about it a little. ....Come to think of it, there is no harm in trying it. Moreover, as one of the elements of our Strategic Initiatives is to carry out research in Hindu scriptures, this could be considered as part of the research. What do you think?...Where is the *Yagya* going to be held?"

"He is thinking of holding it right in the front yard of his house." Daddyji says.

"I will authorize the expenditure, but we do not want Nautiyal Industries' name to be associated with it. Let him, whatishisname, be the front man."

• •

A rectangular *Yagya Vedi* of brick masonry has been constructed in the front yard of Dinesh Jain's house with all the other accessories in place. In the early morning of February 5, 1952, the *Kamyakarma Yagya*, in support of the Indian cricket team, starts in earnest. Dinesh Jain's Guruji starts the *Yagya* with chanting of sacred Sanskrit hymns. All the four priests are in attendance. As the fragrance of incense burning in the fire permeates in the neighbourhood, people stop by to see and ask for the purpose of the *Yagya*. A radio has been set up in the sitting room to listen to the running commentary of the cricket match.

On February 6, at 9:30 A.M., the radio is turned on and the noise of thousands of spectators filling the Chepauk Stadium, Madras, comes on with the English accented voice of the commentator, Vizzy, the Maharajkumar of Vizianagram, in the background saying, "Good morning to all our listeners; England has won the toss and has decided to bat."

This is a five day match. In between, an additional day is allocated as the rest day. Each team may bat for maximum of two innings each, if the time permits. The team that scores more runs, in aggregate, is declared the winner. However, the team, that scores more runs in one inning than the runs scored by the other team in both their two innings, is also declared the winner.

Dinesh Jain comes out of his sitting room to the front yard and whispers in the priest's ear, "Pandit ji, the match has started; England is going to bat." The priest immediately looks for a brass plate containing specially formulated *samigri* and sprinkles it into the *Yagya Vedi* and pours a few tablespoons of *Ghee or* clarified butter. The flames leap up, and he loudly recites a few more *slokas* in Sanskrit.

In the afternoon, the news of the death of King George VI is announced. The next day, February 7, being the rest day, is declared the day of mourning. On February 8, the third day of the match, England is all out for 266 runs. Mankad takes 8 wickets for 55 runs, a record. Dinesh Jain walks out of his sitting room and comes out to give the news to the priests; they smile with pride as if they are the ones who bowled out England for a relatively small total.

Next day, when I am leaving school, my friend, Suraj joins me for walk home, and we start talking about the cricket Test match. He asks, "Do you think the *Yagya* is going to help India win the match?"

"I don't know. Mummyji went to see the *Yagya* and noticed that they were using vegetable oil instead of *Ghee*. This can be a serious infraction of the *Yagya* procedures. She brought this to the attention of Dinesh Jain, and he immediately went out and brought two tins of real *Ghee*."

Suraj is quiet for a while and then says, "Can I also come and see the *Yagya*?"

"Sure."

When we reach home, we go across to Dinesh Jain's house. The *Yagya* is going on; the cricket radio commentary is in full swing. It is nearing the end of play, and there is a roar from the crowd. The commentator is speaking at the top of his voice doing his best to be heard over the noise of the crowd. And then, the noise dies down, and, the commentator says, "Pankaj Roy is out from a ball by Tettarsall, caught by Watkins for 111 runs."

The day ends with India scoring 206 runs for the loss of 4 wickets. All the English batsmen have played their first innings and scored 266 runs. On the other hand, only four Indian batsmen have played their first innings and have already scored 206 runs. So, comparatively, they are doing much better than the English team.

As soon as Daddyji reaches home, he walks across the street to talk to Dinesh Jain. They shake hands and Daddyji says, "Dinesh, if India can play like this tomorrow also, I think we may have a chance to beat England."

Dinesh Jain replies, "Guruji was here in the morning, he says he has checked the horoscopes of the Indian players and the alignment is perfect. He is confident that India will win this Test match."

"Well, then, why did India not win the other Test matches before?" Daddyji asks.

"This team has five different players than the previous team—Amarnath, Gopinath, Mushtaq Ali, Divecha and Sen. So the amalgamated horoscope of this team is different than the ones that played in previous Test matches."

Daddyji replies, "Let us hope your Guruji is right."

Saturday, February 9, is half day at school. It is the fourth day of the Test match. Suraj also walks home with me to listen to the radio commentary of the cricket match. When we reach home, Daddyji is already at Dinesh Jain's house—he had taken the day off. The roar of the crowd coming from the radio is deafening; we can hardly hear the commentator's voice. We all have our ears to the radio. A few other neighbours have also come in. Both Suraj and I are not able to understand the commentary in English. I look at Daddyji. He says, "The Indian batsmen are on fire; they are beating the English bowling to bits."

With an unbeaten 130 by Umrigar, India declares their first innings closed at 457 for the loss of 9 wickets just before tea break. The Indian team is now 191 runs ahead of the English team. So they feel that they have enough of a lead that the English team can be put to bat for their second innings. There is only one day left in the match and if the Indian team can bowl the English team out within one day and restrict them to a low score, India can win.

Everybody is shaking hands, and Dinesh Jain goes out to tell the priests that India has taken a lead of almost 200 runs in the first innings. They accept the compliments with folded hands and smiling as if it is all due to their efforts at the *Yagya*.

Suraj looks at me and says, "Hey Vikram, the *Yagya* worked."

Daddy hears the comment and says, "Boys, the match is not over yet. England still has to bat, and we have seen them do better in the second innings. So wait before you start celebrating."

Dinesh Jain, who is standing nearby, says, "Surinder, are you on our side or theirs?" A light banter goes on for a while, and we all go to our respective homes.

February 10 is a Sunday; the school is closed. This is the last day of play. Daddyji and I are ready by 9:30 A.M.; Suraj also arrives as we are having breakfast. Mummyji comes in the dining room and is surprised to see all three of us ready to go somewhere. She asks, "Are you boys going to school today?"

As soon as I hear these words, I know what is coming. I look at Daddyji. He replies, "Today is a very important day for the fifth and final Test match. We are all going to Dinesh Jain's house to listen to the cricket commentary."

"I think all of you are spending too much time on cricket. Vikram and Suraj, if you listen to the cricket match commentary all day, when are you going to complete your homework?" Mummyji asks.

I reply, "Mummyji, I have already finished my homework; I could not sleep because of the sounds of the priests singing the hymns all night, so I decided to finish my homework."

When we enter Dinesh Jain's house, we see an elderly man with a white beard and saffron robe sitting on the floor, chanting hymns. "Guruji, this is Surinder Mehra; I told you about him." Dinesh Jain says. Daddyji moves towards Guruji and joins his hands in *Namaste* towards him.

He holds Daddyji's hands and says, "God bless you. Dinesh tells me that you donated the funds to conduct the *Yagya*. This will bring a positive effect not only on those present here but on society at large—and on the India's cricket team, of course." And then he laughs. Suraj and I also do *Namaste* to Guruji and move towards the sitting room where the commentary has already started, and the crowd is roaring in the background.

The English wickets fall in quick succession, and it becomes apparent that they are not going to survive the day. Just after lunch, a light blue car stops in front of our house. We can see it from the window of Dinesh Jain's house. "Daddyji, see there is a car outside our house," I say.

He gets up to look outside and says, "Oh, Hari Nautiyal and his son Veer are here." And he runs outside to welcome his bosses.

When they walk into the verandah, all four priests and Guruji are reciting the hymns in unison. Hari Nautiyal and Veer just do *Namaste* and come into the sitting room. Daddyji introduces them to Dinesh Jain; the situation in the match and the excitement of the anticipation of the outcome is so overpowering that no words are spoken. Everybody is trying to listen to each word spoken by the commentators. With fall of each English wicket, the crowd goes berserk. Finally, the English team gets a reprieve; it is lunch break.

We all have a quick lunch at our house and are back with our ears to the radio at Dinesh Jain's house. The crescendo of the singing of hymns is getting louder, and, to hear the commentary over the sound of the hymns, Dinesh Jain turns the radio even louder. Being a Sunday, many neighbours just walk in to listen to radio commentary and join in the excitement. England keeps losing wickets. In the end, it seems that every time the priests say *Swahaa*, when depositing the *Samigri* in the fire, an English wicket falls; the last three wickets fall for five runs. England is all out for 183 runs just before tea break. India wins by an innings and 8 runs—this means that England played their two innings, while India played only one of their innings and still scored more runs.

The commentators are speaking at the top of their voices in order to be heard over the roar of the crowd. Everybody in the room is clapping, shaking hands and embracing one another. Dinesh Jain says, "This is the first Test match India has won after the twenty-fifth attempt." He then goes out and gives the good news to the priests and Guruji, "We have won... India has won. We did it, we did it," The priests join their hands and raise them towards the heavens.

Guruji, while caressing his white beard, says with a mystic smile, "We live in an enfolded, illusionary, Universe. It always unfolds as it should to reveal the scenes of *Maya*. Win or lose, it is just an illusion hidden in the folds of the Universe."

Hari Nautiyal looks at him with his hands joined in *Namaste* and says, "How right you are Guruji; if only we could look behind *Maya* and see what is in store for us."

After a while, we all walk out of Dinesh Jain's house. As Hari Nautiyal is getting into his car he says, "Surinder, I wish Kevin Bond was here; I would have really rubbed it into him. Anyway, I will send him a cable in London. Oh, I forgot to tell you, the British High Commissioner, Sir Michael Sharp, has invited us for a party at his residence. Well, now, I can walk in with my head high. You know Surinder, you were right; winning the Test match against the English team is making me feel like a Winner."

• •

A special issue of LESTWEFORGET Magazine is published to celebrate India's first ever win in a Test match—and that too over England. The cover page of the magazine announces: **The Golden Sparrow Won**

India was once known as Golden Sparrow for its cultural, spiritual and material riches.

What a coincidence that I should write the above passage on April 2, 2011; the day India wins the Cricket World cup. Mission accomplished! Sorry, I am mixing the past and the present.

5
CRUTCHES
Delhi: 1952

As I am walking in the colonnade of the outer circle of Connaught Place, I see a car running on only two wheels; the other two have fallen away. Slowly, the white round columns of the colonnade start to collapse. All the people around have only one leg left; one having fallen away. All the birds have only one wing left. Half the stars in the sky have disappeared. The Moon is still there. The sky is still there. The Earth is still there. I look down at my feet and find that I am the only one left with two legs. A man walks out of York restaurant on one leg and says pointing towards my legs, "Young man, this is the age of singularity. You must get rid of one of your legs."

I start to run away and slip on a banana peel and fall out of the dream. I am awake but burning with fever. I hear Mummyji's voice. It is early morning.

Mummyji has put two small wet towels on my forehead to bring down my fever. One has slipped off. I am so hot with fever that I want to take my *paijama* off. One leg comes out, but I cannot find my second leg. One of my legs has disappeared. Did I lose one leg when I fell out of the dream, or did I leave one leg behind in the dream? I do not know.

I shout in panic, "Mummyji, Daddyji... I am not able to find my leg." Both of them come running.

Mummyji asks, "Vikram *beta,* what are you talking about?"

"Mummyji, I am not able to find my right leg," I repeat. She panics and takes off the bed sheet covering my legs and is relieved to find the leg still there.

She says, "Vikram *beta,* the leg is there; it must have gone to sleep."

I reply, "No Mummyji, it is not there; I cannot feel it."

Panic sets in. Mummyji and Daddyji look at each other with concern in their eyes. Daddyji says, "I am going to bring Dr. Trivedi." And he rushes out.

A little while later, I can hear the motorcycle racing out on to the road. In the meantime, Mummyji massages my right leg to wake it up, but nothing happens. She calls our servant, Chottu, to bring some warm *Ghee*. She applies it to my leg and massages again. Still there is no sensation. Her face is contorted with worry. I drag myself up in the sitting position and lean against the headboard of the bed. I try and move my right leg, but I feel as if it is not there. We are waiting for the doctor to arrive. Mummyji is still massaging my leg when the three long and three short beeps from the motorcycle announce Daddyji's arrival.

He walks in followed by Dr. Trivedi. The doctor is an elderly gentleman— not as tall as Daddyji—wearing a grey jacket, black pants and half-moon spectacles perched on his nose. He takes out his stethoscope, thermometer and a flashlight from his medical bag. He puts the thermometer under my tongue and the stethoscope on my chest. After a few minutes, he takes out the thermometer and looks at it rolling it in his hands trying to read the temperature. He purses his lips and shakes his head. He touches my forehead and says, "He does not feel that hot. There must be something wrong with the... "

He does not complete the sentence, and then says, "Surinder, please arrange for two large towels and cold water and get some ice from the market as fast as you can."

"Chottu, go and get some ice from the bazaar," Mummyji tells him and goes out of the room to get the towels and cold water. I am getting nervous. I am surprised that the doctor has not checked my leg.

As the doctor is getting ready to cool me down with cold towels, I point to my right leg and say, "My leg is not moving." He looks at me as if he has not heard me.

Daddyji realizes and repeats what I have said, somewhat, loudly.

Dr. Trivedi replies, "Oh, I did not know that. Surinder, why did you not tell me?"

Daddyji replies, "Doctor sahib, it was the first thing I told you." Apparently, Dr. Trivedi is hard of hearing.

"It is all right. I will check it," Dr. Trivedi says. And as he starts to examine my left leg, I point out my right leg to him. He quickly changes legs. He lifts my right leg at the knee joint and hits it gently with a small hammer. There is no reflex. He scratches it with his nails and looks at me for reaction. I nod my head sideways, indicating no sensation. In the meantime, Mummyji has brought in cold water and towels.

As I see the long towels being soaked in water, I am reminded of, my friend, Gurmail. Many years ago, when we used to live in the E-type Quarters, I had watched Gurmail, who had high fever, being cooled down with long wet towels, and, later that day, we had learned that he had died of Typhoid.

Dr. Trivedi takes off my shirt and covers me with a wet towel. I start to shiver. After a while, I feel wetness in my *paijama*. I assume that water from the wet towels has leaked, but I realize, later, that I have wetted myself. I am gradually realizing that not only is there no sensation in my right leg, but there is lack of sensation in my excretory system also. I muster enough courage and ask, "Doctor, do I have Typhoid?"

Dr. Trivedi replies, "You will be fine… you will be fine." He takes out a pen and his prescription pad and scratches something and says, "Surinder, please bring these as soon as possible."

The motorcycle is kick started and Daddyji races again to the bazaar to pick up the medicines at the chemist's shop. Dr. Trivedi is trying his best to cool me down from the waist up, while Mummyji is massaging my right leg. I doze off, and, as I am about to fall into another dream, I hear the beeps of the motorcycle. Daddyji comes in with a bag full of medicines. Dr. Trivedi looks at the medicines, opens his bag and takes out a syringe and a needle. Holding the syringe in his right hand and the medicine bottle in his left hand, he sucks up the liquid from the bottle into the syringe, and then he raises the needle up to squirt some of the liquid out, one drop at a time.

Now he seems ready to poke me. I am not sure if it is going to be in the arm or the buttock. As he moves towards me, he looks at Daddyji and says, "Surinder, please remove his *paijama*," pointing towards the right side. Daddyji turns me over a bit and pulls down my *paijama* enough for Dr. Trivedi to insert the needle in my flesh. I wince in anticipation of the pain, but there is no pain. After a few seconds, Dr. Trivedi takes out the needle and looks at me with a smile and asks, "Did it hurt?"

I reply feebly, "No. There is no sensation in my buttocks."

Dr. Trivedi replies, "Oh, I did not know that. Surinder, you did not tell me this, did you?

Daddyji looks at him and is about to say something, but decides to keep quiet. Clearly, Daddyji does not seem happy with Dr. Trivedi, his forgetful nature and impaired hearing.

Mummyji asks, "Dr. sahib, what has happened to Vikram's leg. Will he be all right?"

Dr. Trivedi replies, "I have given him an injection. It will bring down his fever and, with that, his leg should become normal. Just keep putting ice cold towels on his body. It is a hot day today. His body must be kept cool. Give him just milk and glucose biscuits but no solids. I will come by in the evening."

He starts to collect his instruments as he is speaking and places them in his medical bag. Daddyji picks up his bag and goes out with him to drive him back, but Dr.Trivedi decides to walk back to his house, where his clinic is also located.

After Dr. Trivedi leaves, Mummyji says, "My Vikram *beta* has been struck with an Evil Eye. I keep telling you not to brag about your achievements, but you people don't listen." As soon as I hear this, I am worried about my cricket career."

I am feeling a bit better, but I can see lines of anxiety on my parents' faces. In the meantime, my younger brother, Kishi, and younger sister, Suneeta, are awake. They both seem disturbed to see me lying in bed covered in wet towels. Mummyji takes them in the other room. Daddyji is sitting beside me on my bed staring at the wall. And then, he gets up and starts to pace up and down. After a while he says, "Kamla, I am going out for a few minutes to talk to Karnail Singh."

When Daddyji reaches his house, Karnail Singh is sitting in the verandah reading a newspaper. As he sees Daddyji, he gets up to greet him and says warmly, "Oh, Surinder, *yaar,* how nice to see you. Come on have a seat."

Karnail Singh can notice anxiety on his face. When Daddyji is seated, Karnail Singh asks, "Surinder, you seem worried. Is there something bothering you?"

Daddyji replies, "Karnail *yaar,* Vikram has had fever for the past few days, and this morning his right leg lost all sensation. Dr. Trivedi was in to see him and said that everything will be all right, but I am really concerned. Fever is very common among children of his age, but paralysis of the leg is very worrisome. I am feeling helpless. I don't know what to do."

Karnail Singh creases his forehead trying to think hard, and he stands up and says, "I know what to do. We should take him to the hospital. You know, Sir Ganga Ram Hospital has just opened. My cousin is a doctor there. Let us take Vikram to Sir Ganga Ram Hospital."

Daddyji likes the idea. They immediately get up and walk over to our house. On the way, they ask a taxi driver, at the taxi stand, to come to our house. As soon as they are home, Daddyji tells Mummyji, "Kamla, Karnail Singh has a very good suggestion. We are going to take Vikram to Sir Ganga Ram Hospital."

Mummyji is very worried to hear that they are taking me to the hospital.

She says, "Why? Dr. Trivedi said Vikram will be all right. I am not going to let him go to the hospital. Who is going to take care of him there? If you are taking him to the hospital, I am also coming with you."

Both Kishi and Suneeta hear this and come out of their room, and say, "Daddyji please don't take Vikram *Bhaiya* to the hospital." And they both start weeping and saying in their own way, "We will put wet towels on him and make him all right."

Daddyji replies, "Kamla, you should stay at home for Suneeta and Kishi."

I am scared. I still remember the one legged people in my dream.

The taxi arrives and beeps the horn. Both Daddyji and Karnail Singh lift me gently, take me out and make me sit in the rear seat of the taxi. Daddyji sits with me at the rear seat, and Karnail Singh sits at the front beside the driver. The taxi driver asks, "Sahib, where are we going?"

"Take us to Sir Ganga Ram Hospital."

"Sahib, where is this hospital?"

Karnail Singh says, "It is in Rajender Nagar," and gives him directions to get there.

As the taxi drives away, I can see Mummyji standing, scared stiff, holding on to Kishi and Suneeta gently waving her hand.

In about 15 minutes, we are at the hospital. Karnail Singh goes in and comes out followed by two men carrying a stretcher. They gently lift me out of the rear seat of the taxi, make me lie down on the stretcher and take me inside the hospital, followed by Daddyji and Karnail Singh. As we enter the hospital, there is an office where all the patients are supposed to report. Daddyji gives all the particulars to the man at the counter. After a while, my name is called. The two men wheel the stretcher into a room. Both Daddyji and Karnail Singh follow. As I lay on the stretcher, they both sit down on a wooden bench near me. The smell of tincturiodine, mercurochrome and phenyl pervades everything.

After a few minutes, a doctor arrives. Both Daddyji and Karnail Singh exchange greetings. The doctor introduces himself as, Dr. Sunder. Karnail Singh says, "My cousin Dr. Jeet Singh also works here. You may know him."

Dr. Sunder replies, "Yes, of course." He removes the stethoscope from around his neck and asks, "…Now what is the problem with our young friend here?"

Daddyji explains to him what has happened. While Daddyji is still talking, Dr. Sunder has started checking my leg. He then takes out a thermometer and installs it under my tongue. After a few minutes, he takes it out, reads it, and writes down something on the piece of paper stuck on a clipboard.

He says looking at Daddyji, "Can I talk to you?" And he walks out of the room followed by Daddyji. Karnail Singh, also, walks out just behind them, leaving me alone in the room for awhile.

I can hear them talking, as they leave the door open. All I can hear is the word *admitted*. I am not sure what that means. I can hear them talking to each other for a few minutes.

As Daddyji comes back in the room, he says, "Vikram, Dr. Sunder wants us to stay here in the hospital for a day or so. They want to give you some medicines to make you well."

I just nod my head, but inside me I am scared, and I say, "What about Mummyji, She will be waiting for us?"

He replies, "Yes, that is what I am thinking about."

In the meantime, Karnail Singh says, "Surinder, I will go back home and let Kamla know what has happened, so that she does not keep worrying. You stay here with Vikram. I will be back in the evening, and we will take him home."

Karnail Singh leaves.

Two men come into the room and say, "Dr. Sunder wants the patient to be taken to a room on the other side of the hospital." They wheel the stretcher to the far side of the building.

I am transferred from the stretcher to a bed. There are many other beds in the room with other patients lying in them. Due to nervousness, illness and high fever, I have an urge to go to the bathroom. I call Daddyji, who is standing nearby, and whisper to him.

He moves closer to the bed and is about to lift me to take me to the bathroom, when a Sister, in a white uniform, comes into the room and says, "Oh, sir, please do not move the patient. It is our job."

Daddyji says, "He wants to go to the bathroom."

Instead of taking me to the bathroom, the Sister brings a white coloured pot, pulls my *paijama* down and slips the pot under my buttocks and says, "You can do it in the pot."

My face, which is already red with high fever, becomes even redder with shyness. But, as much as I do not want to do it the presence of the Sister and Daddyji (thank God Karnail Singh had left earlier), the call of nature takes upper hand, and I feel relieved afterwards—embarrassment or no embarrassment. After all the cleaning, and after the pot is removed, I begin to feel better. It appears that the medicine, Dr. Trivedi had given in the morning, is having an effect. I am feeling a lot cooler, but I still feel numbness in my right leg. I can see that Daddyji is feeling more relaxed due the presence of the Sister in the room. And the fact that we are in the hospital, he feels confident that everything will be all right. The room is nice and cool. Everything looks new. As the Sister is going about her duties, attending to other patients in the ward, Daddyji strikes a conversation with her.

He says, "Sister, I want to thank you for looking after Vikram. I can see from his face that he is already feeling better. You have a very nice facility here."

The Sister replies, "Thank you. We try to do our best and make our patients as comfortable as possible."

Daddyji says, "You know, many years ago, when we were in Lahore, I once visited Sir Ganga Ram Hospital for some blood Tests. And now, here we are again making use of your facilities."

The Sister replies, "I am also originally from Lahore. There, also, I used to work in Sir Ganga Ram Hospital."

Daddyji says, "You know Sister, I have been sitting here and wondering: Who was this great soul who set up this hospital, where the rich and the poor alike can come and be treated?"

By the time I settle down, it is late afternoon. It has been almost seven hours since I came out of my dream, but the vision of the one-legged people still haunts me.

Dr. Sunder comes in and starts his round of checking up on his patients. When he reaches me, he checks my eye lids, my temperature and legs. Left leg is fine, but the right leg still has some problem. When he lifts and moves it, I feel pain, and I almost jump off the bed.

After the checkup is complete he says, "Well, I am happy with your progress, Vikram. When you came here in the morning, you had very little sensation in your right leg, but now you have pain; which is good news. This means that your neuro-muscular system is working. Feeling is back in your leg. Your fever is down. I want you to stay here overnight, and if you are making progress like you have been, we will discharge you tomorrow morning." And then he turns around to the Sister and says, "Sister Nanda, I would like Vikram to get off the bed and start walking a little."

Dr. Sunder and the Sister Nanda gently help me get off the bed and stand on the floor. I am relieved to be standing up on the cold floor. I almost feel energized with the cool sensation traveling up my body. Sister Nanda holds my right arm to give support to the right side of the body. As soon as she touches me, I feel as if a divine healing energy is flowing through me. I take my first step by moving my right leg forward. I am hesitant to lift my left leg, as this will be the test of my right leg. I wait and take a deep breath.

Sister Nanda says, "Vikram, see there is God Krishna standing in front of you; walk to Him. See, all His energy is flowing to you. Imagine you are strong and healthy. Lift your left leg and walk towards Him." And, as if by divine intervention, I lift my left leg and move it forward. I feel extreme pain in my right leg. I wince with pain and look down at my leg with tears in my eyes.

And as I look up, I see Mummyji standing in the door and saying to me, "Come walk to me, Vikram *beta*." And I hop, skip and jump into her arms. She and I are both in tears. Sister Nanda and Dr. Sunder are standing watching proudly, as another of their patients is recovering.

Mummyji holds me by my right arm, and I limp back towards my bed and sit down on the side of the bed. She has brought some food for Daddyji and has come ready to stay with me at the hospital for the night.

"Where are Kishi and Suneeta?" Daddyji asks.

She replies, "They are being looked after by Karnail Singh's wife."

Daddyji says, pointing towards them, "Meet Dr. Sunder and Sister Nanda. They have been looking after Vikram."

Mummyji looks towards them with folded hands saying, "Thank you, and God bless you both."

Sister Nanda replies, "Thank you. It is all in the hands of God; we are just His agents."

Dr. Sunder and Sister Nanda move away to attend to other patients. Daddyji eats a bit of food that Mummyji has brought. He is looking tired and haggard with his unshaven beard.

Mummyji says, "Listen ji, I think you should go home now. I will look after Vikram for the night."

He replies, "No, Kamla, I will go home, take a bath and come back, and then you can go back home; otherwise, Kishi and Suneeta will miss you."

Mummyji says, "All right, whatever you say."

After a few hours, Daddyji is back looking fresh and ready to look after me for the night. "Kamla, you should prepare to go home now. It is getting dark." Mummyji gets ready to leave. Daddyji walks with her out of the hospital and gets her into the same taxi that had brought him to the hospital. When he is gone out to see off Mummyji, I fall asleep.

• •

When I wake up in the morning, there is a new Sister on duty. She is being addressed as Sister Rose by other patients. I feel the urge to go to the bathroom. I look around for Daddyji. I am not able to see him around. I do not want to call Sister Rose to help me with going to the bathroom because, I know, she is going to make me go in the white pot. I hated it last time; having my *paijama* pulled down by Sister Nanda. I keep squeezing harder and harder with hands between my legs, hoping to see Daddyji come in the room and help me walk to the bathroom. As luck would have it, Sister Rose starts to walk towards me.

She comes, stands beside me, feels my pulse, and, while looking at her watch, she is counting the pulse beat and asks, "How are we feeling today?" She can see me squeezing my legs together. Her eyes meet mine and the secret is out.

She says, as Daddyji is walking into the room, "Vikram, do you want to go to the bathroom?" I am kind of non-committal, and then I decide to say yes; but it is too late. I let go and feel warmth below both my buttocks. I am afraid to be found out, but in another way I am relieved. In fact, there are two reasons for my relief. One: The call of nature has been satisfied. Two: And this is the more important of the two; I feel warmth equally under both my buttocks and legs; that means that I have regained sensation in my right leg.

I am so ecstatic that I shout, "Daddyji, I can feel my leg. It is warm on both sides."

Daddyji and Sister Rose, who are standing by my bedside, have no idea what I am talking about.

Sister Rose lifts the sheet covering my legs and says, "Let us have a look at your legs." She is shocked to see the bed sheets and my *paijama* all wet. She says, "I just asked you if you wanted to go to the bathroom. Vikram, I do not expect a boy of your age to do this."

"Sorry, Sister Rose," I say sheepishly, "It will not happen again."

She replies with a stern voice, "I know it will not happen again. We will not let it. We are going to send you home later today, you rascal."

Dr. Sunder comes in the ward for his rounds. As he is walking by, Sister Rose asks him to come to my bed. After exchanging pleasantries, he says, "Sister, let us see how far Vikram can walk."

I get up from the bed and stand beside it on my own, though, feeling week but energized at the same time. With Daddyji standing beside me, I take a few steps using my right leg but with a limp. Dr. Sunder seems pleased and issues the discharge papers. Along with the papers, he gives verbal instructions. He explains, "The fever has affected the muscles of Vikram's right leg. He is fortunate to have recovered so quickly. It will need regular exercise and checkups, every week at the hospital, to bring it up to full strength."

Daddyji asks, "Is there somebody who can come to our home to help us with the exercises?"

As we are winding up the conversation, Sister Nanda walks by and says, "Hello, Vikram I am happy to see you go home. Where do you live?"

Daddyji replies, "We live at Rohtak Road, just across from where a cinema is under construction."

Sister Nanda replies, "I also live nearby."

Daddyji jumps at the opportunity and asks, "Sister, as you know, we are taking Vikram home today, and he is going to require expert care and exercises to make him regain his strength. Will you be able to help us at home in your spare time?"

Sister Nanda replies, "I will think about it. Please give me your address, and I will let you know by tomorrow. If I cannot help, I will find somebody else for you."

As we are about to get up, Dr. Sunder hands over a pair of crutches to Daddyji saying, "These may help."

When we reach home in a taxi, Daddyji reaches over the driver's shoulder and beeps the car horn three times. Mummyji, Kishi and Suneeta come out of the house, and as soon as they see us, they run out to the taxi. Mummyji helps me out of the taxi. Daddyji takes out the crutches and hands them over to me. At first, I feel awkward, but realizing that I have no choice, I put them under my armpits and start to walk.

When Suneeta sees me walking with the help of crutches, she asks, "Why is Vikram *Bhaiya* walking like this?"

Mummyji replies, "Vikram has hurt his leg, so he needs support from the crutches."

In the evening, the doorbell rings. Chottu opens the door and my friend, Suraj, walks in, and in his usual slow and deliberate manner asks, "Auntyji, Vikram did not come to school, so I thought I should find out if everything is fine."

Mummyji tells him the whole story, and I show him my crutches. Suraj seems very perturbed to find out that I may be unable to walk for an extended period of time.

"Vikram, how are you going to play cricket now; you will lose your place in the school team," he says.

I reply, "Suraj, don't worry, I will be fielding with my crutches under my arms and batting with one crutch under one arm and the cricket bat in the other." And we both laugh.

While we are talking, Daddyji is writing something on his writing pad. After he is finished, he hands over a folded paper to Suraj and says, "Suraj, can you please hand it over to the school principal. I will also come to see him in the next few days."

After Suraj leaves, Daddyji gets the newspaper and reads it to me to keep my mind off my leg and also to continue our lessons in English. After dinner, as usual, we listen to the news in English from the All India Radio, Delhi.

Next morning, life has to go on. Daddyji gets ready for work, as usual. Mummyji also has her work to go to; she is the manager of the Galaxy of Stars orphanage run by the Nautiyal Family Trust, but she has decided to take sometime off until I recover.

Before leaving for work, Daddyji says, "Kamla, you should write a letter requesting a leave of absence for two weeks. I will take it with me and hand it over to Veer Nautiyal at the office, and I will also explain the circumstances to him."

After Daddyji leaves for work, the doorbell rings. Mummyji opens the door, and there is Sister Nanda standing at the door. Before Sister Nanda can say anything, Mummyji recognizes her and is very pleased to see her and says "Come in Sister, so good of you to come by."

Sister Nanda walks in and says, "Mrs. Mehra, Vikram's father had asked, if I could help in the treatment and homecare of Vikram. I have come to tell you that I will be happy to help for about one hour a day. My timings will depend on my commitments at the hospital. Oh, and one more thing, I want to tell you that you don't have to address me as Sister Nanda while we are at your home. You can just call me, Your Honour." And they both burst out in laughter, and so do I, although I really do not know what 'Your Honour' means.

•   •

Days come and go, but I am not going anywhere. I sit in the verandah in the morning, Sister Nanda comes to make me do exercises, I eat lunch, have a nap, do the homework that my friend, Suraj, has brought the previous evening, and then it is evening again and Suraj brings more homework, takes back what I have done and the cycle goes on and on and on and on and on and on .... I am exhausted.

For the last several days, I am sitting in the verandah watching ants make an anthill. Every day it is a bit larger than the previous day. I watch them carry grains of sand and, one grain at a time, the hill is taking shape. The whole process is so orderly that I get the feeling that they are able to communicate with each other, somehow, but how? Small little creatures carry stuff and move around from one place to another—not one but hundreds of them. I watch intently how the ants move on fragile little legs with two little things sticking on the side of their head.

As I watch them, I am thinking:

God has given an ant six legs. I had two, and He has taken one away. What a travesty of justice.

I start to pity myself. This fateful day, as I am watching the ants and think-ing, our servant is sweeping the floor of the front courtyard and, in the pro-cess, wipes away a part of the ant colony that is building the ant hill. Little ants are spread all over the place. Some are lying sideways, while others are upside down, moving their bodies and struggling to straighten up. They keep trying and, finally, succeed, and, in a short time, they are back to work, moving in line towards the anthill.

My frustration is growing by the minute.
I am thinking:

Why six legs to them and only one to me? And then... I come to the realization.... But I have two hands, two crutches and one leg. That makes it five implements—only one short of an ant. But they seem to have something more—the will to get up and move again after they had been wiped out by our servant, Chottu.

Something blows up in my brain. It must be my frustration mixed with the inspiration from the ants. I slowly raise myself up from the chair on one leg, holding the round pillars in the verandah. I bend down to pick up one crutch at a time and install them firmly under my armpits and move around in the verandah. The verandah is about six inches higher than the front courtyard floor. I lower myself on to the courtyard floor and slowly walk out of the house on to the street. This is the first time, since my illness, I have ventured out on my own. Chottu notices this and comes running out after me trying to give me support. I push him aside and keep walking to the end of the street.

Chottu goes running inside calling for Mummyji. She is in the bathroom taking a bath. As she hears that I have walked out on my own, she quickly comes running out in her bath gown with her hair tied over her head and a towel wrapped around it and shouts standing at the front gate of the house, "Vikram *beta,* what are you doing? You will hurt yourself. Come back." I look back momentarily. The voice of anguish and concern just floats past me–through one ear and out the other. I keep walking.

As I reach the end our street, I turn right on to Rohtak Road–barely able to maintain my balance on the stone and dust sidewalk as trucks, buses, cars, bicycles and pedestrians whisk by me. As I am walking, I see a beggar boy on the sidewalk. He is sitting in a small buggy made of wood and four wheels. I am wondering why he is sitting in the buggy and not on the sidewalk. I pause to catch my breath and give relief to my legs and arms.

As I look down, I notice that he has no legs below his knees. I ask, "*Bhaiya,* how did you lose your legs?"

He replies, "I had leprosy. It became so bad that they cut off my legs below my knees to save my life."

"What is your name?" I ask.

"Himmat," he replies.

As he extends his right hand up to ask for alms, I notice that some fingers of his hands are missing, wasted away by leprosy. I take out some coins from my pocket and drop them into the tin pot in his buggy. The hollow ringing sound from the coins striking the tin pot reverberates in my ears again and again, as I stand there pondering his condition and comparing it to mine. A song, from Hindi film, Boot Polish, is playing on the radio in the shop nearby.

Nannhe munne bachche terii muthi mein kaya hia; (Hey, young man, what are you holding in your hand?)
Muthi mein hia tuqdiir hamaaaari; (I am holding my destiny in my hand;)
Muthi mein hai tuqdiir hamaaari ; (I am holding my destiny in my hand;)
Hamne kismet ko bas mein kia hai ; (I have, at last, tamed my Destiny.)

As the melody works itself through my ears into my brain, I start to hobble forward concentrating on the words, enjoying the melody and looking at my hands. Is my destiny in my hands? I am wondering. And then, I notice the beggar in the buggy following me. Before I know it, he overtakes me pushing forward with his hands pushing the ground and propelling the buggy forward. I can see that *he* has his destiny in his hands. I decide to have a race with him. I hobble forward with a sense of purpose in my crutches, and we both reach the *Halwaii* shop at the same time. I sit down on the bench outside the shop. He orders a cup of tea with the coins that I had given him. I also order tea. I see fresh *samosas* being fried. I am feeling hungry from the exercise and the exhilaration of the moment and order a *samosa* each for me and the beggar boy.

As we are finishing tea and samosas, Mummyji arrives all perturbed and worried.

She says, "What are you doing Vikram? You will get sick again."

The beggar boy looks up, gives a smile and propels the buggy forward with his hands, humming the song and says, "Vikram, *yaadrahe, Muthi mein hai tuqdiir hamaaari.*"

Meaning: Vikram, remember, our destiny is in our own hands.

I stand up on my own and say, "Mummyji, want to race?" And I hobble home ahead of her.

When I reach home, I take my usual seat in the verandah and start to watch the line of ants moving diligently doing their job. One thing is very clear that they have some way of talking to one another; otherwise, how would they maintain an orderly flow of work?

As I am looking down at the ants, Mummyji comes and stands beside me and asks, "Vikram, what are you looking at?"

I reply, "Mummyji, I am trying to find out how ants talk to one another?"

She replies, "See the two little things sticking from their heads; they send messages through them. God has given them special powers of communication. They just know what the other ants are thinking."

I look up at Mummyji and say, "Mummyji, how do you know this?"

She replies, "Have you forgotten? I am a teacher." And she goes inside the house.

I am thinking: *I wonder if I can have the same power as the ants—and know what other people are thinking.*

• •

My crutches have become my friends and constant companions. I now have three friends: Suraj, Ram and Shyam. Suraj is my school friend; Ram is my right crutch and Shyam my left crutch. Every morning, I look after Ram and Shyam by cleaning and massaging them. When I am walking with them, I am careful that they do not step where they can get damaged.

In a month or so, my right leg has gained enough strength that I am able to walk without crutches, but I have a limp. When I walk without crutches, I do miss my friends, but I am happy that they are having a rest.

One day, when Sister Nanda comes to give me treatment, she brings a walking stick similar to what, my grandfather, Pitaji, has. "Have you brought a new stick for Pitaji?" I ask.

She replies, "This is for you. You should hold it in your right hand to give support to your right leg when you are walking."

I look at the stick and then at Sister Nanda and say, "Sister, I have names for my crutches: Ram and Shyam. I want to give a name to my walking stick also."

She replies, "I think it is a splendid idea. Have you thought of a name?"

I think hard about it and say, "I have already given two of the best names to my crutches. Sister Nanda, do you mind if I name it after you? After all you have done so much for me."

She replies, "Name after me? No…No…You should give it an English name. Your two crutches are masculine names. Let us give your stick a feminine name. Let us call it, Ginny."

I ask, "What does it mean?"
She replies, "Nothing, not all names mean something. It is a mysterious name with magical powers. Who knows Ginny may work magic for you."

I agree to name my walking stick, Ginny.

The same routine carries on. I sit in the verandah with Ginny in my lap and watch the ants do their work. The ant hill has really become big, and Chottu is now very careful not to disturb the ants.

• •

I start going to school. The first day, Daddyji takes me to school on the motor-cycle. As we reach the school, some of my friends, including Suraj, are standing outside. Suraj comes forward to help me get down from the motorcycle.

Daddyji parks his motorcycle and goes in the school. Suraj and I, slowly, walk towards the front gate. There are three steps to climb to reach the front yard of the school. I stand and stare at the steps. I have climbed one step at home before but not three. Suraj senses my hesitation and moves alongside me to help. I look at him with a smile and determination on my face. He understands and gives me a smile and a nod. I lift my left leg and plant it on the first step, and lift myself and plant my weak right leg gently also on the first step; and then, the second and the third step. As I reach the third step, I stand there and look around with a sense of accomplishment. It reminds me of the newspaper pictures of Sir Edmund Hillary and Tenzing Norgay beaming with smiles, when they reached the top of Mount Everest last year in May, 1953.

I walk to the classroom and put down my satchel on the desk. Accompanied by Suraj, and a few other class fellows, I walk slowly towards the prayer ground behind the school. After a while, my other class fellows go ahead as they are walking faster. Suraj and I slowly walk and stand at the rear of the line of students of Class 7A.

The prayer group, standing on the stage, starts the prayer hymns. With hands joined in front, I also start to sing, but my eyes are open. As I look down, there are many ants moving in line and going into a crack in the brick paving. I am reminded of the extraordinary communication ability that Mummyji told me ants have.

As I am standing in line, I see Daddyji come out of the principal's office and walk towards the school gate. I decide to read his thoughts and send him a message similar to how an ant does. I think of him and send a thought: Daddyji turns back and looks at me. As he is about to walk out of the school gate, he pauses and looks back.

I think I can read all these negative thoughts running through his mind.

He is thinking:

Oh, God, I hope Vikram remains hail and hearty at school. This is his first full day at school. What if his limp remains with him for the rest of his life? What a handicap. He will have a hard time finding a job.

I had expelled these thoughts from my mind the day I had met Himmat, the beggar boy.

• •

When Daddyji reaches his office, the peon is waiting outside his office. "Good morning sahib, Mr. Nautiyal would like to see you right away," the peon says.

Daddyji places his briefcase on his chair and goes to Hari Nautiyal's office. He knocks at the door and walks in.

Hari Nautiyal is talking on the phone and signals to him to take a seat. Daddyji sits down and tries to guess who Hari Nautiyal is talking to as the conversation is peppered with words like 'Verinag Ashram' and 'Hindu scriptures'. After Hari Nautiyal is finished with the phone call, Daddyji gives him a questioning look.

Hari Nautiyal says, "I was talking to Suresh Kapoor; he is with the Delhi Intelligence Bureau. Some time ago, I had told him about the research we are sponsoring at Verinag Ashram; he phoned to say that we should keep all the work, being done at Verinag, confidential. In addition, he wants us to get their prior approval of all the foreigners planning to stay at the Ashram."

"Oh, I never thought that we were doing research of importance to national security," Daddyji says.

Hari Nautiyal says, "Well, if you think about what we are trying to accomplish, it is nothing short of magic—just imagine communicating by Brain Waves, or *Divya Drshti* as it is known in the Hindu scriptures. Suresh thinks that we must keep it under wraps. He says that if we are successful, it would be equivalent to the making of an Atom Bomb."

He pauses for some time and then says, "Surinder, I want you to go to Verinag to talk to Swamiji. Let us think about it over the next few days and formulate a strategy. In the meantime, you should book your airline tickets."

Daddyji had been thinking about it ever since I had been stricken with the problem with my leg. He asks, "Mr. Nautiyal, I had written to Swamiji about, my son, Vikram's illness. He has suggested that I should bring him to Verinag. Do you mind if I take him along? I will bear the cost of his ticket."

"Oh, sorry, I forgot to ask you; how is he now?" Hari Nautiyal asks.

Daddyji replies, "He has started going to school, but I am really worried about his future."

"Surinder, the company will bear all the expenses of Vikram's treatment. I hear he is a very promising cricket player; let us make him well. We want him playing cricket soon."

Daddyji's eyes fill up after hearing these words of encouragement. "Thank you Mr. Nautiyal," he says and leaves.

6

FEAR OF FLYING
Delhi: 1952

In the evening, when Daddyji reaches home, he tells us all, "I have a pleasant surprise for all of you. I am going to Verinag Ashram in two weeks, and I am taking Vikram with me for treatment. We are going by air."

As soon as he says this, a war breaks out. Mummyji is up in arms, "No, either we will all go, or nobody will go."

Daddyji replies, "Kamla, taking the whole family by air will be too expensive. Also, there is limited room at the Ashram. You know that it takes two days to get to Srinagar by train. Don't you remember that the train only goes up to Jammu, and then we have to go by bus to Srinagar? Moreover, the company is paying for both airline tickets. When I told Hari Nautiyal that I want to take Vikram along with me for treatment, he told me that the company will pay for Vikram's ticket also. Kamla, we are going to be spending only ten days with Swami Ravi Anand at Verinag Ashram. People say that Swamiji is very knowledgeable in Ayurvedic treatments. We have already tried the Allopathic medicines, but nothing has worked well. I am worried about Vikram's future. Not only that he cannot play cricket, but, with his limp, he will have a hard time getting a job when he grows up. What problem do you have with our going to Verinag Ashram?"

I look at her trying to read her thoughts. The real problem is that she is afraid of the plane falling from the sky and losing both Daddyji and me. I don't like her to be worrying all the time.

Two days before we are to leave for Srinagar, I decide to take action. This morning, I keep lying in bed pretending to be asleep. As the summer vacation has started, Daddyji and Mummyji think I am just lazing around and pay no attention to me. I was hoping that they would be concerned with my extended stay in bed and ask how I was feeling, but nothing of the sort happens. I decide to do something more drastic. I start moaning as if I have pain. This act of mine gets immediate attention.

Mummyji comes over to my bed and asks, "Vikram *beta,* what is the problem?"

I touch my right leg, and reply, "Mummyji, I have some problem with my right leg. I think I do not have much feeling in my leg."

Mummyji calls, "Listen ji, come quickly, Vikram is having trouble with his leg."

Daddyji comes rushing into the room. "Which leg?" He asks with panic and urgency in his voice, "We will see… Vikram move your legs… Can you move your legs?"

And he removes the bed sheet covering my legs and wants to see me move my legs. At this moment, I am wondering how far I should take this pretense. Should I or should I not move my leg. As I am thinking what to do, the time is ticking.

Daddyji takes it to mean that I am not able to move my legs. He looks at Mummyji, their eyes meet and their faces go white. Panic has set in. He rushes out in his *paijama* with the motorcycle key in hand. I make a split second decision.

I shout, "Daddyji, my legs are moving."

He comes in. Mummyji says, "I think you should bring Dr. Trivedi. We should not take a chance with his leg."

He rushes out again, and there is the sound of the motorcycle racing out to the road with plenty of beeps of the horn.

In about half an hour, there is the sound of the motorcycle giving three beeps. It stops outside. Dr. Trivedi walks in with his bag in hand, followed by Daddyji. I wonder what he is going to do. I suddenly realize that last time I saw him; he poked a needle into my buttocks. I am feeling nervous. I hate the look of a needle. I can feel my heart beating faster.

After a checkup, Dr. Trivedi announces, "Well, Vikram has no fever, but, as a precaution, I will give him an injection." And as he takes out the long needle and, as he is preparing it, something tells me that I should tell the truth.

I blurt out, "Daddyji, I want to tell you something. I was just pretending. I did not want Mummyji, Kishi and Suneeta left alone. Mummyji is always worrying about something or the other, and she is so worried about my going with you that I had to do something."

They all look at me in amazement. Daddyji shows a frown and is about to say something, when Mummyji says, "See my Vikram *Beta* is so concerned about me." She kisses my forehead with affection and then caresses my hair.

Dr. Trivedi says, "Vikram, you should never feign sickness. The body sometimes believes it to be true, and it really becomes sick. I am sure you have read the story of the shepherd boy who cried wolf; one day you may really be sick and your parents may not believe you."

I look down with my face red. Daddyji gives me a stern look. He and Dr. Trivedi walk out.

When Daddyji comes in after seeing off Dr.Trivedi, he is in a terrible mood. He lashes out at me in a burst of anger that I have never seen before, "Vikram, I did not expect such irresponsible behavior from you. I want you to come with me to Verinag for your own good. Do you realize that if your ruse had been successful, you would have jeopardized your chances of recovery? Swami Ravi Anand is known for curing cases like yours with Yoga and Ayurvedic medicines. And don't worry about your mother, brother and sister. They will be fine."

• •

On the morning of June 12, 1954, Daddyji and I are up early to go to the aerodrome. I am so nervous that I must have visited the bathroom half a dozen times. Our flight is at 10:00 A.M. A taxi arrives at 6:00 A.M. to take us to the aerodrome. The taxi driver and our servant, Chottu, place our baggage in the dickey of the taxi. Kishi and Suneeta are still asleep. Mummyji comes out to the street to see us off; she has a silver tray in her hand; clay-*Diya* burning in it; a small silver statue of Lord Krishna and some flowers adorn the tray. She performs *Aarti* by moving the tray in a vertical circular motion and chanting hymns invoking the mercy of God for my full recovery and a safe flight. After a brief ceremony of feeding us both *Parsada*—a spoonful of curd and sugar each, Daddyji and I take our seats in the rear of the taxi. Ginny, my stick, which has now become my fourth friend, is sitting right beside me. After checking that everything has been loaded in the taxi, we drive away, with Mummyji waving at us. I am choked with tears, but I do my best to control myself. As I look back, I see Mummyji wiping her eyes.

As there is hardly any traffic this early in the morning, we reach the aerodrome by about 7:00 A.M. The taxi driver parks the car and helps us carry our luggage inside. It seems that we are a bit early for the 10:00 A.M. flight. It is the first time that Daddyji has come to the aerodrome. As we enter the aerodrome building, Daddyji looks around to find out where we should be going. The taxi driver, who brought us into the building, seems to know a lot more than Daddyji. He guides us to an area where a man in uniform is standing behind a counter. He looks at us and can see the confusion on Daddyji's face. He politely waves at us to come towards him. The taxi driver places the luggage on a large weighing machine. Daddyji presents the tickets to the airline man. He takes out a register and checks something in it, writes something on a few papers and gives us a piece of paper and our tickets back to us and says, "Boarding will be at 9:00 A.M." Daddyji pays the taxi driver. He asks the airline man, "Which plane are we going to be flying in?"

He replies, "You will be flying in a Douglas DC-3 Dakota, sir." Daddyji nods his head with confidence, as if he knows the plane well. We move into a waiting area set aside for departing passengers and take our seats. Daddyji senses discomfort on my face and in my fidgety movements. He decides to engage me in small talk.

He picks up a brochure lying on the table and starts to read it and tells me what is written in it, "You know Vikram, till last year there used to be seven airline companies in India. Our government passed a law, The Air Corporations Act, 1953, nationalizing all the airlines into one–The Indian Airlines. It has 99 aeroplanes…" He keeps on talking, but I have no recollection of what he said after that.

I start gazing into the future. In addition to reading other people's thoughts, I have discovered a new pastime since I have acquired Ginny, my walking stick. I find that the future is a wonderful place to be. You can imagine yourself to be wherever you want, whoever you want to be, and whoever you want to be with. There is just one problem: sooner or later you have to come back to where you left off–the present. And that is exactly what happens, as I am sitting far away in my thoughts; an announcement on the loudspeaker brings me back. I am not able to understand what is being said on the loudspeaker.

I ask, "Daddyji, what is the time?" Before he can answer the question, I answer it myself, "Oh look at the clock on that wall. It is 8:30."

Daddyji is reading something he has brought from the office. I return back to the future. I start daydreaming:

I see our plane taking off into the clouds. We are sitting together. I am sitting by the window. The fans of the plane are rotating real fast–just like the ceiling fan at home. I am wondering if the fans of the plane lift the plane upward, then why the ceiling fan cannot lift the house up into the sky. The clouds are getting thicker. We are surrounded by the clouds. It is getting dark in the plane. Every now and then, I can see some hills in the distance. What if the plane crashes into one of the hills? I imagine the plane moving towards one of the hills…

Ginny, my walking stick falls off my lap on to the floor making a rattling noise. I am rattled back to the aerodrome chair. Ginny always comes to my aid, whether I walk or dream. Sister Nanda was right. Ginny has magical powers. Ginny just saved us from a sure crash in my daydream.

The loud speaker is blurting out something; I am unable to understand. Daddyji stands up, and says, "Vikram, let us go. We have to board the plane." We both get up from our chairs. He picks up his small briefcase containing some official papers. I follow him to the door that leads outside where the plane is parked. The airline official, who checked our tickets earlier at the counter, is standing at the door to check our tickets again. He waves us towards the aeroplane. As we approach the plane, we realize that there are landing steps to climb in order to get into the plane. I look at my right leg, and we stand and stare at the steps in consternation. There are five steps to climb.

I hear a voice inside me, "Come on Vikram move. I am with you." I look down at Ginny, as if she said something. I lift my left leg and place it on the first step. As if by magic, Ginny moves and plants itself firmly on to the first step, with my right leg following. The rhythm is set. One after the other, I climb the five steps and before I know it, I am the first one in the plane. As I stand and look back, Daddyji and many other passengers are looking up with smiles of admiration. One by one, all the passengers take their seats.

The air hostess makes sure that everybody has buckled their seatbelts. I am seated by the window with Ginny beside me. The plane's engines start. The noise is loud and the plane is vibrating. Ginny is feeling the vibration and starts to rattle a bit. Is she afraid, I am wondering? I am not sure about her, but I know I am afraid. As the plane starts to run, I hold on to Ginny. After a while, the plane lifts up in the air. I hold on to Ginny real tight. Soon, we are in the clouds. I fall asleep, having been up since 5'oclock in the morning.

7

ASHRAM

We land in Srinagar. As we are waiting at the baggage claim area, Daddyji is looking around to see if somebody from the Ashram has come to pick us up, and he sees somebody in the distance he recognizes.

He says, "Oh my God. Look Vikram... there is Max Hoffer, my Canadian pen friend."

He is so excited that he leaves me behind and moves forward towards Max Hoffer. Not to be left behind, I move after him. When he reaches him, Max is talking animatedly to somebody in a military uniform—a foreigner, an *Engrez*. Daddyji touches Max Hoffer's shoulder. He looks around and says, "Can I..." and then stops and says with amazement, "Surinder, my God, you look the same. It has been almost 11 years." Daddyji and Max shake hands and embrace each other.

Max says, "I am here to pick you up, but I was not really sure how I would recognize you."

Daddyji says, "Max, what a surprise; how did you know we were coming?"

Max replies, "I wrote to you in my last letter that I am in Srinagar with the Canadian peacekeeping contingent. Swamiji sent me a message to pick you up and bring you to the Ashram."

Daddyji suddenly remembers that I am also with him. He looks around. I am standing right behind him watching the drama unfold.

He points towards me and says, "Meet my son, Vikram."

Max extends his hand, and I extend my hand in an awkward sort of way.

He says, "Young man, you may not remember me, but we have met before. I was present when you took your first steps... Oh, and meet my colleague, Lt. Col. Jean-Guy Carriere, Canadian Army. He keeps the peace around here between India and Pakistan. He is with the United Nations Military Observer Group. He will also accompany us to the Ashram. He and I will spend the day there with you and come back to Srinagar in the evening."

Lt. Col. is a big man with a moustache, wearing a green coloured Canadian military uniform and a United Nations armband. Lt. Col. extends his large hand towards Daddyji and says, "Pleased to meet you Monsieur." They shake hands nodding their heads in acknowledgement.

We move into the area where our luggage has been brought in from the plane. There are many porters milling around us, vying for the job of carrying our luggage to the waiting station wagon sent by the Ashram. Two porters bring the luggage to the station wagon. The driver and Max Hoffer sit on the front seats, and Daddyji, Lt. Col. Jean Guy Carriere and I sit on the rear seats of the station wagon. I am sandwiched between the two of them, with Ginny in my lap. Due to the large body of the Lt. Col., I am having trouble fitting Ginny in between my legs. The driver offers to store Ginny in the luggage compartment behind the rear seats. I politely refuse. Some of our luggage is placed in the space behind the rear seats and some is placed on the rooftop luggage rack. All this is being supervised by the driver of the station wagon. When he is satisfied, he shouts, "All aboard! Shall we move, sir?"

Max Hoffer shouts back, "Yes, Sergeant Badri Nath, we are ready to move."

Daddyji looks amused at the military type commands and looks at Max Hoffer.

He explains, "Sergeant Badri Nath is retired from the Indian Army. He was in Hari Nautiyal's unit. We were all together in Burma during World War II."

"Yes, Mr. Nautiyal told me," Daddyji says.

After about fifteen minutes drive through Srinagar, the first stop is at a petrol pump to fill the station wagon. As they are filling petrol and checking under the bonnet of the station wagon, Daddyji gets out for some fresh air. It seems that a particular shop attracts his attention. He walks towards the edge of the sidewalk to have a better look at the sign board of the shop. He then comes back to the station wagon and says, "Excuse me gentlemen, I am just going across the street to look at a shop. I will be back in a few minutes."

'Kachroo Travels–Proprietor Ram Kachroo' is the name on the sign board that attracted his attention. Ram Kachroo was the Guide during our trip to Srinagar in 1943. He is certain that this is the same man. He steps in the shop and asks the man at the reception, "I would like to see Mr. Kachroo. Please tell him an old friend of his, Surinder Mehra, is here."

After a minute or so, Ram Kachroo walks out of his office cabin with a look of curiosity on his face. As soon as they see each other, their arms open and they embrace like long lost friends. Ram Kachroo says, "Professor Sahib, what a pleasant surprise to see you. Where have you settled after partition?"

He replies, "We are settled in Delhi... Tell me about yourself. When did you start this Travel Agency?"

Ram replies, "About five years back. I now have offices in Jammu and in Delhi. Also, now that there is calm in the fighting, tourists are beginning to come to Kashmir. We plan to have offices in Calcutta and Bombay this year, and with the grace of God, all over India next year. We have been appointed agents for both Air India and Indian Airlines. We have also applied to BOAC and Pan American. We plan to be the largest travel agent in India. Professor Sahib, now that we are free from the yolk of the British, and once our differences with Pakistan are settled, India will grow very fast. We want to participate in that growth."

Daddyji replies, "Ram, you sound like a business tycoon. I wish you the very best."

Ram replies, "I still remember the day we were sitting under a Chinar tree in Nishat Garden in April 1943, when you quoted Shakespeare: *there is a tide in the affair of men, which if taken on flood leads on to fortune.* I should tell you that I have thought about this quote ever since. I have just been waiting for the flood of opportunity. I think I see it coming, and I will take it on."

Daddyji replies, "You will be surprised to know that I have gone far away from Shakespeare. From a professor of English, I have become a business executive with Nautiyal Industries."

They say goodbye with promise to keep in touch. And while he is walking back to the petro pump he is thinking:
In spite of all the fighting and devastation in Jammu and Kashmir, people like Ram Kachroo have risen up with optimism and confidence in the future. It seems **Sone Ki Chidiya**—*the Golden Sparrow—will soar again one day, in the not too distant future.*

••

Everybody else is standing outside; I am the only one sitting in the car. I take Ginny out from between my legs and place her beside me to give her some room to breathe. "Come on Vikram, get up and move out of the station wagon. I want some fresh air," the voice of Ginny echoes in my ears. I slide across the seat towards the car door and come out of the car. It is a sunny day. A cool breeze is blowing—a relief from the hot Delhi weather. As I am standing looking, a convoy of green army trucks passes by. Lt. Col. is standing nearby observing the trucks move on. The convoy is followed by a green colored army jeep with the blue flag of the United Nations. Lt. Col. waves at the occupants of the jeep. The jeep turns into the petrol pump area. There is an Indian driver of the jeep in military uniform and two *Engrez* men also in military uniform. The Lt. Col. speaks to them for a few minutes, and the jeep leaves.

Daddyji is back. Everybody takes their seats. Sergeant Badri Nath shouts "all aboard", and without waiting for a reply, puts his foot to the floor and we drive off towards Verinag Ashram situated close to the origin of the Jhelum River.

After a few minutes of quiet ride, Daddyji asks, "Colonel, how are the peacekeeping operations going?"

He replies, "Oh, comme ci comme ca… you know, so- so. We have our challenges some days. It is not easy for only 250 military observers to keep an eye on such a long border."

"How many observers are from Canada?" Daddyji asks.

"Canada has contributed 50 observers and support staff," the Lt. Col. replies.

"What other countries have provided personnel?" Daddyji asks.

"United States of America has contributed most of the rest. There are a few observers from Australia and New Zealand also. But America is withdrawing their observers."

"Oh, why is that?"

"Well Monsieur, politics is not my forte. It is better for a military man to stay away from politics. Max is our political spokesman; maybe he can tell you a little more."

There is a bit of lull. Everybody is quiet. It seems that Max is also not willing to volunteer any information. And then, quite unexpectedly, the driver Sergeant Badri Nath joins the conversation.

He says, "I have heard that the Americans have started giving aid to Pakistan. Therefore, their impartiality, in the matter of Kashmir, is in question. This is the reason why they are withdrawing from the peacekeeping mission."

After this comment, there is silence for the next five minutes. It appears that the Canadians don't want to make any comments about their neighbours and cousins, the Americans.

Finally Max speaks up, "Surinder, have you heard about PL-480?"

Daddyji replies, "Yes I have, what about it?"

"Well, in that case, you should know that, under that law, America is going to provide massive amounts of food grains to India and other countries to promote peace and goodwill."

"Yes, but it is not going to be free. India will make payment to America in Indian rupees," Daddyji replies.

"Yes, but all the money that America receives from the sale of grains will be spent in India on other aid projects." Max replies.

"Well, that is a good gesture on the part of America, and we should be grateful to them, and by the way, to our Canadian friends also for providing food and other aid under the Colombo Plan."

"We are pleased to help." Max says with a smile.

For a while, the Canadians talk about the weather, at which they seem to be good. The Lt. Col. explains, "There are four seasons in Canada: winter, winter, winter and winter." All the Indians are quiet. Realizing that we did not get the joke, he goes on to tell us in detail about weather in various parts of Canada.

"Oh, the Chinaar trees," he says, "make me homesick. You know, back home, these are known as Maple Trees. It snows here like Canada, but that does not make me homesick." He laughs and carries on, "I am not much of a skier back home. I don't really like snow."

After listening to the Lt. Col., everybody goes quiet again.

As we are getting closer to the Ashram, the conversation shifts to spiritual matters.

Max Hoffer turns his neck to look at the rear seats and says, "Surinder, this part of the road, we are traveling on, is where the travelers usually fall asleep and have strange dreams."

I am only dozing, but the Lt. Col. and Daddyji are both fast asleep and snoring. After hearing Max say something, Daddyji wakes up and says, "Max, did you say something?"

"Yes, I said: this is the part of the road where the travelers usually fall asleep and have strange dreams. Researchers from the Ashram have carried out surveys and found that 90% of travelers fall asleep and have strange dreams."

Daddyji says, "Yes, I know. I receive all the reports. And you know the reason for the travelers falling asleep is suspected to be the excess of oxygen in the area due to the presence of a thick forest of Pine trees."

As we are nearing the Ashram, Sergeant Badri Nath has to wake us all up. We had all fallen asleep driving through the particular stretch of road that is known to induce sleep and peculiar dreams. The Lt. Col. says when he wakes up, "Tebernac... I have been in Kashmir for over a year, but I have never fallen asleep in a vehicle in this manner, and I have never had a dream riding in a car. What a weird dream it was!" He describes the dream:

"Hello Monsieur, I am Adolf Hitler."

"Adolf Hitler, you are supposed to be dead. What are you doing here in Srinagar?"

*"I am looking for the **Manoastra**, the weapon that can control the peoples of the world. We Germans have studied all the original Hindu Scriptures written in Sanskrit. We have unearthed the Secret, and it is to be found in the valley in Srinagar."*

Herr Hitler, the weapon you refer to has already been made and tested. It is called the H-Bomb.

I know Monsieur, I already know about the H-Bomb. The days of physical destruction to conquer the world are gone because everybody has the same weapons. What I am looking for is a means to control the minds of people.

But, Herr Hitler, you are dead. What good is it for you to find this weapon that you talk about?

Monsieur, have you not heard about reincarnation? I will be born again. I have scores to settle.

The Lt. Col. says, "I hope he does not come back."

"Come on Jean Guy, it is just a dream. Don't take it seriously. Both Surinder and I had a dream, somewhat, like you had, when we were driving back in a bus back in April 1943." Max says looking towards the rear seat where Daddyji and the Lt. Col. are seated.

Daddyji adds with a nod of his head, "Yes, that was quite a disturbing experience for me, and I kept thinking about it for years afterwards. And it became uncanny the day I found out about the dropping of Atom Bombs on Hiroshima and Nagasaki."

• •

When we reach the Ashram, we all stumble out of the station wagon and look around at the magnificent view of the snow covered mountains far away. The Ashram is located atop a hillock that overlooks north and east. A few men from the Ashram come out to unload our baggage.

As we are standing around straightening our legs, a tall man, with grey hair and wearing white *kurta* and *paijama,* comes out of one of the rooms of the Ashram. He starts walking towards us. From his gait, and the looks he is getting from the people standing around, it is obvious that he is the Swamiji that everybody has been referring to. Everybody, except me, starts to move towards him. He waves at other people and starts to walk towards the direction that I am standing. Ginny is in my hand. I look around and there is nobody else in the vicinity but me. I start to get a bit nervous. I think Ginny can feel the tremor in my hand. "Come on Vikram, be brave. What are you afraid of? He is just a Swami not a *Howwya* or a bugbear." Ginny's voice rings in my ears. I am not sure how I would greet him. I have seen people greet Swamis by touching their feet, but I am not going to be able to do that because of the problem with my right leg. As Swamiji comes and stands in front of me, I join my hands to do *Namaste,* with Ginny hanging on to one of my fingers. He places his right hand on my head, and blesses me by reciting a Sanskrit Mantra. I do not understand what it means, but, I guess, it is meant to cure the defect in my leg.

Swamiji then walks to where Daddyji is standing and they shake hands warmly. Daddyji says, "Swamiji, after eleven years, you still look the same." Swamiji laughs and says, "Nice to see you all; welcome to Verinag Ashram."

After the introductions and formal remarks, Daddyji and I are directed to our living quarters. There are two beds in one room along with a study table with two drawers and a chair. There is a quilt and a blanket on each bed. When we enter the room, our luggage is already in the room. We had brought our own holdalls containing our own bedding, but we just leave them unopened as the bedding is provided. There is an attached bathroom with a pot containing water and a commode toilet. Everything is neat and clean but sparse. Both Daddyji and I decide to lie down and rest a little. It is almost 2:00 P.M. I have been up for about eight hours. My right leg is stiff. I lie down with Ginny beside me. After a few minutes, I hear the sound of snoring; Daddyji is deep in sleep. Here we go again—more dreams, I am thinking. Fortunately, after a few minutes, there is a knock on the door and a man announces, "Sahib, the lunch is ready." The man leaves after the announcement. Daddyji is still snoring. I get up from my bed, with Ginny protecting my right flank.

I shake Daddyji, holding his shoulder with my right hand. "Lunch is ready," I say to him. He gets up, combs his hair and straightens out his clothes. As I am standing beside the study table waiting, I open the top drawer. There is nothing else in the drawer except a photograph. I remove it and start to look at it.

Daddyji sees me looking at the photo and asks, "Whose photo is it?"

"I don't know," I say.

He walks over and looks at it and says. "This is Hitler's photo. I wonder why a photo of Hitler is in the Ashram." He takes it away from my hand, places it in his briefcase, and we go for lunch.

The kitchen and dining area are in a separate building. Max, the Lt. Col. and Swamiji are already sitting in the dining area. There are five tables with six chairs to a table. We join the rest of them on the same table. A brass tumbler full of water is at each seating position. After Daddyji takes his seat, he opens the buckles of his well worn leather briefcase and gently slides out Hitler's photo and places it in the centre of the table. Naturally, other people sitting on the table take notice, while they are engaged in conversation.

As soon as they see the photo, there is silence for a moment, and then somebody asks, "Who is this?"

Daddyji keeps silent. Max says, "Looks like Hitler, does he not? There is again silence. Swamiji has a serious, but mysterious, look on his face.

Daddyji, finally, breaks the silence and asks, "Swamiji, whose photo is it? It looks like Hitler's, but if you look carefully his features are Indian."

Swamiji, finally, says, "Surinder, you are right. This is not Hitler's photo. This is the photo of an unknown Indian freedom fighter. His name was Adarsh Rai Nautiyal, Hari Nautiyal's father. He went to Singapore in the late 1800's to work there. After making a lot of money, he returned to India and set up his own business. In the 1930's, he left everything to his son, Hari, and started working towards freeing India from the British rule. It is said that he hated the British so much that when Hitler attacked England in 1940, Adarsh Rai Nautiyal openly started supporting Hitler. He believed that the enemy of the enemy is a friend. So much so that he started dressing like Hitler, including his hair style and moustache and started calling himself Adrarsh Hitler. In 1943, he went back to Singapore and fought against the British alongside the Japanese, and it is believed that he died there. This photo was apparently taken during that time."

Everybody is spell bound by the story. There is silence. The servers start to bring lunch to the table, and we all start to eat.

After lunch is finished, Max asks, "What is the explanation for the dreams that people are having when travelling on the road to the Ashram."

Swamiji replies, "The locals believe that Adarsh Nautiyal's soul is still roaming these areas, and, every now and then, enters people's dream. It is not a scientific explanation, but dreams do not have a scientific explanation. And one more thing is worth noting. It was Adarsh Nautiyal who started providing financial support to this Ashram and started the Mind Research Institute here that has now become world famous. My guruji, Swami Shiv Narayan, founded this Ashram in the 1890's. Some people are of the opinion that the dreams people have travelling on this road are because of the research we are doing in long-range brainwave communication. The fact is that we really do not know."

By the time lunch is finished, it is 3:30 P.M. Both Max and the Lt. Col. are ready to go back to Srinagar.

"Surinder let me know when you are going back to Delhi. I will meet you in Srinagar before you fly back," Max says, as he is getting up.

8

MIND OVER MATTER

Next morning Daddyji and I meet Swamiji in his office. The first topic of conversation is my leg. After listening to the background of how I developed the problem in my leg, Swamiji closes his eyes and goes into meditation for a few minutes. Both of us just sit there and watch him reciting a mantra for what feels like several minutes. After he is finished, he rubs his face with both hands and opens his eyes.

"Our body is a servant of our brain," Swamiji says in a slow and deliberate manner and looking into my eyes to emphasize the point, "It does whatever our brain tells it to do, but it has capabilities far beyond we give it credit for. If you place limitations upon yourself through negative thinking, the body immediately senses it and puts limitation on its capabilities." He asks me, "Vikram do you understand what I said?"

I am not sure if I did, but I just nod my head to indicate that I do.

He carries on, "It is unfortunate that you have developed this problem with your leg, but it is going to become normal soon. You must believe it. In fact, you must start to act and think, as if your leg is normal, and you will see that you will be fine. I have asked Tyagiji, our Yoga instructor, to teach you some Yoga *asanas*… Oh, and one more thing: you must part company with your friend and guide sitting beside you," he says, pointing towards my walking stick, Ginny. He gets up and says, "Please follow me, I will introduce you to Tyagiji."

We walk across the grassy plot on a walkway paved with pebbles from the river Jhelum and lined with colorful flowers on both sides. *Yogdham*, the hall where Yoga classes are held, is a stand alone building with windows on all four sides and a sloping roof like all the other buildings that I have seen in the area. As we enter, we are greeted by a man wearing white *kurta* and *paijama*.

Swamiji introduces Daddyji and me to Tyagiji, "Meet Vikram Mehra; he is the one I told you about. And you have heard about Surinder Mehra, our Executive Director; here he is, in person."

Tyagiji says, "*Namaste,*" with hands folded and with a slight bow.

"Well, we will leave you with Tyagiji," Swamiji says, and both he and Daddyji walk out of the hall.

Tyagiji hands me over a pair of shorts and says, "Vikram, you can go in there and change into shorts." As I start to walk away with Ginny in my right hand, he says, "You can leave the stick here. Try and walk without it."

I am startled. I have not walked without Ginny for the last few months. Nevertheless, I, reluctantly, leave Ginny leaning against the wall. As I am walking away, I look back to see if Ginny is fine, and I see it sliding down along the wall towards the floor with Tyagiji standing beside it. I run back to give her support and prevent it from falling. I am barely there in time to hold it and stop it from sliding to the floor.

"Well done, Vikram! You can move real fast. It seems that you are very attached to the stick."

I place Ginny securely against the wall and go to the change room. As I am changing into a pair of shorts, I am wondering about what Swamiji had said earlier about the influence of mind over body. My being able to run so fast, without feeling any pain, gives me renewed confidence. When I go out after changing, I see Ginny lying beside the mat on which I am supposed to do my *Yogabhyaas* or Yogic exercises.

Tyagiji tells me, "I put it there."

As I sit in the lotus pose, I hear an echo in my head that says, "Well done, Vikram. That was quiet a run. And listen to me carefully. Swamiji is right. You must part company with me. You can make it on your own. Do not worry. I will always be with you watching over you, guiding you whenever you need me."

After completing my *Yogabhyaas,* I feel energized. I get up and change back into my normal clothing, pick Ginny up on my shoulder and walk out of the hall with Tyagiji. I still have a limp, but my legs feel strong.

"See Vikram, you are carrying me now, instead of me carrying you." Ginny's voice echoes in my ears. Tyagiji goes his way, and I walk over to Swamiji's office.

Daddyji and Swamiji are still having their meeting.

I stand at the door and ask, "May I come in, sir?"

Swamiji looks up and sees me standing with Ginny on my shoulder and says, "Look Surinder, who is here. Come in Vikram; have a seat there," pointing to a chair on the far corner of the room, so that I cannot hear what they are talking about.

I make myself comfortable. As the discussion between them is going on, I look up sideways and down to while away time. I see something moving on the concrete floor; it is a line of ants moving towards the wall and disappearing somewhere in the crevice. I am reminded of the ability of the ants to communicate with one another without a sound. I decide to listen in to the conversation between Daddyji and Swamiji. I am not able to make out anything. And then, I start to sense what they are saying—no sound but just a sense that I just know what they are talking about.

Daddyji says, "Swamiji, Hari Nautiyal wants to make sure that we are not giving away the research you are doing in long-range brain wave communication to other countries. He does not want any more foreigners admitted to courses or research projects in this subject. For the last many years, there have been a lot of foreigners studying at the Ashram. He wants this cut down to no more than ten percent of the total admissions. We are letting various universities in India know about what we are doing here. We are offering scholarships to encourage them to send their brightest students to the Ashram for short periods of time. Brain wave communication is expected to be the final frontier in human communications. It will be very helpful in leading India to the forefront of nations of the world."

Swamiji replies, "Surinder, you should tell Hari Nautiyal that when we exchange ideas with foreign students who come to study here, they learn from us, but we also learn from them. We gain by sharing knowledge and not by hoarding it."

Daddyji responds carefully to Swamiji's frustration, "Swamiji, let me tell you the whole story. We have been approached by the Intelligence Bureau. They think that the subjects of your research are of national importance; therefore, your research at the Ashram must be treated as confidential, like at any other national research laboratory. In fact, the government will be sending some senior civil servants to the Ashram for studies. The good news is that monetary grants will provided to the Ashram by the government. Hari Nautiyal has asked me to convey his gratitude to you. He will also be visiting the Ashram, in the company of some dignitaries, in the near future. Oh, and one more thing: all the applications should be sent to me before granting admission to any new candidates."

Swamiji appears perturbed to hear this. He says, "Surinder, I am a simple minded Yogi. I do not want to get involved in IB, MI5, MI6, KGB and get into the alphabetic soup."

Daddyji replies, "I will convey your concerns to the Trustees of the Ashram."

The routine at the Ashram is like clockwork. One activity follows the other, and before I know it, the day is over. There are 33 students and researchers at the ashram. The classes are going on all day. Daddyji attends some of the classes to familiarize himself with the workings of the Ashram.

During my stay at the Ashram, I have repeatedly heard Swamiji use the word *Mannosancharan*. One night, when we are getting ready to go to bed, I ask, "Daddyji, what is *Mannosancharan*?

"Oh, so you have been listening... Swamiji has coined this term. It means being able to read other person's thoughts or plant thoughts in other person's mind at long distances through your brain or mind. It can be translated into English as: 'long-range brain wave communication'."

I reply, "I also want to learn this technique. You know, Daddyji, I think I already know how to read other people's minds. I learned it from ants."

Daddyji gives me a strange look and says, "Ants? ...Well, why don't you talk to Swamiji in the morning?"

"Daddyji, can you please ask him?" I plead with him.

Next day I ask, "So Daddyji, did you talk to Swamiji about me?"

"Yes, I did, but he says you are too young to get into all these things. You should concentrate on your studies. When you are in College, you can come here one summer. Right now the techniques are not well developed."

• •

We are sitting down for dinner. Swamiji is in deep thought. I have no idea what comes over me; I spontaneously start repeating 59049, 59049, 59049............ At first, they keep talking, as if they are not hearing me. I start speaking a little louder, louder and much louder. Daddyji looks at me with a look of annoyance on his face and says, "Vikram, what are you doing?"

Swamiji also gives me a strange look, but tells Daddyji, "Let us find out what Vikram is saying."

"Tell us Vikram... What is it that you are talking about?

"59049. Swamiji is this not the number you had in mind, when you were talking to Daddyji a little while back?" I say with sparkle in my eyes.

Swamiji replies, "What is the number again?"

I repeat, "59049."

Swamiji says with a look of surprise, "Yes, this is the number we were talking about earlier in my office. You must have heard it. In any case, yes, this is the number. All right Vikram let me ask you something. Why is 59049 a special number? "

I think about it for a while and reply, "It is 951 less than 60000." He starts to scratch his head and says carefully weighing his words, "What is the significance of 60000 minus 951?"

I reply, "Nothing really but 59049 is significant."

"Why?" he asks.

"It is 3 raised to the power of 10; but, Swamiji, why were you and Daddyji talking about 59049?" I ask.

"This is the amount of money we spend in a year for everybody to live at the Ashram. Are you satisfied now?" he replies.

"One more thing, sir: Why is the expenditure number 3 raised to the power of 10, and not some other number? Why did it work out to exactly this number and no other?" I ask with a mystic smile.

"Vikram, I think you are being a nuisance. Can you please stop this now," Daddyji says with emphasis on *now*.

I am glad that Swamiji intervenes, "Wait a minute, Surinder. I think he has a point. I will have to study the numerological significance of this number."

After dinner we retire to our rooms.

The next day, again, we are in the dining hall sitting down for dinner. Swamiji is wearing his usual white attire and a smile. He sits down with his gaze fixed on me and with a slight smile on his face. He says, "Surinder, your son is a *Mannosanchari*."

Daddyji looks at Swamiji with a puzzled look. "What is that?" he says

"I just made up a new word. A *Mannosanchari* is a person who practices *Mannosanchar*. Yesterday night, Vikram was successful in planting a number in our minds that we had never heard of, and he made us believe that we knew the number as 59049. Remember, last night I said that 59049 was the amount of money we spend every year running this Ashram. Well, I went back to my office last night and checked the number; it is 65536."

"Swamiji, this number is 2 raised to the power of 16," I say.

Swamiji takes out a piece of paper from his shirt pocket and looks at it and repeats it, "Well, the number is 46656."

"Swamiji this number is 6 raised to the power 6. This is a real coincidence that you are spending this exact amount of money to run the Ashram." I say.

Both of them look at me puzzled but with a smile. Daddyji takes the piece of paper from Swamiji's hand and reads the number aloud, "It is 56466."

I laugh and say, "Well, finally you got the right number."

"Vikram, you really swarmed us with numbers. How did you do this?"

"I just planted the numbers, close to the real numbers, in your mind. I have been telling Daddyji that I can enter the minds and dreams of people, but he does not believe me." I say laughing.

"Surinder, is he telling the truth, or is it some kind of a mathematical trick you two are playing on me?" Swamiji says.

"Swamiji, I know that Vikram makes claims that he can read the mind of other people, but I have never taken it seriously. I know he is very good in mathematics, and he can play games with numbers."

"Vikram, how did you get to be so good in mathematics?" Swamiji asks.

"Our mathematics teacher, Mr. Madan, holds a special class for those students who are good in mathematics. In that class he teaches us how to play tricks with numbers. Swamiji, I can really read minds and plant thoughts in the minds of other people." I say.

Daddyji is looking at me annoyed and says, "Vikram, as I told you earlier, I want you to concentrate on your studies."

Swamiji intervenes and says, "Surinder, mind reading is not a bad thing. We all do it and do not even realize it. We have done experiments and found that ordinary people were able to read other people's thoughts about 25% of the time. This is a very common social skill that we humans practice unknowingly. Young people can read each other's minds even better. As we grow older, we learn to hide our thoughts to gain advantage over others. However, those who are close to each other, such as husband and wife or close friends, can read each other's mind 50% of the time. And there are some people who can read the minds of strangers 75% of the time. Vikram is one of them. What we are trying to achieve with our work at the Ashram is to devise or discover a methodology, whereby, strangers can read each other's mind 100% of the time or as close to it as nature would permit. We believe that our ancient forefathers had the mind reading ability. However, as life became more complex, we humans evolved into concealing our thoughts in order to create social order. Can you imagine the chaos in the world, if everybody could read everybody else's thoughts?"

At the conclusion of the long and enlightening explanation, Swamiji gets up and says, "Well, you have to leave early tomorrow. It has been a long day. Let us retire for the evening."

As we are getting up from our chairs, he starts to speak again, "Surinder, a thought has crossed my mind." And he pauses for a while, scratching his right cheek and carries on speaking, "I think you should let Vikram stay at the Ashram for an extended period of time; let us say one school term. He seems to have a natural gift of mind reading that will be of great value to us in our research, and he will enhance his capability also. At the same time, we can carry on with the treatment of his leg."

Daddyji appears shocked; his face turns white and mouth is wide open, and he is speechless. He takes some time to gather his thoughts and says curtly, "He is too young to stay in the Ashram and miss a school year. We will see what happens in the future." And we get up and go to our rooms.

When we reach our room, Daddyji does not talk to me. We go to sleep. The next morning we are up early, "Good morning Daddyji," I say. He carries on packing his suitcase. He does not reply. I know that he is annoyed with me for showing off my mind reading skill to Swamiji against his wishes. I am afraid to say anything more and quietly take a bath and get ready for breakfast. Daddyji gets ready after me and walks out to go to the dining room, while I am still sitting on the edge of the bed waiting for him. I get up and start following him. He enters the dining room; I also enter the dining room. He picks a table to sit at; I go and sit on the same table. Breakfast is served. It is milk, roti, honey and curd. We both start eating. Swamiji comes in and sits down beside us. Daddyji looks at him, nods his head and keeps eating with his head down.

Swamiji looks at me, and, as our eyes meet, he flickers his eyelids towards Daddyji as, if asking, "What is wrong with him?" I just make a face and keep quiet.

After breakfast is over, we all get up and walk out of the dining room. The station wagon is waiting outside with our luggage loaded and is ready for boarding to take us to Srinagar. We are to take the 2:00 P.M. flight to Delhi. Daddyji walks towards the station wagon, still ignoring me. I walk behind him with a limp and Ginny on my shoulder.

A voice rings in my ears—Ginny's voice, "Vikram, it is time to show that you matter. Your father is being a pig, and you should teach him a lesson."

"Come on Ginny. Don't call him a pig; that makes me a pig too," I say in my thoughts.

"Sorry, Vikram, I do not mean it literally. I will tell you what you should do. Stop walking and stay where you are, and let your father go sit in the station wagon and see what he does." Ginny's voice rings in my ears. I follow her instructions and stop walking. Swamiji comes and stands beside me. Daddyji comes and stands near us and says goodbye to him and goes and sits down in the rear seat of the station wagon and shuts the door. Sergeant Badri Nath, the driver, goes and sits in the driver's seat, waiting for me to enter the station wagon. Nevertheless, I keep standing and hold my ground. I think Swamiji senses the game I am playing. A few minutes pass.

"Now you will see him come out; just watch; 1, 2, 3..." And before she can say... 4, the rear door of the station wagon opens. "See, what did I tell you?" Ginny's voice rings true. Daddyji steps out of the station wagon with a smile on his face, holds me by my right hand and walks me to the station wagon.

"Vikram, ultimately parents have to give in to their children." Ginny's voice rings in my ears.

Our journey to Srinagar is uneventful. There are three of us in the station wagon. As we are travelling through the stretch of road, where travelers usually fall asleep, we decide that we will keep talking and not fall asleep. We reach the Srinagar Airport at about 11:00 A.M. As soon as our station wagon comes to a stop in front of the airport building, a swarm of porters surround us. Sergeant Badri Nath gets out and picks two of them to carry our luggage inside. At about the same time, we see a military jeep come to a stop in the parking lot. Max Hoffer comes out and walks towards us. After exchanging pleasantries, we all walk into the airport. Sergeant Badri Nath helps us to check-in our baggage and get us our boarding passes. It seems that all the airline staff knows him personally. Later, we find out that the Sergeant is well known for distributing gift baskets full of apples to the airline staff. After we are checked in, the Sergeant says goodbye.

Max, Daddyji and I sit in one corner of the building and wait for our flight to be called.

"Surinder, I will be going to Canada for a while on official business within the next few months," Max says.

Before Max can finish what he has to say, Daddyji interrupts with excitement, "You must stop in Delhi for a few days and stay with us." And then he asks, "Why are you going to Canada at this time of the year? You usually go in winter."

Max replies, "Well, I have been asked to become a member of a committee to look into the peaceful uses of atomic energy."

Daddyji says, "I had read about it and wondered at the time: How can the destructive atomic power be used for peace? Does this duality not appear in conflict?"

Max replies, "Well, this will all be looked at by the committee. The main aim is to spread the use of atomic power to generate electricity."

They keep talking, while I have a little nap until Daddyji wakes me up, "Vikram *Beta*, time to board the plane."

We board the plane at about 1:00 P.M. After everybody is seated, we wait and wait and wait, until somebody asks one of the hostesses, "Miss, what is the delay?"

"Sir, we are waiting for some V.I.P.'s to arrive. It should not be much longer."

It is almost 2:30 P.M. The passengers are feeling uneasy. Somebody asks one of the hostesses, "Who is the V.I.P.?"

"Sir, we have not been told who the V.I.P's are; however, we have been told that it should not be much longer."

Soon thereafter, there is commotion on the ground just beside the aircraft. A group of two men and two women board the plane and take their seats near the front. After they are seated, there is a ripple of whispering rumour flowing through the plane, "Film actor Jeet Kumar and actress Rani Roy, the heart throbs of those days, are travelling in the plane."

Nearly everybody lifts their bums and cranes their necks to have a look. I also try to do my best to have a glimpse, so that I can tell my friends at school that I travelled with the film stars. It seems the pilot realizes that as soon as the plane takes off, the passengers will be coming to the front of the plane to have a glimpse of their favourite film stars, thereby causing disturbance near the front seats. He requests the film stars to take a walk through the plane to meet the passengers, so that there will be fewer disturbances during the flight.

Jeet Kumar and Rani Roy are gracious enough to accede to the pilot's request. One by one, they take a walk in the aisle, smiling and shaking hands with some of the passengers. I am seated in the aisle seat with my stick, Ginny, resting in my lap. As Rani Roy is walking past me, she notices my stick. I think her maternal instincts just get the better of her after seeing a 12 year old boy sitting with a walking stick in hand.

She stops in her tracks. "Hello," she says in her sugary voice and asks, "What is your name, darling?" And she shakes a lock of her dark silky hair away from her eyes. She sounds exactly the way she sounds in her movies. My face is flush with blush.

"What happened?" she asks pointing to my leg.

I can hardly get a word out of my mouth, "Fever. I had fever," I say.

To my utter surprise and delight, she caresses my cheeks and then holds my chin and says, "Sweetie, you will be all right just like the little boy, Pashi, in my last film *Jyoti*." She slowly moves on. I look to my left. Daddyji is fast asleep, having missed the biggest happening in my life. No witness, there is no witness, I am thinking. Nobody is going to believe me that Rani Roy touched me.

As always, Ginny comes to my help. Her voice echoes in my ears, "Vikram, I saw everything—you lucky boy. Wake up your father. What better time to use his photographic skills than now?"

I shake Daddyji by his arm, "What is it Vikram?" he asks.

"Picture with Rani Roy," I say softly. He quickly takes out his Kodak 'Brownie' D box camera. As Rani Roy is walking back to her seat, I raise Ginny up to make her notice me. Her eyes meet my pleading eyes. She bends down with her cheeks against mine, and 'click' 'click' goes the 'Brownie'; the picture captured in the camera and in my heart for ever.

I am re-living, in my mind, the drama of Rani Roy touching my cheeks and the picture taken with her. I do not even know when the plane takes off, and I fall into sweet slumber.

I wake up from my reverie by the sound of the thud of the tires of the plane touching the runway of the Willingdon aerodrome, New Delhi.

As we are travelling home in a taxi, Daddyji says, "Vikram, your mother will be in a fit of anxiety. We are two hours late."

He is right. As the taxi turns into our street, we can see Mummyji standing at the front gate of the house along with Kishi, Suneeta and Suraj and looking towards Rohtak Road anxiously awaiting our arrival.

The taxi driver asks, "Sahib, which is your house?"

"That one with the 'reception committee' standing outside," Daddyji replies sarcastically.

The taxi driver says, "Sorry sahib, I could not understand what you said."

By this time the taxi is almost in front of his house, "Stop, stop… right here," he says.

As the taxi comes to a stop, the 'reception committee' rushes forward to meet us. As soon as I see Suraj, I am anxious to tell him about my 'encounter' with actress, Rani Roy. Alas, I have to wait for that. First, Mummyji embraces me and gives me kisses on my head and cheeks and enquires about my leg.

"See, Mummyji, I can walk without Ginny," I say, with Ginny on my shoulder.

Next Suneeta and Kishi are after me, "Vikram *Bhaiyya,* what have you brought for me?" each of them asks.

I point out towards Daddyji and slip out to play with Suraj.

"Suraj *yaar,* you will not believe this. In the plane, I saw Rani Roy along with Jeet Kumar," I tell him with excitement.

"What are you saying? I don't believe it. You are a lucky boy. Now tell me, tell me, did you see her from up close?" Suraj asks, holding me by my shoulder.

"You are talking up close! Oh, Suraj *yaar,* you are not going to believe this. She actually touched my cheeks." I tell him with hyperbolic excitement.

Suraj is beside himself, "Tell me, how does she look in person?"

"Suraj, you are not going to believe this also. Her hair is like strings of velvet, her eyes like two shinning diamonds, and when she touched my cheeks, her fingers felt like as if rose petals were touching me. And her fragrance reminded me of the day we were in the Rose Garden of the Moghul Gardens."

When I finish speaking, Suraj has his gaze fixed at some point in the future and says with his head high and full of confidence, "Vikram, one day, I will be rich. I promise you. I will be filthy rich, and Rani Roy will act in a movie of which I will be the producer."

I say tapping him on his shoulder, "Suraj, wake up; let us play some street cricket."

He looks at me with surprise and says, "How can you play cricket? What about your leg?"

I raise my hands up and say, "Look, Suraj, I can walk without Ginny."

"Oh, my God, this is a miracle. Show me; I want to see you walk," Suraj says.

Suraj and I walk to the end of the street up to Rohtak Road. I still have bit of a limp.

Suraj says, "Are you going to start playing cricket now?"

"Swamiji told me to gradually ease into playing cricket. So I will see you at the cricket practice after school tomorrow."

Next morning, as I am getting ready to walk out with my cricket bat in hand, Mummyji says, "Vikram, do you remember what I told you?"

"Yes, Mummyji, I do."

"What?" she asks.

"I have to drink lots of milk, if I want to be a Test player in cricket," I reply with a smile.

She says, "Vikram, youstupidboy, I told you to stop bragging about your achievements; otherwise, you can be struck with Evil Eye."

"I know, Mummyji, I was just joking with you. I have learned my lesson."

9

MAX GOES TO DELHI

There is a knock at the door. "Telegram, sahib," the postman announces. We are having dinner. Anxiety lines appear on Mummyji's forehead. Daddyji gets up and goes to the door to sign for the telegram. He quickly scratches his signatures and starts to bolt the door, but the postman is still standing and waiting with a meek smile. Daddyji thrusts his hands in his pocket looking for some change. Mummyji, knowing that he does not have any money in his pocket, takes some out from her purse and goes out to hand it over to the postman as a *Baksheesh* or tip. Daddyji notices anxiety on her face.

He says, "There must be some good news in the telegram; otherwise, the postman would not have waited for the tip."

"How does he know what is in the telegram?" I ask.

"They have their own ways. If there is bad news, he will never wait for the tip," Daddyji replies.

He starts to open the envelope and says, "I know who the sender of the telegram is. It is Max Hoffer."

He then opens the envelope and reads the telegram aloud. "Arriving Delhi August 13, 4:00 P.M. Staying at the Claridges. Request meeting 14th morning. Max."

He goes in and looks for Mummyji, "Kamla, Max is coming to Delhi."

She asks, "Why is he coming? Did you know he was coming?"

He replies, "When we met in Srinagar, I had asked him to stop in Delhi on his way to Canada."

She asks, "You never told me that; how are we going to accommodate him?"

Daddyji replies, "Kamla, he is not going to live with us; he is staying at the Claridges Hotel. I want to invite him to have dinner with us the evening of August 15."

It seems Mummyji is allergic to Max Hoffer's name. As soon as she hears that Daddyji is going to invite him, she makes her usual face to express displeasure. Daddyji, sensing it, adds, "We will also invite your brother, Daulat Ram, and brother-in-law SK. It has been a long time since we have seen them."

She seems to accept the bitter with the sweet.

On August 14, Daddyji rings up the Claridges Hotel from his office to talk to Max. They decide to meet for lunch at the hotel. At about 12:00 noon he roars out of the parking lot of the Scindia house on his motorcycle and heads south on Queensway. He rolls into the parking lot of the hotel within ten minutes. After pulling the motorcycle on the stand and locking the ignition, he walks towards the entrance to the hotel. As he is walking up the steps, he notices from the corner of his eye that there are two men playing tennis on the lush green grass court. He stops and has a closer look. One of the men is no other than Max; the second man is one of the other guests staying at the hotel. In the mean time, Max also notices Daddyji standing at the entrance steps. He waves his hand and shouts, "It will be another ten minutes."

Daddyji waits for him in the hotel lobby. After a while, Max walks in wiping perspiration from his face, saying, "Surinder, I will take a quick shower and be down in ten minutes."

• •

As they are sitting down for lunch, Max says, "You know, Surinder, I have been invited by the Canadian High Commissioner to join him to watch the Independence Day celebrations at the Red Fort tomorrow."

"You just read my mind. Max, I was going to invite you to join me to watch the celebrations. I have two journalist passes. And after that I was going to invite you to have dinner with us in the evening at our house," Daddyji says with a disappointed look.

"Well, I can still come to dinner and meet your family. I am free tomorrow evening," Max replies.

"It is a deal, as you North Americans say. I will pick you up here at 6:00 P.M. tomorrow, as long as you don't mind riding on the rear seat of my motorcycle."

"It is a deal," replies Max with his right hand meeting Daddyji's right hand—as if it is some kind of an international deal being sealed by the shake of hands.

As the lunch arrives, the conversation shifts to more serious topics.

"Surinder, I have heard that you are restricting the number of admissions by non-Indians to Verinag Ashram?" Max asks, as he is chewing on a piece of Tandoori chicken.

Daddyji keeps quiet, continuing chewing his food and composing a response at the same time.

He starts to say, "Well… " And then picks up a glass of water to take a sip; he is trying to gain time. He continues, "As I was saying… Max, have you been to the Ashram lately?"

Max breaks a piece of a Naan, dips it in the gravy of *Rogan Josh* and says before putting it in his mouth, "Yes. I visited the Ashram last week. I wanted to discuss with Swamiji the possibility of some friends of mine from Canada staying at the Ashram next year. He told me that they should fill an admission application, and then you will decide who gets admitted."

Daddyji wipes his lips with the cloth napkin and says, "Yes. That is the new policy to limit the admissions from foreign countries. There is a lot of interest from Indian Universities to send their students to the Ashram. Therefore, we have decided to give them a chance first. However, we will gladly admit a few visitors from Canada. After all, we are eating Canadian wheat. For all we know, the wheat from which *this* Roti is made could have been grown in Canada." And they both break into a laughter.

After lunch, Daddyji returns to his office, and Max returns to his room.

• •

Next morning, the 15th of August, Daddyji has a journalistic assignment at the Red Fort to report on the Independence Day celebrations for his magazine, LESTWEFORGET.

After completing his assignment, he returns home at about 2:00 P.M.

"Chottu, I have to leave at 5:00 P.M. Make sure that the motorcycle is clean and shinning," he tells our domestic servant.

Daddyji dresses up and is ready to leave at 5:15 P.M. As usual, Mummyji is worried on a number of fronts: the food for guests, cleaning and getting the house ready, especially, to impress a foreign guest. And another thing is uppermost in her mind. August 15, being a day of celebration, there is a lot of traffic on the roads; she is concerned with Daddyji going on his motorcycle to bring Max home.

"As Daddyji is about to kick start the motorcycle, she says, "Listen ji, why don't you go in a taxi?"

"It is fine Kamla; the weather is good. I should be back in about 90 minutes. Moreover, Max will like it. When one is riding a motorcycle, one gets a different perspective of a city." And then he looks at me and says, "Vikram, you go help Mummyji to organize things." He kicks at the starter paddle and roars away.

We all dress up and are ready for the guests, especially Max. I have Ginny resting in the closet. The first to arrive are: Daulat Ram, Uncle SK and their wives. We have not seen them for months. In fact, they have not seen me after my illness, and neither are they aware of the fact that I had developed a problem with my leg. It was a conscious decision by my parents; they did not want a whole bunch of relatives descending on us to ask about my well being, and they did not want to burden me with the stigma of a serious illness. As soon as the guests settle down in the drawing room, they notice that I am walking with a limp.

Daulat Ram is the first to notice, and he asks, "Vikram, what happened? Fell down from the bicycle?"

As I am about to open my mouth to say something, Mummyji says, "*Bhaji*, he got injured playing cricket. The doctor says it is a minor sprain. It should be fine in a few days." After this bit of inquisition, I walk out to play in the verandah with Kishi and Suneeta.

The relatives are catching up on the news and are enjoying pakoras and tea as appetizers. After a while, Mummyji comes out and stands at the front gate—as she usually does when waiting for Daddyji.

Earlier, Daddyji reaches the Claridges Hotel, picks up Max at the appointed time and heads home. While driving back, he decides to take a detour to show Max the area around India Gate and Rashtrapati Bhavan—the President's residence—and the circular Parliament Building. It is about 7:00 P.M. The air has cooled down and the motorcycle ride is most pleasant. They are both shouting at each other over the roar of the motorcycle and the rushing breeze to have a conversation. Daddyji is giving a running commentary, while they are passing by the important landmarks.

Max has seen these landmarks on his previous trips but only riding in a car or a military jeep. "Surinder, I think motorcycle is the best way for sight seeing. When you come to Canada, I will certainly return the favour and give you a similar tour of the area around the Parliament buildings in Ottawa, but make sure you come in the summer; riding a motorcycle in the middle of winter will be unsafe because the roads are slippery with ice and snow!"

At about the time that Mummyji is standing at the front gate of the house waiting for Daddyji to arrive, and I am playing with Krish and Suneeta on the road
in front of the house, Daddyji is riding the motorcycle on the last leg of the
journey home. They are riding down the slope from Pahargunj area down to
Rohtak Road. As I look up, a man is walking by with his bicycle in hand with a
punctured front tire. This brings back old memories, when our bicycle tire was
punctured near my school. Strangely, a thought comes to my mind. A thought
that has never occurred to me since Daddyji has bought the motorcycle: What if
the tire of the motorcycle gets punctured?

I turn around and ask, "Mummyji, do tires of motorcycles also get
punctured?"

She is not at all happy to hear this strange question from me and tells me
with irritation in her voice, "Vikramyoustupidboy, why do you come up with
these strange inauspicious utterings?"

Unbeknown to us, when Daddyji is throttling the motorcycle down the slope of
Pahargunj, the ride becomes very bumpy. "Oh, the road is really bad," he shouts
to Max. After a minute or so, as the bumpy ride continues, Max shouts back,
"Old chap, you have a flat."

Daddy hears what Max has said, but he has no idea what he means by 'flat'.
He thinks that Max is enquiring if we live in a flat.

Daddyji replies, "No, we have an independent house."

Max shouts back, "What I mean is your tire has lost air. It is flat."

"Oh, do you mean punctured?" Daddyji asks.

Daddyji brings the motorcycle to a stop on the side of the road. They both
get down, and, sure enough, there is no air in the tire. Daddyji looks around;
every shop is closed, being Independence Day holiday. They stand there pondering what to do. Max is rather enjoying the experience. He is looking around
taking in the surroundings. Buses, cars, rickshaws and bicycles are rushing by.
Daddyji is feeling helpless.

Max asks, "How far are we from your house?"

Daddyji replies, "Oh, about one mile."

"Why don't we push the motorcycle home? That seems to be our only alternative," Max says.

Daddyji pulls the motorcycle off the stand and starts pushing the motorcycle, with Max walking beside him. With the punctured flat tire, pushing the
motorcycle is even harder. After only about ten minutes, Daddyji is, himself,
out of air. He stops and lifts the motorcycle on the stand. They are in front of

a *Jhuggi* colony where labourers are living in thatched huts. Smoke is coming out of coal and wood burning stoves. Men folk are sitting outside their huts smoking *Biddies*, children are playing and aroma of food being cooked is permeating to the outside. Max stands there watching with the interest of a tourist, while Daddyji is looking for somebody to push the motorcycle home. He walks towards the nearest *Jhuggi* and starts a conversation with two men sitting outside in their undershirts and *Loongies*. Max follows him.

"*Bhaiyya*, our motorcycle has broken down, is anybody interested in pushing it to our house?" As he is saying this, he takes out some change from his pocket to show the color of money to tempt them. Max is standing and looking at the goings on. Two labourers get up from their *charpoys*. The presence of an *Engrez*—a white man— among them fascinates them. They can sense an opportunity to make money.

"How far do we have to go, sahib?" they ask.

"We live just across from the Liberty cinema," Daddyji replies.

"Sahib, it will cost you five rupees," one of the labourers says.

"That is too much. It will only take you one hour going and coming. I will pay you one rupee," Daddyji replies and starts to walk away.

The labourers know that the two sahibs need them badly. They cannot imagine the sahibs pushing the motorcycle that far on their own. They stand their ground and let Daddyji walk away. After taking a few steps, Daddyji stops and looks back. The labourers are sitting back on the *charpoy*.

Max is watching all this with interest. And, as Daddyji is still looking at the labourers and deciding what to do, Max goes to the motorcycle, takes it off the stand and shouts loudly, "Come on Surinder, let us move. We are getting late," and he starts to push the motorcycle. As the labourers see them walking away, they run to the roadside and shout, "Sahib, how about two rupees?"

Daddyji waves at them to come and push the motorcycle. One of the labourers says, "Sahib, we want the payment in advance." Daddyji take out two rupees and hands it over to him.

The two labourers push the motorcycle in tandem; one holds the handle bars and the other pushes from the rear.

"Max, you are a good bargainer. That was a good technique—walking away," Daddyji says.

"I used to teach the art of negotiation to the Foreign Service officers back home in Ottawa. You know, the fundamental principle of negotiation is that you must have a fall back position and be willing to walk away from the deal," Max says with the tone of a professor teaching his class.

Daddyji replies, "Max, your principle may work for negotiations at the United Nations, but here in the crowded bazaars of Delhi things work differently. You take what you can get."

Max replies, "Well it did work here, did it not? You saved three rupees."

"Max, we have not reached home yet; let us see what happens," Daddyji says.

After about ten minutes, the labourers stop. They are huffing and puffing. "Sahib, this motorcycle is very heavy. With the punctured tire it is very hard to push. We want another three rupees," both of them speak in unison.

Daddyji stops and looks at Max and says, "See, there go your principles of negotiations. What do we do now?"

Max replies, "This is unethical on their part. You should tell them a deal is a deal."

"Max, this is not United Nations where you make deals in writing; here we practice Darwin's principle of Survival of the Fittest," Daddyji says with smile and anguish on his face.

Max replies jokingly, "I think we should hire them as our negotiations consultants when setting up the framework for Atoms for Peace conference at the United Nations."

Daddyji agrees to pay them another three rupees, payable when they reach home.

In the meantime, all hell has broken lose at home. It is now 8:30 P.M. Daddyji was expected back at about 7:30 P.M. Mummyji has pulled the alarm. She has gone to the ultimate authority, her brother, Daulat Ram; who it is believed, can get anything done in Delhi.

"*Bhaaji*," she pleads with tears in her eyes, "He has not come back."

Daulat Ram knows when his sister is in anguish. He gets up and walks out of the house and walks down the street looking up at the sky. The rest of us are standing in front of the house, looking on with curiosity. In fact, he is not looking at the sky; he is looking at the wires on top of the poles. He is trying to find out; who has a phone in the neighbourhood? To his dismay, not only that there is no phone, there is not even a telephone pole on our street.

After walking up and down the street, he comes back and says, "Kamla, you should get a phone installed. Is there any phone nearby?"

"Yes *Bhaaji*, there is a phone in the next street in the house of the income tax officer, Raj Sharma. Sometimes we use his phone."

Daulat Ram looks surprised and says, "I know him. I have met him at the Gymkhana Club."

They walk to his house in the next street. Raj Sharma is sitting in his verandah reading a newspaper. He is in his mid forties, with a touch of grey at the temples and wearing a white *kurta* and *paijama*. As Daulat Ram and Mummyji enter the front gate of his house, he looks up from the top of the newspaper and stands up to greet them with the newspaper still in one hand.

Mummyji introduces Daulat Ram to him. They both recognize each other, having met at the club a few times. "Raj *Bhai sahib*, can we use your telephone please?" Mummyji asks with a sense of urgency in her voice.

Raj Sharma senses that something is wrong and asks, "Kamla ji is everything all right?"

Daulat Ram replies instead of Mummyji, "Surinder had gone to the Claridges Hotel to pick up a guest. He was supposed to have been back by 7:30 P.M. It is now...," he looks at his watch, "almost 8:30; he has not come back yet. We are getting worried. I was thinking of ringing up the Hotel to find out if the guest is still in the hotel."

Daulat Ram looks up the telephone directory to find out the phone number of the hotel. After a great deal of trying and connecting to several wrong numbers, he finally connects with the hotel. He is told that Max is not in the hotel, and that he was seen leaving the hotel with somebody.

Raj Sharma consoles them, "Because of Independence Day celebrations, the traffic is bad today; I am sure he will be back soon. If there is any problem, let me know. I know the *Thanedaar* of the Karol Bagh Police Station. If required, I will contact him for help in locating Surinder. Let us wait for another hour or so."

In the meantime, the two labourers, Max and Daddyji are making steady progress along Rohtak Road. They have reached near the *Gundha Naala*, the open channel that is the main collector sewer. It is a landmark in the area where all buses stop. A lot of people get down there to change buses to get to their destinations; therefore, there are a few shops selling eatables and soft drinks. Because of the heat, long walk and a little bit of anxiety, they are feeling thirsty. As luck would have it, they come across a stall selling freshly squeezed sugarcane juice. They stop.

"Max, would you like a glass of sugarcane juice?" Daddyji asks.

"I am game," replies Max.

Daddyji shouts and asks the labourers pushing the motorcycle to stop.

"Two glasses of Juice," Daddyji tells the shopkeeper.

"Are you not going to offer juice to your employees," Max says pointing to the two labourers standing and waiting at a distance.

"No. Those two can pay for their own juice. The bastards are already robbing us. I am not paying for their juice."

Ignoring what Daddyji says, Max calls the labourers in his own Hindi language to come here, *"Bhaiyya, eedhaar Aywooo."*

"Hey Max, don't spoil the labour relations in India. This is not Canada," Daddyji says laughing.

The two labourers turn the motorcycle around and walk over to the juice shop.

"Two more glasses of juice," Max tells the shopkeeper pointing to the labourers.

The labourers are delighted to be offered juice. They just cannot believe it. They know that it is the *Engrez* sahib who invited them; the Indian sahib would never have offered them anything. As they are sipping, one of them says looking towards Max, "Thank you, sahib."

Daddyji is surprised to hear English words come out of his mouth and asks, "You know English?

"Yes sahib, I learned a little bit when I was in the Second World War."

As soon as Max hears the word *War*, he tries to speak to the labourers in mixed English, sign language and broken Hindi, "Where, where?"

The labourer understands and says, "I was in Egypt, Tunisia and Libya. General Montgomery was the commander. We beat the Germans and the Italians."

Max is absolutely flabbergasted to see a piece of history pushing a motorcycle. "Surinder, is there no pension or rehabilitation programs for the veterans of the War?"

"I do not know. I have heard that over two million Indians took part in World War II. There must be something but likely not enough. I will look into it. On second thought, I will do a feature on the Veterans of the Wars in LESTWEFORGET, the magazine of which I am the editor."

As Daulat Ram and Mummyji are walking back home after making the phone call, Daulat Ram is trying to engage her in interesting small talk to keep her mind off her anxiety. He tells her, "Kamla, Raj Sharma is well known in the business circles for his Diwali party. Every Diwali, he invites some of the well off people in his region to his house for a dinner party. Being Diwali day, they all bring gifts. The story goes that his guests bring baskets of fruits and sweets, with expensive gifts hidden underneath to gain his favour at income tax time. His nick name is Giftcollector. He insists that he throws the Diwali party to keep the highest taxpayers happy, at his own expense, as an act of patriotism."

This diverts her mind for a little while, as she says, "We have noticed that on every Diwali evening, there is row of cars waiting to enter the street."

As the caravan of the two labourers, followed by Max and Daddyji, enters our street, Daddyji runs to the motorcycle and starts to beep the horn in his characteristic way: three short beeps followed by three long beeps. As soon as we hear the beeps, we know that Daddyji has arrived. We all rush out and see the two labourers pushing the motorcycle, with Max and Daddyji walking behind them. Mummyji is standing at the gate ready to pounce on him for dropping her in the sea of anxiety, but, when she sees Max; she controls her emotions.

Max is introduced to uncle SK and Daulat Ram.

When introduced to Mummyji he says, "I hope you remember me. We met a long time ago." And he joins his hands in the traditional Indian *Namaste* greeting.

The two labourers are standing on the side watching. Daddyji, realizing that he still owes three rupees to the labourers, takes out money from his pocket and goes over to them to make the payment.

They refuse to accept saying, "Sahib, it was wrong for us to try and take advantage of you after agreeing to an amount. Inspite of that you offered us juice. We are waiting here not for the money but to offer our apologies."

One of them lifts his shirt to expose his stomach, and says thumping it, "Sahib, it is this empty stomach of ours and the pangs of hunger of our infant children that force us poor people to resort to cheating. "And they join their hands in *Namaste* and walk away.

Max appears bewildered by what he has witnessed.

Everybody settles down comfortably in the drawing room. After a while, Chottu brings in soft drinks to the dismay of the men folk. Uncle SK says, "Surinder *yaar*, after all the anxiety we went through, we require something stronger."

Daddyji gets up to get a bottle of VAT 69 Scotch whisky out of the bedroom cupboard. The women folk get up and move to the other room. Chottu gets the sign to bring in four glasses, water and soda water. There is no ice in the icebox, so Chottu is dispatched to fetch some ice from the store.

As the effect of VAT 69 begins to take hold, the conversation picks up and is moving in all sorts of directions. Daulat Ram is very interested in Max and his profession. He sees him as a potential client or someone who may lead him to new foreign clients. He asks a number of questions about the Atoms for Peace program.

At one point Max says to him, "Sir, you are remarkably well informed about the goings on in the nuclear industry."

Daulat Ram replies, "I represent foreign companies in India. I have to know what is going on in the world. I have read and heard that the nuclear industry will grow, and, no doubt, the companies from the advanced countries will be at our doorstep wanting to sell machinery and know-how to India. We are here to help them steer their way through the maze of bureaucracy."

"What is the name of your company?" Max asks.

Daulat Ram has a stack of business cards in his pocket. He takes a card out and hands it over to Max. He reads the name aloud, "India Connections (Private) Limited; it is a very catchy name."

Daddyji and uncle SK, who are sitting nearby sipping their drink and quietly listening to the conversation, complain, "*Bhai Sahib*," addressing Daulat Ram, "You changed the name of your company and never told us."

Daulat Ram explains to Max, "The name of our company used to be Government Liaison Services. We changed it to a more modern sounding name. The old name implied that we only deal with the government, but we provide services related to private companies also."

"This is very interesting," Max says and puts the business card in his pocket.

After the dinner is finished and everybody is ready to leave, Daulat Ram has already figured out the next step. He says to Max, "Mr. Hoffer, I will drive you back to your hotel."

"Are you sure? I can take a taxi. I do not want to impose on you unless it is on your way," says Max.

"There is no problem. Moreover, it will give us time to get to know each other better," replies Daulat Ram.

This conversation is going on while everybody is walking out of the house to the street to board Daulat Ram's car. Daulat Ram and Max sit on the front seats. Uncle SK and his wife, Devika, and Daulat Ram's wife, Nirmala, are seated in the rear seats. After a few minutes of drive, the passengers in the rear seats start dozing.

Max and Daulat Ram are engaged in a vigorous conversation. Max, realizing that Daulat Ram is interested in the nuclear industry, wants to know about the status of nuclear industry in India. He thinks that the knowledge will help him in his next assignment at the United Nations. Daulat Ram is, in turn, interested to know if Max can give him references or names of some companies that can be his future clients.

Max fires the first shot, "Is your company dealing with any foreign companies in the nuclear field?"

Daulat Ram is not willing to reveal the names of his clients. Although he has been approached by the French to act as their agent, he considers it unethical to divulge the information. "No nothing specific," he says. But he realizes that he will have to trade some information. He decides to give Max some information that he himself is not directly involved with. He says, "I have heard that the British arc providing a research reactor to India."

Max replies, "Yes, that is correct. I am aware of that."

"What is your position in the Canadian government?" Daulat Ram asks.

Max replies, "I am a civil servant in the Department of External Affairs."

Daulat Ram says, "Mr. Hoffer, I have been wondering for a while about the Atoms for Peace initiative being supported by the developed nations such as America, Canada and Britain. They have all acquired nuclear weapons themselves and now..."

Max interrupts him before he can finish the sentence, "Let me correct you. Canada does not have nuclear weapons."

Daulat Ram continues "Yes, of course, you are right. Pardon me." After a brief pause, he says, "Are they introducing the concept of peaceful uses of atoms out of guilt, fear, or do they want to cash in on the new technologies?"

Max replies, "To be honest, it is a little bit of all the three reasons you mentioned. They do not want the proliferation of nuclear weapons, so they are promoting the peaceful uses of atomic energy; and yes, there is business component also."

Daulat Ram says, "Is it not unfair on the part of these countries to form a nuclear weapons club and expect the others to remain under their thumb forever? Moreover, when you give access to nuclear technology for peaceful purposes to other countries, they will, no doubt, want to build weapons also. So how is this initiative going to stop proliferation? Is it not better to just lock up the nuclear technology and deny access?"

Max replies, "Yes, this is a contradiction that is hard to explain. The United Nations Conference on the Peaceful uses of Atomic Energy is taking place next year in Geneva. Let us see what agreements are reached."

At this time of the night, the traffic is very light. They reach the Claridge's Hotel in 45 minutes. After dropping off Max, Daulat Ram heads towards uncle SK's home to drop him and his wife off.

IO

SOCIETY WITH SECRETS
1954

The peon brings an envelope to Daddyji's office. He opens it and finds a hand written note from Hari Nautiyal: *Meet me in my office at 11:00 A.M. today.* This is the first time he has received a note written, personally, by Hari Nautiyal. In fact, he has never before seen his handwriting. Daddyji realizes it must be something very confidential that he wants to see him about that he has written the note himself, or maybe he wants to terminate his services, he wonders.

At 10:55 A.M., Daddyji picks up a writing pad and walks over to Hari Nautiyal's office. His personal assistant is sitting outside at his desk. As he sees Daddyji approaching, he gives him a signal to go into the office. Still, Daddyji knocks at the door twice. "Come in," a voice says. Daddyji turns the door knob and walks in. Veer Nautiyal is already there. Hari Nautiyal gestures to Daddyji to take a seat. Seeing the serious atmosphere in the office, he is feeling a bit apprehensive.

Hari Nautiyal takes out an antique looking book with a well worn binding and begins to speak, "Sorry to ask both of you to come in at such short notice. Tomorrow, I would like both of you to join me for a brief journey out of town to attend a meeting. I will brief you as we are driving to the venue. Please be in the office by 8:30 A.M. We will go together. Veer, you will drive as no car drivers are permitted there. But both of you will have to be sworn to secrecy. Do you agree?" He looks at them for their reaction; it appears positive. He then gives them the Hindu holy book, Bhagvad Gita, to take an oath of secrecy.

The next day, Daddyji leaves home at 7:30 A.M. When he reaches the office, Hari Nautiyal and his son, Veer, are waiting in their Jaguar car in the parking area of the office at the rear of Scindia House. Daddyji notices their car, parks his motorcycle and goes towards them. Hari Nautiyal signals to him to get into the rear seat.

Veer, who is in the driver's seat, asks, "Where are we going, Papa?"

Hari Nautiyal replies, "Let us take a circle of Connaught Place first, and then take Barakhamba Road."

Veer starts the car and follows his father's instructions. As they are maneuvering to get out of their parking lot, Hari Nautiyal notices a Jeep start its engine and follow them. Hari Nautiyal says, "Veer, stop on the side, and let the Jeep overtake us."

Veer follows the instructions and stops. The Jeep passes by, but they wait for five more minutes before the Jaguar moves towards the inner circle of Connaught Place. Hari Nautiyal looks around as the car is moving.

Veer asks, "Papa, what are you looking for?"

"I want to make sure the Jeep is not following us," Hari Nautiyal replies.

Once they have driven around the inner circle of Connaught Place, the Jaguar turns on to Barakhamba Road.

Veer asks, "Papa, where are we going?"

"Take us to our farm house in Gurgaon," Hari Nautiyal replies.

Once they are outside the city, Hari Nautiyal says, "Veer, please stop on the side of the road."

They wait for five minutes; no other vehicles pass by. He seems satisfied that they are not being followed, and they start moving again. The drive is now smooth, except for an odd cow or a dog crossing the road.

Hari Nautiyal says, "Well, we have a few minutes before we reach our destination. Let me brief you on what this is all about. In the summer of 1944, I met a group of Indian physicists. Actually, I was introduced to them by Swamiji. They had all studied nuclear physics at Cambridge and wanted a Sponsor to support their research efforts in India. We all met at the Ashram in Verinag. I had come home after spending some time with the Army at the Burma front. It was a great meeting, a very fruitful one. They all talked very passionately about the power of the atom; I had no idea what they were talking about. They wanted to establish a nuclear research establishment. But we were at war; the British were the rulers. After some thought, I decided to provide some financial help. After a year or so, the news of the dropping of the atom bombs on Hiroshima and Nagasaki convinced me of the power of the atom. I talked to a few other businessmen and politicians, and they all agreed that we should pursue the research in nuclear physics. We formed a secret group and named it *Shakti 9,* although at that time we had only eight members, Swamiji suggested that we should use the number 9–being an auspicious number. Today is the 10th anniversary of our first meeting at Verinag. Six of the eight members are attending the meeting today–plus the two of you. I think, now, you know enough for today."

Daddyji is so surprised to hear all this that he is quiet, but Veer asks, "Papa, you kept it all a secret for so long; does Mom know about this?"

Hari Nautiyal replies, "Well, we had all taken an oath of secrecy, so I did not even tell your mother. And remember, you have also taken an oath of secrecy."

At about 9:45 A.M., they reach the farmhouse. Veer stops the car and goes out to open the gate. The guards and the servants had been given the morning off. Veer drives the car up to the front entrance of the house. Swamiji is sitting in the veranda in his trademark white attire. The sun is shining on the white marble floor and the reflecting light brings out his angelic looks.

As soon the car stops, Swamiji stands up and comes out to greet us. He appears to be surprised to see Daddyji and Veer Nautiyal at this meeting. After the initial greetings are over, he asks, "Who else is expected to attend?"

Hari Nautiyal replies. "I do not want to take any names standing here. They should be here soon. Swamiji, you must be surprised to see Veer and Surinder. I will explain their presence when we meet inside."

Other members of the group start arriving a little before 11:00 A.M. They all move indoors. Hari Nautiyal takes them on a short tour of the house. The drawing room is a polygon with nine sides–a nonagon design based on Swamji's belief that nine is an auspicious number. There is a large fireplace occupying one of the nine sides. A double-leaf door made out of carved wood at the main entrance to the house occupies another side. There is a single leaf carved wood door at each of the other seven sides of the nonagon leading to a ring corridor that has kitchen and bedrooms connected to it.

"We have nine acres of land right now; number 9 is considered very auspicious by Swamiji. When we bought the land, we had fifteen acres, but on Swamiji's advice, we severed six acres and sold them off," Hari Nautiyal tells them.

After the tour they all settle down in the drawing room.

Hari Nautiyal starts the formal meeting, "Friends, by now you have all met my son, Veer, and Surinder Mehra. Surinder is an executive director of Nautiyal Industries. Both of them have taken an oath of secrecy. I have full confidence in their abilities. I think time has come to introduce new blood into our group. As you will see on the proposed agenda, we have a lot to accomplish over the next ten years. Veer and Surinder will be our right and left hands and will help me take care of many formalities that we will have to complete."

"Friends, 1954 will go down, in the scientific history of India, as the year when *Anushakti or* atomic energy got its own home in Trombay. The construction at the Atomic Energy Establishment has started. Something that we all conceived in 1944 has come to fruition."

As soon as Hari Nautiyal finishes the sentence, Chandubhai Patel, a freedom fighter, and now an influential politician, takes off his white Gandhi cap, puts it on the table and rubs his bald head with his right hand. Everybody comes to attention when Chandubhai Patel takes off his cap; he makes this well known gestures only when he is about to make a profound statement.

He clears his throat and starts speaking, "I will come to the point. I do not like beating around the bush, as our erstwhile rulers used to say; I like to uproot the bush if I do not like it. The so called developed world has got the big stick with which they can rule the world. It will not be long before China also makes the Bomb. All our research should be aimed towards making ourselves strong and preserve our hard fought freedom. At the end of the day, it is: *Jiss Ki Lathi Oos Ki Bhense*—it is brute force that counts. I think I have made myself clear."

Sumitra Mukherjee is a popular politician from Calcutta. She grew up in poverty. Having seen the effects of centuries of starvation, she is strongly in favour of nuclear research but, first, to help fill the stomachs of people. She says, "We must not waste precious resources to make bombs. We should first give electricity to the masses so that they can pump water from the ground to irrigate their lands."

Chandubhai Patel assures her, "Sumitra ji, Bhakhra Dam is under construction, and other dams are also being planned. India is going to have plenty of electricity. Moreover, *Anushakti* or nuclear power gives us both types of powers, the electrical power and the explosive power. Sumitra ji, let me tell you one thing. If the Chinese are able to make the atom bomb before us, we will all have to learn Chinese in a hurry."

Cyril Dastur, the nuclear scientist, raises his hand to get permission to speak, being the youngest of them all. He speaks almost in desperation, "We can do both—make electricity and the bomb. Our problem is hardware. We have the theoretical know-how, but we lack the equipment to carry out research. We can make do with paper and pencil, and make atoms fly in our imaginations only for so long. Somehow, we have to get our hands on a nuclear reactor."

Hari Nautiyal says, "Cyril, have patience. We are going to get one in a few years. You already know that construction of British supplied, 1 Megawatt, nuclear reactor–which has been named *Apsara*–is going to start next year. Once it is ready, you can break as many atoms as you like. You and your friends told us ten years ago that you will be self-reliant by now, but you have not been able to. So we had to go back to the British for assistance–so much for self-reliance and self-rule. Just imagine, a mere seven years after independence, we are back to the British for help."

Chandubhai Patel knows of Hari Nautiyal's penchant for all things–British, including his 1954 Jaguar car parked outside. But he also knows that it is due to Hari Nautiyal's connections, within the British Establishment, that the Aspara reactor is becoming a reality. But he does not like the last taunt about 'going back to the British and so much for self-reliance and self- rule.'

Not only Chandubhai Patel, even Swamiji is not happy to hear the caustic remark by Hari Nautiyal. He gets up, caressing his beard with his right hand, and starts to speak.

"We, Indians, have known about atomic secrets millenniums before today. If you read the Vedas, the secrets are all there. It is just that due to a thousand years of rule and oppression by foreigners, we have lost touch with our ancient scriptures. This is what we are trying to restore at Verinag Ashram. In the last ten years, hundreds of scholars from the, so called, developed world have visited the Ashram in search of ancient secrets. When you are dealing with the minutest particles of the universe, you are getting close to God and, at that level, science and spirituality become one. Let us close our eyes for five minutes and get in touch with the infinite."

When they open their eyes, there is a strange glow on their faces. There is silence in the room. Swamiji slowly bends down and takes out a bronze statue from his bag. It is about one foot high. He places it in the centre of the table in the middle of the room. The only person who recognizes the significance of the statue is Cyril Dastur. It is a statue of Goddess Kali with one hand stretched towards the sky carrying, what looks like, a ball with smaller balls going around it.

Cyril Dastur says, "This is a model of an atom; but Goddess Kali carrying an atom?"

"Astonished? This was discovered in a temple in south India. It is estimated to be 3500 years old. You see what I mean? We had knowledge of atomic physics that long ago." Swamiji says, with a mysterious smile on his face. He then looks at Hari Nautiyal and says with sarcasm in his voice, "My lord, I rest my case. If given adequate time and resources, we will catch up."

Hari Nautiyal smiles at Swamiji, while taking out a sheaf of papers from his briefcase. He gives one to each of the seven people sitting in the drawing room.

"Friends, this is the action plan for the next ten years. God willing, we will all be sitting here in 1964 with the satisfaction of having accomplished what we set out to do."

There are only a few typewritten lines.
1. Two nuclear power plants.
2. Get our brightest students admissions in universities of nuclear countries to study nuclear science and technology. Scholarships to be provided by us.
3. After completing studies, help them get jobs in nuclear establishments of those countries to gain practical experience.
4. After 3 years of job experience, they are to return home.

As they are reading the contents of the single sheet of paper, he says, "Friends, we have contacts in the countries of interest. They will help us. As far as financial assistance is concerned, I, and my friend, Mohan Singh—who is known as the wealthiest man in Punjab—will take care of that."

Mohan Singh gives a glance of approval at Hari Nautiyal.

Sumitra Mukherjee asks, "I see 'two nuclear plants' written on top of the list. May I ask, how do you propose to fund the purchase?"

Hari Nautiyal replies, "Sumitra ji, the western nations with nuclear technology want under-developed countries like India to develop nuclear capability for peaceful uses such as electricity generation. They will make loans available at favourable terms."

Sumitra, still not satisfied, asks, "Nautiyal sahib, the loans have to be paid back; how will we do that?"

Hari Nautiyal is a bit irritated by the persistent questioning by Sumitra Mukherjee. He says, "This will all take five to ten years; by that time India's economy will grow and we will have enough resources to pay back the loans. We have friends in America and Canada who have also promised to help in this regard."

After the meeting is over, Hari Nautiyal takes the agenda papers back from them, takes a matchbox from his pocket, goes to the fireplace and sets fire to all the papers. After the papers are turned to ashes, he takes his seat.

Hari Nautiyal concludes the meeting by saying, "Friends, at this time we will have to be content with a 1 MW reactor, but negotiations are on going with Canada for the supply of a, more powerful, 40 MW reactor. God willing, after the United Nations Conference on Peaceful Uses of Atomic Energy next year, we will be on our way to getting the CANDU."

Mohan Singh, the tall Sikh businessman from Karnal, who has been quietly listening asks, "Oh, Nautiyal sahib, what is this Kandoo?"

He replies, "It is a complicated long name. Maybe Cyril can tell us."

"It stands for **CAN**ada **D**euterium **U**ranuim," Cyril tells them.

Hari Nautiyal continues, "Friends, God willing, we will restore the *Golden Sparrow* to its ancient glory; maybe not in our lifetime, but certainly in the lifetime of our children."

The meeting is adjourned at 12:00 P.M sharp. There is no lunch; only water from Hari Nautiyal's personal thermos is offered. One by one, they all leave.

II

THE UNTOUCHABLE ATOMS
1955

Soon, my memories of grade 8 will fade in the haze of time like other memories. In the class, Mr. Partap Singh, who teaches us just about everything, except mathematics, is going through the formalities to be completed by all the students.

He has a stack of forms in front of him. He lifts the stack above his head with his right hand and announces, "Students, you should have your parents or guardians complete the form and bring them to school before the grade 8 examinations start. In this form you will indicate your preference for either science or arts subjects, when you start grade 9."

He then asks two students to distribute the forms to each student.

In the evening, as Daddyji reads the form he says, "Vikram, I spent years studying English literature–hundred or two hundred year old plays and poems. Maybe they had relevance during the British Raj but not any more. This is the age of science and technology and of development. The whole country has to be developed; buildings, roads, power plants, dams and bridges have to be built. We will require thousands of scientists and engineers. In place of Shakespeare and Dickens, Newton and Galileo will be our new friends. Instead of Merchant of Venice and David Copperfield, Newton' Laws of Motion will be our new literature."

Daddyji selects the science subjects for me, signs the form and gives it back to me.

After carefully placing the form in my satchel, I ask, "Daddyji, what is science?"

"Science is the study of God's creation—all the nature around us, the Sun's heat, the light and the sound of lightening and the thunder, the Stars, the Moon. To understand God, we must study science."

"Daddyji, have you studied science?" I ask.

He replies, "When I was in high school, my interest was mainly English literature, although my father always stressed that I should take more interest in science and technology. But, ever since I have come back from our trip to Verinag Ashram, I have bought some scientific books, and I plan to educate myself."

"Daddyji, after you become knowledgeable in science, will they start calling you *Sciencewala* instead of *Shakespearewala*?" And we both laugh.

• •

Grade 9 has started in earnest. Between the swing of the pendulum, the focal point of convex lens and the pungent smell of H_2S gas, it seems that I am beginning to learn the make up of the world around me.

This day, our physics teacher, Mr. Chandra, gives a lecture that could shake the very belief system of India. He tells us, "Students, you will find it fascinating to learn that every thing is made of tiny things known as atoms. They are everywhere and they constitute everything."

As Mr. Chandra is finished saying this, a peon knocks at the class door. Mr. Chandra asks him to come in.

As he is signing some papers, I begin to think:

Not only that I, Krish, Suneeta, Daddyji and Mummyji are made of atoms but even the air in between. Even, Chottu, our servant and Rampiyari, our sweepress, who cleans our toilets, are made of the same atoms. Imagine the untouchable sweepress made of the same atoms as the rest of us! This could shake the very foundation of the class system and the sanitation system of the country. Is it possible that the untouchables are made of the same atoms as the rest of us? Unbelievable!

My reverie is interrupted.

He always teaches us using a provocative story. I am not sure if the stories are real or made up to emphasize the particular physical process that he wants us to remember. Mr. Chandra carries on with his atomic theory, "Students, you are not going to believe this. I started my career as a teacher in a school in Lucknow. There were a large number of students from Brahmin families in my class. They were very caste conscious. In one of my physics classes, I told them about atoms; what I just told you. The word got out to the parents that I am equating the Brahmins to the untouchables. The Brahmin parents came to the school to lodge a complaint against me. I was instructed by the school principal to tone down my atomic theory or lose my job."

From then on, whenever I see Rampiyari or Chottu, I look at them intensely to find out: why they are they and I am I? I mean, why Chottu and Rampiyari are made to do what they do, and why I do what I do, if we are made of the same atoms. I am trying my best to find the difference. Chottu works all day long and gets to eat his meals sitting on the kitchen floor, after we are all finished eating. He works till late at night, goes to bed when everybody else is asleep and gets to sleep on the floor of a small cubby hole under the staircase. Rampiyari goes from house to house cleaning and carrying all the garbage to the dump, where the municipality is supposed to pick it up everyday but never does. She goes from house to house, at lunch time, to collect food from each of her clients so that she can feed her family at lunch and dinner time. So, my mind is back to the atoms; I come to the conclusion that all of us could not have been made from the same atoms, if there is so much disparity between us.

I decide to put up my hand in the next physics class. "Sir, I have a question. If we are all made of the same atoms, then how is it that there is so much disparity between Rampiyari and me?"

Mr. Chandra has answers to all the questions, but on this one he stumbles. He answers the question with a question. After a great deal of thinking and starting and stopping, he asks, "Who is Rampiyari?"

"Sir, she is our *Jamadarni*—the sweepress."

"This is not a physics question. Do you know Shastriji, our Sanskrit teacher? You should ask him," he replies.

In the next Sanskrit class, after Shastriji has finished the coursework and there is time for questions, I put up my hand, "Sir, if we are all made of the same atoms, then, how is it that there is so much disparity between our, *Jamadarni*, Rampiyari and me?"

Shastriji has to think about this one, and after a while replies, "*Atma* or soul never dies. It moves from birth to birth changing bodies like clothes. What bodies you get to wear in a particular incarnation depends on how you performed in the previous births. Clothes or bodies are made of atoms, but *Atma* is not made of atoms. It is formless, massless and can pass through a plate of steel, and fire cannot burn it. *Atma* is not governed by the laws of science, as we know them."

I am intrigued to hear the explanation offered by Shastriji comparing Atom and *Atma*—both somewhat similar sounding words. But this provides me with more food for thought. Whenever our servant, Chottu, brings food to the table, I wonder what bad things he must have done in his previous birth to deserve this life. And the same thoughts come to me when I see Rampiyari cleaning the toilet and carrying the garbage in the bamboo basket on her head. So much so that I begin to wonder, what I must have wrought in my previous birth to be stuck with one leg shorter than the other.

I start watching my every move to make sure that I do not step on the wrong side of the Gods, who are going to decide on my next incarnation. I start following the teachings of Mr. Chandra. In addition to teaching physics, he is also our civics teacher. In the civics class he teaches us how to be 'Good Boys'—in other words, how to be on the right side of God. Wash hands before eating, cut nails regularly, take bath everyday, use a latrine, do not urinate on the street, keep your surroundings clean, throw banana peels in the litter box, help the frail and the elderly and tell the truth. These are the directive principles emphasized in our civics class. We are given a Red Cross book in which we are required to record which of the edicts we followed, and which we did not. I consistently score 100%, being fearful of the consequences in the next incarnation.

This is when I start to think deeply about the meaning of life and the part that atoms play. The word Atom Bomb has found its way into popular lexicon by now. I have become preoccupied with the thought: If we are all made of atoms, can we explode like an Atom Bomb?

This is when I decide that I am going to become a Physicist.

12

RED CAP

The radio is sitting in one corner of the drawing room on top of a small round table. It is adorned with an embroidered table cloth for the dual purpose of decoration and to prevent dust from getting into its innards. Our family is sitting in the drawing room waiting for the yearly finale of *Binaca Geet Mala* 1955 to start.

It is a countdown radio show broadcast from Radio Ceylon featuring sixteen of the best *filmi* songs of the week. The show is sponsored by Ciba Geigy, a Swiss firm, the makers of Binaca toothpaste in India. All over India, every Wednesday at 8:00 P.M., people gather around a radio, whether at home or in front of a *paanwala* shop, waiting for those iconic haunting words: *Amin Sayani Peish Kartei Haien Binaca Geet Maala*. Meaning: Amin Sayani presents Binaca Geet Mala.

I am sitting on the sofa chair closest to the radio. My friend, Suraj, is sitting beside me. He comes over to our house on most Wednesdays. At first, we study together and then listen to *Binaca Geet Mala*. Mummyji and Daddyji are sitting on the long sofa set against the far wall. Chotu, Suneeta and Kishi are sitting on the carpet, talking and just playing around and laughing. The exterior door of the drawing room is open. The drapes are hanging from the curtain rod and are slowly swinging as a light breeze is blowing. The noise being made by Kishi, who is being especially boisterous, is bothering me. I have to move my left ear closer to the radio to hear what is being said.

The program starts with the blowing of the bugle and the usual haunting words of Amin Sayani. There is a lot of suspense in the air about which of the film songs is going to be the topper of 1955.

About ten minutes into the program, our old friends, Karnail Singh and his wife, knock at the door and walk in. Apparently they had been invited for dinner.

Karnail Singh has recently returned from his visit to Russia. He was visiting as part of a delegation of Indian businessmen following a visit by Prime Minister Jawaharlal Nehru. Daddyji is very keen to hear first hand about Karnail Singh's impressions of Russia.

As soon as they are seated, Karnail Singh takes out a bottle from a bag he is carrying. "Surinder, I did not forget you," he says, and puts the bottle on the centre table. Daddyji picks up the bottle and holds it as if he is holding the treasure of Sindbad in his hand.

"Chottu, get up and bring two glasses and a bottle of soda water," Daddyji orders. Upon hearing this cue, Mummyji gets up to go to the kitchen to cook the accompaniments, such as fried fish and chicken tikka. Karnail Singh's wife also accompanies her. In the meantime, the countdown of the best song of the year is on, and I am not happy with the noise around me. I am leaning over towards the radio, and my left ear is almost touching it.

"Vikramyoustupidboy, move away or you will get electrocuted," Mummyji says, as she walks in with the first installment of fried fish and chicken tikka.

The countdown is on. Daddyji and Karnail Singh have no interest in *Binaca Geet Mala*. They are engaged in a rather loud conversation of their own. From their talk I conclude that they are drinking an alcoholic drink known as Vodka. They are talking loudly, so much so that the rest of us are having a hard time following the program.

"Listen ji, at least let us hear the top song," Mummyji says. Everybody stops talking. There is calm in the room. The bugle announcing the top song is sounding. Amin Sayani announces with much fanfare, "The top song of the year 1955 is *Mera Joota hai Japani* from the movie 'Shri 420'." The song starts to play on the radio.

Mera joota hai Japani;
Yeh Pantloon Englishtaani;
Sur pe laal topi Russi;
Phir bhi dil hai Hindustaani.

The name of the movie refers to Section 420 of the Indian Penal Code in which theft and deception is a punishable offense. So the story is about a fraudster or a trickster.

English translation of the lyrics:

My shoes are made in Japan;
My pants are made of English style;
The red cap is Russian;
Still, my heart is Indian.

At the conclusion of the radio program, Karnail Singh and Daddyji start discussing the lyrics of this song—which I find surprising because they paid no attention to the song while it was playing on the radio.

Karnail Singh, who is now a deputy Secretary in the Ministry of Commerce, says, "Surinder, we must give credit to the Japanese. A mere 10 years after being hit by two atom bombs, they are exporting shoes to India. So much so that shoes made in Japan have found their way into a popular Hindi song. It seems that the lyricist, Shailendra, is well up on the fact that Japan exports shoes to India, among many other goods." And they both have a laugh.

Daddyji adds, "Look at us. We, in India, are still trying to get our first Five Year Plan completed. Anyway, Karnail, tell me something about your trip to Russia. Why do Russians like us so much? Pundit Nehru visited Russia in June and now both Bulganin and Khrushchev are in India."

Karnail Singh picks up his glass of Vodka, takes a sip and says, "Surinder, I have fallen in love with this drink called Vodka. It gives one so much energy that one feels as strong as a horse." And they both laugh again. I cannot understand the joke. It appears that Vodka is getting the better of both of them.

Karnail Singh has a longer sip of Vodka this time. He seems a bit tipsy. After a great deal of thinking he says, "You know, I think Raj Kapoor's movies are our best ambassadors to Russia. You will not believe this. But I was surprised to find that his movies were being screened in Moscow when we landed there. When people saw us on the street, they would ask us about Raj Kapoor. They love the songs in his movies, especially the one about the Russian red cap; the one that just won the top spot in *Binaca Geet Mala*. I think Russians like us because of Raj Kapoor."

Daddyji asks, "Karnail, why do Russians like Raj Kapoor's movies so much?'

Karnail Singh replies, "I think 'Shri 420', and other earlier films, produced and acted by Raj Kapoor, such as Awaara and Boot Polish, have become hits in Russia because of their pro-poor and pro-working class themes that matched with the mood in Russia at the time. Raj Kapoor has become one of the most admired actors in Russia, along with Charlie Chaplin. During a visit by Raj Kapoor to Russia, people on the streets used to stop him and ask him to sing the famous songs of his movies. He had a difficult time explaining to them that the songs were sung by, the playback singer, Mukesh, and not by him."

Daddyji picks up a few pieces of chicken tikka with his fingers, deposits them in his mouth and takes a few more sips of Vodka and says laughing, "I think we should appoint Raj Kapoor as India's ambassador to Russia."

Karnail Singh says, "The story goes that the movies of Raj Kapoor, in particular, and Indian films in general, have gone a long way in forging friendly relations between Russia and India. After years of trying by the KGB to bring India into the Russians orbit, the cultural exchanges have done the trick."

Daddyji adds, "You know, the Americans and the British do not like this; they are concerned with India moving closer to Russia. The visit by Prime Minister Jawaharlal Nehru was such a big success, that the newspapers of Western countries called it an Elephant and mango diplomacy because of the two elephants and crates of mangoes that were presented as gifts to the Russians–they are just jealous."

Karnail Singh asks, "Is your employer, Nautiyal Industries, doing business with Russia?"

Daddyji replies, "No, not at this time, but I have heard Mr. Nautiyal talk about it."

After getting their food from the dining table, both Karnail Singh and Daddyji are back in the drawing room. Daddyji, usually, likes to chew his food thirty two times, but today he is talking with his mouth full.

He says, "Karnail, I think I agree with you. This Vodka is something else. I already feel energized. Let me tell you one thing, Karnail, the Americans are not far behind in wooing India."

"What do you mean?" Karnail Singh asks, while chewing the flesh off the leg of the tandoori chicken.

Daddyji replies, "I have heard from my sources in the Ministry of External Affairs that preliminary plans have been made for our Prime Minster's visit to America and Canada in 1956. And I will let you in on a secret: I am trying to get on the delegation as a journalist."

Karnail Singh stops chewing the bones that he is so fond of. He looks at Daddyji with a smile, and says, "Oh you lucky man. How did you swing that?"

"Well, it is not a done deal yet. There is going to be a lot of competition among journalists to be on this trip."

Mummyji walks in and stands in the drawing room waiting to find a gap in the conversation so that she can get in a word. As soon as Daddyji finishes speaking, she says, "Please take the dessert as soon as possible so that Chottu can finish his work. He says he has to go to a meeting."

Daddyji stops eating. And with a look of utter disbelief, looks at Mummyji, and says, "Who has to go to a meeting?"

She replies, "Chottu says he has a union meeting."

Incredulity—both on the faces of Daddyji and Karnail Singh—is such that they put their plates down on the tables beside them. There is silence—as they both digest this information, along with Vodka and chicken tikkas. After about a minute, when it has sunk in, Daddyji calls out loudly with anger in his voice, "Oh, Chottu, can you come in here? I want to talk to you."

Mummyji senses trouble. She knows that, lately, Chottu has become very militant and has even refused to do some work and has been very particular about his hours of work and days off.

She says, "Please take it easy with him. It is becoming very hard to find domestic help now-a-days. The neighbours are telling me that the domestic servants have formed a union; also, that they prefer to work in factories where they have regular hours and have the protection of labour laws."

Chottu walks into the drawing room in a somewhat defiant mood and comes and stands with both hands on his waist. After hearing what Mummyji has said, Daddyji is at a loss for words. After clearing his throat a few times, he finally says, "Chottu I have heard that you have joined a union. Is this correct?"

He replies, "Yes sahib. All the domestic servants in this area have formed a union. It is like a union of factory workers. We want to have reasonable working hours and, at least, one day off in a week. Also, the union has decided that the families who mistreat their domestic servants will not be able to find one to work for them."

Daddyji asks, "Who is your leader?"

Chottu replies, "He is a man from the big union. I do not know his name."

Daddyji says, "You can go now."

As they carry on discussing politics, Suraj and I get up and move out of the room into the verandah. "Vikram, I will be going home now. My parents must be waiting for me," he says.

As he starts to walk away, Mummyji calls from the dining room "Vikram and Suraj, come in and have your dinner."

Suraj replies peering through the curtain, "Auntyji, I am going home. My parents must be waiting for me." I walk out with Suraj to just outside the front gate, and he picks up his bicycle and rides away.

I go in, pick up my food from the dining table and go and sit in the drawing room where Karnail Singh and Daddyji are sitting having their meal and still deeply engaged in political talk.

Karnail Singh says, "Surinder, I think, the Communists are taking over our country. Now we know why the Russians are so friendly with India. They want to spread Communism in India. How dare these domestic servants form a union? Next thing we know, the sweepers will be forming a union. Who is going to do the work? This way, we will become workers and workers will become the bosses."

Daddyji replies, "Karnail, times have changed. There is nothing wrong with our domestic servants asking for better working and living conditions. They are human beings like the rest of us. You know, there are unions in America also; that does not mean that America is going to become Communist. At our company, Nautiyal Industries, the workers are free to join a union. But, as things stand today, they are treated so well that only a few have joined the union."

13

THE PARTY
1956

Daddyji is sitting in his office dictating a letter to his stenographer. There is a knock at the door. Veer Nautiyal walks in and says, "Surinder, are you interested in buying a car? I have a 1950 Hindustan 14 model that I want to sell. I can assure you that you will get a good deal. I will give it up for five thousand rupees."

Daddyji is pleasantly surprised. He has been toying with the idea of buying a car but not that soon. The price is attractive, and he knows the car; Veer has driven it to work many times. Whenever he has seen the car; its sea green colour has fascinated him.

Veer can see that Daddyji is interested, and he says, "Surinder why don't you take the car home today and show it to your family."

Daddyji thinks for a few seconds and says, "Thank you, I will take it home." And then, suddenly, he says, "Veer, there are two small problems: I do not know how to drive a car, and I do not even have a driving license."

"Well, driving license is no problem. I can get you one in fifteen minutes. See that building across the road; that is where you get driving licenses. In fact, I will send my assistant, and he will bring one for you even without you going there for a test. The fact that you do not know driving is a more serious problem. I would not want you to be in an accident. We want you to be with us for years to come."

Daddyji thinks about it and says, "I have an idea. If your driver can bring the car to our house one day, and if my family likes the car, then I will get a learner license, learn driving from your driver and get a driving license. How does that sound?"

On a Sunday, at about 11:00 A.M., a car stops in front of our house. It beeps the horn twice to announce its arrival. Daddyji, of course, knows about it, but has not told anybody; he wants it to be a surprise. I am sitting in my room doing my homework. My grandparents, who are back from Simla, are resting in their room. Daddyji peeps outside when he hears the beep of the car horn. He walks to the kitchen, where Mummyji is busy cooking, and tells her, "Kamla, come outside quickly and bring Suneeta and Kishi also." As he is walking out, he tells me also to come out. When we are all outside standing by the car, he says, "Boys and girls. Do you like this car?"

The sea green colour of the car, whitewall tires and pink flowers in the background growing in flower pots on top of the boundary wall of our house, form a very sleek looking scene. The sun is shinning. I look up and see a flock of sparrows flying circles around us, as if looking down at us inspecting the scene. I keep looking up following the flight path of the sparrows going round and round. Why?

I am thinking: *why are they looking at us. Is there an omen, a signal?*

And, then, they swoop down in formation and sit on the parapet of the roof of our house, chirping. My other family members are so engrossed in looking over the car that they do not notice. I see my grandmother, Beyji, standing near the gate, watching me and smiling.

She says, "Vikram, the day you were born, the same sparrows flew circles around our house in Lahore. See the one over there with the golden wings; it is the same one. She used to come to our house everyday, and I used to give it bird food. They are telling us that it is a good omen, and they have all come to bless us."

Daddyji and Mummyji look back at Beyji, and they realize that they had forgotten to tell my grandparents to come out. In the meantime, my grandfather, having heard all the noise and commotion, also walks out with his steel tipped walking stick in hand, just in case.

There is a buzz in my head. I know it is Ginny, my walking stick, calling. Having seen my grandfather bring his stick out, she also wants to come out and join the fun.

To show due respect to his father, Daddyji tells him, "Pitaji, we are planning to buy this car; Do you like it? We need your blessings."

Our servant, Chottu, and sweepress, Rampiyari also come out to see the car. And before we know it, dozens of residents of our street are out gathering around the car.

Daddyji looks around at everybody, and asks loudly, "As this is going to be the first car on our street, do you all like it?"

There is a resounding yes... yes... yes from the whole crowd. One of the children says, "Uncleji, I have never been in a car; can I have a ride?"

Daddyji asks, "Children of the neighbourhood, who wants a ride?" Many hands go up. We all pile up; one on top of the other–there must be nine of us.

One of the neighbours says, "Come on, you can pack more. There are only nine children in the car; I can accommodate my wife and my three children just on my motorcycle, and still have room left over for grocery bags. The way our population is growing, we must learn to accommodate at least ten passengers in one car." Everybody laughs.

Within two weeks of the arrival of the car, the motorcycle has been disposed off through a broker. Our servant, Chottu's, work load has increased and Mummyji is worried–in case he reports her to the union. At the time we owned the motorcycle, his first job in the morning used to be to clean and shine the motorcycle. Now he has to clean and shine the car, and, of course, the whitewall tyres have to be washed everyday. Boxes of Simonize polish and cakes of soap are being consumed like you would not believe. But somehow, Chottu is very enthusiastic about looking after the car. His whole attitude towards his work has changed. We are all pleasantly surprised, but we are not able to think of a reason. Until one day, he tells Daddyji, "Sahib, one day, I want to be a car driver." Then we find out the reason for the change in him; he is dreaming of learning to drive our car.

I have started admiring Chottu's foresight; he wants to improve his lot by adding an additional skill to his, already, many skills. To be honest, I must give credit to Chottu for my own ambition to learn to drive. As I am growing up, my urge to be mobile using a mechanical device is growing. I have learned to ride a bicycle, but with my one leg being still shorter than the other, it is not easy; and the difference between the legs is even more visible on the bicycle. So much so that, I have seen younger boys making fun of me and calling me names like 'Timur the Lame'–hence the urge to learn driving. Once in a while, I sit in the driver's seat of the car to see how I fit in.

In a close-knit neighbourhood like ours, being the only one to own a car can be a liability. An unforeseen problem has arisen. Just in the first month of ownership of the car, Daddyji had to drive two grooms to their weddings, and one expectant mother to the nursing home in the middle of the night.

One day, the unthinkable happens. One of our neighbours, Kesriji, comes to our house and asks to borrow our car. Is it not unthinkable? In a place where people are reluctant to lend their bicycle to anybody; imagine somebody having the gall to ask to borrow your car.

He says, "Surinder ji, I have to attend a very important party at the Delhi Cantonment coming Sunday. There will be high ranking army officers and officials of the Defense and Foreign Ministries. They are my clients, and I want to present a prosperous image to them. I could take a taxi, but that would not be in keeping with the image I want to project..."

And then, he is quiet for a while to let Daddyji digest the information. I guess he does not want to shock him, or maybe he wants to let him draw his own conclusions. He then takes out two packets of sweets he has brought from Delhi Sweet House—one of the most desirable sweet shops in all of Delhi—and places them on the table. I think, after this, Daddyji has a pretty good idea about what Kesriji is looking for.

Daddyji says, "Kesriji, we are busy next Sunday. We are expecting some guests." He thinks that Kesriji will be deterred by this statement of his—after all, how can he drive Kesriji to the Cantonment, when he is himself busy with his family?

Kesriji has a plan in mind. He had already figured out what Daddyji was going to say. He says the unthinkable, "Surinder ji, I know you are busy, and in any case, I would not think of giving you so much trouble as to ask you to drive me that far. I am wondering if I can borrow your car for the evening. Please do not worry; I have hired a professional driver to drive me there."

'I am sorry Kesriji. I cannot lend the car to you. We might need it ourselves."

Now Kesriji, having exhausted all his plans, uses his trump card. Having heard of Daddyji's weakness for going to parties attended by important people, he says, "Surinder ji, the party will be well attended. I have heard that central government ministers, members of the diplomatic corps, and even the Prime Minister might attend to felicitate some army officers. And you know that *Armywallas* are known for throwing lavish parties. Drinks will be flowing like water. As the Russians are also attending, there is bound to be Vodka. I am telling you this because your magazine may want to cover this important diplomatic and political function. In your capacity as a journalist, you should not have any trouble getting an invite."

Although, Daddyji knows why Kesriji is throwing this bait to him, he sees some benefit in going to attend the party. For the last many days, he has been talking of visiting America and Canada. He thinks that, in the party, he may meet some V.I.P., who may further his cause.

Kesriji's wish is granted.

• •

On Sunday at about 6:00 P.M., Daddyji and Kesriji set a course to Delhi Cantonment, which is located at the other end of the town.

In the party, everybody is talking of going abroad; the most used words in the party are: abroad and foreign. The party is well attended, though. Kesriji was right on. Apart from the army officers, bureaucrats, and politicians—there are ambassadors, high commissioners and other assorted diplomats and, last but not least, a few journalists and businessmen are also present.

The Russian ambassador is standing with some people gathered around him. He is talking about Raj Kapoor's movie, Boot Polish, and the middle and upper class Indians' obsession with getting their boots polished every day. The whole of the diplomatic corps agrees that, in their respective countries, nobody polishes their shoes everyday—well, maybe, once a month.

Demetri Sovolov, the Russian ambassador's aide, who is standing there, says, "Comrades, just imagine, how much petroleum your country can save if you use less boot polish. It has been reported by the Planning Commission of India that the consumption of boot polish has gone up since the release of the film, Boot Polish. Another bad and wasteful habit I have seen in India is that everybody washes themselves and their cars and motorcycles everyday. Just look at the amount of water and energy you people waste. No wonder you have to import heavy water from Canada. In Russia, sometimes, we do not take a bath for a month."

There is a Holy man in the party, a Sadhu; who is listening to all this quietly, but he is not able to remain quiet anymore.

He says, "God bless you all. I am Swamiramanathansubramunuim from Kangra hills. I only wear slippers made of wood that do not need polish and last forever. I meditate for a month at a time; therefore, I need to take a bath only once a month. All these modern Indians, who bathe every day and polish their shoes everyday, have forgotten their heritage. It is all the fault of the British; who encouraged us to take a bath everyday, but bathe once a week themselves. It is they who taught us how to make shoes that need polishing everyday. It was a conspiracy hatched by the British to encourage us to polish our shoes everyday, just to increase the export of British made boot polish to India. They have ruined our country. This is why Gandhiji wanted everything made in India and stop imports and become self sufficient."

Daddyji is making a mental note of all that is being said. To a sober person, all of the above sounds like nonsense—the product of gallons of alcohol working its way through the veins. But, at the moment, most of it makes perfect sense to him, having himself had a few drinks of Vodka.

Daddyji nearly collides with one of the guests, as he turns around to walk away from the circus being conducted by the Russian diplomat, Dmitri Molotov.

"Oh, pardon me," the man says. Daddyji looks at him trying to hold on to the glass of Vodka that nearly got toppled out of his hand. The man moves his own glass to his left hand, and extends his right hand, "I am Alexander Graham Bell. I am with the Canadian High Commission."

Daddyji extends his right hand and says with a laugh, "If you are Alexander Graham Bell, then, I am William Shakespeare of Lahore...Tell me, any relation to *the* Mr. Bell of the telephone fame?"

"No, not really... maybe a distant relative." They both have a hearty laugh.

Daddyji suddenly comes to attention, as he sees his 'passport' to Canada standing right in front of him. He introduces himself, "Really, I am Surinder Mehra representing the magazine, LESTWEFORGET. I know another Canadian diplomat. His name is Max Hoffer."

"Well, well, well... what a small world. You know, Max has been posted to India as the Deputy High Commissioner. He should be here in the next few months."

As Daddyji hears this, he can see himself boarding the plane to America and Canada. He is sure that Max will somehow help him achieve his dream. As he is standing there dreaming of his plane taking off and flying him across the seven seas, another man joins them.

He extends his hand of friendship to Daddyji, "Hi, buddy, I am Wilbur Wright with the United States Information Service."

Daddyji looks at him with a look of exclamation, raising his finger towards him and just about to ask, if he is related the Wright Brothers, the inventors of the airplane... when Wilbur Wright says, "Well, I get asked this question all the time. But I am not related to *the* Wilbur Wright, but I wish I was."

And they all laugh and have sips out of their respective glasses. Daddyji is convinced that it is either the Vodka doing the tricks on him, or somebody is pulling a practical joke on him; meeting the namesakes of two of the most famous inventors on the same day seems impossible.

The dinner is being served. All three serve themselves and go and sit down on the same round table. As the other two are eating, Daddyji stops eating and just watches the other two eat. After a great deal of thought, he asks, "Gentlemen, I am curious about one thing. Two of the most important inventions of the recent past–the telephone and the airplane– were made: one in Canada, and the other in America. What is the reason behind it? How is it that you people are so inventive?"

"Wilbur says, "Wait a minute, let me correct you. Both the inventions, you refer to, were, in fact, made in America. Mr. Bell just happened to live in Canada."

Alexander immediately refutes the statement made by Wilbur, "No, Wilbur, you are wrong. The first, and the now famous phone message, 'Come here, Mr. Watson, I want you' was transmitted at the home of Alexander Graham Bell in Brantford, Ontario, Canada. Yes, the subsequent patents may have been granted in America."

Daddyji, sensing the issue developing into an international incident, says, "Gentlemen, please control yourself; otherwise, we will have to refer the matter to the United Nations Security Council." He bangs the mock gavel on to the table, and all three break into a laughter.

After the drunken laughter subsides, Wilbur says to Daddyji, "Ah... sir, I forget your name ...please do not mind... I am very bad with names."

Daddyji says sarcastically, "To refresh your memory, my name is Surinder, but you may call me, sir."

Wilbur asks, "Sir, to keep things simple, do you mind if I call you Sam?" And he continues, "Sam, you were kind enough to ask us why Americans and Canadians are so inventive. We think that Indians are very inventive also—may not be in mechanical fields, but you people are way ahead of us in the extrasensory fields, such as meditation and mind reading. We have heard that you have research projects underway in Long-range Brainwave Transmission and Mind Reading, which can make all the research in the field of telephony look primitive."

Daddyji is surprised to hear the interest the American man has in what they are doing at Verinag Ashram. He remembers Hari Nautiyal had told him to keep the subject, of Brain Wave Communication, confidential. He smiles and nods his head, but does not say anything more.

As the party is coming to an end, and the people begin to leave, the three of them exchange addresses and telephone numbers. When Daddyji is ready to depart, he goes around the lawn to look for Kesriji, who is engaged in a drunken stupor with, the Russian diplomat, Demtri; trying to convince Demitri to help him import goods from Russia and both of them will share the profits.

"Come on, get up Kesriji, we have to make a move now," Daddyji says, as he drags him to the car.

As they are driving back home with Kesriji fast asleep, Daddyji is happy that Kesriji talked him into going to the party. He feels that he may have made life-long contacts that will prove useful in accomplishing the mission of the *Shakti 9 group*, and his own ambitions.

Wilbur and Alexander had come to the party in the American Embassy vehicle with CD license plates, driven by an Indian driver. Most cars owned by foreign missions are driven by Indian drivers because the foreigners do not feel comfortable driving in the chaotic traffic in India with people, animals, and vehicles of all stripes competing for space on the roads.

It is late at night and having had their share of alcohol both, Wilbur and Alexander, fall asleep as soon as the car starts to move. As the car is driving through Dhaula Kuan area, a hoard of goats runs across the road, and the driver has to suddenly apply the brakes. The jerk is enough to throw both, Alexander and Wilbur, forward, and they hit their heads on the front seat. By the time the car stops, it has crushed a number of goats.

A number of nearby shanty dwellers are still awake. And after hearing the sound of the accident, they all come out to the main road. The driver also comes out, but tells Alexander and Wilbur to stay in the car and lock the doors. The owner of the goats is up in arms, when he sees five of his goats crushed under the wheels of the Chevrolet Impala. People gather around the car and are looking in through the widows. The word is out that the occupants of the car are foreigners. Some of the people see the plates and realize that it a car owned by an Embassy.

Daddyji has started his trek home a few minutes after the diplomats. Although they live in different directions, some of the route is common. As luck would have it, Daddyji's car reaches the point of the accident as the crowd is beginning to swell and starting to beat on the windows of the locked car. He has no choice but to stop his car. By this time, Kesriji also wakes up. Daddyji turns off the engine of his car, and Kesriji and he get out of the car to investigate the cause of the riot. Kesriji is a big man. He walks through the crowd ordering them to move away, with Daddyji following him. When they reach the diplomats' car, the crowd has started to rock the car in a rhythmic motion in order to overturn it. They are demanding that the occupants of the car come out. Seeing the two foreigners in the car, they can sense a handsome payoff for the goats.

Daddyji and Kesriji look inside the car. Both Alexander and Wilbur are sitting scared and looking out. Daddyji knocks at the window and pushes his face at the glass of the car window. Alexander recognizes his face. Daddyji waves at him to be patient.

Kesriji shouts at the top of his voice, "Friends, the occupants of the car are diplomats, and they are under protection of the Government of India. If any harm comes to them, you will all be in trouble with the police. Please move away. If there has been any damage, you will be compensated."

After listening to an authoritative voice, the crowd starts to move away from the car. As the time goes by, other cars from the party, that are taking the same route home, also stop there. And finally, a police jeep comes to a stop nearby. Daddyji looks into the diplomats' car and signals them to come out. One police inspector and two constables come and take charge. Alexander and Wilbur step out of the car and wipe perspiration from their foreheads. Alexander seems fine, but there is a small bump on Wilbur's forehead. Daddyji asks him to press on it with his hands to keep the swelling down. The two constables use their canes to push the crowd back.

Daddyji moves forward to explain, "Inspector sahib, these gentlemen are American and Canadian diplomats. None of them was driving the car."

The inspector turns around, looks at Daddyji and asks, "Sir, who are you? Why are you speaking for them? Please stand aside and let us do our work."

"Who was driving the car?" the inspector asks.

Alexander replies, "I was driving."

Daddyji looks at him, wondering if he is still drunk. Alexander knows that if the police get hold of the driver, the poor man will rot in jail for months before he will get a hearing. He knows that it was not the driver's fault. In his case, he knows that he has diplomatic immunity and nothing will come of the case, after he pays a few rupees to the owner of the goats as compensation.

The inspector asks him to show his driver license. He takes out his International license and hands it over.

"Sir, do you have any other papers?" the Inspector asks.

Alexander takes out his diplomatic identification and shows it to the inspector. The Inspector takes a look at it and asks, "Sir, have you been drinking? And he moves closer to Alexander to smell his breath. Both Alexander and Wilbur are reeking of alcohol. Kesriji senses a problem. He suspects that the inspector is trying to make a case to extract some money. The Inspector knows very well that he cannot do much in this case; the best he can do is to create a nuisance for them and hope that he might get a few rupees.

Daddyji seizes the opportunity to do something special for the diplomats to forge a relationship. He says to the inspector, "Inspector sahib, let them go. We will take care of things." And he takes out some rupee notes from his wallet and hands them to the owner of the goats. The idea is to show the colour of money to the inspector. The inspector gets the hint and starts to move towards his jeep and goes and sits in it. The two constables follow him and so do Daddyji and Kesriji.

As the inspector is about to light his cigarette, Kesriji takes his own lighter out and lights it for him. As the inspector takes in a deep breath and exhales the smoke, Daddyji extends his right hand and says, "Thank you inspector sahib. I am the editor of the magazine called, LESTWEFORGET. Let me know if I can be of any help to you." At the same time he slips some rupee notes to the inspector. The constable, who is driving the jeep, turns the ignition on, and the jeep drives away.

Both Wilbur and Alexander are standing beside their car watching the drama. They did not see the exchange of money between the inspector and Daddyji. Wilbur opens his wallet and takes out some money to compensate Daddyji for what he had paid to the owner of the goats–who is long gone.

Daddyji says, "Gentlemen you are guests of India. For us, a guest is like an incarnation of God."

Both Wilbur and Alexander thank Daddyji and Kesriji, and they all drive away to their respective homes.

When Daddyji reaches home, he sees a big crowd in front of our house. Our family, Kesriji's family and many neighbours are standing and talking. When Daddyji did not reach home by 11:00 P.M.–the time he said he would be back by was 10:00 P.M.–both the families got panicky and called some neighbours for help in deciding how they should go about looking for them. As they were about to call the police, the characteristic beeping of Daddyji's car horn could be heard from far away at that time of the night. As soon as the car stops and they come out, their respective wives blow up at them, with the neighbours trying to talk to them and trying to find out the cause of the delay.

Mummyji is upset with him, so he is not able to tell her anything about the party. All night he is so excited that he is hardly able to sleep. He sees unlimited possibilities in the contacts he has made last night. He is excited about telling this to his boss, Hari Nautiyal. He cannot wait to get to the office in the morning.

The next morning, as soon as he reaches the office, he, straightaway, goes to the office of Hari Nautriyal and talks to his personal assistant to make an appointment.

"He has a meeting at the ministry of defense all morning," he tells him.

As soon as Daddyji turns around to walk back to his office, he sees Hari Nautiyal walking towards him at a distance. He looks at the personal assistant, and then at Hari Nautiyal, confused.

In the meantime, Hari Nautiyal has reached the front desk of the entrance to his office and says, "Oh, the meeting got cancelled; the defense secretary is down with malaria," and then looks at Daddyji and asks, "Surinder, are you here to see me?"

Daddyji replies, "Yes, Mr. Nautiyal, if I may?"

Hari Nautiyal opens the door to his office and gestures to Daddyji to follow him.

After they are seated, Daddyji tells him all about the happenings of last night.

Hari Nautiyal listens to it very intently and says, "Well done, Surinder. I think you should nurture these connections. These diplomats can be very useful to us in more ways than one."

Daddyji says, "Yes, I agree with you. Also, I have learned that Prime Minister Jawaharlal Nehru will be visiting America and Canada, and these diplomats can help me get a place in the delegation as a journalist."

Hari Nautiyal says, "Surinder, America is going to take over Britain's place as the world leader, and Canada is showing leadership in peacekeeping and is also a country with nuclear capability. I think both the contacts will pay dividends for years to come. I authorize you, as one of your official duties, to develop contacts with, not only these two diplomats but, the diplomats of Britain and Russia also. I will issue an order authorizing the expenditure. In fact, I would go so far as to say that you should plan a trip to America and Canada to coincide with the Prime Minister's visit."

• •

About half a mile from where Daddyji and Hari Nautiyal are sitting and planning how to use and extend the newly made contacts with the American and Canadian Diplomats, Wilbur Wright is sitting down talking to, Bobby Schwartz, the Counselor for Public Affairs in the Embassy of the United States of America. Wilbur Wright works for the United States Information Service (USIS), whose function is to understand, inform and influence foreign publics in the promotion and furthering of the national interest of the USA. At this point in time, USIS is very active in India trying to increase contact with the local population to counter the growing Russian influence in India.

Wilbur says, "Bobby, this man we started calling Sam; his real name is," he takes out a piece of paper from his pocket and continues; "...Surinder Mehra. He says he is the editor of a small magazine, LESTWEFORGET–a magazine with nationalist flavor. I have made enquiries. In fact, it is owned by the well known Nautiyal Industries, and Surinder is a senior executive of the organization. I think he will be a very useful person to have on our side."

Bobby says, "Wilbur, you have my permission to follow up on this contact. Utilize the usual procedures."

Wilbur, who has been with USIS for only three years, is barely thirty years old. He has a bachelor's degree in library science and a master's degree in International Affairs. Before being posted to India, he has been trained in Indian culture and Hindi language. After his meeting with Bobby Schwartz, he goes to his office at the USIS building. The first thing he does is type out a letter to Daddyji to his office address thanking him for his help and promising to get in touch very soon. At the same time, Bobby Schwartz goes to his secretary, and gives her a piece of paper asking her to add the name of Surinder Mehra to the list of names to be invited to different embassy functions.

Daddyji has become a part of the, proverbial, Diplomatic Circuit–with all its connections.

14

DIPLOMATIC CIRCUIT

After a few days, Daddyji receives a letter. The quality of the envelope and lettering shows that it is from a western embassy, and, of course, USIS is printed in bold letters. Indian typewriters usually produce broken, disfigured and, sometimes, tilted alphabets. The quality of the envelope is so good that he holds the envelope in his hand for about a minute as he hesitates to tear it. For this reason, he foregoes his usual way of tearing the edge of the envelope, instead; he goes to the kitchen where a tea kettle is sitting on an electric heater. He turns the electric heater on and lets the steam from the kettle soften the glue. He then slowly peels the closure flap of the envelope off, and takes out the thick bond paper with dark lettering; with USIS printed in blue and with an imprint of the American flag. There is something about it that he likes. He starts to read the letter. The letter is from Wilbur Wright thanking him for his help at the time of the accident. He folds the letter, puts it back in the envelope and places it in the top drawer of his desk.

In a few days, he receives a similar letter from Alexander Bell of the Canadian High Commission, but it is a little more than that. It contains an invitation to attend a cocktail party.

In early May 1956, Daddyji receives a letter from Max Hoffer that he will be joining his new posting at the Canadian High Commission on June 1. Daddyji is absolutely delighted. He seems to have developed a special relationship with Max, both sharing the same birthday, and the dream that they still talk about whenever they meet.

Soon thereafter, he receives an invitation from the Canadian High Commission for a cocktail party to introduce Max Hoffer. He cannot wait to see him.

Daddyji is one of the first guests to arrive at about 7:00 P.M. He parks his car across the street from the High Commissioner's residence and beeps the car horn three times—a habit he picked up from his motorcycle days. Max and a few others are standing in the front lawn, chatting. Daddyji comes out of his car and walks towards the residence. Max does away with the normal diplomatic protocol and walks out to the street. They embrace each other like two long lost brothers. After the long embrace and back slapping is over, Max Hoffer's wife, Jane, who is standing watching the two of them, comes forward and gives a polite embrace to Daddyji, who is somewhat embarrassed; not being used to it.

She says looking around, "Oh, where is your beautiful wife?"

Daddyji replies, "I am coming here directly from my office. To see her you will have to come to our house."

She replies with a giggle, "I am looking forward to it."

Other guests start arriving, and soon there are almost a hundred guests under the colorful tent erected on the front lawn of the High Commissioner's residence. Daddyji notices that almost the same guests attend all the diplomatic parties. There is predominance of diplomats of other countries, journalists, well known businessmen and a few civil servants from the Ministry of External Affairs.

He sees Wilbur Wright of the American Embassy from a distance and goes over to meet him. Wilbur is standing talking to a Russian diplomat, Demetri.

After the initial niceties, Demetri asks Wilbur, "So how is the planning going on for the Prime Minister's visit to America? You capitalists are copy cats. We had the Prime Minister visit us in Russia last year, and you want to do the same thing. So when is the visit going to take place? I hear the dates keep changing."

As the conversation is going on, another American walks over. Wilbur introduces him only to Daddyji, as he already seems to know Demetri—for whom he does not appear to have much use as is obvious from the cold shoulder he gives him.

"Bobby, meet Surinder Mehra, the editor of LESTWEFORGET magazine. He is the one who was very helpful to us after the accident."

Bobby extends his hand towards Daddyji with a wide grin on his face and says, "I am Bobby Schwartz. Pleased to make your acquaintance. We are very thankful to you for helping Wilbur get out of that messy situation."

Demetri slowly moves away and joins another group.

Bobby watches Demetri leave, and he keeps talking to Daddyji in his long drawn way of pronouncing each word, "Tell me about your magazine. I have not had the good fortune of reading it."

Daddyji replies, "Mr. Schwartz…"

Bobby immediately says, "Oh, please call me Bobby. As you probably know, we Americans gave up the British traditions about 175 years ago."

Daddyji continues, "Well, if you say so, Bobby. LESTWEFORGET was set up a few years ago as a magazine to keep reminding our own employees and the public at large about the sacrifices that had to be made to gain Independence—and hence the name LESTWEFORGET. There is a Hindi version also. The name is *Yaadrahe*—meaning, Remember. Both are distributed, free of charge, to all the employees of Nautiyal Industries and many other organizations, such as libraries of schools and universities. It is published once a month."

Bobby says, "How much readership do you have?"

Daddyji replies, "We print and distribute ten thousand copies of each edition."

"You know, Surinder, I used to work for a small local magazine, like yours, in a small city in the South, named Marietta, in the state of Georgia. After the national magazines spread their wings; it closed down. The reason I am telling you this is because the name of that newspaper was also, Remember—which I think you will find interesting. Now don't get me wrong. By telling you this, I am not suggesting that your magazines will close down. All I am telling you is that there is a trend towards reading national magazines, so you should try and grow your magazine to the national level."

Daddyji likes the way Bobby speaks; each word appears to flow out smoothly from his mouth, well rounded and well thought out. He replies, "Well, we are planning to turn our magazines into national magazines. The names will remain the same."

There is bit of a pause, while Bobby scratches his right ear lobe and says, "I have an idea." There is another pause. Daddyji is waiting to hear the idea. Bobby looks around and takes Daddyji by the arm and walks to the far end of the tent, leaving his fellow American, Wilbur Wright, behind.

"My young friend, have you heard of PL 480? Why am I asking you this? You are a journalist. You must know what it is. You see all the food grain coming to India from America is being sent because of an American law known as Public Law 480. As you probably know, the food grain is not free. The only difference is that all the payment for it is made in Indian rupees that stay in India. My young friend, our accounts are overflowing with the PL 480 rupees. Some of this money is available as interest free loans to private enterprises in India like yours. If you want capital for growing your magazine, we will be happy to help."

Daddyji is surprised to hear Bobby make this offer. He has always seen the Americans as very generous people, but to offer a loan at the first meeting surprises him. Many questions flash through his mind in a matter of a few seconds. He replies politely, "I appreciate your offer. I will talk to the Chairman, Mr. Hari Nautiyal, and get back to you in a few weeks." And suddenly, he utters something that appears to have fallen from heaven into his brain, "Bobby, I would like to invite you and your wife to have lunch at my house next Sunday. I will also invite Wilbur."

"Thank you, kindly. This is so gracious of you. There is no Mrs. Schwartz. I am a bachelor," Bobby replies.

As Daddyji is driving home after the party, he is thinking and gets lost in his thoughts. As the effect of Champagne–that has become his favourite drink, instead of Vodka, since he has taken to the diplomatic circuit–puts him in a giddy mood; his old friend Shakespeare drops into his thoughts. Daddyji begins to do some jolly talk to himself:

"I must hob nob in this world of give't and take't. . . this is . . .a . . .tide . . .I must . . .take on flood. . . this is going to. . . take me to the shores of America. . . America. . . everybody . . .wants to go to America.

As these thoughts are swirling in his mind he starts to sing America … America… I am coming… I am coming… everybody wants to go to America… in the tune of one of his favourite tunes of Kundanlal Saigal, the late iconic Indian singer of his youth, *Aye Dil-e-Bekarar Kyon*…meaning: … Oh… my dear why are you getting so impatient?

He keeps singing and driving until he reaches Sarai Rohella railway station, and, by the loud whisles of the steam engines, he realizes that he has overshot his house by a mile.

"Oh this *Shumpain* is going to get me into trouble one day," he mutters to himself.

When he reaches home, as usual, he is late, and Mummyji refuses to talk to him.

The next morning, he is sitting in his office waiting for the meeting to start. He is eager to tell Chairman Hari Nautiyal about the offer Bobby Schwartz has made. At precisely 10:30 A.M., he gets up and walks over to the boardroom.

When he reaches there, it is empty. He waits and waits, and there is no sign of the Nautiyals. He looks at his watch. It is almost 10:40. He decides to get up and find out what the matter is. As he walks over to the door, he finds both father and son, the Nautiyals, standing outside and they shout at him, "Surprise!" He is startled, but then gets hold of his wits and looks at them with a questioning look.

Hari Nautiyal laughs, saying, "Remember last time you told me that it is auspicious to be late by 11 minutes. So, here we are at precisely 10:41."

Jokes aside, they finally sit down to discuss business. The purpose of the meeting is to review the Business Plan prepared by Daddyji to take the magazines to the next level, and turn them into national magazines. As the question of financing comes up, Hari Nautiyal says, "Arrangements have already been made with our bank. Let us plan to publish the first copy on August 15, 1957, exactly ten years after the first Independence Day."

After Hari Nautiyal is finished speaking, Daddyji tells them about his meeting with Bobby Schwartz and the financing offer he had made.

Hari Nautiyal says, "I am surprised to hear this." He is quiet for a while, and, after a great deal of thought, continues, "Surinder, arrange a meeting with him. Invite him for lunch at the Imperial... on second thought; let us invite him to the new Ashok Hotel. I was invited at the opening; I tell you, it is a fine example of Indian craftsmanship."

Daddyji suddenly remembers and says, "Mr. Nautiyal, I have already invited him to my house for lunch this coming Sunday. I would like you all to come to our house also. I think lunch at the Ashok Hotel may not be necessary."

Hari Nautiyal agrees to the suggestion, "I think it is a splendid idea."

Driving home after work, he is feeling very satisfied that he is going to be entertaining American diplomats, and one of the top Indian business families in his home. He is sure that this is what Shakespeare meant by hob nob and give't and take't to move up in the world. As he reaches home and gives the good news to Mummyji, she breaks into one of her anxiety attacks.

"It is already Tuesday... guests are coming on Sunday. And she starts to count on her fingers; 1+2+2+2... 5 guests... no... no, I mean 7 guests. Tell me, tell me... how many guests are coming?" She just goes and lies down on the bed. Daddyji knows the drill. He just keeps quiet and lets the storm pass, and then he says jokingly, "Kamla, do you not remember the golden rule of how to win friends and influence people? It is through their stomachs. The great Chanakya, the political scientist during the Mauriya dynasty, said so 2,000 years ago."

At school I tell my friend, Suraj, that we are having Americans to our house for lunch this coming Sunday.

"Oh *yaar,* your Daddyji is so well connected. So what will you make for lunch? Will you serve *humburgers?*" he says, using the Punjabi pronunciation.

"I don't really know. Why don't you also come? As you have never seen an American, this is your opportunity," I say teasing him.

"Oh, come on Vikram, I have seen Americans before. Have you forgotten the two American girls, in red skirts, accompanying the Cola trucks when we were in primary school?"

"Oh, how can I forget—especially the one with blonde hair?"

Suraj asks, "How is it that India never plays cricket matches with the Americans?"

I reply, "I think they don't play cricket in America."

"Oh, why is that? Were they not a British colony at one time?" Suraj asks.

I reply, "I don't know; why don't we ask them, when we see them on Sunday?"

• •

On Sunday, it is very hot. Daddyji has turned the cooler on early in the morning so that the house will be cooled by the time the guests arrive. My friend, Suraj, is the first one to arrive at about 11:30 A.M. He is dressed in all white clothes and well polished black leather shoes. "Suraj, you are looking so white that you are looking like an American," I tease him.

At about 12:30 P.M., Bobby Schwartz, Wilbur Wright and his wife, Anita, arrive together in a car with CD plates. As the diplomats come out of the car, the word spreads in the neighbourhood. Necks are craning out of the windows to take a peek.

Mummyji gets introduced to Wilbur's wife, Anita.

"Is this not an Indian name?" she asks. "My daughter's name is Suneeta, it rhymes with Anita."

Anita smiles politely, "I would love to meet her."

Everybody is talking to everybody, as they all find seats. And then there is the usual two beep horn to announce their arrival. The Nautiyal family of four has arrived. Daddyji runs outside; a long blue Pontiac car is gracing the pot-holed road in front of our house. He leads them into the house. There are again introductions all around.

Finally, everybody is seated. Daddyji asks the ladies for their choice of J.B. Rose or Cola. This reminds Bobby that he has brought some bottles of red wine with him, but they are left in the car. He quietly gets up, goes out and brings in a cardboard box.

"Ladies and gentlemen, I present to you the genuine red American wine straight from Napa Valley California–the best suited with Indian curry," he says lifting the box up.

Anita is the only lady who wants red wine. The other ladies opt for either J.B. Rose or Cola. The menfolk, on the other hand, all opt for red wine; although, Daddyji has Golden Eagle beer at home.

Meera and Bina Nautiyal get up from their seats to move to another room. Mummyji is busy in the kitchen. Anita, after she sees the other two women get up, also gets up and follows the other two ladies to the dining room. As this is all going on, Daddyji realizes that there are no glasses in which to serve wine. Bobby has opened the box and takes out a few bottles. He looks around to find something to take the cork out with, and finally, takes out a contraption from his pocket and pulls the cork out of the bottle. Without waiting any further, he begins to pour wine into the glasses that are meant for beer.

Suddenly, the hum of the cooler, and the whirling sound of the ceiling fans stops. The electricity has gone off. It is nothing new for us. It happens to us almost every day. But for the guests, who live in the New Delhi area around Connaught Place, this almost never happens. After a few minutes, it begins to become warm and then hot, especially for those who are drinking wine. Some hand-held fans are provided. Some of the guests pick up newspaper and magazines from the tables to fan themselves and get some relief from the heat.

Daddyji feels bad that his guests have to go through all this and to make small talk, he says, "See Bobby, what we have to go through in India. Do you have rationing of electricity in America?"

"Very rarely."

"In addition to food aid, I think we need some electricity aid also. I was wondering if America and Canada can send us some dams and nuclear reactors," Daddyji says, trying to introduce some cool humor in an otherwise hot atmosphere.

Bobby, not to be left behind, adds with a laugh, "I will send a cable to Washington tonight and convey your request. By the way, Surinder, America is already helping India with the design and construction of the Bhakhra Dam. My friend, Harvey Slocum, is the Chief Engineer. He shuttles between New Delhi and Bhakhra. There are over fifty American engineers stationed right here in New Delhi to help with the design. Do you know where Kaka Nagar is?"

"Yes," Daddyji replies.

Bobby continues with his story telling in his charming drawl, "That is where I live also. If you go there on a Sunday afternoon you will see American engineers and their wives sitting on the roof top sunbathing and trying to get a tan."

"Yes, I have noticed that whenever we have visited our nephew; he works in the Bhakhra Design Directorate and lives in the same flats."

All of sudden, the hum of the ceiling fan and the cooler comes back. Everybody looks up at the ceiling, as if thanking God for the little mercy known as electricity.

"It usually goes off for two hours, but today the electricity is back in just half hour. I think the Delhi Electricity Board must have found out that we have V.I.P's sitting in our house," Daddyji jokes.

Mummyji calls me to the kitchen and tells me to go to the drawing room and announce that lunch is on the table.

"No, tell Chottu to do that. I am not doing it," I say and walk out of the kitchen.

Eventually, she goes and requests the guests to move to the dining room to have lunch. Daddyji gets up and shows the way. Kishi, Suneeta and I are standing in the verandah. When Daddyji sees us, he brings us into the dining room and introduces us to the guests. I, being the tallest, attract everybody's attention. As they are placing food on to their plates, some of them make small talk with me. Bobby stops by me on his way back to the drawing room, with his plate in hand, and starts a conversation with me—with Suraj looking on. I have no idea what he is talking about. The way he speaks English is so much different than what I am used to that I just smile and nod.

To my utter surprise, Suraj, who can hardly utter two words of English, asks Bobby, "Sir, do Americans play cricket?"

Bobby replies, "No, I don't think we do."

Veer Nautiyal, who is standing nearby, says, "Bobby, America was a British colony once; so how is it that the Americans don't play cricket?"

"It is true that America was once a British colony, but we did not catch their bad habits—like playing a game of cricket for five days. Who has the time?" Bobby replies with a laugh.

The men sit down in the drawing room, and the women take their seats in the dining room. Daddyji comes around with a plate full of *Chapaaties*, with Chottu following with a number of glasses full of water or Cola.

As they pass in front of Wilbur, Daddyji says, "Wilbur, you see these *Chapaaties*; these are made of wheat from Kansas, Coca Cola is made in Atlanta,

Frigidaire is made in Detroit, and the wine is from California. And, in the not too distant future, we will be receiving electricity from Bhakhra Dam built with American help. Oh, and the light blue car standing outside was also made by General Motors in Detroit. I hope you are feeling quite at home." They all break into laughter.

At the same time the above conversation is going on, I am standing in the verandah with Suraj. Mummyji asks me to go into the drawing room to announce that the desserts are on the table.

"No, Mummyji, not me. Ask Chottu," I say.

"Come on Vikram, you are a big boy now. You are training for public speaking. Let me see you go in there and speak a few words," Mummyji says, challenging me.

To make matters worse, my sister, Suneeta, who is standing nearby, says trying to tease me, "Vikram *Bhaiya,* I can go, if you are feeling shy like a little girl." Suraj also joins in pushing me to go in. Finally, I decide to take up the challenge.

As soon as I enter, they all break out into laughter. It seems to me as if they are laughing at me. My cheeks go read. I look around and then down at my pants to check if there are any reasons for them to laugh at me. I find none. My presence is not noticed by anyone.

The conversation is continuing... In response to what Daddyji had said earlier, Wilbur puts down his plate on the table, rises up, takes a bow and says, "We are happy to help our friends. Any time we can be of assistance, please let us know."

After I hear what Wilbur has said, I realize that the joke must have been on something said before. I stand my ground. After Wilbur sits down, I muster enough courage. I have decided that, today, I shall make my mark as a public speaker.

For the last three months, I have been training with Daddyji for the interschool elocution contest. I decide to put it to practice. "Gentlemen," I say loudly. Everybody looks at me. One at a time the voices stop and there is silence. I am surprised to see that my voice has such power that when I speak, people listen.

Daddyji looks at me annoyed—as if telling me with his looks to get lost.

I continue loudly and with confidence, "Gentlemen, may I have your attention please. The desserts have been set up on the dining room table. Please serve yourself at your convenience."

To my surprise, they all get up and move towards the dining room. Ice cream, sliced mangoes, *rassagollaas and burfee* adorn the dining table. The last two have been decorated with silver leaf. The Americans look at the silver covered desserts—not sure how to, or whether or not to eat them. Mummyji explains to them what each of the desserts is made of. Still, they seem apprehensive in eating silver, in case it is poisonous. Hari Nautiyal comes to the rescue; he mutters something in Bobby's and Wilbur's ears about the silver leaf being good for men, and they both willingly pick up one each.

As they are sitting in the drawing room sipping tea, Bobby asks, "Surinder did you have a chance to talk to Mr. Nautiyal about the offer I made about the loan? The money is going fast as many Indian enterprises are taking advantage of the loan offer."

Daddyji looks at Hari Nautiyal, who puts down his cup of tea, wipes his lips with a cloth napkin, clears his throat and says, "Bobby, I appreciate your offer. At this time we have already made commitments to our banks for financing our activities going forward. If there is need in the future, we will contact you."

As soon as Hari Nautiyal is finished speaking, his son Veer starts, "We have another suggestion. Nautiyal Family Trust has created a scholarship program to offer financial and other assistance to some of our brightest students to pursue post-graduate studies in universities in America, Canada and the U.K. We can offer assistance only in rupees. You are aware of the foreign exchange problem India is having; if you can help in that regard we will be grateful."

"I think we should be able to work something out in that regard," Bobby says.

All the guests are ready to depart by 2:30 P.M. One by one, they all thank Mummyji for arranging such a sumptuous lunch at short notice. Bobby Schwartz is the most eloquent of them all, "Mrs. Mehra," he says bowing down to shake her hand, "I shall ever be thankful to you for opening your home to us. This is the first time, in my two years in India, that I have visited an Indian home. I had heard of the legendry Indian hospitality; today, I have experienced it first hand. I hope, one day, I will be able to reciprocate your hospitality."

Mummyji replies very softly, "We are delighted to have you as our guests. You are very kind with your comments."

• •

Informal contacts between Daddyji and the American diplomats continue. He is even invited to attend the foundation stone laying ceremony of the new American Embassy building. The Chief Justice of the United States, Earl Warren, who is visiting India, lays the foundation stone on September 1, 1956.

Max Hoffer and Daddyji get together every now and then to keep in touch. The more he meets the American and Canadians diplomats, the more he desires to visit these two countries; this desire is well known to his American and Canadian friends. During his contacts with the diplomats, he comes to know that the Prime Minister's visit to America and Canada has been finalized for the month of December, 1956. His dream is to visit the two countries as a journalist member of the delegation. Despite his contacts with the diplomats of the two countries, and his boss Hari Nautiyal's contacts in the Government of India, he is not selected to accompany the delegation.

In consultation with Max Hoffer of the Canadian High Commission and Bobby Schwartz of the American Embassy, it is decided that both Hari Nautiyal and Daddyji may visit America and Canada at the same time as the Prime Minister's visit as journalists, but not as part of the Indian delegation. This decision is finalized in September, 1956. They have three months to make arrangements. As for the requirements for Visa to Canada, there is no requirement for the citizens of India, both being Commonwealth countries. The Americans readily agree to give them the visitor visas. Moreover, they are happy to find out that both their friends, Bobby Schwartz and Max Hoffer, will be visiting their respective countries to coincide with the Prime Minister's visit. As the dates of the Prime Minister's visit are finalized, they also make tentative airline reservations. The program is to depart from Delhi on December 11; arrive in New York on December 13, via London, and arrive in Washington D.C. on December 14; two days before the PM and his entourage is scheduled to arrive. The PM, accompanied by his daughter Indira Gandhi, and his delegation are scheduled to land in Washington D.C. on December 16. The PM has meetings in Washington from Dec 16 to Dec 20. On December 20, he travels to New York to address the United Nations and then on to Ottawa, Canada, on Dec 22. On December 24, the delegation flies back to India via London and West Germany.

"Surinder, are you sure you want to be in Washington and Ottawa in the middle of winter? Ottawa usually has snow at that time of the year; unless, of course, you want to see white Christmas," Max Hoffer says to Daddyji on the phone one day.

In the heat of the excitement of a foreign trip, they had forgotten about the cold weather. As soon as Hari Nautiyal finds out, he cancels the trip. He suffers from arthritis, and he does not want to take chances with his health. Now the question arises: Would Daddyji like to go alone? That possibility is vetoed by Mummyji; her main concerns being the danger of flying over ocean, and catching pneumonia in cold weather!

It is decided to postpone their trip to some time in the summer of 1957.

15

MANTRA SADHANA

Early in 1957, Swami Ravi Anand arrives in Delhi for his yearly 'pilgrimage' to escape from the winter of Kashmir, and to meet with the Trustees of Nautiyal Family Trust, the main financial supporter of Verinag Ashram. He is staying as a houseguest of Nautiyal family. Chandubhai Patel, Hari Nautiyal and Tirath Bhatia—a senior civil servant—are the Trustees. They are all looking forward to hearing about the exciting research that is being carried out at the Ashram. The focus of the research is the ancient Hindu scriptures and long-range brain-wave communication. Veer Nautiyal and Daddyji are also attending as senior executives of Nautiyal Industries. The meeting is set for Sunday at noon. It is a cool day, but the sunlight pouring through the expansive windows of the sprawling Nautiyal residence on Curzon Road is making the drawing room comfortably warm. Everybody has arrived by the appointed time. Swami Ravi Anand is wearing his trade mark attire- white *kurta*, *paijama* and a white *Pashmina* shawl. Daddyji notices a glow on his face that comes from a sense of satisfaction and contentment from within. All the trustees have been receiving periodic reports about the progress of the research. The subject of the research is so esoteric that the trustees, except Hari Nautiyal, are skeptical about the claims being made by Swamiji. They have, up until now, gone along with Swami Ravi Anand's contention that it is worth the effort. The interim reports have been very positive; therefore, there is a strange sense of anticipation, and Swamiji knows it.

He closes his eyes for a few seconds in meditation and starts to speak. He says, "For the last 25 years or so, the Nautiyal Family Trust has been providing both financial and moral support to the Long Range Brain Wave Communication Institute at Verinag Ashram. I would like to thank them for their patience. A Canadian friend has suggested that we name the research program: BrainCom. I have accepted the suggestion, and I will, henceforth, refer to our research projects as Braincom 1, 2, 3, etc. I think time has come to reap the benefits of 20 years of research. There have been two research projects underway: One is to enhance the mental capacity by means of *Mantra Sadhana* or meditation by means of a *Mantra*; we will call this Braincom 1; second is known as Brain Wave Communication or *Mannosancharan;* this means communication between humans by means of ethereal vibrations through brain waves; we will call this Braincom 2."

He pauses for almost thirty seconds to let those present absorb what he has said and to gather his own thoughts.

He continues, "We have all heard or read the story in *Mahabharat*, the great Hindu epic. When the battle between the Panduvs and the Kauravs is about to start, King Dhritrashtra, the blind father of the Kauravs, asks his aide, Sanjay, 'Tell me what is happening on the battlefield.' Sanjay, an accomplished *Divya Drishti Sadhana* practitioner, starts to describe the scene on the battlefield that is hundreds of miles away. Today, I am happy to inform you that we are closer than ever in acquiring the same capability. If there are any questions, please do not hesitate to ask." He pauses.

Tirath Bhatia, who had been shifting in his seat, clears his throat gently to attract attention to himself. Swamiji looks towards him and nods.

Tirath Bhatia says, "I have read the brief reports that you have been sending. I, and others present, would be delighted to hear in your own words the progress that has been made."

Swamiji replies in his usual confident manner, "I think it will be better if you see a live demonstration. Tirath ji, would you like to participate?"

Tirath Bhatia hesitates, at first, and then replies, "Yes. I will be honoured."

Swamiji is happy that one of the skeptics is going to participate in the demonstration and says, "All right then, you can write anything you like on a piece of paper and look at it intently for a minute or so. I will draw what you have written on another piece of paper. You should do this exercise in another room of the house, not here. Also, you can say any words you like in any language, also in another room out of my hearing range, and I will reproduce the sounds as closely as possible."

Tirath gets up and looks at Hari Nautiyal for permission to go to one of the rooms of the house. Hari Nautiyal nods at his son, Veer, who gets up and leads Tirath Bhatia into a room at the rear of the house.

"Veer, can you please get me a piece of paper." Veer goes to another room and brings a writing pad and a pen and hands it over to Tirath Bhatia. He accepts the writing pad, but for some reason, politely declines to accept the pen and takes out his own pen to write with—probably to allay any possibility of collusion. Veer leaves the room. Tirath Bhatia thinks for sometime and then starts to write and fills the whole sheet of paper with his writing. He looks at it carefully, and when he is satisfied, he folds it and gently places it in the right pocket of his trousers. As he is getting up from the chair, he thinks of something and sits down again. He takes out the paper he had written on from his pocket and tears it up into pieces and puts it back in his pocket. He then removes another blank paper from the writing pad, folds it and puts the blank paper in the left pocket of his trousers. He walks out to the drawing room, where others are sitting and waiting quietly. Swamiji is in meditation with his eyes closed.

He senses Tirath Bhatia's entry into the room and gradually opens his eyes and says to him, "Please have a seat beside me and look into my eyes." Tirath Bhatia pulls a chair and sits across from where Swamiji is sitting. Swamiji looks into his eyes, while saying a mantra in Sanskrit, and gives a hand sign to Veer to give him a sheet of paper and something to write with. After he receives the paper and a pen, he gets up and asks to be taken to another room.

After a few minutes, he comes out of that room with a paper in his hand and gives it to Tirath Bhatia. As Tirath Bhatia is reading it, Swamiji says, pointing to one of the complex mathematical expressions, "Tirath ji, one of the formulae you wrote earlier is a bit incorrect."

Tirath Bhatia carefully looks at the paper and says, "Swamiji, I did not write anything on the paper. I left it blank."

He then takes out the blank paper from his left pocket and hands it over to Swamiji, who takes one look at it and says, "Tirath ji, this is the second paper; where is the first paper that you tore up and placed in your pocket?"

Tirath stands up and takes out the shreds of paper from his pocket. Everybody in the room is spellbound. Tirath Bhatia shakes his head in amazement and says, "Swamiji, I cannot believe it. This is just unbelievable. What amazes me most is that you found the mistake in the complicated formula—the mistake I had deliberately written in. Tell us the secret. How did you know that there is a mistake in the formula? It is a complicated mathematical expression."

"Well, it is no secret, and Mr. Nautiyal knows that I am a physicist. I completed my BSc. at Hindu College, right here in Delhi, and then I carried on further studies at Cambridge for two years and received my MSc. Degree in physics. This is why I was able to find the mistake in the formula you had written. What you should be asking is: How was I able to know that you had torn up the first piece of paper you had written on," Swamiji replies."

Tirath Bhatia is feeling embarrassed at having tried to play a trick and having been caught at it. He says with a sheepish smile, "How did you learn the technique?"

Swamiji replies, "After a great deal of effort. It is a long story." He had been instructed by Hari Nautiyal to keep the technique of Braincom 2 confidential amongst as few people as possible.

"Chandubhai Patel, who has been listening intently, asks, "How did a highly qualified physicist like you get involved with the Ashram?"

Swamiji replies, "I was interested in Hindu scriptures, while I was at Hindu College. I had taken courses in religion and also studied Sanskrit. The interest continued, or rather it increased during my years at Cambridge. I found, and my other Indian colleagues also found, that being away from home increased our interest in Indian cultural heritage. In due course, I started holding classes in Hindu Scriptures. I was surprised to find the interest that students from countries other than India had in Hindu religion. In fact, most of my students were from Canada, America and Germany. Without naming anyone, I can tell you that some of my students have gone on to become world renowned in their respective fields. Many of my students used to work day and night to complete their assignments. When they used come by to attend my class in the evening, they would be dead tired. One day, I showed them how to relax by means of *Mantra Sadhana*. After only a few weeks, they began to tell me the benefits they were experiencing. I was not surprised. One of them told me jokingly: future generations will owe a debt of gratitude to India and to you, Swami Ravi; that is what they all started calling me affectionately. Why so, I asked, and he replied: Buddy you are responsible for some of the breakthroughs in Atomic physics, and you don't even know it. He told me later that as a result of *Mantra Sadhana* and study of some of the scriptures, he was able to analyze the research data in a way that would not have been possible otherwise."

"How did you happen to start the research institute at Verinag Ashram?" Tirath Bhatia asks.

Swamiji replies, "I had originally intended to complete my PhD. in physics at Cambridge, but the War started, and I returned home. Our family Guru, Swami Shiv Narayan, started the Ashram in the 1890's and started research in Hindu Scriptures and adaptation of the information contained therein to everyday life. At some point, he met Mr. Adarsh Nautiyal, Mr. Hari Nautiyal's father. Since then, the Ashram started getting support from Nautiyal Family. Swami Shiv Narayan left for his heavenly abode in 1939. Upon my return from England, in 1940, I met Mr. Hari Nautiyal. When he learned of my scientific background and knowledge of Hindu scriptures; he suggested that I take over the reins of the Ashram. After giving it considerable thought and the fact that he agreed to give me complete freedom of operation, I accepted. And here we are today 17 years later."

There is silence after an overpowering performance by Swamiji. Hari Nautiyal, who has been listening quietly, says, "Thank you, Swamiji, for taking the time to give us a live demonstration. When we set upon this path, our aim was to make the findings of our research available to our countrymen for prac- tice in their day to day life. As it turns out, the foreigners are more interested in what we are doing than our own people."

At this point, Swamiji removes a file from his briefcase. After thumbing through some papers, he says, "Just to give you an idea of the degree of interest from other countries, we have, in the last three months alone, received a hun- dred and seventeen inquiries. The most significant among them are the ones from the United States Information Service, and the Embassy of the USSR. I have received official invitations from both the countries to visit them for giving lectures in the near future."

Hari Nautiyal is intrigued to hear this. He gets up and goes over to where Swamiji is sitting to have a look at the letters from USIS and the USSR. After looking them over, he says to Daddyji, "Well Surinder, it is none other than, your friends, Bobby Schwartz and Demetri... what's his name."

None of the others, except Daddyji and Veer Nautiyal, are interested in what Hari Nautiyal has said.

Chandubhai Patel is a no-nonsense man, and he asks a very pointed ques- tion to Swamiji, "What are the practical benefits of the findings of your research?"

Swamiji starts to say something, but Hari Nautiyal looks at him and gives him a slight nod of his head and takes over the reply to the question. He says, "In the recent past, huge technical innovations have been made by the west- ern countries. India has been left behind. We have to play catch-up. It will require import of large amounts of machinery and know-how to even begin to keep pace. Our strength over the centuries has been spirituality. Braincom 1 and Braincom 2 will be our exports to western countries–the exchange of Technology for Spirituality. This should certainly improve our image in the world and bring in valuable foreign currency."

Chandubhai Patel takes off his Gandhi cap and places it on the table beside the sofa he is sitting on. Hari Nautiyal knows that when this happens, Chandubhai is not happy with what he has heard, and that fireworks are about to start.

Chandubhai says with irritation in his voice, "Nautiyal sahib, I do not understand this new idea of yours. How can you export spirituality? Are you going to sell our scriptures, or are you going to convert Christians to Hinduism. How will that bring in foreign currency?"

Hari Nautiyal senses irritation in his voice, and says in a calm and calculated manner, "Chandubhai, your concerns are understandable. The plan is for Swamiji to visit some countries and give lectures at various institutions. Now that he has been invited to the USA and the USSR, we will take advantage of this offer. In this way the benefits of our research in Braincom 1 will be conveyed to international audiences. We do not plan to offer training in Braincom 2 as a part of this campaign. Based on initial response, we expect a large number of foreign nationals to visit India to attend training classes in Braincom 1. As the word of the benefits spreads, we expect that thousands of people will be visiting India. This boost in tourism, combined with the fees for classes, will bring in large amounts of much needed foreign currency. In addition, this will also improve India's image. Today, in foreign countries, we are known as the land of snake charmers and starving millions. How far we succeed, we do not know. We think it is worth trying. It certainly cannot do any harm."

Hari Nautiyal looks around and finds smiling agreeable faces. The Trustees give their blessings to the strategic plan. As soon as the meeting is over, lunch is served, and after lunch, Tirath Bhatia leaves.

Chandubhai looks out the window and says, "Nautiyal sahib, it is a nice sunny day. Look at your beautiful rose garden. Why not enjoy the sunshine and also smell the roses."

"It will be my pleasure, Chandubhai. Please follow me."

Hari Nautiyal leads all of them to the lawn in the rear of the house. There are six chairs placed in a circle. Three are in shade, and three are in sunshine. Chandubhai picks the one in sunshine and lowers his large frame down, takes off his Gandhi cap, closes his eyes, and, in about half a minute, he is snoring. This is not the first time Hari Nautiyal has seen this drama from Chandubhai. He is known to do this to disarm people first and then ambush them with diatribe. Being the elder statesman that he is, others take their seats and carry on their conversation in whispers. This goes on for about five minutes, and then Chandubhai is awake as abruptly as he had fallen asleep.

He looks around the grounds and at the house with a mock sense of surprise and says, "Nautiyal sahib, you are lucky that your father bought this house during the depression years. Today this must be worth a fortune." And then he comes to the point. "I like that you have done well in the last few years since Independence. Your companies have fully participated in the development carried out during the First Five Year Plan; and now that the Second Five year Plan has started, you will do even better. You know, sometimes, I wonder who benefitted the most from India becoming Independent. The answer is: the business community. The common man still has to stand in a queue outside the ration shop. Look at the freedom fighters like me: What have I got from Independence? I do not even have a government job that will give me pension or provident fund. Who is going to look after me in my old age? The Party says it will, but the Party has to depend on donations from businessmen like you. So ultimately, Nautiyal sahib, I will be sitting at the doorsteps of the businessmen. They call me a power broker, the party bagman, the Kingmaker, and all kinds of high sounding names, but, at the end of the day, I am the servant of the business community."

Hari Nautiyal has heard all of this before and knows what Chandubhai is looking for. He says, "Chandubhai, what are you saying? You are our *Maibaap*, our Provider. You need not worry about mundane matters like money. Your Second Five Year Plan will start right away."

"Nautiyal sahib, you are a generous man," Chandubhai says with a broad smile. He then turns his attention towards Swamiji and says, "I am not happy with the English name, Braincom, you have given to *Mantra Sadhana*. You should have used the Hindi names."

Swamiji replies, "We had to come up with catchy English names to market it in the western countries. We will still be using Hindi names when we start to teach the techniques."

Chandubhai nods his head in agreement and fires off another question, "This demonstration you gave today is very impressive, but this technique in the wrong hands can be very dangerous. Do I understand it correctly that you were able to read Tirath's thoughts, and that you could penetrate his mind? If this is so, then sitting here I feel that I am mentally naked. We will have no privacy left. A man's mind is his most private domain, and if you can open the door and look in; we will have no place to hide. This research should be treated at the same level as nuclear research is treated by the western countries—absolutely confidential and Top Secret. I am meeting with somebody at the Prime Minister's Secretariat tomorrow, and I am going to bring up this point."

Hari Nautiyal, who has been listening intently, says, "We have already been contacted by the Intelligence Bureau. They have asked us to treat the technique of *Mannosancharan* or Braincom 2, at the same secrecy level as nuclear research being carried out at Trombay."

It is late afternoon, and the shadows are lengthening. Chandubhai's chair is now partly in shade, but his head is still in light. He is still massaging his bald head, as if to get some light into his head in the waning moments of sunshine. Hari Nautiyal is sitting in a chair in the shade that is right across from him. It presents an eerie sight; the dark body of Chandubhai in the dark, and his dark face brightened by sunlight.

Hari Nautiyal is thinking: *I hope he gets enlightened by the sunshine!*

He knows that Chandubhai still has something churning in his mind; as he is still rubbing his head with his hand moving in circles.

Then finally, the hand movements stop. Chandubhai has figured out what to say. He says, "Nautiyal sahib, you are a well traveled man. You have visited many parts of the world, some during the War and others afterwards. A man's perspective is widened by travelling to other countries. I have been like a *Koop Ka Mandoop*; like a frog who lives in a well and thinks that there is water everywhere. Now that you are planning a world tour for Swamiji, I am wondering, as a Trustee of the Ashram, if I can also be a part of the delegation?"

Hari Nautiyal replies, "It is all right with us, but will you be able to take a month off from your busy political life? The general elections are around the corner. I think we should plan a trip to America later this year after the elections, in July or August. Chandubhai you should get your passport ready and after talking to the Americans, we will let you know the program."

Chandubhai replies, "We politicians always have our passport ready; you never know when the opportunity may present itself."

It appears that he has got everything he wanted. He gets up. The rest of them also get up and take leave of Hari Nautiyal. As they are walking out, they see a white lady in saffron coloured sari strolling in the front lawn of the house. As Swamiji notices her, he goes over to her and asks her to come and meet everybody.

"Meet Svetlana," Swamiji says, "she is visiting our Ashram. She is from Russia."

There is a look of disbelief on the faces of everybody, except Hari Nautiyal's because he already knows of her presence in the house. She takes a few steps towards them, with her hands folded in *Namaste*, and with a broad smile that brings cheer to the faces of all of them standing there.

"Are you enjoying your stay at the Ashram?" Daddyji asks just to make some small talk.

She surprises everyone by her command of the English language. She speaks immaculate English, with a thick Russian accent that adds a little sensuality to her voice. Even Chandubhai, who was making a face showing disapproval of her association with the Ashram, is now trying to get in a few words of his own. As they are talking, Hari Nautiyal's wife, Meera, comes out of the house and, after exchanging a few pleasantries, takes Svetlana to go shopping.

There is silence for a while, and then Chandubhai speaks directly to the point, "Swamiji, she does not look like an ordinary Russian lady interested in Hindu scriptures. I hope she is not planted by the Communists to steal our secrets. It is known that senior civil servants are going to be staying at the Ashram for training in Braincom 1. This presents an opportunity for her to come in contact with them. Surinder, did you know about this?"

"Her name is not on the list of those living at the Ashram," Daddyji says.

Chandubhai asks, "Nautiyal sahib, did you know about this lady staying at the Ashram?"

Hari Nautiyal seems somewhat flustered by the question. He clears his throat by coughing mildly, trying to compose his thoughts and then replies, "Yes, I knew about her. In fact, I am the one who sent her to visit the Ashram. She was recommended by a business contact at the Russian Embassy."

"Oh, I did not know that you have business contacts with Russia," Chandubhai says, rather surprised.

Hari Nautiyal replies, "At this time, we are exporting textiles and sugar to Russia. We are looking to expand our business relationship with them. I was asked by the Russians to allow Svetlana to visit the Ashram. I sent a telegram to Swamiji about it. She stayed there for two weeks, and she will be going back to Russia in few days. As our business negotiations were at a delicate stage, I did not tell any of the executives including, my son, Veer."

Chandubhai is not happy with the situation. He is concerned, having heard of the stories about the KGB using seduction as a tool of choice in their espionage activities.

He says, "You are all wise men. Just a word of caution: *Istri-pralobhan*—the temptation or enticement by women—is the greatest weakness of man."

At last, Hari Nautiyal comes to the conclusion that he has had enough of preaching by Chandubhai and says curtly, "Chandubhai, you have made your point."

Chandubhai walks over to his waiting car, the driver opens the door, and he takes the rear seat. As he pulls the door shut, Veer, Hari Nautiyal's son, brings to him a cloth bag and says, "Chandubhai, here are some home made *Roties* made from *Makki* flour; I thought you may like to take some home."

Chandubhai accepts the bag, opens it a little to look in and takes one *Roti* out for the others to see and starts eating. On his way home, after he is finished eating one *Roti*, he takes the rest of the *Roties* out of the bag, and is happy to notice a stack of crisp hundred rupee bank notes underneath.

Thank God for the Five Year Plans and Makki Roties, he is thinking.

16

FOOD FOR VOTES

As the car is meandering through the traffic towards his flat in the Khan Market area, Chandubhai breaks into an itch at the unmentionable parts of his body. It has happened a few times before also, whenever he takes home 'contributions' from Hari Nautiyal. *Is it God punishing me for accepting 'contributions'?* He is thinking.

"Madho, I want to stop at the temple near our flat," he shouts at his driver.

As the car stops at the temple, he picks up the bag and gets out of the car. On his way in, he buys five rupees worth of sweets at the shop next door, as offering to the Gods. Holding the bag tight to his body, he goes in, rings the large brass bell hanging overhead and goes and stands in front of the Idols of the Gods. There is a lineup in front of the priest. He is accepting the offerings and asking the purpose of the offerings. Chandubhai waits for his turn. Meanwhile, the itching is making him uncomfortable, and considering the location of the itch on his body, all he can do is shift from one foot to the other to get some relief. Finally, his turn comes. He hands over the offering to the priest, who looks up and recognizes him and says, "Chandubhai Patel, we are so glad to have a leader of your stature in our temple. Sir, I will do a special prayer for your well being. Please tell me your one wish that you want God to grant you."

Chandubhai is at a loss for words. He is shifting from one foot to the other to induce some relief to the itch on his unmentionable parts. At last, he replies, "Pundit ji, I have come to pray for the success of the Second Five Year Plan for the development of India."

The priest says with a surprise in his voice, "Chandubhai, you are a great man. People usually come here and ask for something for themselves; you are the only one I have come across who is asking something for the whole country."

The priest recites hymns praying for the fulfillment of Chandubhai's wish. At the conclusion of the hymns, the priest makes an offering of sweets to the Gods and gives a small part of the sweets to Chandubhai as *Prasad* or oblation. He accepts it in his folded hands and deposits it in his mouth. He expects the burden of guilt and itching to lighten a bit after having done his bit to please the Gods. The priest brings out a red coloured holy thread that he wants to tie on his wrist, but Chandubhai moves the cloth bag forward and wants him to tie the holy thread on the bag. The priest is surprised, but goes ahead, saying, "Is the Second Five Year Plan in the bag?"

As Chandubhai moves out of the temple, he notices a row of beggars sitting on the ground with their hands stretched out asking for alms. Chandubhai, being a charitable man that he is, gets an idea to do something more to lighten his burden of guilt and itching. He takes out all the *Makki Roties* from the bag and distributes them, one each, to the beggars. He runs out of Roties, but there are still some outstretched hands. The itch is driving him insane. In final act of insanity, he takes out the twenty, one hundred rupee, bank notes and starts to distribute, one at a time, to the remaining beggars. The first beggar looks at it and says, "Oh, sahib, how will I fill my stomach with paper? I want food."

Chandubhai replies, "Oh *Bhai,* you can buy a lot of food with this hundred rupee note."

The beggar laughs, "Eh, sahib, why are you making fun of us unfortunate starving poor beggars by giving us this piece of paper."

And then he calls all the neighbouring beggars and tells them, "Friends, see this man is making fun of us by giving me this piece of paper to eat."

Some of them get up and threaten him. Chandubhai does his best to convince them. But they are not listening, as they have never seen a hundred rupee bank note. At last, he is fed up. He goes and sits in his car and asks the driver to take him home. As he is on his way home, Gods drop another idea in his fertile brain.

"Madho," he calls his driver, while scratching himself to get some relief, "Are you in need of some money?

Madho is quiet and does not reply. He does not believe that this question could be for him. But, then, he realizes that there is nobody else in the car except him.

He asks, "Sahib, did you ask me something?"

"Oh, you idiot, do you see anybody else in the car except you and me?"

"No sir. But I did not understand the question," Madho says.

"I asked you; do you need some money?"

"Sahib, who does not need money," Madho replies timidly.

Chandubhai's itch is reaching unbearable proportions, and, to top it all, his driver is refusing to understand his question. He repeats the question, "I am asking; do you need some money?"

"Yes, sahib."

While the conversation is going on, the driver stops the car in front of the building where Chandubhai lives. Chandubhai looks around; there is nobody looking. He takes out all the twenty, one hundred rupee, bank notes and hands them over to Madho, who takes a look at the stack and is surprised to see so much money.

He quickly hands it back saying, "Sahib, if I get caught with so much money, I will be arrested by the police for stealing."

"All right, take just one of them."

The driver replies, "Sahib, a hundred rupee bank note is too big for me. If I take it to a shop to buy something, the shopkeeper will either suspect me of stealing or think that it is counterfeit; either way, I will be arrested and the police will take the bank note away from me. And when they discover that it is not counterfeit, they will release me but will keep the hundred rupee bank note anyway. So, if I am not going to get anything out of it, then why accept it."

Chandubhai feels trapped. He feels caught between an itch and a stack of hundred rupee bank notes. And, then, another idea strikes him; after all he is the think tank of the political party he belongs to, and he is built like a tank too.

• •

At the very moment Chandubhai is struggling to control his urges to scratch his unmentionables off, Nautiyal family is having high tea in their expansive drawing room, being served by uniformed servants. There is laughter, and the object is Chandubhai.

"By now he must be scratching his clothes off his body," Veer says with a smirk on his face.

"I hope you did not add too much," Hari Nautiyal says.

"Well, dad, I was in a rush, so I just sprinkled some on the *Roties* and some on the bank notes. I think I may have added two or three times the amount we added last time."

"Oh, you rascal, do you know what he is going to do if he finds out. He is going to get us shut out from all government contracts," Hari Nautiyal says, barely able to speak while laughing.

"Dad, he is becoming greedy. Every time we see him, he wants a 'contribution'. Thank God, I did not add the other *Chooran*-concoction—the one that is guaranteed to make your stomach flow like a river."

• •

"Madho take me back to the temple," Chandubhai shouts at his driver. The driver pushes the clutch down to the floor, changes the gear and releases the clutch suddenly; the car lurches forward with a jerk. This is an indication that the driver is upset with the owner of the car.

As the car reaches the temple, Chandubhai gets out with the bag in hand. One of the beggars runs after him, shouting, "Oh, sahib," and baring his stomach and beating it with his right hand, "give me something for our stomach. My wife and children have not eaten anything for two days. Buy us some food."

Chandubhai stops, turns around and looks at the beggar and says nothing. Meanwhile, the other beggars gather around him. He looks around again to take in the scene. There are now hundreds of them gathering. The word is spreading through the grapevine; the crowd of beggars is swelling. Chandubhai sees an opportunity. The General Election is around the corner. He decides to buy food for all of them to get rid of the, twenty one, one hundred rupee bank notes and gain blessings and political capital in the bargain. *Today, I will kill three birds with twenty-one one hundred rupee bank notes, itch or no itch*; he is thinking.

The thrill of being surrounded by the crowd and being the centre of attention turns him on—so much so that, the effect of adrenalin takes over the effect of the itch. He begins to walk with a purpose towards the *Halwaii* shop selling sweets, samosas, roties and all kinds of food. He is waving his hands and goading the beggars to follow him. They are running ahead of everybody. Their mouths are watering. They are imagining eating all the tasty foods that they have ever dreamed of. Days of starvation seem to have come to an end, at least for today. As the crowd is moving ahead, Chandubhai is in the centre of the crowd goading them on.

At last, the destination is right in front. The crowd gathers in front of the *Halwaii* shop. The floor of the shop is built a foot and a half higher than the surrounding ground. Shaadilal, the shop owner, is standing and watching the crowd moving towards his shop. He recognizes Chandubhai.

Seems like a political Jaloos; it seems the election fever is starting early; he is thinking.

Chandubhai tears through the crowd walking towards the shop and is greeted by the owner. Chandubhai tells him to feed the crowd to their heart's content. A few of the employees of the shop come out and ask the beggars and urchins to sit down on the ground. They fall-in like a military platoon. In about fifteen minutes, the flow of food starts.

In the mean time, the word of the Happening has spread to the newspapers. Some reporters have already arrived, with pencils and pads in hand. A little boy about 10 years old squeezes through the forest of legs of the crowd of people and, somehow, manages to reach near Chandubhai. He touches Chandubhai's feet as a mark of gratitude. The boy's pleading eyes meet Chandubhai's eyes. The boy, with hands outstretched, looks at him and pleads, "Sahib, my little sister and my mother are destitute. They are lying in the empty sewer pipe nearby. We have not eaten for days. Can you please get us some food?"

Chandubhai waves at the shop owner and tells him to give some food to the boy.

Meanwhile, the ranks of the reporters are swelling. Some of them have pushed their way to the front of the crowd and are within hearing distance of Chandubhai.

"Sir, can you please tell us, what is going on?" one of them asks.

"Can you not see what is going on? We are distributing some food to the hungry."

"Sir, what is the occasion?"

"Do we need some occasion to feed the hungry? Industrialist Hari Nautiyal is a generous man. He gave me some money to arrange for the distribution of food." Chandubhai announces loudly.

• •

It is 6:00 A.M. Hari Nautiyal is getting up for his morning walk, but before that he must have bed tea. There is a knock on the door, "Come in," he says. The servant walks in with a tray with two cups, a tea pot with a teacosy and three of India's national newspapers. All three have photographs of Chandubhai and similar headings on the front page. The photos show Chandubhai surrounded by beggars and the headline reads: **Chandubhai Feeding the Hungry**

The story reads: Last night, Chandubhai Patel placed an order with Shaadilal Halwaii to provide food to all the beggars and hungry people in the vicinity of a small temple in Khan Market area. Food was distributed to over two hundred men, women and children. Chandubhai was showered with blessings from the recipients. Chandubhai stated that the funds for the food were provided by, Industrialist and philanthropist, Hari Nautiyal. He further stated that Nautiyal family has promised to repeat this charitable act every week at different places in Delhi. The locations will be kept secret to avoid overcrowding.

As Hari Nautiyal finishes reading the statement, he starts to smile and then laugh. His wife, who is still sleeping, wakes up, and asks, "Ji, why are you laughing?"

He tells the story to her, and says, "I have to take my hat off to Chandubhai; he is one shrewd politician. Here we were trying to cut down on making 'contributions' to him, and he has turned the tables on us. He has announced that we will be feeding the hungry every week for God knows how long. He has done a good deed and benefitted his Party at the same time. But I am happy; it is all for a great cause."

Chandubhai's performance at the temple has been noticed by the high commands of major political parties. Compliments are flowing in like the Monsoon flood. It seems Chandubhai, by accident, has hit upon a new strategy to win votes. The Nautiyal family organizes *Lunger* or free food drives every Sunday evening. Other political parties, not to be left behind, are also conducting free food fairs for the hungry. The winners are the starving millions. Some political parties are handing out small pamphlets, with the Party Symbol, along with the food. The hungry, at first, are wondering: why this sudden generosity? As the time passes by, they are beginning to understand the power of their vote. They are not interested in who gets elected, but who will give them food.

17

ELECTION FEVER

Election fever for the second general elections in the history of free India is gradually building up. Political processions are seen on the roads, with the shouting of slogans and colorful party flags being carried by the Party faithful. The name of the candidate or the party is not as important as the Party Symbol. With 80% of the electorate being illiterate, it is the Symbol that the voters are expected to remember—more familiar the symbol the better. Symbols such as Cow, Bull, Bullock Cart, Candle, Hand, Elephant, and Hammer and Sickle, are selected to appeal to the electorate—the Symbols they can remember easily. With over 40 political parties and dozens of Independent candidates taking part, catchy Symbols are at a premium. The noisier the better, is the aim of the political processions. The atmosphere is festive. One cannot find a wall or a light pole without posters. Prior permission of police is required to ensure that two political processions do not intersect and end up in a riot.

After the elections are over, the counting of the votes goes on for about two months. The Indian National Congress wins a majority. Chandubhai Patel, inspite of being an Independent, is given an important political position in the Food Ministry, having discovered the 'Effect of Food on the Voting Habits of the Hungry'.

However, the Americans are in panic. The Communist Party of India has won a majority in the state elections in the southern state of Kerala. And to make things worse, they are also the main opposition party in India's Parliament. At the time that Communism is brewing in India, Americans have become paranoid about Communists in America. American Senator Joe McCarthy had been making claims that a large number of Communists and Soviet spies had infiltrated the American federal government and elsewhere. A Communist victory in one of the major states, with the highest literacy rates in India, sends shock waves both in India and in western democracies.

• •

Preparations for the American trip of Swamiji, Hari Nautiyal, Chandubhai Patel and Daddyji are in full swing. Swamiji has been invited to speak at the George Washington University in Washington D.C. and the Columbia University in New York City. The American diplomats have suggested that they should plan to be in Washington D.C. on July 4, in order to watch the Independence Day Parade. A Visit to England is a must for the two of them. Although Swamiji and Hari Nautiyal have been to England before, Daddyji and Chandubhai are very keen to see the homeland of the erstwhile rulers of India. And Daddyji wants to visit the birthplace of William Shakespeare, his guide and philosopher.

Bobby Schwartz, the American diplomat, calls Daddyji for a meeting to talk about their forthcoming trip. After the Communists have come to power in the state of Kerala, the Americans have become very concerned with India moving towards the Russians.

They meet for lunch at Imperial Hotel.

"Surinder, ever since I had lunch at your place, I have not been able to enjoy Indian food at any other place. Please give my regards to Mrs. Mehra," Bobby says trying to break the ice. He continues, while sipping his drink every now and then and says, "You know, our fears have come true. The Soviets have succeeded. The Communist Party of India has won the election in an important state. What is next?" And he rambles on in his southern drawl.

Daddyji is not sure what he is getting at. *Does he want to cancel our trip?* He is thinking.

He asks, "Bobby, are the details of our trip finalized?"

"Oh, yes, everything is arranged. In fact, Wilbur is going home on vacation, and he is going to accompany you throughout your trip in America. I want to tell you the good news. You will all be the guests of our government."

Daddyji says jokingly, "Are you competing with the Soviets?"

Bobby laughs and replies, "Well, you could look at it that way."

Daddyji says in jest, "Bobby, not too long ago America and Russia used to be allies, and now you two are falling over each other to win the favour of developing countries. Why?"

Bobby replies, "Well, it is all due to their expansionist policy; we want to stop them. They are making the Iron Curtain around them thicker and thicker. …Anyway, let us leave that aside. I just want to make sure you are taking your pad and pencil along with you to write a nice story about your trip to America."

Daddyji finally understands the purpose of the meeting; Bobby wants a good story after the visit.

Bobby is quiet for a while. He is looking intently at the band playing 'Rock Around the Clock' and tapping his feet to the beat. *Is Surinder on our side or theirs*, he is thinking. Bobby loves his Tandoori chicken. He is tearing the bones and the flesh apart and chewing the bones. After he gets the leg bone chewed up, he says, "Surinder, whenever I am eating Tandoori chicken, it reminds me of Southern Fried chicken back home."

Daddyji has been borrowing books from the American Library and reading up on the American way of life before his trip, but he has no idea what Bobby is talking about.

He says, "Bobby, you lost me there. What is Southern Fried Chicken?"

"I will tell Wilbur to take you for a Southern Fried Chicken dinner when you are in America."

18

SANIYA

As Daddyji's trip to America is drawing near, the home front has become the war front. Mummyji is not in favour of Daddyji flying over the seven seas to go to America. There are arguments every night. In the end, I have to step in.

One day, as she is ready to go for her afternoon siesta, I go to her and say, "Mummyji, look at me. See my eyes are becoming blue."

She holds my face, and says, "Let me see. Yes, I think you may be right. You know, my brother, Daulat Ram also has blue eyes."

"I thought only people of western countries have blue eyes," I say.

She replies, "No, that is not true. People from Afghanistan and Iran also have blue eyes. And, you know, when Alexander the Great left India; a lot of his Greek soldiers stayed back and settled in Punjab. This is also the reason why some of us have blue eyes."

This is just a way for me to look into her eyes. Now I want to give her a dream.

"Mummyji, tell me about God *Hanuman*," I ask, "Why do you recite the *Hanuman Chalisa* every morning?"

Her eyes light up. This is the first time I have shown interest in religious matters.

She starts to explain the significance of the *Hanuman Chalisa*, the hymn of God *Hanuman*. "God *Hanuman* is the son of Pawan, the Lord of Winds. He is considered to be the source of power, wisdom and strength. When only ten years old, *Hanuman* could lift hills of twenty miles in circumference and throw them like stones. He could fly in the sky, being the son of the Lord of Winds."

"Mummyji," I say, "Being the son of the Lord of Winds, Lord Hanuman must be the one keeping all the aeroplanes flying in the air."

"Yes," she says, "His devotees feel safe and fearless under his protection. All diseases, pain and suffering disappear on reciting regularly his divine name. He is the conqueror of Wind, the destroyer of all miseries and the symbol of Auspiciousness."

After I have talked to her for about five minutes, she starts to feel drowsy and lies down for her Sunday afternoon nap. In a few minutes, she is sound asleep. In another few minutes, she is going to start dreaming.

I make my move. My imagination is going to become her dream. I go to my room, close my eyes and let my imagination run wild.

I close my eyes and imagine: planes flying in the air, and Lord *Hanuman* flying alongside each one of them. Each plane has an incarnation of Lord *Hanuman* flying beside it keeping it safe. Mummyji is beginning to dream whatever I am imagining. She is watching Daddyji flying in one of the planes with the incarnation of Lord *Hanuman* flying beside the plane. She looks up at the sky smiling and begins to recite the *Hanuman Chalisa*, the Hymn, invoking His blessings and mercy. I am also beginning to fall asleep.

There is a knock at the door. I get up from the bed to answer; lest her dream gets disturbed.

I open the door to the verandah. A girl, dressed in a light yellow *Salwaar and Kameez,* is standing with a small basket in her hand. She is fair in complexion, has blue eyes radiating innocence, and has a slight blush on her cheeks. Her light brown long hair tied in two *choties* or pig tails are hanging lazily by her side. Is she real or is it a dream? I look back into the room just to make sure.

She asks softly, shyly… "Is bibiji home?" She is referring to Mummyji as bibiji–a term used by the servants for the mistress of the household.

I keep looking at her. The front door to the verandah is open. A light breeze is blowing and the curtain at the door is fluttering. The curtain touches, Ginny, my walking stick that is hanging on the wall. It begins fluttering too; striking the wall in the process. As I stand there looking at the girl, the tik, tik, tik …… sound of Ginny striking the wall wakes up Mummyji. She walks out to the verandah.

"Who are you?" she asks the girl.

"Bibiji, I have come to collect the daily bread on behalf of, Rampiyari, your sweepress," the girl says in immaculate English. The words fall out of her lips …as petals from a rose.

Both Mummyji and I look at each other. In the meantime, Rampiyari walks in.

"*Nee,* Rampiyari, who is this girl?" Mummyji asks.

Rampiyari is quiet for a while, thinking … and then she says, "Bibiji she is my daughter."

"You never told us before that you had a daughter. Look at her; she is English. How can she be your daughter?" Mummyji says pointing a finger at the girl.

Rampiyari is again quiet for a while and then tells her daughter, "Go, Sani. Go to other houses; I will join you soon."

The girl walks away and out of our house.

She is certainly not made of the same atoms as the rest of us, I am thinking.

Mummyji is looking at Rampiyari waiting for her to explain.

Rampiyari starts to talk, "In 1943, I used to work as a domestic servant in the household of Douglas sahib, the Deputy Commissioner of Meerut. There was an outbreak of typhoid fever, and Mrs. Douglas died. I kept work-ing for Douglas sahib, and, with the grace of God, we were blessed with a baby girl in 1944."

Mummyji looks at me and says, "Vikram, go to your room."

I turn around and go behind the door and stand there eavesdropping.

And then she turns to Rampiyari, and asks, "What do you mean? Do you mean you got married to Douglas?"

Rampiyari replies, "Bibiji, she was a blessing from God. Marriage is just a custom created by the society. Douglas sahib needed me, and I needed him. I had nowhere to go. You know bibiji, when she was born, Douglas sahib wanted to name her Sandra, after his late wife. I wanted to name her Sandhiya. There were arguments, and, finally, we named her Saniya—a beautiful mixture of two cultures. We call her Sani."

"So where was Saniya all these years? How is it that we never saw her before?" Mummyji asks.

Rampiyari replies, "In 1950, my family, on my mother's side, secured the contract to provide sweeper services in this area. My mother was getting old, so I moved here and took over the business. Douglas sahib sent Saniya to study in a convent school in Dalhousie. She is back in Delhi, and now she is going to attend school here in Delhi. Douglas sahib is trying to get her admission in Lady Irwin School."

Mummyji stands there spellbound due to the incredible nature of the story.

Saniya has gone home, but… but I am gone too.

19

AMERICA, HERE THEY COME

D-day, the Departure day, is drawing near. After my talk with her, Mummyji has accepted the fact that Daddyji is going to America for about four weeks. She is reciting the *Hanuman Chalisa* hymns several times a day.

He is allowed two suitcases on the plane. His penchant for fine clothes has got the better of him; four bespoke suites, shirts, collars, cufflinks and four pairs of shoes have almost filled the two suitcases. Mummyji is more concerned with him having enough underwear for the four week trip.

While she is packing for him, Mummyji asks Daddyji, "Listen ji, are there washermen in America and England?

Daddyji is beside himself and showers her with sarcasm, "No, Kamla, the British have not washed their clothes ever since they left India, and the Americans don't wear too many clothes; have you not seen photos of American women wearing a small piece of cloth around their waist?.... Why do you ask questions like that? How do you think they wash their clothes? Of course, they have laundries and washing machines. Don't worry about these small things; I will manage."

What really gets Daddyji going is when he sees a holdall containing a new quilt and other pieces of bedding lying beside the suitcase. "What is this, Kamla?" he asks

"You are going to a cold country; you should have warm bedding." Mummyji replies.

"Kamla, it is all provided by the hotels we are going to be staying in. I am not exactly going to be staying in an Indian *Sarai*."

A driver has been arranged to drive us around while Daddyji is going to be away. Siyaram, our new driver, is a very friendly man. Our servant, Chottu,

157

has started taking really good care of him. I have figured out why, and I am not the one to be left behind. This is a golden opportunity for learning to drive for both Chottu and me.

I am already imagining driving with Saniya by my side. I have started day-dreaming a lot, and there is only one occupant of my dreams—Saniya.

• •

All the relatives have arrived in the morning. The neighbours are dropping by to offer their good wishes for a safe and pleasant trip, along with a request for one thing or the other they want from America. Daddyji is wise to have a notebook in his lap; he is making a note of all the requests. The majority of the requests are by women for a hair dye that not only makes the grey hair dark but also takes the wrinkles off one's face; nobody seems to know the exact name, though. The closest he can figure out is that it sounds like Oxytoxy. Not to be impolite, he writes the name down.

Daddyji's flight is late at night at 12:40 A.M. By 7:30 P.M., our car is loaded with the luggage. A photographer is on hand to record the occasion for posterity. My friend, Suraj Rajpal, has also arrived. He takes me aside and asks, "Vikram *yaar,* I am not sure when I will get a chance to go in an aeroplane in the near future, but, at least, I can see the aerodrome. Can I also come with you? Maybe, when we are there, I will get a chance to see an aeroplane also."

Garlands of Marigold flowers are seen everywhere. People are asked to get alongside Daddyji, a small group at a time, to get their photo taken. As they go and stand beside him, they pick up a garland and place it around his neck. Eventually, after five or six people have garlanded him, he is covered up to his nose. As soon as I see Daddyji drowning in Marigold flowers, I move forward and relieve him of the burden. Mummyji is sad, but I am happy for the oppor-tunity to be able to learn driving while he is away. After the priest is finished chanting a few sacred hymns, he takes out his astrological almanac. And based on the calculations he had already carried out, he declares that the most auspi-cious time for departure from home to the airport is 17 minutes and 33 seconds past 8:00 P.M; there are only 13 minutes left. Everybody scrambles to get into their cars, and the procession of cars starts towards the Safdarjung aerodrome. There are six cars in the procession.

When we arrive at the aerodrome, it seems that there is a carnival under-way. There are hundreds of people milling about. I am good in arithmetic, thanks to the headmaster of my primary school, Atma Ram. I quickly figure out that, if there are fifty passengers departing and, if ten relatives or friends come to see off each passenger, there would be about five hundred people at the airport. There is a long line-up in front of the Pan American Airways counter. The airport porters carry Daddyji's luggage to the counter, and he goes and stands in the queue as friends and relatives are milling about. As we are waiting, a man in a dark suit comes and stands behind Daddyji. He pays no attention to him; he is looking ahead for his turn at the counter, but, off and on, he looks back towards the entrance door of the terminal building. He is looking for other members of his party.

"Surinder, you are looking very uneasy. What is the matter?" the man behind him says with a mysterious smile.

Daddyji looks back and says, "Oh, my God, Chandubhai, is that you? You look so different in western style clothes. What made you give up the national dress?"

"Surinder, I want to look up-to-date. As they say, when in England dress like the English; when in America dress like the Americans."

Daddyji laughs and, speaking and laughing at the same time, says "Chandubhai, you came up with a new saying. I have heard the one about the Romans but not about the English and the Americans."

Chandubhai, not to be left behind, says, "When we go to Italy, we will dress like the Romans do."

It seems Chandubhai is in good spirits, literally; he smells of it. Swamiji and Hari Nautiyal, along with their entourage of relatives, have also arrived. It is becoming difficult to stand without bumping into somebody. Suraj and I move out of the terminal building and stand on the sidewalk, looking at people coming in and out. A blue bus arrives with 'Pan American Airways' written on it. A few men and women come out, some are passengers and the others are the crew and employees of the airline. The particular objects of our attention are the American air hostesses wearing blue uniforms. As we move closer to look at them, the porters, who are removing the passengers' baggage, rudely ask us to move away. Suraj loses his temper. He tells the attendant, "Talk to us properly... One day I will own my own aeroplane, and you will all be my servants. You will see... I tell you... you will see!"

Along with the dreams of constructing buildings, making movies and casting film star Rani Roy, now he has added another tall ambition—owning his own aeroplane. We will see how he makes out.

After his outburst at the porters, Suraj and I walk to the queue of passengers in front of the Pan Am counter. Daddyji is still standing in the queue where we left him. Upon inquiry, I learn that the weighing machine has broken down.

The mechanics are trying to fix it; there is utter chaos. Being the month of June, it is suffocating and hot.

There are tears, hugs and last minute instructions being given back and forth between those who are departing, and those who are going to be left behind. Finally, Daddyji embraces Suneeta, Kishi and me. He just looks at Mummyji with a smile. She dries her eyes with the end of her sari. Her sister, Devika, consoles her, while waving her hand-held fan to give herself some air and trying to keep her enormous frame stable at the same time. She says, "*Nee* Kamla. He will be back before you know it. What are we for? Let us know if you need us."

• •

Washington D.C. July 4, 1957

All four of them: Hari Nautiyal, Chandubhai, Swamiji and Daddyji are sitting in the dining room of the Willard Hotel preparing to have breakfast before walking over to Constitution Avenue to watch America's National Independence Day Parade. They had arrived the previous day from London after having spent four days in England; one of which was spent at Stratford-Upon-Avon, the birthplace of Daddyji's idol, William Shakespeare. At Daddyji's request, Hari Nautiyal had approved the expense for the stay at the historic Willard Hotel with the history of such notable guests as Charles Dickens; and Mark Twain who wrote two of his books at the hotel. An old friend of Hari Nautiyal, Col. Jake Krieger Retd., of the United States Army Air force, Air Transport Command, is also expected to join. Hari and Jake were at the China-Burma-India theatre during the World War II. Later in the morning, Wilbur Wright of the United States Information Service is expected to come to the hotel and take them to watch the parade; special passes have been arranged for them to view the parade from the area meant for official guests of the American Government.

It is a sunny and hot day. They have ordered their breakfast of toast, omelets and milk; Chandubhai, being a vegetarian, has ordered only mashed potatoes, toast and milk. To the utter dismay of all of them, and particularly Chandubhai, the milk is ice cold.

"Can we get hot milk," asks Chandubhai. The waiter stands politely and just stares at them; he is not able to understand the request. Hari Nautiyal repeats the request in clearer, decipherable English.

"Sir," the waiter says politely, just to make sure that he has understood the request correctly, "Do you mean *hot,* like it is a *hot* day outside?"

Chandubhai has difficulty understanding the waiter's Southern accent, and he looks towards Daddyji.

"Yes, please," Daddyji says, looking at the waiter.

As they are waiting for hot milk to arrive, Hari Nautiyal decides that this is as good a time as any to tell them something he has been wanting to tell, but did not know how to start the topic.

"I would like to tell you something before my friend, Jake Krieger, arrives," he says in rather a matter of fact way, as if what he is about say is an every-day trivial matter. "You know, when we formed our group, *Shakti 9,* in 1944, my friend, Jake, and some of his friends also formed a similar group here in America; they named it *Robus 10*, which also means the same as our group—strength from solidarity. It was not a coincidence. The idea came to us when we were fighting side by side against the Japanese in the Burma Campaign, with Monsoon rains, heat and mosquitoes as our companions. There were Americans, British, Canadians and Indians in our unit. We decided that if we get out of the War alive, we will form a secret organization in each of our countries and work towards influencing public policy and political thought in our respective countries for the benefit our citizens. And we will do everything in our collective power to help each other's people. I should tell you that there are also such secret organizations in England and Canada. The one in England is named *Potestas 10*, with a meaning similar to ours, and in Canada it is named *Canuck 10*; although, I must say, I do not know what the word *Canuck* stands for. Surinder, your friend, Max Hoffer, is the head of the group in Canada."

The other three are sitting with their mouths open listening to the story, as the waiter is standing with four glasses of piping hot milk in his tray, with steam rising. The waiter places the glasses with hot milk, one by one, in front of each of them. Chandubhai is the first to pick up his glass and takes a slurp and makes a sound that receives strange gazes from the three of his countrymen.

"The milk is hot, but there is no body to it. It seems that it is adulterated with water, just like in India," Chandubhai says, looking sheepishly at the others. He gets nothing but blank looks.

A tall bald man, with gold rimmed glasses on a large nose, wearing an immaculate grey flannel suit and with a row of medals adorning his breast, enters the breakfast area. He stops for a moment, looks around and walks purposefully towards their table. When he is a few feet away, he stops. Hari Nautiyal is the first one to look up. He stands up with his hands outstretched. And in no time, they are shaking hands and embracing. Looking at Hari Nautiyal up and down, Jake says, "Well buddy, it has been almost thirteen years. But the good thing is that we kept in touch through the mail."

The rest of them stand up and are introduced to Col. Jake Kreiger. Having just heard that Jake Krieger is the leader of *Robus 10*, they look at him in awe as they shake hands.

"Gentlemen, how are you doing so far in our country? We want to make sure that your visit with us is a memorable one, for I have very fond memories of India. Oh, I still think about the Great Eastern Hotel and the Cabarets that Hari and I used to go to, whenever we were in Calcutta during our rest and recreation breaks. Hari, do you remember the name of the girl?" Jake Krieger says with a laugh.

Hari Nautiyal is red faced, as his reputation among those present is that of a serious minded businessman. He says, "Oh, come on Jake that was long time ago. At our age, memories begin to fade."

"Not mine, my friend. When are you inviting me to visit India? We will go to Calcutta and revisit our old watering holes," Jake says, looking around, talking in a whisper so as not let others around hear it.

The waiter, seeing that a new person has joined the table, comes around and asks Jake Krieger, "Sir, would you like to order something?"

"Bring me some coffee, John," he replies.

"Do you know him?" Hari Nautiyal asks pointing at the waiter.

"Yes, our group meets here often," Jake Kreiger replies, but he is not sure if he should talk any further about the group.

"Jake, I have informed my friends about your group in America, and the ones in Canada and Britain also, including a bit of history. You should know that they are all members of *Shakti 9*, so you can talk freely," Hari Nautiyal assures him.

The waiter brings the coffee and places the cup on the table along with sugar and cream. As soon as the waiter is out of hearing range, Jake Krieger starts to speak as he is adding sugar and cream to his cup, "While we are all together, let me tell you a little bit about the activities of our group. We now have twenty members from a broad cross-section of American society, and from both of our political parties—Democrats and Republicans. Suffice it to say that we are well connected. The whole group is pro-India, and we feel that regardless of the fact that, sometimes, America may take a position that may appear to be contrary to Indian interests, our fundamental and long-term position will generally be in India's interests."

The Indians look at each other, while eating their breakfast, wondering who is going to ask the question, and they all have the same basic question. Finally,

Hari Nautiyal, being well known to Jake Krieger and the head of the Indian group, asks, "Jake, we are all wondering, why is your group interested in helping India and favour India over other countries of the region?"

Chandubhai is not able to restrict his overbearing personality from intervening, and he says in his characteristic and endearing style in his mixed Hindi-English, basically reinforcing what Hari has already said, "Nautiyal ji, why is America giving so much primacy to India-America *jugalbundhi?*"

Jake Kreiger looks at Hari Nautiyal for translation. He clarifies that *jugalbandhi* means working in unison or *making music together*–literally.

Jake Kreiger replies, as he is smiling at the meaning of Hindi word *Jugalbandhi*, "The foreign policy sub-committee of our group has determined that, in the long-term, India will become a major economic and military power in the region, and so will China. Russia and China have taken to Communist political philosophy, which is diagonally opposite to ours. India has adopted a democratic form of government which is similar to our own. Another thing I should like to tell you, gentlemen, is that the American political leadership was very impressed with your Prime Minster, Jawaharlal Nehru, when he visited America in 1949 and 1956. As you probably know, President Eisenhower spent over 16 hours in meetings with your Prime Minister. Your Five Year Plans really fascinated the President, and there is a move afoot for the President to visit India in the near future. In short, it is in America's interest to help India grow to be a major power in Asia and in the whole world. We want the democratic experiment of India to succeed. We don't want any more states in India going Communist."

Chandubhai is suspicious. He is thinking: *It took us hundreds of years to get rid of one white race; now another white race wants to move in with us. I hope it is not another East India Company in the making.*

Chandubhai again asks, speaking in his inimitable style of English, "Mr. Kreiger, how do you propose to help us grow to be a major political and economic power?"

This time Jake Kreiger has no trouble following what Chandubhai has said. It appears that he is getting used to his accent. He starts to reply by addressing Chandubhai by his common name, but, not being sure of how to pronounce it, he looks at Hari Nautiyal for help.

"You may address him as Mr. Patel," Hari Nautiyal says.

"Yes of course, Mr. Patel, please forgive me. You had asked about how America can help. Let me give you a few examples: We could facilitate export of

American food grain to India; which in fact, is already taking place as we speak. The terms for the sale of PL 480 grain to India have already been made very easy. We could and will facilitate admission of students from India to pursue higher studies in American universities with financial assistance, followed by jobs in American firms where they could receive further training before returning home to help build new India. Another way of bringing the two countries and cultures together is to promote cultural exchanges—similar to the one proposed for Swami Ravi Anand to give lectures on ancient meditation techniques. You know, Indians in America are doing very well. Dilip Singh Saund, a Sikh from India, got elected to the House of Representatives from the 29th District of California early this year. Imagine in 25 years or 50 years time, if people from India keep immigrating to America, they will be occupying positions of influence thereby helping both our countries to have... well... what was the word Mr. Patel used?"

Hari Nautiyal replies, "You mean *Jugalbandhi*."

"Yes, yes, that is the word. Both our countries will be *making music together*."

"Maybe we should start a *Sitar and Jazz Quartet* in New Orleans," Hari Nautiyal interjects, laughing.

"Mr. Krieger, how will America benefit from all this? What will you expect us to do in return?" Daddyji asks.

"Oh, please call me Jake. ....Well, I will be honest with you. We are not doing all this in the spirit of altruism."

Chandubhai looks at Daddyji for interpretation of what Jake Krieger has said. Jake, realizing that Chandubhai has not understood the language, takes a breather. Daddyji explains the meaning of the word '*altruism*' to Chandubhai who nods to indicate that he has understood the meaning.

Jake Kreiger carries on, "As I was saying, America has a lot to gain from the steps that I just stated. By attracting young bright students from India to live among us, we will be making a lot of new friends, who will go back to India and promote America and our way of life and convince their fellow countrymen that democracy is a better alternative to Communism. Also, a prosperous India is a big market for our goods and services. Our companies will be selling goods in India, and Indian companies in America. So you see it is a win-win situation for both our countries. Oh yes... there is only one thing we expect in return, and it is a safe passage to India for our Hollywood films."

As soon as Chandubhai hears the word 'Companies' and 'films', the smoke of his suspicions starts to rise again.

He is thinking: *Oh, the bloody East India Company all over again.* Being a devout Hindu, he is suspicious of the proliferation of Hollywood films and its effect on Indian culture.

Chandubhai has reason to be full of suspicion. But his other three colleagues are all smiles ready to be part of the rosy scenario painted by Jake Kreiger. Swami Ravi Anand, who has been listening quietly, has suddenly come to life. He loosens his tie, which he has probably worn for only the second time in his life, clears his throat, and starts to gently recite "Oooooooommmmmmmmmmmmmm, Ooooooooooommmmmm, Oooooooommmmmm," the primal Hindu sound. He repeats it three times, closes his eyes and starts to recite mantras in Sanskrit. "Please close your eyes," he says in between. There is silence on the table. They all close their eyes.

He starts to speak, "I am looking at *Kaal,* the fabric of time, where the past and the future is etched in all directions. I see the future... I can predict that Wilbur Wright will be appearing soon."

They are all puzzled at his pronouncement, as they were all expecting him to make a profound statement. They open their eyes, and there is Wilbur Wright, the American official, standing in front of them to take them to the 4th of July parade. Swamiji had seen Wilbur Wright standing in the far corner of the dining hall talking to somebody and decided to lighten up the conversation.

They all break out in laughter and get ready to join in the 4th of July celebrations.

• •

After attending the parade, they all go back to the hotel; Jake Krieger and Wilbur Wright go back to their respective homes, promising to come back to take them around the city by night. They are all to meet in the lobby of the hotel at 7:30 P.M. After a few hours of rest, Swamiji comes out of his room barefoot and knocks at the doors of the rest of his group and asks them to come to his room. He wants to talk about his lecture and demonstration of *Mantra Sadhana* or Braincom 1 that he is presenting the next day. He is nervous. It is one thing to lecture on your own turf, but completely another thing to do this at one of the famous universities of America. In fifteen minutes, they all gather in Swamiji's room. He is pacing up and down visibly disturbed about something. He is covered from head to toe. "It is too cold," he says with a tremor in his voice. "The cooler in the room is blowing too much cold air. I am not used to stale cold air. If I have to give a lecture tomorrow, I want to sleep outside in fresh air."

Hari Nautiyal gets up and turns off the cooler in the room, and says, "Swamiji, it is easy to turn off the cooler, but I do not know how we will arrange for you to sleep outside."

And then, suddenly, he jumps up, and says, "I have an idea. There is a balcony outside my room. You can sleep there if you like, Swamiji."

"We will look at it at night when we come back."

At 7:30 P.M. they all come down the elevator to the main lobby of the hotel. While they are waiting for Jake Kreiger and Wilbur Wright to arrive, Daddyji walks over to the hotel concierge and starts to ask him when and where Charles Dickens and Mark Twain had stayed at the hotel—this being the reason why he had requested Hari Nautiyal to stay at the Willard in the first place.

Chandubhai sees Daddyji talking to the concierge and shakes his head and mutters to other members of his group, "Oh, the British have left, but their remnants, in the form of people like Surinder, are lingering among us. First he drags us all to the birthplace of Shakespeare, and now he is wasting time asking about other English authors. In school I read the novel, David Copperfield, but I did not see anything special that Shakespeare has written in it."

As he is speaking to the others, Daddyji is standing behind him and listening to what Chandubhai is saying. He is so incensed that he says in a caustic tone, "Chandubhai, David Copperfield was written by Charles Dickens and not by Shakespeare."

"Oh well, whatever... what does it matter? How does that affect the price of rice and lentils in India?" Chandubhai replies in a rhetorical tone.

In the meantime, Jake Kreiger walks in followed by Wilbur Wright.

The program for the evening is to have dinner and watch the fireworks. It appears Wilbur has got it all planned.

Wilbur says, "Bobby Schwartz had instructed me that I must take you to a Southern Fried Chicken dinner. We have to find out how you folks like it compared to Tandoori Chicken. So we are going to hop into two taxies, and we are going to be treated by Colonel Sanders tonight."

Chandubhai has no idea what Wilbur is talking about and neither do Swamiji and Hari Nautiyal, as they were not present when this conversation took place between Bobby Schwartz and Daddyji. He asks, "Who is Colonel Sanders?" He is looking at Hari Nautiyal, wondering if Colonel Sanders was also with him during the Burma Campaign in World War II. Wilbur explains to Chandubhai that Colonel Sanders is the owner of a chain of restaurants all across America. The six of them get into taxis—three in each taxi. Jake Kreiger, Daddyji and Wilbur Wright get into one taxi and the rest in the second taxi. They then realize that there should be one American in each taxi to show them some landmarks along the way. Jake Kreiger and Swamiji exchange places. The street around the hotel is jam-packed with people enjoying the Independence Day. Being a hot sunny day, the Americans have shed their clothes and inhibitions. Daddyji and Swamiji both have their eyeballs popping out at the scantily clad women moving around, and some of them still lying on the lawns trying to soak in the sun in its twilight, while Chandubhai looks away from the temptations.

In about ten minutes, the taxis stop in front of a restaurant. They are led in by Wilbur Wright. The Indians had expected a regular restaurant, but they are surprised to find a counter with one man and one woman in uniform and a few tables. There is a small lineup. Wilbur points towards the tables, and they all take their seats. Wilbur asks Daddyji to come and look at the menu on the wall behind the counter. Well, it turns out there is not much of a choice; there is only one type of chicken; all you can choose is the number of pieces. There is meal for two, three and so on. Wilbur and Daddyji confer and decide to order enough chicken for six people; bread, salad and French fries are included with the order of chicken. The only thing that is familiar to Indians is ice cold Cola. Both of them pick up the cartons full of chicken pieces, bottles of cola and plunk them on the table. As the cartons are being unpacked, they realize that, as usual, they have forgotten about Chandubhai, the vegetarian.

"Mr. Patel," says Wilbur, "It is very hard to get pure vegetarian food in America. I am really sorry."

Chandubhai says, "I understand. See, there are plenty of vegetarian dishes here. Here we have bread, French potatoes and salads. This will do for me. During the fight for Independence, I was jailed by the British for months at a time. All we were given to eat was rice and water. This is a feast compared to that. Moreover, I am really happy to be eating a common American meal rather than eating in a high class hotel."

After they had taken some bites, Wilbur asks, "So gentlemen, what is the verdict? How do you like Southern Fried chicken?"

Daddyji replies, "Well, it is different and tasty. I like it. As far as comparing it to Tandoori chicken, it will be like comparing ice cream to Indian *Kulfi*. They are both milk products and frozen and tasty."

Wilbur replies, "Very well said, Surinder; you should be a diplomat."

Hari Nautiyal has business on his mind. He says, "I am wondering about starting an Indian restaurant in Washington. Jake what do you think?"

"Hari, you know, Washington is a very cosmopolitan town. People eat out a lot. I think an upscale India restaurant will do very well."

Hari Nautiyal announces with hands up in the air, "Gentlemen, we shall have an Indian restaurant up and running here by next year. And if it is successful, we will open Indian restaurants in all major cities in America. Jake, would you like to be my partner?"

"Let me think about it. I will let you know," Jake replies.

Daddyji asks, "Will the American government allow that? Would we not have to ask for permission?"

Hari Nautiyal replies, "It is not the American government I am concerned with; it is the Government of India that will make us climb Mount Everest before they give us permission. Well, we have Chandubhai, our Minister on Special Duty in the food ministry, sitting right here with us. Let us ask him."

"Well, Hari you know better than anybody else about the foreign exchange crisis we are having. So if you are looking for dollars to invest in America, you are not going to be able to get permission from the Reserve Bank of India," Chandubhai replies.

Hari Nautiyal is quietly chewing his food, while in deep thought, and says, "Friends, at this time, as far as I know, there is only one Indian Company who has an office in America, and that is Tata. Just look at all the American companies that are doing business in India. And look at Bata, a Czech company that has become synonymous with shoes in India. I want Nautiyal Industries to establish a presence in America. We export a number of products to Britain. We can try and sell the same products—made of silk, cotton, brass and jute—in America also. What do you say, Jake? Do want to be our agent in America?"

"I like this idea better than starting a restaurant. Let us say that you can count on me."

Chandubhai nods his head to give his blessing. Nautiyal Exports (America) takes birth in a small Southern Fried Chicken restaurant in Washington D.C.

After dinner, they drive back in taxis to the Willard Hotel and walk over to Constitution Avenue to watch the fireworks display—along with thousands of Americans. At 10:00 P.M. sharp, the fireworks start and carry on for half an hour.

"This is just like the *Diwali* festival in India," Chandubhai says looking up.

Hari Nautiyal clicks a few pictures. After the smoke has settled, they walk back to the hotel. It is almost 11:00 P.M. Jake and Wilbur take their leave and the rest of them go up the elevator to their rooms.

As they reach their floor and are getting out of the elevator, Hari Nautiyal asks, "Swamiji, are you going to sleep in my balcony?

"No, no, I will be fine in my room. I feel much better after the walk tonight. I just needed some fresh air."

• •

One of the lecture theatres at George Washington University is overflowing, with some students sitting on the steps of the sloping floor. Swamiji is dressed in full 'battle gear'. Instead of his usual white attire, he is dressed in saffron coloured *kurta-Paijama* with a long saffron coloured mark on his forehead. He wants to conform to the image of a traditional Swami from India. There is a table on the podium covered with a table cloth with *Om* printed on it, both in English and the traditional Hindu symbol of *Om*. A large silver plate has incense burning in it; the fragrance is gradually permeating through the lecture hall. The sound of whispering between the attendees is merging with the supernatural fragrance of incense to create a celestial and serene atmosphere. Swamiji and others, including Wilbur Wright and Jake Kreiger, are all sitting in the front row. Swamiji has his eyes closed and is in deep meditation.

Wilbur leans slightly towards Swamiji, whispers in his left ear and gets up to go to the podium.

A voice crackles through the speakers, "Ladies and gentlemen, it is my honour to introduce, Swami Ravi Anand from India. I assume that you all have had time to read the introductory material that has been distributed earlier. He is going to give a talk on *Mantra Sadhana*, also known by the acronym Braincom 1."

While Wilbur is speaking, Swamiji gets up and walks up the two steps to the podium. After Wilbur is finished with his brief introduction, he moves away from the microphone, and Swamiji takes over. For about thirty minutes he introduces the concept of a mantra, what it is, and how it stills the mind and provides deep relaxation. In conclusion, he invites the audience to join him in a brief demonstration of Braincom 1. Afterwards, there is a question and answer session, and the event is over by 11:30 A.M. After the formal session is complete, many attendees approach Swamiji for a more detailed discussion and express interest in visiting the Ashram in India for formal training. At this stage,

Daddyji moves up on the podium alongside Swamiji, and hands out the address and other terms for gaining admission to the Ashram in India. They had brought twenty copies which are quickly grabbed by those present. Others are given a location by the representative of the University, where the information will be posted on the student notice board.

After the lecture, they all go for lunch in the university cafeteria to do 'post-mortem' of the day's events.

"Swamiji, judging from the response of the students attending the lecture, I think you are about to become a celebrity," Wilbur Wright says.

"Well, I think, time will tell," Hari Nautiyal adds.

"Wilbur," Jake says, "If it is all right with you, I would like to take these gentlemen out to meet a few friends of mine. Do you have any plans for the evening?" This is a way of telling Wilbur that he is on his own for the evening.

"Well, I was going to see some friends also. And I was wondering if I should take our guests along. You have taken a load off my mind."

After lunch, Hari Nautiyal, Chandubhai, Swamiji and Daddyji are dropped off at the hotel for the afternoon siesta. Wilbur drives away in a taxi. Jake Kreiger is driving his own car. He parks his car on the street and walks in with them into the hotel lobby.

"We are meeting some friends of mine at about 7:00 P.M., is it all right if I pick you all up at 6:30 P.M.?" Jake Kreiger says, while he is trying to pat his hair down—the few that are left on his bald shinning head. Looking at him, trying to settle his hair down, Hari Nautiyal and Chandubhai, instinctively, start to follow what he is doing. Swamiji, after his successful lecture, is in a playful mood and says, "If you gentlemen practice *Mantra Sadhana* regularly, your hair will grow again."

They all break into laughter. Jake Krieger adds, "Swamiji, this is a typical American marketing idea. In your next lecture in New York, you should tell the audience about this. Do you know that growing hair on bald heads is the second most sought after product made in America?"

"Daddyji asks, "Which is the first one?"

Jake Kreiger looks around mockingly and says in a whisper, "I rather not say. I leave it to your imagination." And he walks away saying, "See you at 6:30 P.M. sharp outside on the sidewalk."

As they all walk to the elevator, they are still discussing what the first most sought after product in America might be.

20

THE MEETING

They are all dressed in suits and ties. Three of them are wearing dark suits of various shades and stripes, except that Daddyji decides to wear a white Sharkskin suit with a red tie. They are dressed to the hilt on a hot July day. As four of them are standing on the sidewalk in front of the hotel, waiting for Jake Kreiger to arrive, they are receiving glances from the passersby. But they want to put their best foot forward—so much so that Daddyji is wearing white shoes to go with his white suit. He has even brought the white powder along from India to rub on the shoes to make them standout.

Hari Nautiyal looks at Daddyji's white shoes and says, "Surinder, very stylish shoes. Where did you buy these?"

Daddyji looks down proudly at his shoes and replies, "These shoes were made by a cobbler, named Nathu Ram, located in the Reghar Pura area in the western part of Delhi. Nathu Ram claims that he used to be frequented by the military personnel of Britain and America during World War II. The sign on his shop boldly advertises: *Our shoes are walking in all corners of the world*."

Hari Nautiyal agrees, "Yes, of course, I remember now." And then he suddenly comes up with another business idea, "Surinder, this can be a great export item—shoes Made in India. Imagine: If we flood the American market with Indian made shoes."

Then Hari Nautiyal changes the topic and says with a mysterious look, "Swamiji, I have a question for you. Let us see if you can foretell the number on the building that Jake is taking us to."

Swamiji looks at him with an equally mysterious smile and replies, "So you are testing me." He then takes a deep breath, closes his eyes for a few seconds and says, "Twenty one."

At that very instant, Jake Kreiger's car glides to a stop beside the sidewalk. They open the doors and get in.

When they are all seated, Jake says, "We are going to meet some people that you may be surprised to see. You may have seen some of them in the newspapers. I want you to understand and be convinced that our Group, *Robus 10*, is connected to the highest levels of the American establishment. I will not tell you anything more; I don't want to spoil the surprise element."

They all look at each other, wondering what Jake has in store for them. After a few minutes' drive, Jake points to the Potomac River on the left side of the car. He slows down to let them look at the scenery. After a few more minutes of drive, the car stops in front of a large house in the Georgetown area of Washington D.C. They all get out of the car and look around to take in the scene. The number on the house is *21*. All four of them look at each other. Hari Nautiyal nods at Swamiji to acknowledge that he had foretold the number correctly. Jake Kreiger steps forward to ring the door bell but before he can press the button, the door opens and they all walk in. A man in a dark suit leads them to a room at the rear of the house. It is a large and oblong room. Ceiling-high bookcase lines one of the walls and paintings adorn the other wall. The ceiling is of ornamental plaster with two chandeliers. The floor is dark hardwood with rugs. It is richly furnished.

As they walk in, followed by Jake Kreiger, all four of them have their mouths open in disbelief. They could not have imagined in their wildest dreams what they see. Hari Nautiyal looks back at Jake Kreiger with a facial expression, as if he has been caught naked. There are so many surprises that they stand still for a while looking at each other.

Daddyji is the first one to speak, "Oh, my God, Mr. Rankin... Mr. Bond... *you*... here?" And then he looks at his friend Max Hoffer, the Canadian Deputy High Commissioner for India, and his old friend, and says, "Max you... what are you doing here? You never told me you were coming to Washington."

All of them mingle and talk to each other like long lost friends.

While this is all going on for a few minutes, two men sitting on a sofa near the window at far end of the room are watching with a smile. Due to all the excitement, they have gone unnoticed by the Indian delegation.

Jake Kreiger brings some order to the room, "Gentlemen, please be seated," as he points to the sofas and chairs closer to the two men seated at the far end of the room.

After they are all seated, Jake Kreiger introduces the Indian delegation to the two men; pointing first towards the two men and then to the Indian delegation. "Mr. John Cooper and Mr. Samuel Coolidge …they are members of our American group, *Robus* …and I think they do not need any further introduction… and I am pleased to present the members of the *Shakti* group from India. ……Hari Nautiyal, a prominent businessman of India; Chandubhai Patel, one of India's influential politicians; Swami Ravi Anand, a world renowned proponent of meditation and other spiritual techniques for the enhancement of human potential—and he can also tell the future—and, last but not least, Surinder Mehra, an executive with Nautiyal Industries."

After the two names—John Cooper and Samuel Coolidge—are mentioned, the members of the Indian delegation realize that they are sitting amongst two of the most influential Americans; they have read about them as being referred to as 'Boston Brahmins,' in addition to being in businesses such as movies, real estate and finance; and John Cooper's name has also been mentioned as the Democratic Party candidate for the next President of America. Brahmin refers to scholarly class in the class system of India. And Boston Brahmins refers to old wealthy Boston families of British origin some of whom had business ties with the British East India Company.

Both John Cooper and Samuel Coolidge get up and walk towards the Indian delegation; there are warm introductions and hand shakes.

The Indian contingent is overwhelmed.

They all take their seats.

As Jake Kreiger starts to speak again, Hari Nautiyal whispers something to Swamiji. He raises his hand before Jake Kreiger can utter the next word, and says with a mysterious smile, "Mr. Kreiger, as there are a number of Brahmins present in this room—Mr. Hari Nautiyal and I are the Indian Brahmins, and Mr. Cooper and Mr. Coolidge are the Boston Brahmins—I would like to say a Hindu prayer before we proceed any further."

As soon as Swamiji finishes speaking, there is laughter from one and all.

After they settle down, Jake Krieger looks around for any objections to the Hindu prayer that Swamiji had suggested. There are none. "All right Swamiji… go ahead."

Swamiji closes his eyes and recites mantras in Sanskrit for about a minute, and then requests everybody to repeat after him the Word, *Om.* And he starts, "Ooooooommmmmmm, Ooooooommmmmmmm, Ooooooommmmmmmm."

It is not clear how many of those present repeated after Swamiji, but it appears from the sounds that most did repeat in one form or the other. Some even recited *Om as… Amen.*

Jake Krieger continues, "Although, you know them from your past association, still, let me present David Rankin and Kevin bond, members of *Potestas 10*, our affiliated group in Britain. And then there is Max Hoffer, whom some of you know too well; he is the head of our affiliated group in Canada, *Canuck 10*."

The members of *Shakti 9*, the Indian group, look at each other shaking their heads and then they look at David Rankin, Kevin Bond and Max Hoffer, and say "Well… what a surprise!"

Jake Kreiger continues, "I want to keep it short. The purpose of having Mr. Cooper and Mr. Coolidge is to demonstrate to all of you that *Robus 10* has the ears of the political and business leaders of America at the highest levels. The fundamental purpose of the American group, *Robus 10*, the British Group, *Potestas 10* and the Canadian Group, Canuck 10, is to spread democracy in the world and counter Communism. And, as I have been told, the purpose of the Indian group, *Shakti 9*, is to make India strong and uplift its population from the shackles of poverty. I want to say to the members of *Shakti 9* present here today that we are with you. We have, as I stated to you when we met yesterday, a plan that, we think, will go a long way in achieving our goals."

There is a knock at the door, and Jake Kreiger stops talking. Trolleys carrying refreshments are wheeled in by two uniformed waiters. As the trolleys approach the Indian group, their sense of smell is picking up familiar fragrances of *Samosas, Pakoras and Dhokla.* Chandubhai is the first one to feel it. He turns to Hari Nautiyal and whispers, "Oh, the *khushboo* of *samosas, pakoras* and *Dhokla*; only if we could…"

"Chandubhai, you seem to be homesick. Don't hope for what you cannot get."

When the covers are taken off the trays, Chandubhai's dream comes true. The trays are full of what he had imagined. After eating tasteless, bland baked potatoes and French fries for the last many days, the presence of his favourite Indian delights is too much for his sense of self control. He gets up to have something to eat, but Hari Nautiyal pulls him down gently to the chair and whispers, "Chandubhai, we are in America. We should wait until we are asked to get up to have tea and snacks."

"Gentlemen, let us break for a few minutes to refresh ourselves. In addition to American snacks, we also have some surprises for our friends from India," Jake Kreiger announces with a smile.

After consuming some *Dhokla,* a snack from the Indian state of Gujarat, Chandubhai's home state, the apprehensions that he had voiced the previous day seem to have evaporated. As Jake Kreiger resumes his talk, Chandubhai nods his approval at every sentence. After a few minutes, Chandubhai gets drowsy, and, every now and then, he dozes off with his head drooping down, and then he, suddenly, straightens out with a jerk, opening his eyes.

Jake Kreiger rambles on. "To summarize, we, *at Robus 10,* have a Five Point Action Plan to help India. Number one is food aid. Number two is to facilitate admission of students from India to American universities. Number three is the placement of Indian students, after they have graduated from an American university, in suitable American enterprises. Number four is to make immigration of people from India to America, as permanent residents, easier. Number five is to open up the American market to exports from India. And as I understand, Britain and Canada also have a similar plan." Jake Kreiger pauses. Looks around and asks, "Any questions?"

Hari Nautiyal raises his hand and says, "India has dire need for power, and, as we have heard, nuclear reactors are one of the ways to fulfill the need. Would you be able to help us in that regard?"

Hari Nautiyal deliberately uses the word *Power* and not electrical power. He has other kind of power in mind–the one that comes with owning a nuclear bomb.

Jake Kreiger replies, "Yes. That is being addressed under Atoms for Peace initiative announced by President Eisenhower in December 1953 in a speech at the United Nations. The way things look; it is a buyers' market. All the countries with nuclear capability want to sell their technology to the developing countries; therefore, we will be competing with our friends from Britain and Canada. Under the circumstances, you should have no trouble procuring nuclear hardware for peaceful purposes."

Hari Nautiyal is thinking: *They themselves want to own nuclear weapons and want to give us reactors to make electricity so that they can pull the plug anytime they want and leave us in the dark with hurricane lanterns, with no oil.*

Chandubhai is dozing. But it seems he has read Hari Nautiyal's thoughts because he is suddenly wide awake and says, "Oil is what we need more than anything else. We cannot make *Samosas* if we do not have oil......... no, no ...no sorry ...sorry, you ...know, I still have the taste of tasty *Pakoras* and *Dhokla* you served us. But you know what I mean. Can America help us with oil?

175

Jake Kreiger replies, "You probably do not know this, nowadays, even America has to import oil from the Middle Eastern countries. The best we can do is to put in a good word for you with the Shah of Iran."

The others laugh, and Chandubhai settles down in the comfortable sofa and starts to dream of *Dhokla*.

Hari Nautiyal says, "Jake, the Five Point Action Plan is very similar to the plan our group, *Shakti 9*, put in place a few years back."

Daddyji raises his hand to speak. He says, "On a lighter note, I must tell you that in 1948, I hatched a plan to avenge what the British did to us for over two hundred years. This plan has some components that are similar to your plan. We named it Operation *Vilayat*."

Kevin Bond and David Rankin of the British group, *Potestas 10*, get very excited after hearing about Operation *Vilayat*. "Surinder, we would like to know what you have in store for us. During all our stay in India, we never heard about this, although, I know that *Vilayat* is a Persian word meaning, *foreign*, and Britain was referred to as *Vilayat*. "

"All right," Daddyji says, "I will tell you briefly. First: We must beat Britain decisively in cricket because nothing will hurt the pride of the British more than being beaten at their own game. Second: We must indianize the English language by adding Hindi words into it and call it *Hinglish*. Third: Export Indians to Britain in such large numbers that parts of London begin to look like Karol Bagh area of New Delhi. Fourth: Open so many Indian restaurants in Britain that instead of fish and chips, the national dish of Britain becomes Butter Chicken, and instead of Guinness, the British start to drink *Lassi* in their pubs."

Both Kevin Bond and David Rankin laugh their heads off. David Rankin says, "You know what old chap, the Operation *Vilayat* is already underway. What you told us is already taking place. The Five Point Action Plan, Jake just talked about, is going to hasten it. And watch out Jake, if you go ahead as planned, New York is going to start looking like Bombay. But that is what we want, is it not? So many Indians will be living in America and Britain that the flow of dollars and pounds back to India will keep the urge to embrace Communism at bay. We would have accomplished what CIA and MI6 would not be able to do in a million years."

• •

After the meeting is adjourned, they all engage in small talk. Max Hoffer urges them, "Gentlemen, you must visit Canada. I have a meeting at the UN, and I know Swamiji has a lecture in New York at Columbia University; after that we can all fly to Ottawa. Surinder, remember, I promised to give you a motorcycle ride around our Parliament Buildings."

They all look at each other, and Hari Nautiyal says, "Thank you, Max, for the invitation, but we are in a rush to get back to India. As you probably know, we are bringing out the inaugural issue of our magazine, LWF, on August 15, the 10th anniversary of the Independence Day of India. We promise you, we will make it to Canada another time."

As John Cooper and Samuel Coolidge are walking out, they stop to have a chat with the Indian group. They are especially interested in Swamiji.

John Cooper says to Swamiji, "I have heard and read a lot about your technique of meditation. One of these days, I would like to learn more about it."

Swamiji is not the one to miss this opportunity, and he says, "Why not today. If you have time, I will be happy to show you how it works."

"Are you sure?" John Cooper says and also asks Samuel Coolidge to join him.

A room is arranged for them and, for the next hour or so; the others are waiting and chatting while Swamiji is teaching the art and science of Mantra Meditation to two of the most influential Americans.

When they are back at their hotel, and are walking through the lobby, Swamiji whispers to Hari Nautiyal, "I have made the connection—a connection that would last for years to come."

21

HOSPITALITY

After a successful stay in Washington, the next stop is New York City. The purpose is to see the countryside and other cities along the way. They ask the hotel to pack some sandwiches, bottles of cola and water in an ice box, and they set course to New York City in a rented station wagon. As they are driving, Chandubhai is fascinated with the signs by the roadside that read 'Motel'. At first, he is hesitant to ask, but having passed so many of them he asks, "Wilbur, what are these places named motels?"

"These are small hotels along the road that tourists travelling by motor car use to stay either overnight or for a few days. You will notice that they park their cars just in front of their rooms." Wilbur points out to one of the motels that they are just passing.

"Are motels like Inns?" Chandubhai asks Wilbur.

"Yes, you could say that."

"Why don't we have motels in India?" he asks, looking at Hari Nautiyal.

Hari Nautiyal laughs and says, "Chandubhai, people in India do not travel by road that much. Moreover, there are very few cars and not enough roads."

"Let me tell you something interesting. My father used to own a *Sarai* in Ahmedabad in Gujarat province. *Sarai* in English is known as Inn, is it not? Let us ask our resident expert in English language," Chandubhai says, looking at Daddyji.

Daddyji replies, "Yes, Chandubhai, Indian *Sarai* is very much like an English inn of the olden days."

The car windows are slightly down. The breeze is blowing in. The noise of the wind blowing is such that they have to shout to be heard, and they are not able to have much conversation. As they all had to get up early to start their journey, they are a bit sleepy. Hari Nautiyal, realizing that Wilbur is the sole driver and it is a long drive, is trying to keep awake and engage him in conversation. He had read about Americans falling asleep at the wheel and having accidents.

Chandubhai, as usual, is dozing off, and every now and then, looks out enjoying the moving landscape. But his mind is moving faster than the car. He is way ahead of everybody; not in space but in time.

Chandubhai has one son, Kantibhai, who is 35 years old and runs a small restaurant on the ground floor of their ancestral home in Ahmedabad, India. Their house is near the train station. Sometimes, passengers come to town and they have no place to stay. Kantibhai has a deal with the coolies and the *Tongawallas* to bring any such passengers to his shop for food and lodging. He has a four bedroom flat upstairs from his restaurant. He rents out two rooms whenever he can find a suitable customer. When Kantibhai started renting out rooms, Chandubhai did not like it. But now, as he is travelling in America and seeing hundreds of motels, a plan is slowly germinating in his fertile mind. Ever since the meeting, where Jake Kreiger had stated that it will become easier for Indians to immigrate to America, he has been thinking. And now, after seeing such a demand for motels in America, he is wondering: *why not let Kantibhai immigrate to America and buy a motel or two or three or four.......* He has his eyes closed with a smile on his face and is counting on his fingers.

And then he opens his eyes and says, "Guys."

Hari Nautiyal is the first one to notice. He says, "Chandubhai, in a few days you have picked up the American slang. I am impressed; calling us guys."

Chandubhai replies, "Ever since we have landed in America, I have been hearing American people say... guys, guys, or honey, honey, so the word slipped off the tip of my tongue. Also, thank God, I did not call you guys, honey. Anyway, what I want to tell you is that the words *Motel* and *Patel* rhyme. Moreover, our family is already in the hospitality business. My son, Kantibhai, runs a kind of a motel in Ahmedabad. Well, instead of motor cars the passengers come there by Tonga. I guess you could call it a *Totel*. I have decided that I will ask my son to immigrate to America and buy a motel. Wilbur, do you think this is possible?"

Wilbur replies, "Yes sir. It is possible. In America anything is possible, if you are willing to work hard, and you have *Goddess Lakshmi* on your side." They all laugh on hearing reference to Hindu *Goddess Lakshmi*, the Goddess of wealth, from Wilbur."

Daddyji says, "Wilbur, I did not know that you believed in *Goddess Lakshmi*."

"Surinder, we Americans are Capitalists, and we are all disciples of *Goddess Lakshmi*, the Goddess of wealth." Then he says, looking slightly towards the rear seats where Chandubhai is seated, "Mr. Patel." He always addresses Chandubhai as Mr. Patel, in view of his position and their age difference.

Chandubhai replies, "Yes, I am awake." And they all laugh again.

Wilbur continues, "Mr. Patel, I have an idea. As you seem to be very interested in motels, would you like to stay in one tonight? That way you can have a first hand look at how they look and operate."

"I think it is a great idea. Let us do it."

Hari Nautiyal, who has been looking forward to staying at the Waldorf, says, "But Wilbur, we have a reservation at the Waldorf."

"Not to worry, Mr. Nautiyal, I will call them and take care of that. There will be no charge for tonight. Don't forget I had made the reservations in the name of the American Government. We will stay there tomorrow night."

After a few minutes of driving, Wilbur steers the car off the main highway to the side road where a number of motels are located. He selects one, and drives to the entrance to the office that is located on the left side of the single storey building. The sign in front of the building reads: Royal Motel; Neat and Clean Rooms Available. They all get down and stretch their bodies to take the kinks out, having been sitting in the car for a number of hours. Wilbur leads them to the entrance door and holds it open for the rest of them to enter the motel.

As soon as Chandubhai steps in, he starts to look around and is trying to pick up a fragrance that is testing his taste buds. He is hesitant to say anything lest Hari Nautiyal again make fun of his longing for Gujarati food. But he is absolutely certain that *Kathia Wadi Alloo* is being cooked very close to where he is standing. As they are all standing near the front desk waiting for somebody to attend to them, Chandubhai looks towards one of the corridors and starts to walk following the scent. Other members of his party are surprised to see him disappear into the adjoining corridors. Wilbur follows him, followed by others. Chandubhai stops in front of one of the doors. He is standing there trying to smell a crevice of the door. There is muted sound of a conversation floating out of the room along with a fragrance that seems to be the object of his attention. As they are all standing there, Chandubhai says pointing to the door, "I can bet my life that there are *Kathia Wadi Alloos* being cooked in there."

As soon as he is finished talking, the door opens and a man walks out. He is taken aback when he sees five of them standing outside his door, but, at the same time, he is also pleased to see some of his own kind. He extends his hand and says, "My name is Hasmukhbhai Patel, I am the owner of this motel. Sorry, you had to wait. I just left the front desk for a few minutes."

As soon as Chandubhai hears the word *Patel*, he extends his hand and says, "I am Chandubhai Patel, *Kem Chho Hasmukhbhai.*" Meaning: how are you Hasmukhbhai?

They all walk back to the front desk. Chandubhai and Hasmukhbhai are talking to each other animatedly in Gujarati; not only that Wilbur is not able to understand what they are talking, neither are the others. After a few minutes of talking to each other, like the long lost brothers, the two Patels settle down. It turns out that Hasmukhbhai hails from Kathiawad area of the state of Gujarat. They all get their rooms, but Hasmukhbhai refuses to charge them anything.

He says, "This is the first time anybody from my country has come to stay here. So I am not going to charge you any rent. You are our guests. As we say in India: *Atithi Devo Bhava*; do you know what it means? A guest is like God."

After a great deal of persuasion, he agrees to accept half the daily rate. In the meantime, his wife, Ketki, also comes out and is introduced to everybody.

Hasmukhbhai tells her, "Ketki, please cook some more food; we have five *Gods* to feed."

They all laugh.

"Only the fortunate ones have guests," she says, and goes back to her room to cook more food.

They all go to their respective rooms to freshen up and rest a little before dinner. It turns out that Hasmukhbhai and his wife live in one of the rooms of the motel.

Hasmukhbhai explains to them, "Evening time is very busy. This is when people like to turn in after a long day of travelling. Morning is also busy because it is in the morning that most people checkout."

Chandubhai is beside himself with joy at having found a fellow Gujarati to talk to, and, on top of that, in the motel business. "Thank you, Wilbur, for bringing us here. How did you know? Had you stayed here before?"

"No, Mr. Patel, I had no idea. It is just destiny," Wilbur says, and looks at Swamiji.

"Swamiji says with a smile, "Chandubhai, Wilbur is right. Destiny has brought you in contact with Hasmukhbhai. Who knows, what is in store?"

For dinner, they decide to get together in the motel's office, just behind the counter, so that they can watch the front desk and eat at the same time.

During dinner, guests are checking in one after the other. Chandubhai is keeping a mental note of how many guests have checked in. After about an hour, he notices that Hasmukhbhai is beginning to tell the would-be guests that the motel is full. After a while, when it is dark, Hasmukhbhai goes and switches on the FULL sign. After dinner is finished, they all get up to retire to their respective rooms.

Chandubhai asks, "Do you people mind if I stay back to have a chat with Hasmukhbhai?"

Hari Nautiyal replies, "It is all right with us."

The rest of them, including, Hasmukhbhai's wife, Ketki, walk away.

After some small talk with Hasmukhbhai, Chandubhai comes to the point. He says, "Hasmukhbhai, if you don't mind, please tell me how did you get to America, and why did you choose to get into the motel business?"

He replies, "My uncle came to America in 1949 as an illegal immigrant. He worked in motels just outside Baltimore as a cleaner for a few years, saved some money and bought a small motel. In a few years, the small road on which the motel was situated was turned into a major highway. The traffic on that highway increased so much that his motel was always full. With the money he saved, he bought another motel a few miles away. He needed help. Rather than hire anybody locally, he sponsored me. I arrived in September 1953. I worked for him for three years, and he helped me buy this motel. I have owned this place for only about a year."

Chandubhai says, "I have been thinking, ever since I arrived in America, about how to help my son settle here. I want my son, Kantibhai, to move to America and buy a motel. I think I can arrange for his immigration, but there is the problem of converting rupees to dollars. What do you suggest?"

Hasmukbhai laughs and replies, "Chandubhai, with your status and connections you should have no problem, but there are other ways also. We are sending money to India regularly, while we are building a house and trying to start a business there. You give us rupees in India in exchange for dollars in America. It is a bit expensive, though."

Chandubhai asks, "How expensive?"

Hasmukhbhai replies, "The unofficial exchange rate is eight rupees to a dollar, but, for you, it will be six rupees to a dollar. Chandubhai, we are like brothers. You have status and connections, and we have dollars. We should help each other to get ahead. You help us, and we will help you; it is win-win, as the Americans say."

Chandubhai gets the point and asks, "I agree with you Hasmukhbhai. Let me know if I can be of any help."

Hasmukhbhai starts to speak and then keeps quiet, saying, "I am not sure whether I should impose. But just for your information, we want to set up a small factory in India to manufacture manhole covers for export to America. For that we require permission from the state government and the central government."

Chandubhai takes his eyeglasses off and rubs his eyes—a way of gaining time to think about what has been said. In fact, at the same time, he is also secretly admiring the initiative of Hasmukhbhai.

He says, "Hasmukhbhai, you know, I like this plan of yours to set up manufacturing for export. You let me know the details, and I will definitely help you to get the permission from the government. Oh, and I have one suggestion. Why don't you take my son, Kantibhai, as your partner; it will solidify our relationship."

The deal is finalized with a shake of hands. And, unbeknown to the rest of the world, thus starts one of the world's largest acquisitions of the hospitality business in the history of the world, and the start of the *outsourcing* of the most sacred of the American infrastructural items, the *Manhole Cover*. With this historic shake of hands, over the next 50 years, most of the motel business of America would gradually pass into the hands of the Patels of India!

The next day they all drive to New York, and check into the Waldorf-Astoria Hotel on Park Avenue. As Daddyji was keen to stay at the Willard in Washington D.C., Hari Nautiyal's dream was to stay at the Waldorf–Astoria so that he can tell his rich friends back in India. The lecture by Swamiji at the Columbia University is also a success. They spend a few days visiting the New York City landmarks such as the Empire State Building, the Statue of Liberty, and the newly completed United Nations Headquarters. One full day is spent in shopping around the Time Square. On July 14, they head back to Delhi via London.

As the plane is on its final approach to the Sufdarjung Aerodrome, New Delhi, Hari Nautiyal says to himself: "Only time will tell what have we wrath......"
The rest of them are still dozing.

22

LABOUR OF LOVE

While Daddyji is enjoying his trip to America, I am doing things I had only dreamed of. It is summer holiday time. I am home. After lunch, most days, I sit in the front verandah and wait for the queen of my dreams, Saniya, to come and collect the daily bread on behalf of her mother, Rampiyari.

Today, as soon as she comes in, I get up, give her a smile and quickly go in and get her four *roties* instead of two that she is entitled to.

She smiles, shyly, and says, "My mother told me that I am supposed to collect two *roties*; you gave me four."

"It is fine; we have so many in our Frigidaire," I say, trying to impress her.

"Oh, you have a fridge?" She says. "My Papa in Meerut also has a fridge."

Everyday, I have to think of new things to talk about. After two or three days, I seem to be running out of ideas. Whenever she comes to our house, I am very careful to hide my limp. It is a good thing that I had been practicing English language skills with Daddyji; it is proving very useful. Having grown up with her father, who is English, and having studied in a convent school, her English language skills are excellent, but I can also manage very well.

"Have you hurt your leg?" she asks me one day, to my utter surprise.

At first, I was concerned that she may not like me with my limp. In fact, the effect is quite the opposite. She listens to my story with keen interest and sympathy and is very interested to meet my crutches, Ram, Shyam, and my walking stick, Ginny. I have a Cadbury chocolate bar in my pocket; I take it out and offer it to her. She hesitates at first, and then accepts it, opens the wrapper, breaks the chocolate into two and gives one piece to me. As I go in to pick up my crutches; Mummyji comes in the room.

"What are you doing, Vikram youstupidboy?" She asks.

My face goes red. My heart starts to beat faster and faster. She does not know that I have been talking to Saniya for the last few days—every time she used to come to pick up the roties.

I start to stammer, "Oh... oh... SSSSaniya is outside. She wants to meet Ram, Shyam and Ginny."

She goes outside to see what is happening. I follow her carrying my three friends. Saniya is sitting on one of the chairs eating the chocolate bar. Mummyji looks at her with a frown. I can read her thoughts: *"How dare the daughter of our sweepress sit on one of our chairs and eat a chocolate bar."* She is thinking.

As Mummyji walks into the verandah, Saniya stands up and says, "*Namaste, auntyji.*" This comes as a bigger shock to Mummyji, being addressed as auntyji by the daughter of her *Jamadaarni*—the sweepress, an untouchable. Her face is red and blue like fire. I am thinking of ways to douse the fire before it incinerates my sprouting relationship with Saniya.

I do some quick thinking, like a military Commander under sudden attack, and decide to carry out a strategic retreat. I look at Saniya trying to send her a thought, and signal her with my eyes to leave. She suddenly says, "*Namaste, bibiji,*" and quietly moves out of the house. I am relieved, but I know that, sooner or later, there will be an inquisition. What an intelligent girl she is, I am thinking. Instead of addressing her as auntyji, the word that inflamed Mummyji, she says bibiji—the word that a girl of her station is expected to use.

I have not seen Saniya for a number of days now. Her mother has started coming to collect the daily bread. Whenever she comes, I am sitting in the verandah hoping to see Saniya. I feel like asking her, but something is holding me back— lack of courage and fear of 'what will people say'.

I am learning how to drive; thanks to our driver, Siyaram, and his ingenuity. All the practice takes place in the afternoon hours, when Mummyji is having her afternoon siesta. In order not to wake her up, the car is manually pushed out of its parking spot in our front yard. When it is on the road, it is pushed a bit away from the house before pulling the starter. And then, the practice sessions take place in the back alleys without going to the main roads. As I gain a little practice, we begin to venture a little further away. Monsoons have started early. It is making life a little difficult, but we manage. My aim is to drive by where Saniya lives and let her see me driving the car. She lives with her mother in the tenements with sloping tin roofs near Sarai Rohella railway station. Their laneway is very narrow and full of potholes filled with water. I am not sure if the car can even pass through. During one of my driving lessons, I turn the car into the lane where she lives. I slow down the car right in front of her tenement. It is raining heavily.

"Vikram, if we stop the car, it is likely to get stuck in mud," Siyaram, our driver, says. As he is speaking, I am looking towards her home hoping to have a glimpse. Siyaram is no fool. He had seen me a few times sitting in the verandah and talking to her.

"Are you looking for somebody?" asks Siyaram with a smile and chewing the *paan* at the same time.

I am bent upon seeing her. I keep sitting in the car and looking towards her home.

Siyaram's ingenuity has to be admired. He gets out of the car and goes and knocks at the door of Saniya's home, with the rain pouring on. He is drenched. Rampiyari, our sweepress, comes out. She looks at him and then towards me. Siyaram says something to her, and she goes in and brings a pail of water and hands it over to him. He brings out the pail, opens the bonnet of the car and starts to fiddle. I sense an opportunity. I open the car door and run into the tenement—my clothes wet to my body. What I see breaks my heart. Saniya is sitting on the kitchen floor with her back towards me, and she is washing utensils with the ash from the hearth.

How dare Rampiyari make her work like this at such a tender age? I look at her and send her a thought.

"Saniya, look who is here," Rampiyari says, at exactly the same time I send her the thought.

She looks back. I would like to think she responded to my thought. Rampiyari's message traveled at the speed of sound, but mine travelled at the speed of light. My thought reached her first; I am sure. I want to be absolutely sure; I send her another thought. She stops scrubbing the utensils and just looks at me, and I know she is saying; "I am coming".

I am spellbound.

My soul mate of the seven lives has arrived; I am sure. She gets up and walks over to where I am standing. She looks at me and says in English, "Come in, have some water."

"There is enough water falling from the heavens," I say, looking up at the sky outside. I walk out and stand in the falling rain with my face facing the heavens—drinking to the occasion. I look back, walk to the car, take the wheel and pull the starter; the car engine comes to life. I slip it into gear and move away–looking sideways and waving.

The age of communication by thought has arrived. The Ether vibrates when Saniya and I talk by thought. Whenever a thought from Saniya arrives, Ginny vibrates at her perch on a peg on the wall; I know it is a thought from Saniya. We call each other several times a day. One day, I am sitting in my chair reading a book. A light breeze is blowing. The curtain is swinging in the breeze. Ginny begins to vibrate violently. *A thought from Saniya has arrived,* I am thinking. I try to receive the thought, but there is no thought in the Ether. Ginny is vibrating violently; there is a knock at the door. I get up, and part the curtain, and who do I see? My soul mate of seven lives, Saniya, is standing there. I step forward to touch her on her shoulder; there is nothing there, but she is still there; an image made of thoughts. ...Is it Imagination or Realization by Thought. I do not know.

23

OH, OUR CUSTOMS

Four weeks fly away, as if time had stood still; my soul mate Saniya's thoughts filling the cosmos, obliterating all sense of time.

The flight is scheduled to arrive at 4:00 A.M. The same people who had, four weeks ago, gone to see him off are all gathered to travel to the airport to receive Daddyji. The six car procession leaves home at 2:00 A.M. My sister, Suneeta, and brother, Kishi, are left behind, still asleep, with my grandmother and servant Chottu watching over them. Marigold flower garlands are filling the air in the car with their fragrance. There is something about the fragrance of the Marigolds that stirs my romantic emotions. As the car is racing through the cool early morning Monsoon-*ish* air, my thoughts are filled with Saniya; ...oh, how she must be sleeping unaware of my feelings. I am wondering if I should enter her dreams, but I dare not; lest she wake up from her sweet slumber.

I am jolted out of my imaginary machinations by a sea of cars outside jostling for position by the curb of the airport.

A crowd of people in the airport building are standing around the small door through which the international passengers, with disoriented looks, are trickling out, one at a time. Some onlookers are standing on their toes, and craning their heads to look inside through the small door opening to get a glimpse of their loved ones inside the Customs and Immigration hall. The flight is on time, but we have arrived early. We are waiting, with garlands in hand, looking aimlessly at the door from the customs area watching strangers walk out the door and looking around trying to find their loved ones. Mummyji is silently reciting hymns of the *Hanuman Chalisa* praying to God *Hanuman*—the Lord of the Winds—to guide Daddyji's plane safely to the ground. Uncle Daulat

Ram is talking to Uncle SK standing at the rear of the crowd—typical of Daulat Ram, never a part of the crowd, always above it. He is talking and looking around at the same time, while scratching his chin; this is something he does when he is about to embark on a mission.

I am watching the door from the Customs area and, every now and then, I look back at him. From the expression on his face, and his body language, I can sense that he has made a decision to do something. He moves away from Uncle SK, as aunty Devika approaches. He walks towards a door that leads to the inside of the aerodrome building. As he is walking, he takes out his wallet and slides out a few rupees and his business card. There is a peon sitting outside the door. He talks to him briefly and hands him something. There is a smile on the peon's face. He salutes Daulat Ram and lets him walk through the door and leads him to the back offices of the Customs and Immigration area. Daulat Ram has cracked the outer defenses which, in the Indian bureaucracy, are the most difficult to overcome. Daulat Ram is a past master at lubricating the wheels of officialdom. He knows that inertia is the most difficult obstacle to overcome; after that, once the things are in motion, they continue in a state of motion; one just has to keep removing the friction. Daulat Ram never studied physics, but he certainly knows how to apply the Newton's laws of motion. As he walks deep into the customs area, led by the peon, he comes face to face with a uniformed officer of the Customs Department, who looks at him with surprise and suspicion—finding a foreign body in the sanctum sanctorum of the Customs and Immigration area at the aerodrome. Before he can say anything, Daulat Ram presents his card and says with his hand outstretched, "I am Daulat Ram. I know Commissioner Krishan Khanna. I talked to him yesterday, and he told me that I should see Mr. Chunnilal Khurrana."

Commissioner Krishan Khanna is really known to Daulat Ram, both being members of the Gymkhana Club; they play tennis together once in a while.

The fact that he is being led by the peon, and the name of the Commissioner has come into play, the officer takes Daulat Ram's hand in both his hands and shakes it gently.

"Let me take you to Mr. Chunnilal Khurrana's office," the officer says.

Chunnilal Khurrana is the Officer-in-charge at the time, whose name Daulat Ram had found out after warming the peon's palm.

Chunnilal is sitting in his small office with glass walls on three sides for him to be able to observe the operations of his department. The Customs Officer introduces Daulat Ram as a friend of Commissioner Krishan Khanna. Upon hearing this, Chunnilal stands up and greets Daulat Ram warmly. They both take their seats.

"How can I be of assistance to you?" Chunnilal Khurrana asks.

Daulat Ram replies, "My brother-in-law and three of his friends are returning from a visit abroad. I am here to receive him. I just want to make sure that their arrival is comfortable after such a long journey."

"What is your brother-in-law's name?"

"Surinder Mehra."

"Mr. Daulat Ram, Surinder Mehra appears to be a very well connected person. You are the third person who wants Surinder Mehra to have a comfortable arrival. I have had phone calls from two colleagues in my department. One of them received a call from his mother-in-law that her friend's son, Surinder Mehra, is arriving today and they want things to go smoothly during Customs clearing. The other received a call from his brother that Surinder Mehra is his neighbour and that he is arriving today, and he would like him to have a smooth sailing through Customs. I have come across one or two recommendations for a person before but never three. Who is Surinder Mehra anyway? I would like to meet him when he arrives," Chunnilal says, while both of them have a hearty laugh.

After this long discourse from Chunnilal Khurrana, Daulat Ram comes to the conclusion that he may have to apply a second layer of lubrication. And he says, "Khurrana sahib, you should consider this as a compliment to the Customs Department that even important people are apprehensive when passing under the eagle eyes of the hard working Customs and Excise officials of the Government of India."

Chunnilal Khurrana's face glows with pride when he hears this. He says with humility in his voice, "The Parliament makes the laws, we just enforce them."

"Well, let me tell you who Surinder Mehra is. He works with Nautiyal Industries. Mr. Hari Nautiyal and Chandubhai Patel are also accompanying him. Oh, and you must have heard of Swami Ravi Anand; he is also arriving with them," Daulat Ram says, looking at Chunnilal Khurrana and waiting for his reaction.

"Oh, so this is the Indian delegation that has been in the news lately. I have heard that Swami Ravi Anand has become a hit in America. His technique of *Mantra Sadhana Meditation* has been found to increase the efficiency of the brain and reduce blood pressure. I would love to attend one of his seminars."

Daulat Ram sees an opportunity to oblige him. He says, "If you want, I can arrange a private session for you with Swamiji."

"Oh, that will be fantastic."

The metallic voice on the loud speakers in the ceiling echoes through the Customs hall announcing the arrival of Pan Am Flight 323. After a while, Chunnilal Khurrana gets up and says with sarcasm, "Let us go and receive your brother-in-law and his companions and make sure they have a comfortable passage through Customs. Now, we don't want them hassled by our eagle eyed customs officers, do we?"

The arrival of Daddyji's flight was announced almost half an hour ago. I am standing in the front lines of the crowd with garland in hand, shifting from one leg to the other to relieve pain in my leg and to keep myself from falling asleep. Every now and then, I sniff the Marigolds and get lost in miniature dreams of my love, Saniya. And then, I see Daddyji, along with the other members of his group and followed by Daulat Ram, walking out of the door from the Customs area carrying four bags in both his hands and followed by porters carrying three suitcases.

I am thinking: *Daulat Ram has succeeded in lubricating the wheels of the customs bureaucracy.*

As Daddyji reaches the crowd of people gathered to receive their loved ones, I am the first to garland him, followed by others. Soon he is drowning in Marigolds. I move in and rescue him; taking a whole pile of garlands off his neck. Mummyji is standing behind the throng of people, watching and wiping tears with the end of her sari; except that the tears at departure were that of separation, and the tears today are tears of joy.

We are home by 6:00 A.M.

• •

By about 1:00 P.M. the stream of neighbours starts. Those who had gone to receive him, and those who had placed orders for their favourite products, are hovering inside and around the house, wondering if their particular item has found its way in Daddyji's suitcases. As the neighbours come in, Mummyji tells them that Daddyji is still asleep. She is very particular to explain that due to the time difference, the American time is the middle of the night.

While Daddyji is asleep, Mummyji has opened and emptied the suitcases and handbags. She wants to make sure that he has not been carried away by good neighborly feelings and brought anything extravagant for the neighbours. Especially the hair dye, that the women of the neighborhood had ordered, receives particular attention from her. She wants to make sure that the women of the neighbourhood do not become devoid of grey; lest all wisdom disappear! A search of the suitcases unearths no hair or skin products. In fact, it turns out that, he had bought very little in the form of gifts for anybody, except the immediate family. One strange item is dozens of pens, the type of which we have never seen before. Made of plastic with no nib, it is known as 'Ball Point Pen'.

By the time Daddyji wakes up, it is 7:30 P.M. The neighbours are gone home after waiting. The carcasses of suitcases are lying on the drawing room floor with their tops open, as if they have been ransacked.

Those who come to visit the next day are offered a Ball Point Pen as a souvenir of America. However, when his friend, Karnail Singh, comes to see him, he receives the souvenir of Scotland, a bottle of Johnnie Walker Whiskey; this is in return for a bottle of Smirnoff Vodka that Karnail Singh had given Daddyji, when he had returned from his trip to Russia.

As all this is going on, there is only one thing uppermost in my mind: How to manage an American souvenir for Saniya. Neatly stacked, in one corner of the drawing room, are several items with Max Factor embossed on them. From the multitude of fragrances, I am able to guess that these products are for face make-up. I want to give one of these to Saniya, but how. Should I ask, or should I just take one. Knowing Mummyji, I am sure that she must have counted each and every item that came out of the suitcases.

It is now or never. If I have to steal one for my love, I am convinced that God will forgive me. I finally convince myself that it is all right to take one item. I refuse to call it stealing. Very calmly, I pick one of the round thin boxes, with Max Factor written on it, and place it in my pocket. I look around to check if anybody has seen me, and I find two eyes staring down at me. I look away so as not to lock my eyes with those eyes. I move away near a door and look back; the eyes follow me. I move to the door on the opposite wall; still the eyes follow me. If the eyes belonged to an ordinary mortal, I would have ignored them. But the eyes belong to God Krishna, the Lord Master of Hindu religion, the author of, Bhagvad Gita, the most sacred Book of the Hindus. His picture is hanging on the wall, as if it has been placed there to keep an eye on me. I know that He has seen me; He sees everything good or bad going on in the Universe. The question in my mind is: if I carry on with my act of taking one of the items, will He consider it stealing, and punish me accordingly, or will He consider this as an act of love for my beloved. As the legend goes, God Krishna too used to steal butter to give to his beloved, *Gopiyaan*, the village belles that he used to flirt with. Well, I finally convince myself that it is all right; if God can do it, so can I. As soon as I have cleansed the guilt off my mind, I notice that there are another two eyes looking at me–those of Mummyji. I know from her looks that she has seen me placing the Max Factor compact in my pocket.

"Vikram," she says with surprise in her voice, "Do you know what you have put in your pocket? It is for women, not for men."

I have to do some quick thinking. Do I pretend ignorance and give the compact back, or take a stand and let the truth come out once for all. It all happens in a few seconds. I turn around and look up. The first thing that I see is the picture of God Krishna, still staring at me, but with a smile; it seems as if He is telling me to tell the truth. I have committed one wrong act of stealing, and if I tell a lie now; that will be a second wrong act to conceal the first wrong act.

"Mummyji, I want to give this to Saniya as a present," I say in a calm and collected voice that even surprises me.

"What?" she shouts at me so loudly that Daddyji comes running out of his room, still trying to catch-up on the time difference.

"Did you hear what this son of yours just told me? He wants to give this," she takes it out of my pocket and shows it to Daddyji and continues, "Max Factor compact to Saniya."

Daddyji looks confused. He has no idea what is going on. Mummyji is beside herself with rage at the thought of her eldest son falling in love with the daughter of her sweepress, an untouchable.

"Calm down Kamla. First, tell me, who *is* Saniya?" Daddyji asks.

Mummyji replies, "She is the daughter of Rampiyari, our sweepress."

Daddyji says, "I did not know that she had a daughter."

Mummyji explains the whole story. As the scene is unfolding, I am seeing a smile and a look of pride on Daddyji's face. I think he is impressed with the fact that Saniya can speak good English. He asks, "If she has a white English father, and a dark Indian mother, tell me: is she white or dark?"

I am so excited to see a smile on Daddyji's face that I blurt out, "Daddyji, she is white like milk and red like a rose."

Mummyji is livid after listening to me and shouts again, "What am I going to do with her white colour? Eat it? Don't you understand that she is an untouchable? What will people say when they find out?"

We are all silent for a while, and then Daddyji says, "Kamla, I visited many places during my trip; I had high tea, low tea, and all types of coffees that the Americans are so fond of, but nobody makes tea like you do. Let me have a cup of tea made with your own hands."

Mummyji looks at him, confused, smiles and goes to the kitchen to make a cup of tea.

As soon as she is out of hearing range, he says softly, "Vikram, you rascal ... I never knew you are a romantic."

I blush.

"How long have you known her?" he asks gently.

"Just the time you have been away," I reply. I am relieved that the matter has been, very deftly, handled by Daddyji.

By the next morning, the whole situation has changed. Daddyji calls me into his room and says, "Vikram, you are about to start the final year of higher secondary school. You should concentrate on your studies."

The rest is left unsaid. I get the message, but it goes in one ear and out he other.

Mummyji may have taken the make-up compact from me, but she cannot take Saniya away from me. It strengthens my resolve, just like in the romantic Indian films. What my parents do not know is that Saniya is my soul-mate of seven lives... we have been and will be together for... eternity... infinity. The more it is repressed, the ...fuller it blossoms... love is a many-splendored thing.

24
PANGS OF SEPARATION

I have not seen Saniya for a week or so. She used to come to pick up *Roties*, but she has not come ever since the school has started after the summer vacation. After a few days, I realize that she must have started her school also. I remember her mother had mentioned that her father is trying to get her admission in Lady Irwin School. On way to my school, I start to look for the green school bus, and as if …destiny is conspiring to unite us… after a few days… I see her riding in the green bus as it drives past me. She waves at me… was she real or… made up of figments of my imagination. As I reach my school, my friend, Suraj Rajpal, is loitering outside the chemistry lab, and he comes over to talk to me. I had been telling him about Saniya as my love for her was blossoming for the past few weeks.

"Vikram, your Daddyji has returned from his foreign trip. Tell me *yaar*," he asks excitedly, "what has he brought for you?"

I tell him everything that has transpired, and he says, "Vikram, you are a fool. You should have talked to me before doing anything. Can any parents encourage their son to have a girlfriend? You idiot, matters of the heart are to be pursued in secret. Just try and think of any Hindi movie we have seen. Did the parents of the boy or the girl not oppose their romance in each and every movie? Real life is no different. Look at me. I told you about the girl next door… you know the Bengali girl."

"Oh, the one with the thick glasses?" I ask.

Suraj replies, "No… the one with the thick lips, oh *yaar*… the one who lives in the house left of our house. You know, where two goats are always tied outside."

I nod. He carries on, "You know, I have been friends with her for the past six months. Do you think I told my father and mother about it? If they find out, they would either throw me out of the house, or tie me to the bed."

The school bell rings and we run to the chemistry lab. As we are trying to make crystals of silver nitrate... Suraj and I distill the finer points of romance... by going through the love stories of all the Hindi movies we have seen.

And so my romance with Saniya continues; she riding in the bus, and I walking on the sidewalk. She smiles at me, and I smile back. But once in a while, when I am early, I find her standing at the bus stop waiting for her bus to arrive. We smile at each other and exchange hello... hello... at first... and then... small talk... what is happening at the school... gradually I start to leave the house a few minutes earlier... if it is too early, she is not there... I have to wait. Oh the joy of waiting...... and seeing her walking up the street... as she sees me... her gait becomes faster... and faster... till she reaches the bus stop... almost breathless. ...until one day... one of Daddyji's friend, Hari Singh, who lives just across the road from the bus stop, sees me talking to her. ....As soon as I see him standing at the front gate of his house... looking at me... I know it. ....God always throws obstacles in the way of love...... in every Hindi movie it is like that.

As soon as I reach school, I seek out, my friend, Suraj Rajpal. I describe to him what has happened. He thinks hard and says, "Vikram, my mother says that if you want to remove obstacles from your life, you should repeat the *Gayatri Mantra* eleven times every morning, and your obstacle will disappear."

It sounds like a good suggestion. Every morning, I start to recite the *Gayatri Mantra*, eleven times. From then on, I never see Hari Singh again standing at the front gate of his house... instead... he starts to stand at the bus stop with his young daughter, who has also started taking the same bus to the same school. And I am back talking to Suraj Rajpal looking for new *mantra* to ward off this new obstacle.

And thus, I continue to see Saniya sometime... at the bus stop and...... in the window of the bus, at other times.

25

RISE OF THE HOLY MEN

After returning from their trip abroad, Hari Nautiyal and Daddyji work day and night to ensure the launch of the inaugural issue of LESTWEFORGET Magazine, LWF, on the 10th anniversary of India's Independence, August 15, 1957. The Hindi version, *Yaadrahe,* is also published the same day. Publisher is Nautiyal Publications Pvt. Ltd., and the Editor is Surinder Mehra. The cover is designed to look like the American magazine, TIME. The photograph on the cover of the magazine is that of fireworks, in celebration of the 10th anniversary of India's Independence. In fact, the photograph was taken by Hari Nautiyal on the night of July 4, 1957 in Washington D.C. on the occasion of the American Independence Day celebrations. Apart from the articles about India's freedom struggle, the magazine is devoted to American aid to India and the virtues of Capitalism. The magazine names America as the land of Ice Cold Milk, Hi, Guy, and Honey. It states, in jest, that the Americans serve milk that is too cold for the Indian taste, as the Indians like it hot.

The Editorial emphasizes the need to increase exports to the Western Countries. Export of Spiritual Capital and Human Capital is noted as the key to the solution of India's foreign exchange problems. There is thirst in the West for spiritual wisdom that India has to offer, the Editorial states. House—full attendance at lectures of Swami Ravi Anand, in both Washington D.C. and New York City, is cited as proof. Ever since the visit to America, Swami Ravi Anand has received thousands of letters from people in America and other Western countries, expressing their desire to attend his Ashram to learn MSM (meditation). Large amounts of dollars, pounds, francs and marks will flow into India, if it materializes. Spiritual tourism will result in new Ashrams being built. The editorial states that new trains, roads and bridges will be required to transport thousands of foreign tourists, thus spurring economic activity.

On the one hand, the editorial predicts the in-flow of Spiritual Tourists to India, and, on the other hand, it predicts mass emigration of Indians, of all stripes, to countries such as America, England and Canada. It reports that according to un-named reliable sources in some foreign governments, plans are afoot to increase the quota of immigrants from India. The editorial argues that the emigration of Indians to America, Britain and Canada will increase the flow of foreign exchange remittances back to India; this is expected to ease the balance of payment problem and increase economic activity due to increased consumer spending by the relatives of those who have emigrated. The byproduct of this large exchange of populations of India and Western countries is expected to increase goodwill among the nations of the world. The editorial argues that, in time, the increase in population of people of Indian origin in western countries will increase India's influence in the world.

The editorial ends on a lighter note, however. It states: Lest we forget; we must avenge what the British did to us for centuries, and retrieve our honour. We must beat the British decisively in cricket. It suggests that private sector companies must support cricket in India, and it pleads with the Government of India, especially the Planning Commission, to keep its hands off the game of cricket. The editorial predicts that as India's stature in the cricketing world goes up, the economy of India will rise. This, it says, has been predicted by a group of eminent astrologers and economists engaged by the LWF magazine. A rationale presented in support of this theory is that the self-image of Indian people was trampled so badly by the British that the Indians have lost confidence in their ability. Ascension of the game of cricket in India, and beating the English at their own game of cricket, will do wonders for self-confidence and self-image of the people of India.

The inaugural edition of the magazine flies off the shelves of the newsstands. Newspaper boys at many traffic crossings are carrying stacks of magazines selling them to the people driving their cars, motorcycles and bicycles; a shortage of the inaugural edition of the magazine develops. Extra copies are printed by the publisher to alleviate the shortage but to no avail. An investigation reveals that some newsstands are hoarding the magazine and are selling it as a collector's item for twice the cover price.

American, Canadian and British diplomats send letters of congratulations on the publication of the inaugural issue of the LWF magazine, and especially the Editorial. Russians, though, are not happy to read the contents and arrange to meet Hari Nautiyal and Daddyji.

The Russian diplomat Demetri Sovolov says in the meeting, "Gentlemen, Soviet Union wants to invite Swami Ravi Anand to visit Moscow and Leningrad to deliver lectures about the techniques of meditation."

Hari Nautiyal replies, "Mr. Sovolov, it will be our pleasure to visit Soviet Union, but, at this time, we would like, at first, to organize our affairs here in India to be ready for the influx of Spiritual Tourists. The Tourists from the Soviet Union are as welcome as from the West."

After he is free of the launch and post launch activities for the magazine, Hari Nautiyal convenes a meeting of the *Shakti 9* group. Ever since the launch of the inaugural issue of LWF, he has been receiving calls from members of the *Shakti 9* Group to find out more about his trip to Washington D.C. The meeting is organized at Hari Nautiyal's Farmhouse south of Gurgaon, the same place as the last meeting. The protocol is also the same as last time.

Hari Nautiyal starts the proceedings, "Friends, our mission has been accomplished. I am sure all of you must have read the stories in the newspapers. Our own Swamiji has become an international celebrity. The success of our trip has been beyond our wildest dreams. We received excellent cooperation from similar groups in America, Canada and Britain."

What fascinates the other members of the *Shakti 9* group is the formation of BICA, the consolidated Group that comprises of all the four Groups of the four countries. He explains to them that BICA is an acronym formed from the first letters of: **B**ritain, **I**ndia, **C**anada and **A**merica.

"My friends," he says, "We have been assured of complete cooperation of other members of the BICA Group in providing help towards India's development in all the fields of endeavor. You must realize that history was created on July 5, 1957, the day BICA was formed. BICA is a secret Group; the existence of which must be kept secret."

Chandubhai takes off his Gandhi cap and starts to rub his bald head, a sign that something is churning in his mind. He finally places his cap back on his head and says, "I have already been summoned by the Prime Minister's Secretariat. I was asked why did I not inform them about my trip, and why the Indian Embassy in Washington was not involved. They wanted to know about all the people we met while in Washington. I told them that, apart from an American official who accompanied us, we did not meet any officials and that it was just a private visit as directors of Verinag Ashram."

As expected, Sumitra Mukherjee, who is always suspicious of the motives of the Western countries, asks, "Hari, as you know, nobody in this world does something for nothing. So my question is: What do we have to do to in return for the favours that other members of BICA will do to us?"

Hari Nautiyal is in a joyful mood, having tasted success in both his recent endeavors. He replies, "Sumitra *didi,* all we have to do is let Hollywood movies play in all the theatres in India and discontinue the production of films in India."

He has barely finished his first sentence, when Sumitra jumps up and says, "There is no way I will agree to let American moral values pollute the minds of young Indians and throw our rich cultural heritage to the winds. On one hand, we have Spiritual tourists coming to India, and on the other hand you want to let Hollywood movies shape our future and lose the very spiritual values we so cherish!" By the time she is finished, she is red faced and breathless and sits down with her head in her hands.

Hari Nautiyal gets up from the sofa and walks over to where Sumitra is sitting and says with his hands folded, "Sumitra *didi,* I was just joking. Do you think the people of India will let anything like this take place?"

Sumitra is not giving up. She continues her anti-American tirade and says, "Have you seen this thing called Hoola Hoop?—another American invention that has taken the world by storm. Any place you go, you see young men and women swinging their hips with this thing around their body; it looks so vulgar." The rest of them break into laughter.

S.P. Subramanium, a prominent businessman from Madras, asks, "Hari, seriously, please tell us what do the other groups expect from us?"

Hari replies, "Well, they are not asking for much. They were very frank about the whole thing. Their main expectation is that we will support democracy in India and oppose Communism. Their main fear is the spread of Communism in the world."

Everybody appears satisfied, and the meeting is adjourned at 12 P.M. sharp. As usual, there is no lunch. As they are all standing outside getting ready to board their respective vehicles, Hari Nautiyal opens the rear door of his, recently acquired, light blue Chevrolet, takes out a thermos bottle and offers water to everybody.

Cyril Dastur, the nuclear scientist, himself a connoisseur of foreign cars, notices the new car, and says, "Mr. Nautiyal, I see… you have changed sides. After returning from your trip to America, you have exchanged a British made Jaguar for an American made Chevrolet."

Hari Nautiyal laughs, and says, "We like to spread our business around."

In the meantime, Sumitra walks over to Hari Nautiyal, and says, "Hari, I would like to avail myself of your hospitality; I would like a sip of water from your thermos."

Hari and Sumitra have known each other for a long time, having served time in the same jails during the freedom struggle. He always likes to tease her. He says, "Are you sure Sumitra? This thermos is made in America. I hope this is not going to affect your morals."

"Oh, come on Hari, I am not against America. You know that."

Hari fills a glass of water and hands it over to her.

After she gulps down the water, she wipes her lips with the end of her sari and says, "Hari, I was thinking. Now that admission to American universities is going to open up, I would like my son, Shonaal, to go to America to do his Master's degree in civil engineering. I was wondering if you can help in that regard."

"I will look into it and get back to you," he replies, as Daddyji and his son, Veer, are looking on.

As they are driving back to their office, Hari Nautiyal is thinking: *Sumitra is a hypocrite. She does not like Hollywood movies but would like her son to study in America, immersed in the American culture.*

• •

As the black Lincoln Continental turns into the laneway of the Indian embassy in Washington D.C., it is not able to go any further. There is a lineup of people that starts from the entrance to the building and turns around the corner. Over a hundred men and women are lined up. After noticing the car with the Indian flag, the line parts enough to let the car pass through. Ambassador T.N. Srinivasan gets down from the car, buttons down the coat of his navy blue suit, changes his sunglasses to normal glasses and walks towards the people standing in the line with a beaming smile on his face.

"Good morning, ladies and gentlemen. Well, well, well… to what do we owe the honour of a visit from so many of you on this cold and sunny December morning? This is a real surprise."

One of the young men replies, "Sir, we are here to apply for a visa to India."

In the meantime, noticing the Ambassador talking to the crowd, other Indian officials come out of the building. The Ambassador, accompanied by the First Secretary, starts to move down the line chatting with a few more men and women.

He sees two young girls, walks over to them, shakes hands with them and says, "We are very pleased to see your interest in visiting India. Which parts of India do you plan to visit?"

One of the girls with blonde hair replies, "Sir, our first destination is Verinag Ashram in Kashmir. We are going there to learn meditation. After listening to Swami Ravi Anand's lecture here at the George Washington University, we have become his disciples. Many of our friends have already gone to India and have written to us about their celestial spiritual experiences."

The Ambassador remembers having read a small news item about a Swami giving a lecture but had never heard anything further about it.

As he is walking back to the embassy building, the First Secretary tells him, "Sir, we have noticed a gradual increase in the number of tourist visas in the last few months; most of the tourists are going to attend meditation classes."

After the pleasant walk about and chat with would-be tourists to India, the Ambassador goes in and settles down at his desk to attend to his routine duties. He is feeling satisfied that during his stay in America increasing number of tourists have started visiting India. As he is attending to correspondence in his in-tray, his personal assistant—known as the PA in the Indian bureaucratic parlance—brings in some mail that has arrived the previous day in the diplomatic bag. The PA stands on the opposite side of the desk waiting for the attention of the Ambassador while he is signing some letters. After he is done; he looks up at the PA. Before bringing the latest mail in, the PA has already gone through the mail and made notes for the Ambassador to review and give his comments. The PA picks up one of the magazines that has a slip of paper pinned to it and hands it over to the Ambassador and says, "Sir, there is a note here from the Ministry of External Affairs for you."

The Ambassador picks up the magazine and reads aloud, "LESTWEFORGET," and says, "I have never heard of this magazine before. ....
Oh, this is the inaugural issue." And he starts to turn the pages. While he is doing that, he says to the PA, "That will be all for now." The PA gets up from the chair and walks out. The Ambassador carries on reading. He is fascinated to read about Swamiji and the impression he made in America. What he is really surprised to read are the names of well known Indian Industrialist, Hari Nautiyal, and a politician, Chandubhai Patel, who had accompanied Swamiji. The third name, Surinder Mehra, he does not recognize. He rings the bell on his desk and his PA comes in.

"Please ask Mr. Bannerji to come and see me." Mr. Bannerji is the First Secretary, Political Affairs—a senior member of the embassy staff. After a few minutes, there is a knock on the door, and Mr. Bannerji walks in. The Ambassador asks him to take a seat and hands him over the magazine and asks tersely, "Did you know about this?"

Bannerji reads the cover and says, "No, sir. I have never seen this magazine before."

"Just read the editorial," says the Ambassador.

As Bannerji is reading the editorial, the Ambassador starts to attend to some other papers from the in-tray on his desk.

"Well, this is quite a story. They claim to have information about the forthcoming changes to immigration and visa requirements of not only America but also those of Canada and Britain," Bannerji says.

"If the editorial is correct, then how is it that the governments of these three countries did not inform the government of India? There is a memo here from New Delhi asking us this question. Can you please call your contact at the State Department and find out the authenticity of this information?" the Ambassador asks.

Later the same day, Bannerji confirms to the Ambassador that his call to the State Department confirmed that the editorial is largely correct. No formal orders have yet been issued, but the matter of increasing the quota of students and immigrant visas from India is seriously under consideration.

The number of visa applicants, lining up outside the Indian embassy in Washington D.C., is increasing everyday. After about a week, police have to be called in to control the crowd. The High Commission of India in London, England, also has line ups outside. In Ottawa, Canada, even an early snowfall does not deter the would-be visitors to India from lining up outside the High Commission of India office on McLaren Street; a photograph on the front page of the newspaper, Ottawa Journal, goes around the world with the title "Canadian Santas, India Bound,' and is picked by the newspapers in India.

It appears the World has finally found India.

• •

As the word of the success of Swami Ravi Anand during his visit to America spreads, Swamiji is sought after by Indian politicians of all major political parties. They want to hold rallies to felicitate him for bringing such high honour to India. Prominent politicians want to consult him about their future. Some of them are not able to get appointments for months. As the word spreads in the community of the holy men in the holy cities of Haridwar, Rishikesh and Banaras; many of them draw up plans to emulate Swami Ravi Anand.

"Surinder, we should build new Ashrams and expand existing ones," Hari Nautiyal orders at the Board meeting of the company. Daddyji is busy day and night trying to expand the existing Ashrams owned by Nautiyal Industries and build new ones.

India has become the destination for Spiritual Tourism. The holy men are showing entrepreneurship of a level higher than that of the Indian businessmen. They have not only started expanding their resources in India but have started travelling abroad to find followers among Indians who have settled abroad, and among the residents of foreign lands. All kinds of restrictions are placed on Indian businessmen travelling abroad to find export markets for their products, but the holy men have a free hand. The politicians are afraid to tangle with them; lest they throw a curse or two at them.

After reading the editorial and its pronouncements that the rise in the economic conditions in India is tied to how Indians play the game of cricket, young and old have started playing cricket. There is an exponential increase in the number of Indians playing cricket. The holy men have also joined the game. To do their part, they have searched the depth and breadth of Hindu scriptures to find *mantras and yagyas* that will not only enhance the Indian cricket team's abilities, but degrade those of the opposing teams.

In the months hence, scores of Indian Swamis, Gurus and the holy men set up Ashrams in India and foreign countries to teach the techniques of meditation, yoga and astrology. The holy men of India—and not the businessmen—are the first to venture out of India to show the flag, and put India on the world map as the spiritual leader of the world. It is the holy men of India who are the first to dispel India's image as the land of snake charmers and starving millions by spreading the Vedic knowledge to common people of the world.

Not to be left behind, Chandubhai Patel also decides to consult an astrologer to find an auspicious time for his son, Kantibhai, to move to America and buy his first of many motels; and, soon thereafter, start the export of manhole covers.

Nautiyal Industries sets up a separate export division in his company to export Indian made goods to America.

Doors are thrown open for students from India to study in American, Canadian and British Universities. Indian students move by the thousands.

The middle and the upper classes start to pursue money by fair means or foul, as if there is no tomorrow; the colour of money be damned—black or white. They say money is money; it all looks of the same colour in the dark.

Years hence, it would turn out that it is the off-shore banks that have been the beneficiaries of the money that was made in the dark.
Is this the dawning of the age of ascension of India or of descent into *Kalyug, the epoch of darkness?*

In order to counter the effects of *Kalyug*, the epoch of darkness, the owners of black money have all aligned themselves to at least one Holy man, if not two. Demand for the services of the holy men has increased to such a degree that commoners have no hope; the ones with Rupees, Dollars or Pounds Sterling are the only ones allowed in the sanctum sanctorum of the holy men.

26

GOOD LUCK FLY
1958

I am waiting to leave to go write the first of the final Higher Secondary School Board examinations. Today is the mathematics exam. I am nervous. Mummyji is having a hard time lighting the *diya* due to a strong breeze.

"Come on Mummyji. I am going to be late. I am leaving," I say impatiently.

"Wait. It is almost lighted. Your exam does not start until 10 o'clock. If you leave without taking the oblation, it would not be auspicious."

Finally, our servant, Chottu, comes and is able to light the *diya* for about 30 seconds with one hand cupping the *Diya* and the other holding the matchstick. During this window of opportunity, I quickly take a bit of *Halwa* oblation, place it on my tongue, join my hands in prayer and start to walk away. But she holds me back and thrusts two spoonsful of sweet yogurt in my mouth, and says, "Eating yogurt will bring you good luck, and it is also good for the brain."

This is the final frontier of the secondary school, after which I enter the university. My whole future depends on my performance in the forthcoming exams—or so I am made to believe. Therefore, all techniques are employed to enhance performance, including conforming to superstition and praying to different Gods.

It is 8:40 A.M. My girlfriend Saniya's school bus usually stops at our street at about 8:45 A.M. to pick up two girls, who also go to the same school. I quickly walk up the street and see my friend, Suraj, waiting for me at the crossing of our street and Rohtak Road, the main road.

"Come on let us go," he says.

I reply, "Saniya's bus will be here in a few minutes."

As we are talking, the bus slows to a stop and the two girls get up on the bus. Usually, Saniya sits on the window seat and waves at me. I look at all the windows, but Saniya is not there. Maybe she is seated on the other side of the bus; I am thinking. In the meantime, the bus starts to move. I stand there dejected. As the bus moves a few feet away, a piece of paper flies out of one of the windows of the bus and lands on the sidewalk just ahead of where we are standing. I run to pick it up. Hastily scrawled on it is: "Good Luck–Saniya". I stand there staring at the piece of paper with a smile on my face.

"Come on Vikram, walk fast, or we will be late," Suraj shouts.

As I am walking, I fold the piece of paper and place it in my shirt pocket beside my heart. We keep on walking and cross Rohtak Road just in front of the Liberty cinema and onwards toward the examination centre.

Suraj says, trying to make fun of my extra sensory abilities, "So, Vikram, did you have any dreams last night about the questions in today's exam paper?"

"No, but, I will tell you something very interesting that happened last night. As I was looking at last year's question paper, a fly came and sat down on it. I was just going to swat it, when I noticed that it was not an ordinary fly. It was larger that usual, with bluish golden wings. Out of the five questions on the paper, it hopped and touched three questions and then flew away."

Suraj grabs me by my arm, and asks, "Which ones?"

I say, "I won't tell you."

"Oh, come on Vikram, why not?"

I reply, "Because!"

He says, "Because of what?"

I say, "Because the fly made me promise not to tell anybody."

He says, "You mean the fly was talking to you."

I say, "No, I just sensed it. It was a Good Luck Fly."

He gives me a strange look. There is no more conversation, and we keep on walking.

After a while, he says, "You know what happened just as I was walking out of my house."

"What?"

"You know Sushmeeta, the girl with thick lips, who lives next door to us; you know where two goats are always tied. She and her mother were standing outside their house as I was coming here. She saw me and asked: Suraj, where are you going this early?

I said to her: Auntyji, I am going to write my first exam.

She asked me: which one? And I responded that I was writing mathematics.

She said that for mathematics I would need a very fertile brain, and for that I must drink goat milk. She told me to wait and got hold of one of the goats. She told her daughter Sushmeeta to bring a cup, and she started to milk the goat. In no time, she had half a cupful and said: Suraj, drink this and you will become like the great mathematician, Ramanujam. Well, when she invoked Ramanujam's name, I had no choice but to gulp down the goat milk."

Both Suraj and I go into a fit of laughter.

As we approach the roundabout, we see a small temple on the roadside. A few people are standing and singing hymns. Suraj looks at me; I nod, and we both stop in front of the temple for just a minute to pray for our success in the exam. Suraj has his hands together with his eyes closed, and is saying something under his breath. His palms are reddish in colour, as if he has henna on his hands.

After a minute, we start walking again and take a sharp left turn at the roundabout towards the examination centre.

"Hey Suraj, have you got henna on your palms?" I tease him, as only girls apply henna.

He looks at me surprised and says, "No, I don't have anything on my hands." I move quickly and grab his left hand and pull it out of his pocket. Before I can look at his palm, he pulls it back and puts it back in his pocket.

And then, suddenly, he takes it out again, and says, "Do you want to look at the colour of my hands? Here it is. See. Read your familiar formulas. Which formula do you want? They are all here."

"Suraj, this is cheating. Do you realize that if you are caught with this during the examination, you will be thrown out, and you will fail the exam?"

"Don't worry. I am going to wash off all the writing on my palms before the exam starts."

As we reach the examination centre, we see students crowding around a notice board trying to find out their examination room. We push our way through the crowd; it takes us almost five minutes to reach the notice board. We see three sheets of paper pinned to the notice board. It turns out that Suraj and I are in the same room. We go to the room and stand outside, not knowing what to do. After a few minutes, we decide to enter the room timidly. A few students are already sitting inside. As we are walking in, the invigilator asks to see our roll numbers. After a brief look, he waves us in, and we go in and find our desks. We are pleasantly surprised that we are just across the aisle from each other.

After we settle down on our respective desks, Suraj gets up and goes to see the teacher. I just sit there looking around and thinking: this is where my future is going to be decided within the next two weeks. While these thoughts are swirling through my mind, I see that Suraj is standing talking to the invigilator in his usual flattering style, and the invigilator is laughing and talking as if both have known each other for a long time. Meanwhile, my thoughts wander off. I imagine Saniya sitting beside me; suddenly joy takes the place of fear of the unknown. I can feel the ethereal vibrations reverberate through the room; present and the future intersecting, as it were. All the intricacies of mathematics, or *Arthashastra* as it is known in Sanskrit, melt into the ether surrounding me. There are no barriers; knowledge is flowing freely; there are no questions but only answers.

I am shaken out of my reverie by the invigilator's loud voice. "Students, sit down on your respective seats." He counts the number of students. There are forty eight. He keeps speaking, "We have ten minutes before we distribute the question papers. This exam is being taken by thousands of students all over Delhi at this very time. It will start at the same time all over Delhi. If anybody wants to go to the bathroom, do it now. Once the question papers and answer books are distributed, nobody will be allowed to go out until you have completed the exam and handed over your answer books. You get to keep the question paper. Is that clear?"

Suraj gets up and goes out; I presume to wash all the formulas off his hands.

Question papers and answer books are distributed, and all of us get our heads down and start writing. Before starting to write the answers, I quickly scan the question paper. The three questions the fly had hopped on last night were there. I had prepared them thoroughly. I start to write. As I am near the end of the first question about integral calculus, where we are asked to calculate the area under a curve represented by a long algebraic equation, I am not able to complete the answer. Something appears to be missing. I look across the aisle at Suraj. He is busily writing away. But, as he is writing, he looks at his left hand every now and then. It seems he is looking at something and copying it down. Oh my God. I realize that he did not wash his hands; he still has formulas written on it. This little diversion clears my mind, and I get my head down and quickly write down the answer to the question I am stuck at. As I complete the answer to the question, I hear a buzzing sound. The fly, similar to the one I saw last night, is trying to enter my right ear. I suddenly jerk my head and bring my right hand up to ward it away. As I am completing the maneuver, I see the invigilator leisurely walking down the aisle between the rows of desks Suraj and I are sitting on. At this time, Suraj is looking down and is busy writing, and, every now and then, is looking at his left hand. He has no inkling that the invigilator is coming ever closer to us; and if he sees Suraj looking at his left hand while writing, he would know that Suraj is copying something from his hand. I only have a few seconds to react. I get up from my desk and walk towards the teacher. As I am walking, I have no idea what I am going to say. But even the act of my getting up serves its purpose; Suraj looks up and puts his left hand under the desk.

In the meantime, I am face to face with he teacher, and I say, "Sir, I am thirsty."

"I will ask the peon to bring you some water," the invigilator replies and walks back.

Suraj looks at me, smiles, and we both get back to writing. The fly flies past my right ear, buzzing; it is our Good Luck Fly.

Precisely at 1:00 P.M., the bell rings. "The time is over. Please put your pens down," the invigilator announces. He goes from one desk to the other collecting the answer books. As all the answer books have been collected, the students gather in groups to discuss the questions, answers and how they performed. After a few minutes of comparing notes, Suraj and I move out of the building on our way to our homes. On our way back, we essentially retrace our steps. As we are walking, I grab Suraj's left hand to see if he had washed his hands off the cheat stuff or not. His hands appear clean.

"Suraj," I ask, "Your hands are clean. But when I saw you in the exam room, you were looking at your left hand while you were writing."

He looks at me with a smile and says, "Yes, I was."

I ask, "But, why? You have nothing written on your hands."

He replies, "I had spent so much time writing the equations on my hand and looked at them so many times that even after washing it off, I was able to sense what was written on my hand."

I say, "Well, this is really amazing. Maybe I should also try this technique. I don't think it is cheating as long as we wash it off before the exam starts."

Over the course of the rest of the four exams, both Suraj and I have perfected the art of *"palm reading"*—as we begin to call this technique. We would write down the salient points, that we thought will be useful to have handy in a particular exam, on our palms in washable ink with a pen with a sharp nib. As we experiment, we discover that the trick lies in the use of a sharp nib. We come to the conclusion that, even after washing off the ink, the skin of the palm remembers the layout of what was drawn on it and somehow conveys it to the brain.

• •

After the exams are over, Suraj forgets all about it. But I—having been endowed with and interested in the art and science of the extra sensory ideas—decide to pursue this idea of 'skin with memory' a little further. I am fascinated with the idea that skin has memory. Without discussing it any further with Suraj, I start to experiment with this idea. I am wondering: *Is it just the skin of the palm, or is it the skin all over the body that has the property to remember what is written on it?* Instead of just the palms, I start to experiment with writing on my arms using fictitious figures and words and combinations, thereof, to make it more complicated to remember. The result is the same. I find that the skin of the arms has the same ability to remember as the palms. I decide to name the technique, *skin reading*, instead of *palm reading* so that it is not confused with the traditional palm reading to tell the future. One day, I give a demonstration of my newly acquired skill to Mummyji and Daddyji.

They both look at each other and speak at the same time, "Vikram, we hope you have not been using this technique in your exams."

At first, I decide to deny. But then I notice the picture of Lord Krishna, the Lord Master of the Hindu religion, hanging on the wall; his two eyes looking at me. *Why unnecessarily commit a sin by telling a lie;* I am thinking.

Finally, I reply, "Yes. I used this technique in the exams also, but we used to wash off our hands clean before the start of the exam."

They appear satisfied.

• •

There is about a month before my exam results are to be announced. I am busy filling out applications for admissions to various colleges and universities. But in-between, to keep myself occupied, I start doing some further research in *skin reading*. Gradually, I begin to realize that our skin is more than just a covering for our flesh and bones. In addition to ears, eyes, tongue and nose, it is one of the five sensory organs. It gives us the sense of touch; a perception that is transmitted to the brain, which is then recorded for present and future reference. By following this reasoning, I conclude that it may just be possible to use our skin to transfer information from the skin of one person to that of another person and then to the brain—the skin acting as a conduit to transfer information from one brain to the other. Therefore, theoretically, it may be possible for one man to shake hands with another man, and, with proper technique, transfer thoughts to the other person's brain. I know that Swamiji has developed a technique of Long Range Brain Wave Transmission. If transmission of brain waves at long distance is possible, then it must be possible to transfer brain waves by touch—in fact, it may even be easier. I start daydreaming about this phenomenon. It has become an obsession with me to watch people shake hands or hold hands and wonder about what thoughts are flowing between them. I decide to name the new technique *Handshake*.

The publication of the results of the Higher Secondary examinations is a major yearly event. As the day draws near, most students get anxious and try to find the result before it is officially published; they try and approach a friend or a relative who may be, even remotely, connected to either the Board of Education or a newspaper. A neighbour, four houses down from us, works with a newspaper. There are only two days left in the exam results to be published. I am standing outside our house with my friend, Suraj, discussing the finer points of *Handshake*.

He is very excited to hear that a technique he initiated has been developed into something that may, one day, revolutionize communication between people. But he seems to have a rather interesting use for the technique of *Handshake*.

After listening to me, and giving it some thought, he whispers in my ear, "Vikram *yaar,* you have hit upon a fantastic idea for hooking girls. Just imagine the possibilities—planting thoughts by touch. I think instead of calling your idea the *Handshake* you should just call it the *Hook*."

We break out into laughter saying, "I think we are a bunch of *Sheikh Chillies,* always building castles in the air." Sheikh Chillies are people who build castles in the air.

As we are recovering from our silly laughter, somebody passing by stops and says, referring to the exam results that are due in two days time, "Boys, two more days left. It will all be out in the open for all to see. Don't laugh too much, as the saying goes, or you may have to cry an equal amount,"

Both Suraj and I turn around to look—and lo and behold, it is the *newspaper-wala* uncleji.

As soon as I see him, I immediately realize his usefulness in finding our exam result ahead of time.

We both give him broad smiles and say, "Uncleji, have the Board sent the results to the newspapers yet?"

He looks at us with a naughty smile, and replies, "You boys know very well that I am not allowed to say anything about it."

In the meantime, Suraj whispers to me, "Hook Hook Hook..."

"Hook what?" I say to him. And then, suddenly, I realize that he means that I should try out the technique of *Hook or handshake.*

I move forward towards uncle *newpaperwala,* and he moves towards me, and, to my utter surprise, extends his hand. I extend my hand and the rest is history. What happens next can be compared to the moment described in the literature when Alexander Graham Bell, the inventor of the telephone, said: "Mr. Watson, come here, I want to see you." These famous words started the age of communication by wire. What happened between me and *newspapewala* uncleji starts the age of communication by touch.

We both hold each other's hand in the shake position for a whole minute, uncleji shaking it and wishing us the best of luck, and I smiling at him and looking into his eyes and sending him a request by thought to get us our exam results ahead of the publication in the newspapers.

As we disengage our hands, he says to my utter surprise, "I will see what I can do," and he walks away.

The next day, on his way to his morning walk, he comes into our verandah and gives me a piece of paper with two numbers on it, 569 and 558—presumably, Suraj's and my exam marks. I am absolutely elated; this is the dawn of the age of communication by touch.

As I place the piece of paper on the table, a fly comes buzzing around and sits down on it—my Good Luck Fly.

The night before the exam the results are to be published, Suraj and I are up late at night chatting away to mask our anxiety. In spite of the fact that *newspaperwala* uncleji has given us our marks, we are not sure if they are real, or he is just pulling our leg. We are sitting in our verandah chatting until early morning. At about 3:00 A.M., we hear the first newspaper boy riding his bicycle down our street shouting, "Higher Secondary results are out. Come out and get your newspaper."

As we are getting up, a rolled–up, bundled newspaper, tied with a piece of string, lands in our verandah—thrown by our regular news paperboy. We hurriedly cut the string and open the newspaper, running our fingers down to our roll numbers and our names to look up our marks. The marks *newpaperwala* uncleji had provided were correct; I scored 569 and Suraj 558. We are placed in the top twenty in the whole of Delhi. With all the noise and excitement, Mummyji and Daddyji are also up and so is half of the neighbourhood—many of whom, being summer, sleep outside on their rooftops or on the street under the sky. By the time all the excitement is over, the first siren of the Delhi Cloth Mills announcing the start of the morning shift is sounding, lasting a whole five minutes. At the same time, the Sun's rays are beginning to find their way towards us, just hugging the curvature of the earth and causing a golden hue on the eastern sky, announcing, we hope, a golden future for us.

Suraj picks up his bicycle and goes home. Daddyji is getting ready to go to his office. My brother, Kishi, and sister, Suneeta, are getting ready for school. A flock of golden sparrows are flying a formation around our house. I go into my room and go to sleep.

There are voices. I wake up. It is Saniya's voice. I also hear Saniya's mother's voice—Rampiyari, our sweepress. They are talking to Mummyji. I get up and go out. There she is, my soul mate of seven lives, standing, smiling and looking at me. Is it real or a dream? Saniya walks towards me and gives me a chocolate bar and a soft pat on my right arm, and says, "Congrats, Vikram. My Gosh... such high marks."

"Thank you." I say, blushing.

Mummyji is making a face, in her usual way, expressing displeasure at her son being touched by the daughter of an untouchable. When Saniya and her mother leave, Mummyji says, "Come on Vikram, go take a bath. Right now."

I look at her defiantly and walk away and out of the house. And I keep walking until I reach, my friend, Suraj's home.

Suraj's mother is standing in the street distributing sweets to the neighbours in celebration of Suraj passing the Higher Secondary examinations. There is a carnival atmosphere. As soon as Suraj sees me, he comes running and we embrace and pat each other on our respective backs. As I hear people talk to each other, I find out that Suraj has become the most educated man on his street. One man standing around says, "Suraj, now you can add HSP after your name." Meaning: **H**igher **S**econdary **P**ass."

As the excitement subsides and Suraj and I are sitting on the foot steps of his house, I tell him about Saniya coming to my house to congratulate me and my mother's reaction.

I ask, "Suraj, what am I going to do?"

He, as usual, clears his throat, gives the matter careful consideration and then does not say anything, while I am looking at him in anticipation. He is rubbing his chin trying to churn out some words of wisdom. Finally, he says, "I have been thinking. You know that technique we devised; you named it *Handshake,* and I named it *Hook.* Why don't you try it on your mother to change her mind about Saniya?"

I look at him and say nothing. I am thinking: *Would I like to manipulate my own mother's mind? Maybe for Saniya I would. Others before me have been known to lay down their lives for Love. Indian movies and Shakespeare's plays are full of such stories.*

27

TEMPLES OF SCIENCE & TECHNOLOGY

We are sitting in the verandah. I am sitting idle, contemplating my future, and Daddyji is reading the newspaper. "Vikram, see this," Daddyji says while reading, "Scientists and technologists will be the new Pundits of India. It is a good thing you followed the science stream."

During the days that I was preparing for my Higher Secondary School examinations, the founding fathers of India were passing the historic Scientific Policy Resolution on March 4, 1958. The Resolution promises honoured positions to scientists. Science is going to be fostered and promoted by all appropriate means. Science is hailed as humankind's greatest enterprise, promising to bridge the gap between India and the developed nations.

India has temples at every street corner giving opportunity to one and all to worship their favourite God. The modern God is going to be Science and Technology; the universities, colleges and research institutes will be the new temples and scientists and technologists the new high priests.

Will I be a scientist or a technologist? I really do not know the difference. "Science is an intellectual activity designed to discover information about the universe around us, and technology is the practical application of scientific discoveries." Swamiji says; he is visiting us, one day, after opening a new Ashram in Delhi.

Daddyji adds, "Vikram, with your marks, you will be able to get admission in any college of your choice in Delhi."

While we are discussing my future in science, I am itching to tell Swamiji about the new technique of *Handshake* that I have developed. But I know that Daddyji is not in favour of my getting involved in these kinds of activities.

Swamiji asks me, "Vikram, tell me. Now that you are free of the examinations, have you had time to devote to some new ideas about the extra sensory world?"

I can sense that Daddyji does not like Swamiji enticing me into the world of communication by thought.

I am quiet for a while with a smile on my face. This tells Swamiji that there *is* something I want to say, but I am holding back.

He looks at Daddyji and says, "Come on Surinder, let the boy talk. He is very talented. You should not hold him back. He has shown you what he can do, having scored such high marks. He has a very rare talent that, if nurtured, will one day become an asset to India and the whole world. I can tell you that, one day, *time* will dance on his finger tips. Surinder, you grew up in the world of Shakespeare and Chaucer; let Vikram grow up in the world of Einstein and Fermi. You derived pleasure from the sonnets of Wordsworth; let Vikram study Theory of Relativity and Quantum Mechanics. " And then he looks at me and says, "Vikram, tell us, what would you really want to do in life? Once you know that, then only, we can determine what type of science subjects you should be selecting."

I reply, "Ever since I have learned the fact that we, and all things around us, are made of atoms; I have become a fan of atoms. I strongly believe that everything in the world around us is connected through atoms. I want to discover this connection and its connection to our mind."

Swamiji looks at Daddyji and then at me and says, "I am very happy to hear what Vikram has just said. Well, I have a suggestion. Vikram, you should join the Thomason College at Roorkee. One of my friends, Prof. Suresh Srivastava, is the head of the department of Physics. We were at Cambridge together. He is brilliant in pure physics and also has been working with our Ashram in the study of Vedas and their relevance to modern science. Vikram, you may or may not know this; we are in the process of opening a new Ashram near Haridwar. If you study at Roorkee, it will be only an hour bus ride to our new Ashram."

I reply, "Swamiji, Thomason College is now known as University of Roorkee."

He says, "Well, well… I see that you have been doing your homework. I learned something new today. I did not know about the change in name."

I continue, "Swamiji, to be admitted to Roorkee, I have to appear in an entrance examination also. And before that, I have to complete a one year of pre-engineering course or complete my B.Sc."

While Daddyji is looking on with interest, Swamiji says, "Vikram, you seem to be well informed."

"But Swamiji, there is one problem. My grandfather wants me to become a civil engineer, and I want to be a physicist," I say.

Swamiji replies, "At Roorkee, you can study civil engineering and study physics at the same time. Also, as an added bonus, you will be pleased to know that I am shifting my headquarters to the new Ashram near Haridwar."

"Why is that?" I ask.

Swamiji replies, "That way it is easy for me to travel to various ashrams around India."

Later, I discovered that the main reason was that they were asked by the Intelligence Bureau to move all the research activities to Haridwar due to continual tension on the border with Pakistan. Also, there are plans to send senior civil servants to the Ashram for training in meditation; the location at Haridwar would be more convenient.

• •

After a good deal of deliberations, I join the Pre-Engineering class at the Delhi Polytechnic in the Kashmiri Gate area in the eastern part of Delhi. I select Physics, Chemistry and Mathematics as the main subjects. The choice of study of languages is between Hindi, English literature and Sanskrit; I select Sanskrit to open an unlimited storehouse of knowledge—the Hindu scriptures. I immerse myself headlong into my studies.

Soon after Mummyji finds out about my plan to study at University of Roorkee, her attitude towards me changes. She concludes that as soon as I move to Roorkee, in about a year's time, I will be away from Delhi, and that will be the end of my attachment to Saniya. But none of us have anticipated what was about to happen. As a wise man has said, "*the universe will unfold as it should.*" And unfold it does. I begin to feel that true love is a supernatural force that folds up the obstacles in its way and unfolds new ways ahead. It is sometime in the end January 1959, as I am preparing for the entrance exam for University of Roorkee, that I realize the unfolding of a new path in my destiny. The bus from Delhi to Roorkee goes via the city of Meerut; this is where Saniya's father, Mr. Norman Douglas, lives. But I decide to keep this fact a secret, for if Mummyji finds out; she will surely want to fold up the whole plan. I start to dream about meeting Saniya in Meerut whenever she would be visiting her father, and she, eventually, joining the University of Roorkee to continue her studies.

"Vikram, I think we should visit Roorkee to see the university and the facilities," Daddyji says one day. The entrance examinations for Roorkee are in April. Sometime in the middle of March, just after the festival of Holi, and after finishing my pre-engineering examinations at the Delhi Polytechnic, we decide to take a trip, by car, to Roorkee. Daddyji obtains a letter of introduction from Swamiji for, his friend, Prof. Srivastava.

On the morning of the day of departure, we are up early, and the car is loaded by 9:00 A.M., and we are on our way. Our family members, the car driver, two steel trunks and two holdalls, containing our bedding, appear to be straining the 14 horsepower engine of our small car. But slowly the car picks up speed, and, in about an hour, we reach Modinagar. We find a small restaurant and settle down for breakfast of *Allo Puri and Lassi*.

After breakfast, we move towards our next stop, Meerut. This is the city of interest to me. As we are driving, I start to daydream about how one day, when I start my studies at Roorkee, I will be coming down to meet Saniya during her visits to her father. The cool breeze blowing through the open window beside me puts me to sleep.

The car suddenly comes to a stop, and Daddyji is shouting at the driver, "What is that noise?"

"Sahib, we have a punctured tire."

I am shaken out of my dream, and I am thinking: *Oh, there we go again—another puncture. I have seen a few before in my short life of 17 years.*

Mummyji is very disturbed.

She puts on her usual look of anxiety and utters under her breath, "This is not a good omen,"

Daddyji gives her a stern look and says, "Keep quiet, Kamla."

Daddyji and our driver get out of the car to inspect the damage. "You all keep sitting in the car," he says.

After a while, I realize that we are in Meerut. Well, my curiosity knows no bounds. The driver rounds up a few labourers to help him push the car towards the sidewalk. He gets the spare tire and the jack out of the dickey of the car and asks us all to get out. Mummyji, Suneeta, Kishi and I move to the sidewalk, while the driver starts the procedure for changing the tire, with Daddyji looking on. I, a five foot eleven inches tall able bodied youngman, kind of feel useless standing around watching the driver change the tire.

"Mummyji, I am going for a walk," I say and start to walk a little bit away from the car. After about 100 yards, a residential area starts with large bungalows on large plots of land and entrance gates with *chawkidars* for security. Each of them has a name plate on the gatepost. I walk past one of them, read the name and move on to the second one; and when I read the name, I stop in my tracks. The name on the plate is: Norman Douglas M.A. This is the name of my girlfriend Saniya's father. I look around and pinch myself; just to make sure that I am not dreaming.

I am thinking: *If Mummyji finds out… it will be the end my dream of studying at Roorkee.*

As I look towards the car, I see Kishi and Suneeta walking towards me. I immediately act to maintain the status quo. I start to walk back towards the car and meet them halfway and walk back to the car with them. Inside me, I am itching to see Saniya and tell her: I saw your father's house.

Is it a coincident or an incident of universe unfolding as it should? I am thinking.

The tire is fixed, and we are on our way. Mummyji'a anxiety has now gone to an even higher level.

"What if we have another puncture? We have no spare tire now," she says with anxiety lines etched on her forehead.

Daddyji looks back towards her and says, "Kamla, for once, wish something good."

But she does not let go of her insistence that we get the damaged tire repaired. In the end, Daddyji has to give in, and we stop at a petrol station with a car repair shop and get the tire fixed. As the mechanic is working on the tire, it reminds me of the day, in 1948, when Daddyji's bicycle tire got punctured.

I am thinking: *Three times …three times in my life our tires have got punctured; what is the significance of our tires getting punctured so frequently. Is it that our luck is prone to puncture, or there are too many nails on the roads?*

As the big tube of the car tire is inflated by the mechanic, everybody in our family has smiles on their faces and inflated moods.

We are on our way to the final leg of our trip. Instead of the estimated arrival time of 2:00 P.M., we arrive at Prof. Srivastava's house at 3:30 P.M. The driver beeps the car horn three times to announce our arrival. As we are getting out of the car, a man comes out, greets us, and says, "I am Srivastava, welcome to Roorkee."

Daddyji moves forward to shake hands with him. Prof. Srivastava had already received a letter from Swamiji about the day and time of our arrival.

"Sorry, we are late; we had a punctured tire," Daddyji tells him.

"We were expecting you at around 2:00 P.M.; but, nevertheless, this is not bad by Indian standards." And they both laugh and Prof Srivastava contin- ues, "You see, Surinder, time is a very relative thing as the famous scientist of our century, Albert Einstein, has said. You have heard of Einstein, have you not?"

Daddyji replies sounding apologetic, "I have heard of Einstein, but I have very little knowledge of science. My son, Vikram, is studying science."

Prof. Srivastava asks me, "Vikram, have you started studying the Theory of Relativity in college yet?"

"Yes sir." I reply.

"In that case you must have heard of Einstein's simple explanation of what relativity is," Prof. Srivastava asks with a naughty smile.

I reply, "You mean about the girl and the hot stove?"

"Yes, yes. That is the one. Tell your father about it."

I say, "If you put your hand on a hot stove for a minute, it seems like an hour. Sit with a pretty girl for an hour, and it seems like a minute. That is relativity."

Daddyji, not to be out done because of his little knowledge of science, says, "So, Prof. Srivastava, while you were waiting for us, did you have your hand on a pretty girl, or you were sitting on the stove?"

At first, Prof. Srivastava did not quite get the pun that Daddyji has thrown at him by transposing the words in the famous quote. But as he realizes, he says, "Oh, you naughty man, you got the better of me." And they start another round of laughter.

In the meantime, Mrs. Srivastava also comes out and asks as she overhears the last words, "Who was sitting with a pretty girl?"

Prof. Srivastava introduces us all to her and says, "Oh, we were talking about the old theory of relativity."

After the niceties are done with, we move into the drawing room of the house. Mummyji is in conversation with Mrs. Srivastava, and Daddyji is talking to the Prof. and keeps addressing him as Prof. Srivastava.

"Come on, Surinder, you don't have to be this formal with me. Call me Sid. My full name is Sidhartha. When I was studying at Cambridge, I had a hard time with my first name, so I shortened it to Sid. Oh, for your information, I have made arrangements at the university guest house for your stay tonight. We will have an early dinner, and you can retire to the guest house after that. Tomorrow, I will give you a guided tour of the university."

After a while, as we are finishing tea, there are three beeps of a car horn. Prof. Srivastava gets up to go outside saying, "It must be Swamiji."

We are all surprised to hear that Swamiji is also coming. As they walk in, we all stand up and greet Swamiji, and we are even more surprised to find that Daddyji's boss, Hari Nautiyal, has also arrived with Swamiji.

Everybody is talking with everybody else. There are new introductions being made and hellos and howareyous being exchanged. I am just standing and looking. Eventually, the menfolk settle down in the drawing room and the womenfolk move out towards the kitchen and the dining area. I am neither here nor there; I just stand in a corner putting on a polite smile and listening and just thinking. There is a bookcase in the corner of the drawing room. I start to look at the books. I am surprised that, in the home of a physicist, there are books about Hindu Scriptures, psychology and medicine.

During an interlude in the multitude of conversations going on, Hari Nautiyal notices me standing in the corner just listening to the adults talking. He signals to me to come and sit beside him on the sofa. Although three people are already sitting on the sofa, he moves over, making others squeeze to their left and makes a small seat for me. I have seen him before once or twice but never had a chance to talk to him except for a *Namaste* greeting.

As soon as I sit down, he whispers in my ear while others are carrying on their conversation. He says, "Vikram, we are very proud of you. Swamiji tells me you did very well in your Higher Secondary exams. I am not sure if you know it or not; we have a scholarship program for the children of the employees of Nautiyal Industries. This year we have decided to award the scholarship to you. It will pay for all your expenses for as long as you study at a university in India. If you are selected for admission to a foreign university for further studies, all your expenses will be covered by the scholarship also."

I am so overwhelmed by what he has told me that all I can say is, "Thank you, sir."

After dinner, we go to the guest house, and Swamiji and Hari Nautiyal go back to the Haridwar Ashram.

The next day, after a brief tour of the university, we are also supposed to visit the Haridwar Ashram.

As soon as we reach the guest house, I tell Mummyji and Daddyji about what Hari Nautiyal had told me about the scholarship.

Daddyji says, "Well done, Vikram. The scholarship program is under my department, but I had asked Hari Nautiyal to decide; otherwise, it would have been a conflict of interest on my part to award the scholarship to my own son."

Mummyji gives me a hug and a kiss on both my cheeks and says, "My Vikram is the best in the world."

I wish another person was with us—Saniya.

• •

The rest of the family is fast asleep in no time, being tired from the journey. I have a hard time falling asleep. I keep thinking of how my future is unfolding beyond what I could have imagined. What is causing this? Why is this happening? As these thoughts are going through my mind, I decide to send a sub-conscious thought message to Saniya conveying the news about my scholarship and my wish that I want her with me. I think of the latitude and longitude of Delhi and the message is delivered instantly. Although, I have learned in the physics classes that nothing happens instantly; Einstein's Theory of Relativity postulates that nothing can travel faster than the speed of light. But in the case of Saniya and me, we are one; there is no distance to travel—hence the instant transmission of the message.

Next morning, we are all ready for the guided tour of the university. Prof. Srivastava arrives bright and early. After breakfast, we all squeeze into our car, leaving our car driver behind, and start the tour with a visit to the oldest temple of technology in India, and one of the oldest in the world—the Main Building of, the erstwhile, Thomason College of Civil Engineering. We leave the car on the road and have a leisurely walk down the walkway that bisects the lush green north lawn and lines up with the north door of the building. Standing about 500 feet away, we are able to have a full view of the long white magnificent building with a high dome in the centre.

"This is one of the finest examples of Renaissance Architecture," Prof. Srivastava tells us, "and you will be surprised to know that it was not designed by an architect, but it was designed by a junior infantry officer, Lieutenant Price, in 1852."

As we enter the Main Building, after a brief walk through the north entrance, we are standing under a high dome. There is pin-drop silence. Prof. Srivastava is talking or rather talking in whispers. I am looking up at the dome, spellbound. I am having a strange feeling. Everything is crystal clear. There are no doubts. I feel a strange sense of well being as if this is where I belong; I seem to have arrived. My sixth sense is active. There is a sense of anticipation as if something is about to happen. I am able to read all thoughts around me. I move towards Kishi and Suneeta who are standing near me looking up at the dome, and I sense what they are about to do. Then there is a scream and an echo from the dome, and then another scream, and the two echoes crossing each other; Kishi and Suneeta are playing with the echoes. Fortunately, being a Sunday, very few people are in the building.

As the screams and echoes are reverberating, I look up and see two figures, a male and a female, walking towards us at a distance in the corridor. There is something very familiar in the gate of the female figure. It couldn't be, I am thinking. How can she be here? She is in Delhi. As the figures draw near, I can discern that the female figure is Saniya, and the male figure is white and tall and walking with a purposeful gate. While I am trying to de-puzzle my mind, there is no doubt left.

She is standing in front of me with a mysterious smile, dressed in a pink skirt and blouse, and says, "Surprise! It is me, Saniya. Vikram, you are looking at me as if I am an apparition. "And then she turns and says, "Meet my father, Mr. Norman Douglas."

In the meantime, Mummyji, Daddyji and Prof. Srivastava walk over to where we are standing.

Prof. Srivastava extends his hand and says, "Mr. Douglas, Saniya, how good to see you. What brings you here?" He then turns around and introduces us all to one another. Mummyji immediately grasps the situation, having seen Saniya many times. Daddyji, on the other hand, is somewhat confused and looks at Mummyji, and she mumbles something to him, and he nods and smiles.

Prof Srivastava looks at Daddyji and says, "I have known Mr. Douglas and his family for a long time; I am originally from Meerut. They live very near where we used to live."

Mr. Douglas says, "You know, Saniya suddenly came from Delhi by bus this morning saying that she wants to go to Roorkee to meet a friend. So here we are. On the way, while we were driving, she told me all about Vikram and his family."

As much as I am happy to see Saniya, my main concern is Mummyji. How would she react to Saniya and her father? I am afraid of any awkward situation developing.

After seeing the main building, we all decide to do a walking tour of the rest of the campus. The elders are walking in the front, and Saniya, Kishi, Suneeta and I are trailing behind.

"Saniya, how did you decide to come here?"

"Just like that; this is not the first time I have come to Roorkee. We have family friends here. Who knows, one day, I may get admission here."

After the walking tour, Prof. Srivastava invites everybody to have lunch at the guest house. During lunch, Daddyji and Mr. Douglas have very animated conversations. Daddyji has always felt very at home with Englishmen; now that he sees his own son getting involved with an Anglo-Indian girl, he seems to be taking even more interest. During the course of conversations, it comes out that Mr. Douglas owns large tracts of farmland around Meerut, Roorkee and Gurgaon, and also owns apple orchards in Simla, and he is one of the biggest landlords in the state of Uttar Pradesh. When they are talking about it, I notice Mummyji listening to Mr. Douglas intently. I can sense that the magnetism of the wealth of Saniya's father is folding up the prejudices in her mind against Saniya—the daughter of, Rampiyari, our untouchable sweepress.

After looking at the view of the Himalayas to the north, the immaculate and lush grounds, the students' club, the dining areas, the civil, mechanical and electrical engineering departments and the students' hostels, we are ready to go on to the next leg of our journey; but my journey has just begun. I have decided that this is the temple of science and technology where I will be praying.

As we are walking to the car, Prof. Srivastava looks at me with a smile and asks jokingly, "Vikram, sir. Did you like our institution? Will your highness grace us with your presence as a student in this august institution? Have we measured up to your expectations?"

I smile and reply with respect and humility, "Professor, sir, if you honour me with admission to this temple of technology, I shall serve as a disciple of, *Saraswati,* the Goddess of knowledge, for as long as it takes to complete my education."

With this pleasant exchange, we thank Prof. Srivastava, and say goodbye to Saniya and her father and drive away to the Haridwar Ashram.

As we are driving, I keep thinking about what is it that is making things happen the way I am wishing. The incident about Saniya appearing at the university building is the one that really convinces me that I am doing something that needs to be investigated further. I had some Sixth Sense before, but after arrival at Roorkee it appears to have been enhanced. Is it because of the location of Roorkee being near Haridwar, the spiritual centre of the Hindus? In that case, my Sixth Sense should enhance even more at the Ashram which is closer to Haridwar. Or is it the dome that we were standing under at the main building? I am not sure. Or is it all an illusion? Maybe Saniya never came, and my senses just played a trick on my consciousness. I keep coming back to the saying: *The universe will unfold as it should.* As the breeze is blowing at my face through the open window of the car, I keep going over the phrase, *unfolding of the universe.* What does it mean? *Is the universe in a folded state and then unfolds to reveal the happenings?*

Our car slows down and takes a right turn towards Kankhal, a small town about three miles south of Haridwar. After another right turn onto an unpaved road, we drive for a few minutes, and the car comes to a stop in front of a large wooden gate. Daddyji gets out of the car and walks to the gate. A watchman comes out, has a brief word with him and opens the gate. Our car drives in.

The buildings are nearly complete, but some construction work is still going on. There is one car and one jeep parked in front of one of the buildings. As we are all getting out of our car, Swamiji comes out of one of the buildings and walks towards us.

"Welcome to Haridwar Ashram," he says joining his hands in *Namaste*.

All of us return the greeting in our own way. Daddyji, Mummyji and I return the greeting by *Namaste,* while Suneeta and Kishi tag behind the three of us giving a shy smile.

"Let me show you around," Swamiji says, as we all walk along him, "Let me first tell you about the geography of this place. Our latitude and longitude is approximately 30° N and 78° E. You know, we are only about three miles from Haridwar and practically in Kankhal, the abode of the sages from time immemorial. The Sacred Ganga River is just over there; our land abuts the banks of the river. The famed Gurukul Kangri School, imparting education under the ancient Hindu and Vedic school system, is not too far from here."

He then takes us around and shows us the hostel for 40 people, the Yoga Hall, the kitchen and dining hall, and the administration office. Everything is like a five star hotel. The guest rooms have air conditioners and refrigerators. Another large building is still under construction; we are told it is the laboratory building. It is obvious that the Ashram is not built for common disciples.

After the tour, he leads us all to the centre of the circular central grass courtyard. There is a circular temple building with the statue of *Saraswati,* the Goddess of knowledge and science. And there is a hemispherical structure, made of wood, under construction. He explains, "This location is the best suited for the type of research we are going to be engaged in. This area has the highest concentration of holy people in the world. Morning and evening, there are mass meditations and prayers; therefore, the whole space time continuum is conducive to esoteric ideas." He then turns towards me with a mysterious smile and says, "Vikram, you are good with numbers. Tell me what is the latitude and longitude of this place? I just mentioned it a little while back."

I reply after a little bit of thinking, "I think you said 30° north and 78° degrees east."

Swamiji says, "Good. What is the total of the two numbers?"

Before I could reply, my little sister, Suneeta, says, "108."

Swamiji looks at her and says, "Well, we have another little genius here. All right, then, tell us what is special about 108?"

Suneeta replies, "It is a sacred number in Hinduism. Traditionally, *Malas,* or rosaries of prayer beads, have 108 beads."

Swamiji says with a mystical smile, "Very good. Actually there are 109 beads; the 109th bead is known as the *Meru* bead, the head, which is used as a guide. As you probably know that the *Gayatri Mantra* and all mantras for that matter are repeated 108 times. Also, the average distance between the sun and the earth is about 108 times the diameter of the sun. The most important fact is that there are 108 *Upanishads*, our Vedic texts. If you have interest in mathematics, I can tell you that 108 is a hyper factorial of 3, it is a Tetranacci number, and in Euclidean space the interior angles of pentagon measure 108 degrees."

I ask, "Swamiji, which is the exact point around here whose latitude and longitude is 30° north and 78° east?"

He replies, "I think it is a little north of here, and it is believed that it is on the western bank of the revered *Har ki Pauri ghat* at the banks of the Ganga Canal at Haridwar. And talking about that, I want to remind you that we are all going to visit the *Har ki Pauri* in the evening. So get some rest."

It appears that a true temple of science and technology is taking shape where science and spirituality will interact, and I am determined to be an integral part of it.

As we are walking towards the hostel, another car comes in through the gate. Hari Nautiyal comes out and walks towards us. Pleasantries are exchanged, and we all go to our rooms for a little rest.

After a little while, Daddyji gets up and goes to a meeting with Hari Nautiyal and Swamiji.

There are only three of them in the room. Hari Nautiyal asks, "How are things going on with construction?"

Swamiji replies, "You know how it is in construction. Everyday there is a new problem, but overall we have made a lot of progress in one year. I think we should be done with everything in another three to four months."

Hari Nautiyal tells them, "A few days back, I received a letter from America in which Jake Kreiger writes that the visit of the American President Eisenhower has been set for later this year from December 9 to the 14th. This will be the first visit of an American President to India. Jake and a few other members of the *Robus 10* Group will also be visiting at the same time; not as part of the presidential party but as private visitors. At the same time, a number of American businessmen and reporters will also be visiting. I would like to show this place and the research we are carrying out, to the visitors from America. This will be a great opportunity to win friends in America. There is still a lot of time; we can talk about it again. I just wanted to alert you. Surinder, when we go back to Delhi, you should manage all the arrangements."

Swamiji asks, "How is the magazine, LESTWEFORGET, doing? Are you making money?"

Hari Nautiyal replies, "The magazine is not a money making venture. The purpose of owning magazines and newspapers is to influence public policy and gain stature in public life, and I think, we are beginning to do that. As you know, the Mission Statement of the Civics department of our company is to spend money in the service of the citizens of India and not make money. You know, the ashrams we are building, the research we are doing in meditation and the scriptures, is not to make money but to benefit India. Now, you may ask: why is a private company doing this and not the government? The governments everywhere are hamstrung by politics of the day. It has to please many masters. As you know, the Prime Minister of a country or, even for that matter, the President of America cannot do what he wants; there is the Parliament to answer to, and the newspapers and the public opinion to contend with. This is where the private organizations like ours help to shape public policy."

There is silence for a while after this detailed policy statement by Hari Nautiyal.

After discussing some more administrative matters, the meeting is adjourned.

In the evening, we drive to the *Har Ki Pauri*. As soon as we park our car, three or four Pundits in saffron robes–known as *Pandas*–descend upon us, asking, "What is your *gotra* or the root of the family name? Which part of the country your ancestors come from?"

Swamiji and Hari Nautiyal are in another car and park behind us. As soon as they see the *Pandas* storming us, Swamiji says, "Good luck. See you later." And they walk away.

I had heard of *Pandas* keeping records of the genealogy of people of all castes and creeds for the last many generations. It is a centuries old tradition that is passed on from one generation of the families of *Pandas* to the next.

Daddyji has obviously been here before and knows how to deal with them. He shouts over the voices of the *Pandas,* "We are from district Jhelum; our family name is Mehra." In no time we are led to a small side street. We all follow and are led into a small house with a courtyard. Another *Panda* is sitting there on a *charpoy.* He gets up and asks the same question again, and Daddyji gives him the same information about our family. He then leads us to a small room with shelves on all four walls up to the ceiling. There are hundreds of *pothies* or registers, folded up and bound in red cloth binding, and stacked neatly one on top of the other with code numbers written on their splines. He looks up the codes, gets up on a small step ladder and takes out the appropriate *pothy* or register and brings it down.

We all sit around him as he unfolds the four foot long register on a long wooden platform bed covered with a saffron coloured cloth. He sits down on the bed, crosses his legs, joins his hands in *Namaste* pose and recites a few mantras in Sanskrit and says, "My respected clients, today you will meet some of your ancestors; not in person but through the words they wrote especially for you many a year ago. So please close your eyes and say *Om Tat Sat* three times."

As the Panda is saying all this, my sixth sense is at its sharpest. I can sense the sincerity with which the *Panda* is performing the rites. There is a slight tremor in my body after listening to what he has just said about meeting our ancestors. There is a sense of anticipation. The register is about eight inches wide, three inches thick and four feet long, folded twice to fit the shelves. He opens it and turns some pages and stops. He reads aloud some passages and names from the pages and looks up at Daddyji and asks, "Do you recognize the names?"

Daddyji says, "No."

"Tell me the name of your father and grandfather," he asks Daddyji.
Daddyji replies, "My father's name is Shri Yodh Raj Mehra, and my grandfather's name was Shri Damodar Dass Mehra."

He turns a few more pages and says with a smile and looking over his half moon glasses, "My respected client, I think we now have the right pages."

He then turns the register over to Daddyji to read. Daddyji quickly reads through the words with his finger moving from one line to the other. I move closer to Daddyji to have a glimpse. I find that the writing is in *Urdu* script, which I cannot read. The only thing I recognize are a few dates and numbers. As Daddyji is reading, his expressions are changing, as he runs his fingers down the lines. He mutters, "A secret?"

"Daddyji let us also read, please," I plead with him.
He replies, "Vikram, you will not be able to read this. It is written in Urdu."

"Then, can you please tell us what is written in it?" I reply.

"All right… all right. Let me see what I can do," he replies.

Then he is quiet for a while twisting his lips, thinking. And then, he says, "Let us not look at the past. Let us all write something for the future. He takes out a pen and writes about why we came to Haridwar, who is present, the plate number of our car and the names of his father and brothers. Next, Mummyji writes something and then my turn comes and I write: *Vikram and Saniya forever.* Fortunately, Mummyji does not see what I have written. Daddyji closes the register and hands it over to the *Panda* and says, "Let us go. It is time for evening prayers at the *Har ki Pauri*." As we are all walking out, I realize that something Daddyji read has upset him.

After the prayers, we go back to the Ashram. The next day we drive back to Delhi.

• •

As soon as we are back, I immerse myself in the reality. The entrance examination of the University of Roorkee is in another two weeks. I have hinged my whole future to passing this examination with sufficient marks to rank high enough to be admitted. I am systematically turning each stone, until no stone is left unturned.

The examination centre for the entrance exam is at the Delhi Polytechnic, where I have just completed my pre-engineering course. On the day of the examination, I am up early. After taking a bath, I make notes on my left hand with washable ink; the technique of *communication by touch,* which my friend, Suraj, and I developed a year ago, is being put to the test again. After breakfast of curd and toast—no egg or meat is permitted on the day of the examination so as not to offend any Gods and incur their wrath—I step out into the verandah and, as expected, Mummyji is standing there ready to perform the ritual of the prayer with a silver plate in hand. I quickly go through the motions and run to the bus stop to board Bus number 27 to Kashmiri Gate.

Only two percent of those who appear in the examinations are admitted. In a month's time, a letter of admission from the University of Roorkee arrives, and the die is cast.

As I have thrown my fate in the hands of, *Saraswasti,* the Goddess of knowledge and science; my friend, Suraj, has decided to place his future in the hands of, *Lakshmi,* the Goddess of commerce and wealth. He has started studying towards a commerce Degree at a college in Delhi.

Temples of science, technology, medicine and commerce are coming up everywhere. Sensing the business potential of imparting education to million of people, entrepreneurs have stepped in. Private educational institutions are sprouting everywhere. There are private institutes that train people in the art of typing, and there are, somewhat, more advanced institutes that provide tutoring to students who are planning to appear in entrance competitions for the admissions to the national engineering and medical institutions, and selection for coveted jobs in the Indian Administrative Services, the Indian Police Services and the Indian Army. The populace, in general, has realized that education is the key to the uplifting of the country.

Hari Nautiyal saw it coming in 1947; when he had said that **3E**'s—Education, English language and Ethics—will be the salvation of India. The first two E's are being pursued with vengeance, but the poor third **E**—ethics—has fallen by the wayside.

28
DISCOVERY @ ROORKEE

It is July 1959. The day of departure has arrived. All my belongings have been packed and loaded in the car. Daddyji, Mummyji, Kishi and Suneeta are all going to Roorkee to drop me off for the start of the first year of university. Daddyji is sitting on a chair about to put on his shoes. "Come here Vikram," he says, "try my shoes. Let us see if your feet are as big as mine." I take off my shoes and place my right foot into Daddyji's shoes. It comes as a surprise to us all that my foot is too big for his shoes. I take out my foot. Daddyji stands up and says, "Vikram. There is a saying that when the son's feet become as large as that of the father's, the father should stop telling the son how to run his affairs."

My grandparents are staying back. Pitaji, my grandfather, comes to me as we are all standing in the verandah waiting for the driver and our servant, Chottu, to tie up the luggage to the roof top carrier of the car.

He says, "Yes, your father is right, especially in your case. Vikram, you have done me proud. Ever since my days with the Indian Railways, it had been my desire that one of my sons would study at Roorkee and become an officer in the Indian Railways. My sons could not fulfill my dream, but you will. I am sure, one day, you will rise to be the Chairman of the Railway Board." With this little blessing, he wipes a tear and embraces me.

We all begin to take our seats in the car. My grandmother, Beyji, is standing outside. She calls me and says, "Look, Vikram, look," pointing to the clear blue sky." There they are, the golden sparrows, flying in formation around our house. "See, these are the same sparrows that flew around our house in Lahore when you were born." She never forgets Lahore. Then, she comes close to the car and plants a kiss on my forehead through the open car window; there are tears of joy and separation flowing down her cheeks.

• •

We arrive in Roorkee at about 2:00 P.M. and drive straight to the students' hostel; the name of the hostel had been sent to us by mail earlier. It takes about an hour to complete all the formalities and get me settled in my room—my home for the next year. The plan is for the rest of them to drive down to the Haridwar Ashram, stay there for the night and drive back to Delhi the next day. They are all sad to leave me behind. There are moist eyes but brave faces. Daddyji shakes hands with me and says, "Vikram, as I told you earlier in Delhi, you are a grownup now." There is a little bit of choking in his voice. It seems he is having a hard time saying what he wants to say. Finally, he gets it out, "My son. Let me tell you that this is the beginning of the end of our old relationship and the start of a new one."

"Why Daddyji? Is it because my feet have become as big as yours?" I ask while choked with tears.

He smiles and embraces me. Then there are Mummyji, Kishi and Suneeta, one by one, saying goodbye.

The car starts and moves away becoming smaller and smaller and then it is gone...... There is loud thunder and lightning, and the universe seems to be vibrating... opening the heavens for new discoveries. A downpour starts.

I walk back to the hostel building. My room is on the upper floor. As I reach the top landing of the staircase, I hear two boys talking in Punjabi. My sixth sense has come alive. As I turn around the corner, I see the two of them; they are standing in the balcony looking down. Apparently, they had watched the whole scene on the road as my family was saying goodbye to me. When they hear my foot steps, they turn around.

"You must be the only one around here whose family has come to drop him off. "See," they say mocking and pointing to lots of students arriving at the front steps of the hostel building in bicycle rickshaws on their own. They add, "You obviously belong to a rich family with a car. We hope you are not going to be missing Mummy and Daddy, are you?" And they laugh.

I feel a little embarrassed. However, I extend my hand, and we introduce ourselves, and I give each of them a *Handshake*, my technique of communication by *touch*. I look into the eyes of each one of them passing thoughts of friendship.

As I am going to be meeting hundreds of new people during the course of my stay at Roorkee, I have decided to practice and test the effectiveness of the *Handshake*. We exchange names. One of them is Gupta, and the other is Garg. As we are standing there, many of the new fellow students stop and introduce themselves by their last name only. I find this rather strange. It seems that this is the custom in the state of Uttar Pradesh. After a while, I realize that most of the students have only three or four types of last names—Gupta, Garg, Aggarwal and Mittal.

As I am standing there practicing the technique of the *Handshake*, I decide to bring a little variety in my experiment. I decide that I will give the *Friendly Handshake* to the boys with the last name of Gupta and Garg, and to the others, I will give the *Nasty Handshake*. In order to be able to discern the difference between the two, I have made the *Nasty Handshake* really obnoxious like: *you idiot your face looks like the rear end of a horse.* I practice the *Nasty Handshake* on only four boys on that day; I do not want to make too many enemies at the same time.

The dinner time starts at 7:00 P.M. The dining hall is on the south side of the campus; our hostel is located on the north side. As the time nears, the boys start walking towards the dining hall in bunches of three, four or five. Most boys are wearing white shirts and trousers; some boys are also wearing ties, while others are wearing coats and ties. I am walking with Gupta and Garg; we three have really taken to each other. Some of the others such as Mittal, Mehrotra and Jain, to whom I had given the *Nasty Handshake,* are staying away from me. As they are passing by, "Gupta says, "Hey Mehrotra, the way you are dressed, it looks like you are going for an interview."

Mehrotra replies nastily, "You boys are not properly dressed. You will not be allowed in the dining hall."

"We will see," Gupta replies.

After about a ten minute walk, we are at the front entrance to the dining hall. The entrance is very formal with high ceilings, moldings and Victorian columns; it looks very British. In reality, most of us are intimidated by the building's entrance lobby. What comes as a complete surprise, or rather a shock to us is what follows. As we are about to enter the main door of the dining hall, we come face to face with a six feet six inches tall wiry man dressed in an immaculately starched white coat and pants and a white turban, with the *Turrah* of the turban rising another foot in the air above his head. He has already stopped a number of boys. This is our first introduction to the British Traditions of this great institution, and a collision takes place between the two cultures. He looks at us and says loudly, "Sorry, sorry sahib... tie... tie... You have to wear a tie at all meals at the dining hall. In the evening, you must have a coat also."

One senior boy, who is properly dressed, looks at us nonchalantly and says, "He is the Butler. You either do what he says, or you don't eat," and he walks in. If fact, all the senior boys are going in one by one, looking at us and smiling at our ineptness.

We have to walk back to our rooms to wear a coat and a tie. Upon our return, we have to wait for the next sitting. When we enter the dining hall—being from New Delhi—the opulence does not come as too much of a surprise to me. But to my friends, Gupta and Garg from the small town of Saharanpur—waiters in white uniforms, white tablecloths, forks and knives, jugs of water on the table, neatly rolled white napkins—are a cultural shock. What follows is comical. Most of the newcomers have no idea what to do with all the paraphernalia lying in front of them on the table. One of the boys, (who shall remain nameless, as he later ended up heading one of the largest railway networks in the world) who had learned from childhood to wash his hands before taking a meal, lifts the jug of water and washes his hands right on the table on a plate, spilling the wash water on to the white tablecloth. Another takes hold of the cloth napkin and wipes perspiration from his face. The waiters, who are well-trained and used to this drama on the first day of every year, are standing aside watching with poker faces but are amused, nevertheless.

In praise of the waiters, I can say that they help us all very discreetly and without making any one of us feel small in any way. After each of us finishes dinner, a waiter brings a bowl of warm water in a bowl to rinse our hands; something that even I, with my upper middle class upbringing, had never seen before.

After dinner is over, we walk over to the students' club—another tradition left over by our erstwhile rulers. Most of us, who had played *Peethoo* with used tennis balls, and *Goollie Dunda*, come face to face with billiards tables and white uniformed markers waiting on the students bending over the edge of the green velvety tables, with cue in hand, trying to delicately hit the white ball to make it collide with the red ball and, which, in turn, is to go into the pot with a netting. Traditions ...traditions... we are told must be upheld because this is what makes this Institution great. Brilliant, rustic students from 'small town India' are immersed in the ritzy glitter of this Institution, and, by the time they finish their education here, they are ready to hob nob with the best in the world. God bless the British and Lt. Price, I mutter under my breath, for building Thomason College of Civil Engineering.

At about 10:00 P.M., after a brief stroll by the Ganga Canal, we are back to the hostel, and most boys settle down for a peaceful sleep but not me. I lie down and start to think of Saniya, and I suddenly realize that, the fact that I am thinking of her; she must be thinking of me also. With these pleasant thoughts swirling in my mind, I am not sure when I slip into a sweet dream. My table lamp is still on.

Sometime during my dream, I have a feeling that my Sixth Sense is active again. I have a sense of impending disaster. Although I cannot hear any noise, I sense movements outside my room. I get up to look out of the open window. Sure enough, there are fifteen to twenty figures moving about in front of the building. I conclude that these must be some boys who may have gone loitering in the town. I look at my wrist watch; it is 2:30 A.M. And then, it happens as I am still standing; a man appears at the window.

He whispers, "Open the door. I am your senior student," At the same time, I see some other boys in adjoining rooms being lead out of their rooms. I open my door.

He walks in and says sarcastically with a crooked smile, "Welcome to University of Roorkee... Your senior students have a welcome party planned for you newcomers. Come on, walk out."

I had heard of the innovative ways that the senior students adopted for ragging the freshers at Roorkee. I know that this is it; the ragging is on. What an ingenious idea—get hold of sleepy boys?

My Sixth Sense is now fully deployed.

I extend my hand and say, "Thank you. I would have loved to, but I have fever." The man instinctively takes my hand. I look into his eyes and give him the *Friendly Handshake*.

The expression on his face immediately changes, and he smiles and says, "All right. Give me your padlock and key."

He locks the door from the outside and hands over the key to me through the grill of the open window. In the meantime, almost all the 250 or so boys of our first year class have congregated outside and have fallen-in in three rows like in a military formation. There are a few senior boys commanding the formation, while some others are standing on the flanks, and a few are forming the rear guard.

When everything is in order, the senior boy commanding the formation shouts at the top of his voice, "Parade, Quick March."

A group of about 250 boys of my class follow the order and start to march in formation. The sound of foot steps is heard for a few minutes and then becomes softer and softer as the group marches away... and then dies off.

As I am unable to get out of my room, I lie down, and, eventually, fall asleep.

I start to hear noises outside my door. It is still dark. The boys are back. I look at my watch; it is 3:15 A.M.

Boy, they are back early? I am thinking. *What a short ragging spell.*

I had heard a lot about the ragging at Roorkee. I look outside my window and find Gupta standing outside looking at my locked door.

He is surprised to see me standing inside with the door locked from outside.

He says, "I was wondering where you were."

I hand over the key to him to unlock the door. I walk out and ask, "How is it that you all are back so soon?"

Gupta replies, "Well, how is it that you were left inside. Who locked you in?"

I reply with a touch of white lie, "You know, I told the senior boy, who came to get me: My father is a journalist. And if you take me along, the news of what goes on during ragging might get to the newspapers, and, I think, you will agree that it would not be good for the reputation of the university. So, I suggest that you lock me in and leave me behind."

Gupta seems impressed and asks, "Is your father really a journalist, or were you putting him on?"

I reply, "Yes, my father is the editor of LWF magazine. Have you heard of it?"

Gupta replies, "Yes, who hasn't?"

I ask him again, "But, tell me. How is it that you are all back so early?"

He replies, "Something happened while we were out there, but we were told that what happens in Roorkee, during ragging, remains in Roorkee. I have taken a vow of silence; my lips are sealed. This is the tradition."

Despite my trying to get it out of the other boys, nobody would tell me what happened in the early morning hours by the banks of the Ganga Canal—another one of the Traditions that makes this Institution great.

• •

The classes start in earnest. Civil engineering includes the design and construction of buildings, roads, bridges, dams, canals, sewers, water and public health infrastructure. So, in my first lesson, I expect to learn about one of these subjects. But the first lesson we get is in spherical geometry. Prof. Kulkarni carries on for two hours drawing spherical triangles on the blackboard with long formulas to follow. Some brilliant souls sitting in the front of the class are diligently copying everything from the blackboard, but most of us have no clue what he is talking about. At the end of the class, there is the question period, and I am one of the two students to ask questions. The first one is asked by a boy named Zaidi, and it is about the use of spherical geometry in the calculation of azimuth. After a brief conversation between him and the Professor, I stand up and ask, "Professor, sir, what is the practical application of spherical geometry?"

As soon as I finish asking this question, I realize my mistake. Professor Kulkarni's face glows with pride. Nothing fills the heart of a teacher with satisfaction more than the feeling that his students understand what he is teaching, and that they are asking questions and are engaged. However, in this case, nothing could be further from reality; no disrespect meant to Prof. Kulkarni, but the subject is so complicated for the students, who have been up all night bearing the brunt of ragging, that all the equations might as well have not existed. I am getting glances from my fellow students that tell me without words what they mean.

Prof. Kulkarni gives due thought to my question, and after a thoughtful pause, asks me a question in return. This is a very Indian thing–to ask a question in return for a question.

He asks, "What is your name young man?"

I reply, "Sir, my name is Vikram."

"Vikram what?" he asks.

I immediately realize that in this part of the country, the last name comes first. So I reply, "Sir, my full name is Vikram Mehra."

He says, "All right, Mehra, tell me, where are you standing at this time?"

I reply, "Sir, I am standing in the University of Roorkee."

He explains, "You see, you are standing on planet earth, where University of Roorkee is located. Would this not be the right way to describe your location in the Universe?"

As soon as I hear the word *Universe*, my interest peaks. I immediately come to the conclusion that Prof. Kulkarni and I are going to get along just fine.

"Yes Sir." I reply.

He carries on speaking, "And you all know that the earth is a sphere, the sun is a sphere and the moon is a sphere. All planets are spheres. In fact, there is no flat surface in the Universe. Therefore, for all practical purposes, we also call the universe, a celestial sphere. So, if you want to locate anything, anywhere, you have to know about spherical geometry... Any further questions?"

Professor Kulkarni looks at us with a gentle smile, and there is pin-drop silence. And I realize that if I have to unfold the universe, I will have to master spherical geometry.

· ·

Night follows day and day follows night, and so the time moves on, and one day... I receive a letter from Swamiji inviting me to visit the Haridwar Ashram; he is going to be staying there for the next two weeks. I reply promptly; not by regular post, but by *thought post*, using his own technique of Long Range Brain Wave Transmission.

I close my eyes with his face in my thoughts and think about the time of my arrival on Sunday morning at 10:00 A.M., and the car that is required to pick me up at the main road and transport me to the Ashram. This is the first time; I have used this technique on an experimental basis. Just to be sure, at first, I decide to follow up with a letter, but then I decide otherwise. I am thinking that if he does not receive my *thought post*, I can always walk from the bus stop to the Ashram.

On Sunday morning, I board the 9:00 A.M. bus to Haridwar via Kankhal. I get down at Kankhal at about 9:45 A.M. There is nobody there to receive me. Well, I think, even letters sent by regular post go astray some times; so what if my *thought post* has been misdirected. After all, it is just an experiment. I decide to travel the rest of the distance by foot. As I am thinking about it, my Sixth Sense comes alive, and I begin to read the thoughts of people walking around me, and soon I have a strong feeling that I should wait a little longer for the car to arrive from the Ashram. I stand there looking in the direction of the Ashram and down the winding road leading to it. There is a tap on my shoulder, and Swamiji is standing behind me.

"Hello Vikram," he says, "I had to meet somebody at Kankhal. Your message said 10:00 A.M., and here I am on time."

What follows is so strange that even to me—a practitioner of the Sixth Sense and all the related techniques—it comes as a shock. He takes out a telegram message printed on the regular telegraph paper with my exact message typed on it. He places it in front of my eyes and says, "Surprised?"

"What is this? I ask.

He replies with a mysterious look in his eyes, "This is the telegram you sent me."

"But I never sent any telegram. I just sent you a *thought message*."

He guides me into the car, sits beside me and says, "We will talk about it when we reach the Ashram."

As we get down from the car, I am sure that he is pulling my leg about receiving a telegram from me. We go into his office. He takes me into another room connected to his office.

"See Vikram," he says, "We now have our own telegraph machine with its own address. As soon as I received your *thought message*, I redirected it to the machine for typing."

I am quiet; not knowing what to make of his claim. Then he says with a mystic smile, "Today, I may be indulging in wishful thinking, but, one day, this will come true. When I received your *thought message* confirming your day and time of arrival, I just typed it out on this machine and showed you the paper, just to pull your leg and set a goal for us for the future."

There is sound of the construction work going on. I sit down on the chair opposite him at his desk. He is not one of those Swamis who sits down on the floor and meditates all day. He is a modern Swami of science and spirituality and works on an office desk sitting on a chair.

After some small talk, he asks, "So Vikram, what is new in the extra sensory world?"

This is the opening I have been looking for to talk about my experiments with my communication technique of the *Handshake*.

I give him the complete background of how I stumbled upon the technique after seeing, my friend, Suraj Rajpal, with an exam cheat sheet written on his palms, and all the experimentation ever since.

After listening to all I have to say, he says, "This is very interesting and could be very effective in what we want to do in the near future. This may be the best technique ever invented to win friends or lose them; provided it works. But, Vikram, how do we test the effectiveness of *Handshake*."

I just look at him and say, "Yes, you are right. The problem is that, for this technique to work, the subject has to be completely unaware that the technique is being applied on him."

Then he suddenly gets up and says, "Let me show you the progress we have made since the last time you were here."

The guest residence is now complete and fully furnished, the dining hall and kitchen is complete and operating, and the wood dome is nearly complete. There is a lot of construction underway. Tayagiji, who I had met in Verinag Ashram in 1954, is standing supervising some construction.

He walks towards us, and Swamiji says to him, "Tayagiji, do you remember, Vikram, Surinder Mehra's son? He visited us in Verinag. He is studying at Roorkee now."

"Of course, I remember," And looking at me, he adds, "So, you finally gave up your friend, Ginny," referring to my walking stick I used to have.

"Actually, she gave me up; my leg is fine now." What I did not say is that the day I met Saniya, my leg began to heal, and I had no need for Ginny.

As we are about to move out of the meditation room, I move closer to Tyagiji and extend my right hand; he extends his right hand; I look into his eyes and give him the *Nasty Handshake with the thought: I don't like you talking about my walking stick you idiot. Look at the pox marks on your face.*

His face goes white, and Swamiji and I walk out.

Finally, Swamiji takes me into the sanctum sanctorum of the Ashram—the laboratory building. He shows me the concrete vault built inside the building, and says, "This is where we are going to be conducting experiments in Long Range Brain Wave Transmission. We are going to be testing if the transmission of brain waves is affected by barriers such as concrete or steel. For your information, we have 90% success in being able to view distant unknown objects just by knowing the latitude and longitude of the place. We are close to acquiring the technique of *Divya Drishti* that is written up in the Hindu epic, the *Mahabharat*." After hearing this, I realize why he always talks about locations of places in terms of their latitude and longitude.

I look around the room; different types of instruments are lined up on laboratory counters.

"So Vikram, what do you think about our new Ashram?"

"It is very luxurious for an Ashram. It seems that it is meant for special people" I reply.

He says," It is meant for the VIP's—both Indian and foreign."

As we are about to walk out of the vault, I say, "Well, Swamiji……." And I extend my hand; he is surprised, but he still takes my hand; I look into his eyes and also give him the *Nasty Handshake* with the thought: *You are an egoistic Swami, you are not going to get anywhere with this. His smile suddenly disappears; he looks at me strangely and we walk out.*

Now I wait to see if my *Handshake* technique has worked or not.

As we have walked just a few yards from the laboratory building, he says, "You go ahead to the dining room; I will see you a little later."

He walks towards the meditation room as Tayagiji is coming out, and both meet and start talking. I notice them looking back at me.

I go into the dining room and sit at a table. A waiter comes and leaves a jug of water and a glass for me. After a while, both Swamiji and Tayagiji walk into the room and join me at the dining table. They look at me, but their gaze is very cold. They are talking to each other but ignoring me completely. I am convinced that I have the proof of my technique of *Nasty Handshake* in the two subjects sitting right across me.

After a while, the lunch is served, and, as we are eating, I am wondering how to break the news to Swamiji that he has been tested with *Nasty Handshake*. I do not want Tayagiji to know anything about this technique. The problem is that both of them are not talking to me. After Tayagiji finishes his lunch, he gets up and leaves. Now Swamiji is alone with me.

I quickly seize the opportunity and say to him, "Swamiji how did you like my *Nasty Handshake?*"

He looks at me and says, "You so and so… you got me. Yes it works. After you shook my hand in the laboratory, I sensed that you had said something nasty to me. All right, I agree that the *Nasty Handshake* works, but how do we know that the *Friendly Handshake* works. That is the one we really need in the near future."

I reply, "Well, there is no way to test it here and now, but I will think of something. Meanwhile, you can start using it. As long as you try the *Friendly Handshake,* it is not going to do any harm."

We then get up and walk over to Swamiji's office. I am thinking that there must be some reason why he has asked me to come to the Ashram in the middle of my studies.

Sure enough, he starts the topic for which I believe he has summoned me.

He says, "Vikram, you must have read in the newspapers that the American President is visiting India in early December, and with him there will be a large contingent of American politicians and businessmen. Hari Nautiyal has business contacts in America, and they are also visiting India during the President's visit. They are not part of the President's official contingent, but they are on a private visit. They have expressed an interest in seeing this Ashram and the research we are conducting here. We have a shortage of staff who can speak English fluently. I am wondering if you will be able to take a few days off from your studies to be here at that time. We are planning to invite them to visit us here from December 15 to 18; the President is departing on the 14th."

I reply, "I would like to, but I have to check my time table of classes; Saturdays and Sundays will be fine, but I will let you know about the other days."

He then checks the calendar and replies, "December 15 is a Tuesday. You know, Vikram, this is a great opportunity for India to make lasting friendships with influential Americans. We will need a lot of assistance in the development of India, and Americans and Canadians have the resources. Americans have been friends of India for a long time. Even during the British Raj, they were pressuring the British to quit India."

I say jokingly, "Swamiji, if I am here when your American guests come for a visit, I will give them all my *Friendly Handshake,* and they will all become friends of India for good."

Swamiji smiles and says, "I think this is a good idea."

The next morning, I take the 8:00 A.M. bus back to Roorkee; on the way, I get a brilliant idea.

29

THE AMERICANS ARE COMING
December, 1959

In early November, I receive a letter from my girl friend, Saniya, telling me that her school and all the schools in Delhi have been instructed by the government to close on December 9. Each school has been given a stretch of road where the students are to congregate to welcome President Eisenhower of America as his motorcade passes by. She has asked me to come to Delhi for the occasion; hinting that this would also give us an opportunity to see each other. It is, of course, very tempting. Earlier, Swamiji had requested me to come to the Ashram to help out during the visit of some of their American guests. I check the time table of my classes. As it turns out, it is also the week the Convocation is taking place; therefore, there are no classes. It is settled; I am going to Delhi to see President Eisenhower.

The newspapers and magazines are full of articles about America and the forthcoming visit of the American President. The young and old are talking about it. The upper and middle class Indians are enamored by America and the American way of life. The Hollywood movies are the medium through which they have seen America. The American movies are generally shown during the Sunday morning shows from 9:00 A.M.-12:00 P.M. at some of the cinema theaters in big cities such as Bombay, Delhi and Calcutta. Actors such as Frank Sinatra, Bobby Darren, Yul Brynner, Marilyn Monroe, Sandra Dee and Tuesday Weld, are names that teenagers in India talk about to show off their fascination with America. Movies such as 'The Ten Commandments', 'The Seven Year Itch', 'The King and I' and 'Around the World in 80 Days' are the best ambassadors of America. So when President Eisenhower comes calling, he needs no introduction, especially having served as the Supreme Commander of the Allied forces in World War II. Indians are ready, by the millions, to afford him a warm welcome.

As the country prepares for the arrival of the President, the life at the University goes on. I meet Prof. Srivastava at the end of one of the physics classes, and he says, "Vikram, I am going to the Ashram to see Swamiji on Sunday, why don't you come along also? It is nice and quiet there. You can see Swamiji, and also have some time to catch up on your studies."

It seems like a splendid idea to me; in fact, I am excited to be in the company of a physicist and a Swami. I have had some time to think about the *idea* that had germinated in my brain sitting in the bus on my way back from the Ashram a few months back; what an opportunity to run it by the two learned men.

On Sunday morning, both Prof. Srivastava and I board the 9:00 A.M. bus to Kankhal and Haridwar. As we arrive at Kankhal bus stop, we find that there is nobody to receive us. We wait for about fifteen minutes and then start walking.

"I had sent a letter to Swamiji about our arrival, and he had written back to me confirming that someone will come to receive us," Prof. Srivastava tells me, as we are walking towards the Ashram.

I reply with a serious tone, "Professor Srivastava, sir, instead of sending your message by Indian Post and Telegraph, you should have sent your message by *Thought Post*; it is more reliable."

He looks at me with a smile and surprise, and says, "You mean you also practice Brain Wave Transmission?"

I nod, "Well, sort of."

When we reach the Ashram, we find that there are five or six people, including one uniformed police officer and two foreigners in black suites and dark glasses, standing in front of Swamiji's office. Upon seeing the police officers, both Prof. Srivastava and I stop walking and are not sure whether to walk towards them or not. In the meantime, the two foreigners and the police officer climb in the police jeep and start to drive towards the Ashram main gate. The gatekeeper opens the gate for them, and the jeep drives away leaving a trail of dust behind.

We start walking towards where Swamiji is standing and watching the jeep drive away. As he sees us, he gestures by pointing to his head and putting his hands together in *Namaste*, appearing to be apologizing.

When we are within hearing distance, he says loudly, while still walking towards us, "My friends, I am really sorry. I forgot to send the driver to pick you up from the bus stop. I have been tied up in red tape of the security services. Our

Intelligence Bureau and the American Security Service have been concerned with the security at the Ashram as some VIP's, both Indian and American, are expected to visit the Ashram; you must have seen the two Americans with dark glasses."

After hearing this, I am glad that I decided to accompany Prof. Srivastava to the Ashram. I am excited to be in the thick of an international event such as the visit of the American dignitaries to the Ashram.

Prof. Srivastava asks, "Swamiji, is the President expected to visit the Ashram?"

"No," he replies.

Then, Swamiji looks at me and says, "Vikram, I am glad that you are here. Did you give some thought to..."

Before he can finish the sentence, I reply, "Swamiji, I checked my class time table and there are no classes during the week of December 14; it is convocation time. So, I will be happy to help in welcoming your American guests. Also, I just want to let you know that I am going to Delhi to watch President Eisenhower's motorcade. You know, Swamiji, all the schools are closed so that the students can line up along the route of the motorcade to welcome him."

He replies, "Well, Vikram, I am also going to Delhi. You know, there is a party at the Moghul Gardens at the Rashtrapati Bhavan to welcome President Eisenhower. Hari Nautiyal has been able to get invitations for your Daddy and me."

We move into Swamiji's office, and Tayagiji also joins us. When in the office, Swamiji and Prof. Srivastava start discussing the presentations that will be made to the VIP guests in December. Before this visit, I was not aware of the involvement Prof. Srivastava has had in the research and development of Braincom or Long Range Brain Wave Transmission. It appears from the discussion between the two, that, he has been involved in this subject for quite some time.

Swamiji presents his plan for the December visit by the VIP's. He stands up, walks over to a blackboard on the side wall of the office and starts to speak, "We are expecting twenty guests. Ten are Americans and ten Indians. The guests will start arriving on December 15. We will have a general introductory lecture on Wednesday, December 16, from 10:00 A.M. to 11:00 A.M. After that, I will offer to provide, one to one, training in *Mantra Sadhana or Mantra Meditation* or MSM, as it is now known in the western countries. During that week, Hari Nautiyal and Surinder Mehra will also be here. So, during the time I am busy providing training to the VIP's, you can all keep the rest of them busy with conversation and refreshments. Vikram, this is your chance to practice your technique of the *Handshake*. But make sure you give only the *Friendly Handshakes*," He jokes and he carries on, "After lunch, I will make another follow up presentation. In the evening, a visit has been arranged to *Har Ki Pauri,* on the banks of the river Ganga, for guests to witness the magnificence of the evening prayers in all its audio visual glory. On the 17th, we will have a workshop for those of our guests who are interested in getting deeper into the mechanics of meditation and other metaphysical questions. For others, we have arranged a trip to Rishikesh."

Then, he looks at us and asks, "Any questions or suggestions?"

Well, this is the opening I am looking for to present the *idea* that had germinated in my mind, while the breeze was blowing on my face, during my bus ride back to Roorkee the last time I was at the Ashram.

I raise my hand as if I am sitting in the classroom. Swamiji looks at me and says, "All right Vikram... any thoughts?"

I reply, "Swamiji, you had mentioned during my last visit that this is a great opportunity to make lasting friendships with influential Americans. I think after a year or two of their visit here, their memories of the visit will fade away. If you want their memories to last, we should come up with a method that will periodically refresh their memory of the visit. For that I suggest that we should set them up for Long Range Brain Wave Transmission. Each one of them should be given a personalized *Mantra;* I have named it: *Sambodhan Mantra.*"

I get up from my chair and move over to the blackboard and continue speaking, while illustrating my idea with a chalk. "In this context, by *Sambodhan,* I mean: to address. By that I mean *Mantra* with an address. Every person will have a unique address in the universe in the form of a *Sambodhan Mantra.* After repeating it over a period of time, it will become permanently embedded in their subconscious. So, whenever you want to be in touch with them, you can do that by thinking of the particular *Mantra* given to an individual and using your technique of Long-Range Brain-Wave Transmission. Periodically, you can send friendly *thought messages* to keep your influence on them alive."

After I complete my presentation, I come and sit down on the chair. The three of them are quiet and deep in thought—sometimes looking at the ceiling and sometimes at each other.

Prof. Srivastava looks at Swamiji, and says, "Why did *we* not think of this before?"

Finally, after a great deal of thought, Swamiji says, "I think this a great idea, and it should work. We will have to do some experiments to refine the methodology. You know, Vikram, as far as I know, there is no mention of such a technique even in our scriptures."

I reply, "Swamiji, it is all due to the latitude and longitude of this place that I am able to think of such ideas. It is all due to the sacred number 108-the number that results when you add up the latitude and longitude of this area. I have noticed that ever since I have moved to this area, my Sixth Sense has become much sharper. Moreover, I have begun to realize that everything in the universe is interconnected. The humans are inculcated in thinking of the universe in terms of parts, but, in fact, it is a continuum in which, *Brahman* the creator, pervades everything. Consciousness is present in varying degrees in all matter. So, if everything in the universe has connection to each other, then, it must be possible to communicate with everything; the only thing required is the address. I think, for humans, the *Sambodhan Mantra* provides the address. It is like a unique *manosancharan* or *thought-messaging* address for each person. Also, I have come to the conclusion that *thought messaging* is not in the realm of the material universe. It is beyond the laws of physics as we know them. It is not governed by laws postulated by Newton, Einstein or quantum mechanics. It is free of bonds of time and distance."

After speaking all this; I am quiet. It seems that I have surprised even myself with what I have just said. I am not sure where all the wisdom is flowing from.

After a while, Swamiji says, "Tell me, Vikram, how will we create so many *Mantras,* if a unique *Mantra* is required for each person?"

I reply, "By adding numbers at the end of the *Mantra*. First of all, I suggest that you select a *Mantra* with a high frequency vibration, such as... *Shring*; secondly, add three numerals to it between 0 and 9 using their Sanskrit pronunciation. This will give you 1000 permutations. If you want to have more choice, you can add four numerals after the *Mantra;* this will give you 10,000 permutations. e.g. *Shring Sunya eka Dvi,* using the Sanskrit pronunciation, or *Shring zero one two*, using the English pronunciation. But I suggest the use of Sanskrit."

Swamiji stands up and says, with his hands joined in *Namaste* and with a smile on his face, "All right *Guruji*, we will follow whatever you say."

By about 6:30 P.M. I am back in my hostel room at Roorkee, getting ready to go for dinner.

• •

At first, I decide to send a letter informing my family of my forthcoming visit home, but then, I decide against it, and send a *thought message,* instead, to

Mummyji. On the morning of December 8, I board the bus to Delhi, reaching home at about 3:00 P.M. I know that Kishi and Suneeta must be at school and Daddyji at work. It is quiet; it is Mummyji's siesta time. I decide to sit down on a chair in the verandah and wait for her to wake up. A crow comes and perches at the flower bed located on top of the front perimeter wall of the house and starts to caw. It is sitting just outside the window of the bedroom where Mummyji is supposed to be sleeping. After only about a minute or so, the front door opens and Mummyji comes out and is pleasantly surprised to see me.

She embraces me and says, "Vikram, I knew you would be coming home today; the crows have been cawing since morning announcing your arrival." And then, she looks at me, up and down, and says, "Look at you Vikram; you have become so thin. You must take care of your nutrition."

"No, Mummyji, I have not become thin; I have become taller," I reply.

She says, "I hope you are going to be here for a week; I will give you some proper food and make you healthy. You need some more flesh on your bones."

I reply, "Mummyji, I am here for only two nights, I am going back on the 10th. I am here to see President Eisenhower."

She says, "You know, even Kishi and Suneeta are going somewhere to see the President; the schools are closed tomorrow. So much study time is wasted in welcoming the foreign dignitaries. Your Daddyji is also going to the airport tonight to receive some people from America."

I reply trying to humour her, "Mummyji, the Americans are giving us so much aid; this is our way of thanking them. Moreover, it is an Indian tradition to treat our guests with honour."

"All right… all right… now come and eat something," she says.

In the meantime, Kishi and Suneeta have come home from school, and we all sit down at the dining table to have milk and home made biscuits. As I am about to pick up a biscuit, Mummyji gestures to me to wait; she picks up one biscuit and piles up a mountain of butter on top, and, then, picks up one more biscuit and makes a sandwich and hands it over to me and says, "Vikram, finish this, while I make another one for you."

While I am sitting eating buttered biscuit sandwiches, I am receiving repeated thoughts of Saniya; she is sending me *thought messages* asking me to come and meet her at our usual meeting place.

After eating two buttered biscuit sandwiches, I get up and say, "Mummyji, I am going to, my friend, Suraj's house." The fact is that I am really going to see Saniya. After lying to my mother, I am feeling guilty.

As I am getting up to leave, I look at the opposite wall and there is the picture of God Krishna looking at me, as if he is saying, "Vikram, it is admissible to tell a lie for someone you truly love, especially your soul mate of seven lives. Go ahead. Go meet her." Is it my wishful thinking, or did He really speak to me; I would never know.

I get up and walk away; still looking back at the picture, for I am sure He spoke to me.

When I reach the park where we usually meet, Saniya is already waiting for me.

"I have been *thought messaging* you for fifteen minutes," she says.

"Yes, I know," I reply, "But, Mummyji was feeding me buttered biscuit sandwiches."

She says, "Well, I just want to tell you that our school bus will be dropping the school girls off at Madras Hotel. Every road beyond that is closed; the inner circle and the outer circle of Connaught Place are also closed for the President's motorcade. We can meet at about 12:00 P.M. and walk to the inner circle of Connaught Place near Block A; that is where the motorcade is supposed to pass by."

Next morning, the newspapers are full of articles about America and President Eisenhower. Except Mummyji, everybody in our household is going to see the President in one capacity or the other. Daddyji goes out and brings two additional newspapers, the Statesman and the Times of India, in addition to the Hindustan Times, which is our regular newspaper. He does not want to miss any sliver of news about the American President. Daddyji and I are both sitting in the verandah shivering in the early morning chill of December, sipping *Chai* and turning the pages of the newspapers. The radio is also on—just in case anything of interest is announced on the radio.

While he is reading, he is also giving me a running commentary of anything interesting he finds about the Presidential tour.

He says, "Listen to this Vikram. The President watched a cricket Test match between Australia and Pakistan while he was in Karachi. He is flying to Delhi from Karachi, and is accompanied by his son and daughter-in-law. I wonder why his wife is not accompanying him?"

He carefully reads the President's schedule of activities and says, "Vikram, look here. See this party at the Mughal Gardens; both your mother and I are invited, but she does not want to go. But I am going." He goes on and on reading aloud tidbits of information.

Daddyji has to go to the Palam Airport to cover the arrival of the President for LWF Magazine of which he is the editor. He is busy getting ready, and Mummyji is busy in the usual morning rush of getting everybody ready and packed off to their respective destinations.

At about 11:00 A.M., I walk to the bus stop near the Liberty Cinema to board the bus to Madras Hotel. At this hour, the bus is relatively empty, the rush hours being early morning and evening; the seats are all taken, but there are no passengers standing in the isle or hanging on to the handles at the entrance to the bus. A cool December breeze, mixed with diesel fumes, is blowing across my face, and I am excited with the prospect of spending the afternoon with Saniya and watching the motorcade bring President Eisenhower to the city. As the bus is travelling on Panchkuian Road, a rattling sound accompanied by a bumpy ride starts emanating from the rear of the bus. None of the passengers in the bus pay much attention, as it is not uncommon for the Delhi Transport Undertaking (DTU) buses to make such noises due to the buses being old and the potholes on the roads. They are still known to deliver the passengers more or less on time. After the initial reaction, I go back to my daydream thinking about what to talk to Saniya, where to have lunch with her; the usual thoughts that come to a young man's mind about to go on a date during such an august occasion as the visit of the American President.

After a few minutes of the onset of the rattling sound, the bus slowly comes to a stop. The bus conductor moves towards the driver to find out the cause of the stoppage. A little while later, we are told that the bus has a punctured tire. I do not believe my ears. Another punctured tire, I say to myself, somewhat, loudly along with a suitable expletive! We just had a punctured tire in our car a few months ago while travelling to Roorkee. The bus conductor announces that the bus will not go any further. I walk along the isle to get down from the bus, and, for just a fleeting moment, the idea of asking for a refund of my bus fare crosses my mind, but I wave it away. After getting down from the bus, I start walking and hoping to find a three wheeler scooter rickshaw, but not before I make a mental note of getting to the bottom of the cause and effect of four incidents of punctured tires in my short life of 18 years.

When I reach Madras Hotel, everything works out the way it was planned. A bus full of girls alight, and through the throng of green and white uniformed girls, I am able to recognize Saniya from a distance–the distinguishing factor being her milky white complexion and her blue *billy*-like eyes. She notices me standing some distance away from where the bus has dropped her off. She walks towards me with a purpose in her gait, her blonde hair flying in the breeze, and as she is trying to control her green *chunni* from flying away.

At this moment, time dilates, and I have a brief peek into the folds of the universe and see us having beautiful children. And the next moment, she is standing right in front of me.

After lunch, we take up position in front of Block A of the inner circle of Connaught Place. People of all stripes just keep pouring in. In India wherever there are people, the hawkers are not far behind. Policemen are stationed every few hundred yards to keep the crowds away from the road. Every now and then, a police jeep or motorcycle passes raising the hopes of the people that President's motorcade is about to arrive any minute. Flags of America and India are flying from the lamp posts. A group of people are carrying a banner: *We love you Ike.* All kinds of rumors are passing around. Somebody is saying that the Prime Minister and the President will be riding a ceremonial horse-drawn carriage; another is saying that his uncle, who is a Major General in the army, has told him that they will be riding in a bullet-proof car, and the third says that his aunt's brother has told him that they will be riding in a car with an open top. Nobody really seems to know the time when the motorcade is supposed to pass by. Some people are getting edgy, but I am not complaining with Saniya by my side.

Finally, there is the rumble of the motorcade led by an escort of police motorcycles, and the applause of people from the south side of the area. Everybody is craning their heads to see what is coming. In a minute or so, we see a slow moving caravan of police vehicles followed by a long black car, with an open top, with Prime Minister Jawaharlal Nehru and President Eisenhower sitting on top of the rear seats of the car waving at the crowds. One moment they were there and gone the other. The main motorcade is followed by many other vehicles, and the people slowly start to disperse. Afterwards, Saniya and I go to the Volga restaurant for high tea.

As we are getting up after paying the bill, Saniya says, "Our school bus is going to leave at 5:00 P.M. We have 45 minutes to spend."

As we are walking out, I am thinking: I want to spend 45 years with you, and you are only giving me 45 minutes. As soon as I am finished with my thought, she looks at me and says, "What did you say?"

"I did not say anything," I reply. And then, I say to myself: My God she can even read my thoughts.

She says, with a blush on her face, "I know what you were thinking."

To change the topic, I say, "Saniya, I have an idea about how to spend 45 minutes. How about visiting the Hanuman Temple? It is almost on our way, and, after that, we will walk over to Madras hotel; you can catch your school bus, and I will catch my DTU bus home."

We walk by the Rivoli cinema, and we at are the Hanuman Temple in about ten minute. As we approach the front steps of the temple from Irwin Road, Saniya looks at the 100 foot high building with a spire and comes to a stop. For some reason, she appears uncomfortable.

"What is the matter? Saniya," I ask.

She replies, "Vikram, I want you to know that I have been brought up as a Christian, and my mother is an untouchable, and I have never been in a Hindu temple before."

"So," I reply, "What has that got to do with going into the temple?"

She says, "Well, I am afraid that somebody may say something—you know, with my white colour and blonde hair. Do you think they will let me in?"

I reply, "Saniya, Hindu religion is a very tolerant religion. See the top of the spire; just look at the feature fixed at the top in the form of the Crescent Moon. You know that it is an Islamic symbol on top of a Hindu temple. That should tell you something."

I buy a plate of offerings of marigold flowers and sweets. We take our shoes off just before entering the temple. I, then, hold her by her left hand, and we climb the front steps; slowly walking through the temple, we reach the sanctum sanctorum, which houses the self manifest idol of God Hanuman. Devotees walking through the temple are ringing the big brass bells hanging from the ceiling making a symphony of celestial music. Saniya and I standstill in front of the idol of God Hanuman with our eyes closed and hands joined in *Namaste*. Surrounded by the heavenly vibrations of the tolling bells, and fragrance of the flowers and incense, our souls become one for the next seven lives.

Afterwards, we slowly walk to the Madras Hotel bus stop. We say a silent good-bye and board our respective bus and go home.

Next morning, I take the bus back to Roorkee.

• •

Over the next five to six days, the front pages of the newspapers are dominated by the news of the President's visit. It is reported that hundreds of thousands of people turned out to welcome the American President on his way from the

Palam airport to the Rashtrapati Bhawan—the residence of the President of India—where President Eisenhower is staying.

Over the next few days, President Eisenhower takes part in many public functions. Among them is a civic reception attended by hundreds of thousands of people at the Ram Lila Grounds, just outside the old walled city of Delhi, where he is feted by the Mayor of Delhi.

"Mr. President, you have found an echo in the hearts of our millions," Prime Minister Jawaharlal Nehru says in his speech. In the days and months to follow, the echo echoes many more times in the form of editorials and magazine articles chronicling the voyage of Peace and Understanding by the American President.

• •

On the morning of December 14th, I take the bus to the Ashram to help out Swamiji during the stay of the American guests.

On the morning of December 15, five cars arrive at the Ashok Hotel. Each car has a uniformed driver. Fifteen men board the cars. Ten of them are the members of the American Group known as *Robus 10*. Daddyji and Hari Nautiyal are accompanying them along with three security men. These are the ten Americans, the members of *Robus 10 Group*, who Daddyji and Hari Nautiyal had gone to the Palam airport to receive on the night of December 8. Among them are Col. Jake Krieger, the leader of *Robus10*, and nine others.

Unknown to the Americans, they are about to take part in an experiment for which Hari Nautiyal and Swami Ravi Anand have prepared for the last many years. They are on their way to a tryst with the Celestial Sphere. The effects of which will be felt for generations to come.

30

THE CELESTIAL SPHERE

It is Tuesday, December 15. The fragrance of marigolds is permeating the fresh and cold morning air of the Ashram. Now that all the construction work is complete, the geography of the Ashram has become clearer. The Ashram compound is a circle in plan enclosed by a wooden fence. All the buildings are built along the circular perimeter. The space in the centre is a circular grassy plot. Concentric with the grassy plot is a water pond of 200 hundred feet diameter. The temple of Goddess Saraswati, the Goddess of knowledge, is built on one side of the pond. Exactly in the centre of the circular pond is a hemispherical dome of exactly 30 feet diameter. It is constructed of wood with no nails or any other metallic objects. All the joinery is tongue and groove and natural glue. Four openings in the dome walls at the floor level and clerestory windows at the apex of the dome promote natural ventilation and provide natural light respectively. A metal spire at the top of the dome is in the form of number 108. When standing outside the circular pond, dome and its reflection in water form a perfect sphere. It has been named the *Celestial Sphere* in English and *Aakaash* in Hindi; *Aakaash* means sky. Celestial Sphere is where *Mantra Meditation* lessons will be given to the guests.

At about 2:00 P.M., the sound of car wheels grinding on the gravel road, and the resulting dust cloud, announces the arrival of the guests. The first of the guests to arrive are the Indian guests; they are the members of the Indian secret group, *Shakti 9*. They are received by Swamiji and Prof. Srivastava. As the guests get out of their cars and are stretching themselves after a seven hour drive, the second set of guests drive in. They are the American guests; the members of the American secret group, *Robus 10*. Hari Nautiyal and Daddyji also arrive with the

Americans. As the Americans are coming out of their respective vehicles, one of them comes out and moves towards Swamiji and says loudly, "Hey, Swami Ravi. Long time no see! Remember me?"

Everybody turns around to look at the one who is on such informal terms with Swamiji; who, then, turns around and looks at the American who addressed him so informally. It takes a few second for a sense of recognition to set in, and then, with his mouth open in amazement, Swamiji moves forward towards the American with his arms outstretched and says, "Oh, my God, Jimmy. It has been almost twenty years. I did not know you were coming."

They embrace, and Jimmy says, "You know Swami Ravi, when you visited America a few years back, I saw a photo of a Swami in the Chicago Tribune, and I knew it was you. I tried to contact you, but you had left."

As others are looking on, Swamiji asks, "Jimmy, I lost touch with all our class fellows after I left Cambridge in 1939. What did you do after Cambridge?"

Jimmy replies, "Well, at first, I was at the University of Chicago, and, after that, I have been at the Argonne Laboratory trying to figure out what we are all made of."

Swamiji realizes that others are being held up, and he says, "You all must be wondering what the two of us are talking about. We were students at Cambridge in the late 1930's."

After quick introductions, all the guests are politely asked to gather in the conference centre for registration. The conference centre is round in shape with a number of tables and chairs arranged in a circle. My duties include handing over the registration forms to the guests, assisting them in filling in the forms, and, in general, looking after their comfort. Water and soft drinks are stored in two refrigerators in a small room attached to the conference room. Two waiters are going around with glasses of boiled water and cola. I see Swamiji going around shaking hands with the Americans. I can see from his demeanor and his gaze that he is applying the technique of the *Friendly Handshake*.

As the guests are settling down on the chairs, Daddyji gently requests the guests to fill in the registration forms. I am behind Daddyji handing over the forms and a ball point pen to each guest. The registration form contains very general information such as name, address, profession, business address, residential address and the address of the next of kin; the only peculiar information requested is the Latitude and the Longitude of their place of residence. In fact, this is the same form that is used at all the Ashrams run by Nautiyal Trust. As soon as they receive the forms, the Americans get down to filling the forms, but the Indian guests take the forms and put them away.

Chandubhai, the well known politician, says, "Swamiji, everybody knows me. What is the need for filling the forms?" Swamiji just smiles and keeps quiet.

As they are filling the forms, the Americans are mumbling to each other about the need for writing down the longitude and latitude on the form, as none of them know what it is.

Jake Kreiger puts down his pen, gets up and goes over to Hari Nautiyal, who is chatting with Swamiji, and asks, "Forgive me for asking; why do you want to know the latitude and longitude of the cities we live in?"

Swamiji replies, "It is OK; you can leave it out. We will fill it in."
Jake Krieger asks again, "I am really interested to know the reason you want the information in the first place."

Swamiji looks at him in his inimitable smile and says, "Well, it is just a personal whim. When I was studying in England, a few of us went to see the Royal Observatory at Greenwich. I was fascinated to be standing at the Prime Meridian, the zero longitude. From then on, I started looking up longitudes and latitudes of places. In fact, when I write a letter, I always write the longitude and latitude of the place of my location; sometimes I do not even write the name of the place. Now when I see, think or read about a place, I look up the longitude and latitude of the place to have a feel of where the place is located on earth. I feel that it gives me a much better connection with that place. Once I know the longitude and latitude, I can...."

Before Swamiji can complete the sentence, Hari Nautiyal interrupts and says, "Swamiji, why don't we show our guests around the Ashram?"

Hari Nautiyal does not want Swamiji to continue, lest Swamiji gets carried away and tells Jake that by knowing the longitude and the latitude of the place, he can view the details of the place from a distance. It had been agreed that the fact that the researchers at the Ashram have acquired the power of *Divya Drishti* or Celestial-vision shall remain a secret; the information may have to be used at a later date, if required, as a bargaining chip.

Hari Nautiyal knows that the Americans would give anything for the ability to watch the goings on in the Kremlin by using the technique of Celestial-vision, while sitting in the comfort of the offices of their Intelligence Agency near Washington D.C.

After the formalities are over, the guests are led into the courtyard for a brief walking tour of the Ashram. Swamiji himself conducts the tour, and the centre of attraction is the *Celestial Sphere*. The American and Indian guests, alike, are impressed to see the construction, and, especially, the reflection of the hemispherical dome flawlessly appearing as a sphere. What really floors the Americans is the interior of the dome; the inter-play of the beams of sunlight pouring through the clerestory windows with the steel cable of the Foucault pendulum suspended from the apex of the dome swinging back and forth makes for a very intriguing scene. Everybody stands around the pendulum, looking at the floor watching the pendulum swinging to and fro and knock off, one by one, and every few minutes, wooden pegs placed in a circle on the floor. The Foucault pendulum is used to demonstrate the rotation of earth about its axis. The knocking down of the wooden pegs on the floor demonstrates the relative movement between the floor and the plane of the swing of the pendulum. A peculiar thing about this particular pendulum is that the weight at the end of the long steel cable is a large brass bell, usually found suspended from the ceilings of Hindu temples.

As the pendulum is swinging back and forth, it is making a ringing sound similar to the sounds in a Hindu temple. Everybody is standing spell bound looking at the pendulum swing and the bells toll. My Sixth Sense has become very active as soon as I enter the dome, very similar to the day I stood under the dome of the University of Roorkee. I can sense some thoughts of those standing under the dome, but there is a strange lack of thought noise; something I have not encountered before. It sounds as if the thought processes of those present are at rest. After sometime, it occurs to me that it must be the pendulum... I think... and I think, and it suddenly comes to me that the reason Swamiji has installed the pendulum is not to demonstrate the rotation of the earth, but for another purpose all together.

I am thinking: *Oh my God. What a brilliant idea. I would have never thought of this. No wonder Swamiji is where he is. The swinging pendulum has opened the subconscious minds of those present, very similar to what the hypnotists are known to do; the minds of all the guests watching the pendulum swing are at rest and have become open to suggestions.*

As the pendulum is swinging back and forth, the time seems to have stood still, and I sense thoughts from Swamiji all around me. The thoughts of goodwill and friendship towards India have been planted in the minds of all present, the Indians and the Americans.

Swamiji's voice rings above the ringing of the bells of the pendulum, "Friends, I know you all must be tired after the day's journey. Please retire to your rooms and relax for a while." He continues pointing towards me, "Vikram will be your comfort coordinator for the next few days. We have an action packed program planned for you. I am confident that you all will have a wonderful and peaceful time here. I can assure you that all of you will take with you fond memories of your visit here and will keep them fresh in your mind for years to come."

With their minds open to suggestions, Swamiji's words enter the sub-conscious minds of those present. Unbeknown to the rest of the world, to those present, and to even Swamiji and Hari Nautiyal who had planned all this; the ten Americans are the first of the thousands who will be infused with the *Mantra* to influence their hearts and minds; the beneficial effects of this ritual will be felt by Indians for years to come.

The next morning, the guests wake up to the celestial sounds of *Raga Bhairav*, the morning *Raga*, emanating from the Sitar strings of the world famous Sitar virtuoso Pundit Shiv Shankar accompanied by Ustad Akbar Khan on the *Tabla*. As the high frequency vibrations of the Sitar strings and the beat of the *Tabla* float to the rooms of the guests, they come out, one by one, and stand around the dais. Daddyji, Hari Nautiyal, Swamiji and I are already sitting on the carpet. As the American guests walk towards us, we stand up to greet them.

Jake Krieger, the leader of the secret American group, *Robus 10*, walks up to Hari Nautiyal, and says, "Hari, are we in Heaven or what? Thank you for arranging such a memorable experience."

Hari Nautiyal replies, "Jake, we have arranged nothing but the best of everything for our friends."

As the Sitar concert is going on, the guests make themselves comfortable on the chairs arranged around the dais.

Jake Kreiger leans over to Hari Nautiyal sitting beside him, and whispers in his ears, "Hari, this is quite a set up you have here. What are your long-term plans for this place?"

Hari Nautiyal replies, "This Ashram is strictly meant for training of senior Indian civil servants and important visitors from other countries. We are being flooded with requests from different countries for training in Mantra Meditation."

Jake Krieger asks, "Do you charge a fee for the training sessions?"

Hari Nautiyal replies with a smile, "Yes, generally we do, but it depends on who is attending. Don't worry there is no fee for your group."

They both have a hearty laugh, and they keep on whispering to each other, off and on, through the concert.

After breakfast, everybody is gathered at the conference centre for Swamiji's introductory lecture on Mantra Meditation or MSM. Swamiji, having given this presentation numerous times before, is very convincing about the benefits of MSM.

In conclusion, he says, "The practice of MSM for fifteen minutes a day, at least once a day, has been known to promote peace of mind, increase the analytical ability of the brain and mutual understanding and peace. I will be happy to answer any questions to the best of my ability. After the Question and Answer session, I will be happy to provide one-on-one training in the art and science of MSM."

Jimmy Carson, Swamiji's class fellow from the Cambridge days, gets up, and says, "As I told you yesterday, Swami Ravi and I go back about twenty years. Swamiji and I were studying nuclear physics at Cambridge. The course work was grueling; in addition, we also had to work part-time to pay our way. At the end of the day, the students used to be exhausted. Through a friend, I learned about a private course Swamiji was giving in Hindu Religion. I decided to attend. In the course, in addition to the introduction to Hindu religion, Swamiji would give a brief introduction to Vedic Meditation technique that was very similar to what has been described here today. I started practicing, and with me many others did the same. The results were startling. Only after a week of practice, we started to feel that some unknown power was adding clarity to our power of analysis and thinking. The world of sub-atomic particles gradually started becoming clearer to us all. And when Swamiji found out about it, he remarked that when one is dealing with as sacred a thing as the building blocks of matter itself, one has to meditate and get closer to God, as the sub-atomic world is where God resides. Many years later, as I continued the research work in nuclear physics, I used to think that we owe a debt of gratitude to Swamiji for introducing us to this special technique of meditation; for many of the discoveries that I and some of our other scientists were involved in may not have been possible without the meditation technique taught by Swamiji. This line of thought was reinforced when we read about the fact that Robert Oppenheimer, the famed American nuclear scientist who managed the Manhattan Project that resulted in the production of the first atomic bombs, was a scholar of Bhagvad Gita, and that the first words he uttered after the first nuclear explosion was a *Sloka* from, Bhagvad Gita, the Hindu holy book."

After Jimmy finishes speaking, there is complete silence. Swamiji gets up and says, "Thank you Jimmy for the kind words." And he sits down.

After Swamiji's presentation, all the American guests sign up for the one-to-one training in Mantra Meditation. A place for the ritual has been set up on the floor at the centre of the Celestial Sphere. The pendulum had been removed overnight. The only persons present during the Mantra Infusion ceremony are Swamiji, the guest who is receiving the Mantra and me. A Mantra is customized for each guest. As soon as the guest comes in, Swamiji confirms his name, takes out the form the guest had completed the previous day and writes down on the form the particular Mantra given to that person. The guest is then given the Mantra by Swamiji by sounding it a few times to show the guest the correct pronunciation of the sound, and then the guest is asked to repeat it nine times. After that, the the Mantra is said to have been infused in the mind of the subject. The guest is then told that Mantra is, henceforth, not to be repeated verbally, but only in thought during the process of meditation. The whole process takes about ten minutes. In about two and a half hours, the fourteen guests, who had signed up, are given the Mantras.

At about 6:00 P.M., the guests are transported to *Har-ke-Pauri* by the banks of the sacred river Ganga to observe the *Aarti* ritual and the singing of the hymns at the time of onset of dusk. While the guests are settling down in a designated area before the start of the rituals, Swamiji points out the exact point that he calls: the *Bindoo* or Point108. This is the point in the middle of the main current of the river Ganga, the longitude and latitude of which adds up to 108. He tells his audience that the Christian rosary and the Hindu *maala* both have 108 beads and the average distance of the Sun to the Earth is 108 times the diameter of the Sun.

"Oh, now I get it," says one of the American guests, "That explains the sign with the number 108 on the apex of the Celestial Sphere."

The *Aarti*, a ritual of worship, starts at about 7:00 P.M. The bells in the surrounding temples start ringing with the singing of hymns by thousands of devotees. Hundreds of clay *Diyas*—the lighted earthen lamps—with flowers in them are set afloat on the waters of the sacred river Ganga creating a soul touching spectacle of sound and light, as if the heavens have descended upon earth. A number of American guests are seen to be participating in the *Aarti*.

Upon return to the Ashram, the guests go to their rooms to freshen up and later meet in the dining hall for dinner. The seating arrangement has been planned to ensure mingling of the American and the Indian guests. My job is to ensure that all the requirements of the guests are provided for. Cyril Dastur, the Indian nuclear scientist, and Jimmy Carson, the American nuclear scientist, are on the same table. They know each other even before meeting at the Ashram.

Jimmy says, "Once in a while, I meet some of your scientists who are training at Argonne Laboratory near Chicago. While America, Canada and Britain are supplying nuclear hardware and knowhow, there is always discussion among these countries if India would, one day, be making nuclear explosives."

Cyril Dastur replies, "As far I know, there is no such policy at present, but you never know what the future brings. Our efforts are only concentrated towards peaceful uses such as electrical power generation."

At another table, Hari Nautiyal and Jake Kreiger are talking about future plans for starting more Ashrams around the world.

Jake Krieger says, "Hari, Max Hoffer was telling me that your Ashram near Ottawa, Canada, is already operational."

Hari Nautiyal replies, "Yes, that is correct. It is all due to his efforts. As you know, he has known Swamiji and Surinder Mehra since the 1940's and has been very interested in meditation and Yoga. It is his plan that, after he retires, he will devote all his time to the activities of the Ashram in Canada and other Ashrams around the world."

After dinner, most of the guests retire to their rooms. Swamiji, Hari Nautiyal, Jake Krieger, Jimmy Carson, Charles Berger, Chandubhai Patel and Daddyji meet in the conference centre for a private meeting. The meeting has been arranged at the request of Jake Kreiger.

After everybody is seated, he says, "I want to share some information that has recently come to the attention of the CIA and the British intelligence service, MI6. One day, I just happened to be talking to an old colleague in the intelligence business, and he told me about it. There is evidence that the Russians are experimenting with communication by thought. At first, they brushed it off as hocus pocus, but then they decided to look into it further."

As soon as they hear this, the Indians look at each other.

"Are you sure?" asks Hari Nautiyal.

Jake Krieger replies, "Well, we are not absolutely sure, but that is what we suspect. Our Canadian friend, Max Hoffer, tells us that you are also working on this thing called... well ...I don't know the exact word in Hindi. It means being able to view long distance with divine power."

Swamiji looks at Hari Nautiyal as if asking: should we tell him?

Hari Nautiyal says, "You mean *Divya Drishti*."

"Yes, I think, that is it," Jake Krieger replies, and asks, "How far along are you with this thing ...Do you mind if I call it DD?"

The Indians know that Jake Krieger has got them. If they tell him the truth, they will be giving away the secret, and if they lie to him, and if he finds out, they will lose his trust.

Hari Nautiyal decides to take a calculated risk and tell him the partial truth, "Yes," he says, "We have nearly perfected the technique, but there are still a few kinks to be worked out."

Jake Krieger says, "That means that it is possible to do what we think the Russians are trying to accomplish."

Swamiji replies, "Well, yes, theoretically it is possible and the Russians could have obtained some information from the Germans after the War. We all know that the Germans have been studying the Hindu scriptures and have even translated them from Sanskrit to German and English."

Hari Nautiyal yawns and asks Daddyji, "Surinder, can you please arrange for some coffee? I think we are going to need it to keep awake."

Daddyji gets up and goes out to call a cook to make some coffee, but, after a while, he comes back in and says, "Gentlemen, all the cooks have retired for the night."

Hari Nautiyal says, "Well, in that case, let us have some of the good old cola."

After refreshments, Hari Nautiyal seems to have perked up. It was also a ploy to gain some time to think over the response. He knows that Jake Krieger is, sooner or later, going to ask the ultimate question.

When they settle down, Hari Nautiyal says with pride, "My American friends, I am happy to learn that there is at least one thing in this universe in which we Indians are ahead of you. Otherwise, we have to come to you for everything."

"Hey Hari," Jake Krieger says, "I have always maintained that you guys are ahead of us in matters of the spirit. We are only good in the earthly things. If we join forces, imagine what we could accomplish together!"

Hari Nautiyal realizes that Jake Krieger is trying to humour them.

And then, Jake Krieger asks the ultimate question, "Well Hari, will you guys teach us how to do DD?"

Hari Nautiyal wasn't born yesterday either. He replies, "Jake, when we were together in the jungles of Burma, we made a pledge to help each other's countries, and that is how we came to form these secret groups in our respective countries. Now, I think, the time has come to put our money where our mouth is, as you Americans say. Anyway, we are ready to join forces with you. We will tell you what we know about DD and, in return, you tell us how to make the Atom Bomb."

Hari Nautiyal drops the bombshell (pun intended), knowing that the Americans would never be able to deliver on his demand.

Jake Krieger is silent.

Hari Nautiyal says, "Well, Jake, I made you an offer. The ball is in your court now. Keep in mind that if the Russians succeed in DD, you guys will be sitting ducks. Imagine the Russians sitting in the Kremlin and watching what is being said and done in the White House."

Finally, Jake Krieger looks up at Hari Nautiyal, and then, at his colleagues Charles Berger and Jimmy Carson, and says, "Hari, America has given help to India in many spheres of life. Since our last meeting, the quota of visas for Indian students has been increased, immigration quota has been increased, nuclear know how is flowing to India, and, of course, we all know about PL 480 food aid. Total American aid to India has gone up from four hundred million to eight hundred million dollars a year. We even have Indian engineers being trained in nuclear technology in several American Institutions. But handing over the blue prints for making the Atom Bomb is not in my hands. You know very well that America is trying to stop the proliferation of atomic weapons."

There is obviously an impasse. Everybody is sitting and sipping from their glasses and wondering what to do next. Charles Berger, six feet three inches tall and 250 pounds, is the scion of the world famous Berger family, the largest property owners in the world. He gets up and starts to pace up and down.

"Why do you guys want to possess nuclear weapons? You are a peaceful and spiritual people," he asks.

At this instance, Chandubhai Patel, the quintessential politician, takes his white cap off and starts to massage his bald head with his right hand. This, usually, means that he is about to make some profound statement, and he does.

He says, "My American friends. In today's world, to be taken seriously, a country must possess nuclear weapons. There is a lot of prestige that goes with owning atomic weapons. Moreover, we are hearing reports that China is developing a nuclear bomb. Is that not reason enough? As far as the questions of our being peaceful and spiritual is concerned, we will still be peaceful and spiritual after acquiring nuclear weapons. It is just that we want to be strong enough to deter any rogue state from even thinking of occupying us, having just become independent of the British rule."

Charles Berger is not the one to give up so easily, being used to situations like this while negotiating big property deals.

He says, "I agree with you, but don't you think that prestige and self confidence come with building something yourself rather than being handed something on a platter. We can facilitate the flow of nuclear know-how and technology to India leaving the rest in the hands of the Indian experts. Your engineers and scientists, who are working at several American institutions, are known to be among the best in the world."

The Indian group is quiet.

After a while, Jake Krieger says, "Hari, now that we are here, is it possible to see a demonstration of DD?"

Hari Nautiyal looks at Swamiji and Chandubhai Patel. They both nod.

Swamiji says, "All right, gentlemen, all three of you think of a number and keep it in your mind."

Swamiji, then, takes a piece of paper and writes down the numbers that each one of the Americans had thought of. The three Americans are amused but are not impressed. Swamiji has done this little exercise to prime the minds of the three Americans. All three had received the Mantra in the morning, and Swamiji wanted to establish contact with the mantra to check that it had properly implanted itself. He, then, takes another piece of paper and writes down a long string of numerals and alphabets and hands it over to Charles Berger.

After Charles Berger had a chance to look at it for a few seconds, Swamiji says, "Charles, this is your secret Swiss Bank account number that even you probably do not remember. If you want, I can even tell you the amount of deposits in your account, but only with your permission, of course."

Both Jake Krieger and Jimmy Carson look at Charles Berger. His face goes red at being told of his secret Swiss Bank account.

After a pause to recover from the shock, Charles Berger says, "I am impressed."

Now that Swamiji has established contact with Charles Berger's conscious and sub-conscious minds, he goes a step further, and says, "I can tell you the colour of the leather upholstered chairs in the client room of the Swiss Bank where you signed the papers when you opened the account, and the colour of the blouse of the lady who helped you with the bank papers. Her name was Collette Ducharme, a Swiss French lady."

Charles Berger gets up from his chair and puts up his hands in mock surrender and says, "All right buddy, you got my vote. I think you have something special."

Swamiji stands up with his inimitable smile on his face and says, while looking at Jake Krieger and with a mock bow as if in a courtroom, "My Lord. I rest my case... If there are any questions, I will be happy to answer."

Jimmy Carson, the nuclear scientist, has been very quiet, just observing the goings on. He asks, "How does this, DD, work? Are brain waves like electromagnetic waves? Can you please shed some light on this phenomenon?"

Swamiji replies, "Thoughts and light are not related. In fact, one cannot shed light on thoughts. Light is a physical phenomenon and thoughts are non-physical. Light is governed by the laws of physics, but thoughts are governed by the spiritual laws. In the spiritual world, one does not ask questions; one just follows. All we know is that it works."

There are no further questions.

At 12:24 A.M. on December 17, 1959, history is made. It is agreed that the members of the secret group, *Robus 10,* of America will do everything in their powers to usher India into the nuclear club at an appropriate time, and, in return, the secret group, *Shakti 9,* of India will train American personnel in the art and science of *Divya Drishti* (DD) or Celestial-vision.

Swamiji's fame has spread far and wide. He has acquired a rock star status. Important and influential people from all around the world, including politicians, businessmen and movie stars, travel to India to spend a few days with Swamiji at the Ashram to learn Mantra Meditation; or for just being able to brag that they had spent a few days with Swami Ravi. In 1960, almost 500 of the most influential people in the world pass through the portals of the *Celestial Sphere* having been infused with the *Friendship Mantra*, as it begins to be known. Swamiji's global influence and, through him, the influence of the Indian secret group, *Shakti,* has grown exponentially.

3I

EPILOGUE

Now my written story ends. My single typing finger is taking respite from the worn out keys of the computer keyboard. The jumbled letters of the keyboard are staring back at me begging to be touched one more time.

"One more time," they say, "let us be a purveyor of your thoughts."

"Come on you flibbertigibets," I say, "let me rest. Whatever more I have to say, I shall convey by thought and not by punching on you little tit bits of plastic."

"Sire," they say, "we have stood by you taking all the toil you thrust upon us, and now you abandon us after punching upon us over a million times. Who shall say that this is fair upon us? Pray, let us also find out through your thoughts what happened after your written story ends."

"All right, my friends of the keyboard world, I will make a deal with you. I will let you listen to what I say, but you should know that I have acquired the speech recognition software, and I shall not punish you anymore with the punching of my one finger. Nothing personal my keyboard friends; it is just that the *old order changeth yielding place to new.*"

"Sire," they say, "your Daddyji used to quote Shakespeare, and you quote Tennyson; we find that rather strange."

"Never mind, just be quiet and listen; do you hear?" I say, as I put on my earphones and microphone and start speaking.

• •

Five Americans arrive at the Ashram in July, 1960, to receive training in the art and science of Celestial-vision. After a month's stay at the Ashram, they return to America. There is a regular exchange of correspondence between Jake

Krieger and Hari Nautiyal, but it appears that the Americans have lost interest in Celestial-vision as there is no mention of it in any of the exchanges. As all five Americans have received the Mantra during their stay at the Ashram, Swamiji is able to connect with them by thoughts. He comes to the conclusion that all the five Americans are engaged in intense activity related to Thought Transmission and Celestial-vision. After a great deal of investigation, Swamiji determines that the five Americans are located in the state of Florida in or around a coastal town known as Cocoa Beach, close to the location of the Launch Operations Centre for American space exploration program at Cape Canaveral. The discovery of utmost interest is that the longitude and latitude of Cape Canaveral is more or less similar to that of Haridwar, except that the longitude of Haridwar is east, and that of Cocoa Beach is west of the Prime Meridian; the total of longitude and latitude numbers, the *Celestial Number*, is about 108, similar to that of Haridwar.

"Do you think the Americans are using thought transmission and Celestial-vision in space exploration?" Swamiji asks.

Hari Nautiyal, who is visiting, replies, "Well, you never know. After all, Robert Oppenheimer, the American nuclear scientist, was a scholar of our, holy book, Bhagvad Gita. It is also possible that some American space scientist may be interested in Hindu scriptures. Swamiji, your fame has spread far and wide. Millions of people world-wide are practicing Mantra Meditation. I think I will write to Jake Kreiger and ask him."

A few months later, Hari Nautiyal receives a letter in reply. Jake Krieger writes: Ever since their visit in July 1960, the five men you trained have been trying to replicate what they saw and learned at the Ashram, but with limited success. In case you do not already know, two of them were psychologists, one was a physicist, and two were neuro-scientists. A few months after their return, we decided to build an exact replica of the 'Celestial Dome' that we saw in Haridwar. We found a location on the east coast of America near Cocoa Beach and built an Ashram very similar to the one in Haridwar. We selected this location as its latitude and longitude numbers are very close to the place where your Ashram is located near Haridwar. It just so happens that we are located close to the Launch Operations Centre. Now, do not get any ideas; we are in no way related to space explorations. I should like to tell you that I have moved to Cocoa Beach and have bought an ocean front house very close to the Ashram. We have named the Ashram 'Celestial Dome'. Local people are very curious about the Dome. They, at first, thought that it had something to do with the Launch Centre, but we told them the truth. Some of them have expressed a desire to learn meditation. Maybe, sometime in the near future, you and Swamiji could take a trip to Cocoa Beach and give some lessons and see a rocket launch at the same time.

As Hari Nautiyal finishes reading the letter aloud to Swamiji and Daddyji, they are all looking at Swamiji in admiration as he had independently concluded that the location of the Celestial Dome meditation centre was in Cocoa Beach, Florida.

Daddyji asks, "So gentlemen, when are we going to Cocoa Beach?"

Hari Nautiyal says, "Let me write to Jake Krieger to find out when the next rocket launch is scheduled."

Swamiji makes a face indicating his lack of interest in seeing the rocket launch.

Daddyji senses it and asks, "Swamiji, you don't seem interested."

He replies, "Well, piercing the celestial space with man-made objects makes me uncomfortable. We, humans, should stay within the bounds set by God. There is a lot of work to be done right here on earth. Why waste precious resources launching rockets into space?"

Daddyji replies, "Swamiji, you are a man of science, and science is the exploration of Nature. Man by nature is an explorer. Space is the next frontier."

Swamiji persists, "To me this looks like a rat race between America and Russia. As you know, President Kennedy has set the goal of putting man on the moon within this decade. Can you imagine the moon, the most revered of the celestial bodies in Hindu mythology, is going to be stepped upon? What is the need for going to the moon? Look around us. Half the world is starving for food and shelter, and the Americans are going to the moon. I have no desire to watch these smoking tubes of metal being thrown around the earth."

Daddyji's hopes of seeing a rocket fired into space are dashed even before take-off.

• •

During the Administration of President Kennedy, the relations between America and India are at the peak. Jake Krieger, the head of the American, group, *Robus* 10, writes to Hari Nautiyal that the American Administration of the time believes that India is a key factor in Asia, and it must do more to improve relations with it.

In May, 1961, the American Vice President, Lyndon Johnson, visits India. In November, 1961, India's Prime Minister, Jawaharlal Nehru, visits America for the third time. In March, 1962, Jacqueline Kennedy visits India along with, her sister, Lee Radziwill. Prime Minister Jawaharlal Nehru is reported to have said, "There is a psychological pull of friendship between India and America, and Mrs. Kennedy's visit has added to it greatly."

After completing my engineering degree in June, 1962, I am asked by Swamiji if I would join the research activities at the Ashram. I agree. There are two reasons: First: I am extremely interested in the research in Thought Transmission and Celestial-vision. Second: my girl friend, Saniya, has joined University of Roorkee to study architecture; thus giving me an opportunity to be close to her, as the Ashram is only about an hour by bus from Roorkee.

Later in the year, a very serious border conflict erupts between India and China. On October 20, 1962, China launches large-scale attacks on Indian Army positions at the border inflicting heavy casualties. At about the time China-India conflict is brewing, another more serious conflict between America and Russia has come to a head. On October 22, President Kennedy announces the discovery of Russian missiles in Cuba and a naval blockade of Cuba. It is a remarkable coincidence that the escalation of Chinese border dispute with India and the Cuban missile crisis take place in the same time frame. Russia sides with China in the border dispute with India. America is in a nuclear standoff with the Russians. The Indian leadership is rattled by the Chinese attack and makes a request to America for urgent military aid. America, notwithstanding its immersion in the Cuban missile crisis, responds with an offer of assistance.

Hari Nautiyal sends a telegram to Jake Krieger: *Now you know why we want the BS.* BS is the acronym for Big Stick, meaning Atomic weapons.

His reply arrives: Understood. BS is on the way.

Daddyji is sitting with Hari Nautiyal in his office when the telegram arrives. To them the message, *BS is on the way,* means that America is going to provide nuclear weapons to India. However, after a few days, there are reports that the American Aircraft carrier, *Enterprise,* has arrived in the region. Then, they realize that *Enterprise* is the Big Stick that Jake Krieger refers to in his telegram. Indian political leadership considers it a remarkable response to their plea for help. They are grateful that, in spite of the fact that America itself is at the brink of nuclear standoff with the Russians, the Americans send an aircraft carrier in the region to deter China from making any further incursion into the Indian Territory.

The opposition leaders in India are demanding to use the country's nuclear know-how to make nuclear weapons.

Jake Krieger's letter reports that there are some in America's executive branch who believe that America should be helping India to develop nuclear explosives in order to deter China or Russia from having any designs on India.

1964 is an eventful year in India's recent history. In May, Prime Minister Jawaharlal Nehru passes away. In October, 1964, China successfully conducts its first nuclear test. The Indian psyche is shaken up by the two events.

In November 1964, Hari Nautiyal convenes a meeting of the full membership of the *Shakti 9* group on the 20th Anniversary of its formation. The meeting is held at his sprawling newly constructed farmhouse in Chattarpur on the outskirts of Delhi.

When everybody is seated, Hari Nautiyal hands over the agenda for the meeting to all the attendees. As an unusual act, he proceeds to do a roll call of the membership. As he calls each name, he asks, "Do you speak Chinese?" As it turns out, and, not surprisingly, not even one of them knows how to speak Chinese.

"Well, if our defense preparedness remains the way it is," he says sarcastically, " we will all be speaking Chinese one day, and not in the too distant a future."

He then turns towards Cyril Dastur, the nuclear scientist, and asks, "How is life in the world of atoms?"

Cyril Dastur senses the sarcasm in Hari Nautiyal's voice and replies, "Nowadays we are not that concerned with atoms. We are having problems with neutrons. We are having trouble with the neutron initiator."

"What is that?" Hari Nautiyal asks.

"It kick starts the fission chain reaction that produces heat," Cyril Dastur replies, trying to keep it as simple as possible.

Hari Nautiyal has no idea what Cyril Dastur is talking about. To change the topic, he asks, "So what do your friends at Trombay think about the Chinese nuclear test?"

"It was expected. It was just a matter of time," replies Cyril Dastur.

Chandubhai, the politician, who has been listening with his eyes closed, is suddenly awake at the mention of the Chinese nuclear test.

He says, "Cyril, when do you think India will conduct the test?"

Cyril Dastur replies, "Chandubhai, we still have a lot of work to do before that can happen. Both the Americans and the Canadians are adding a lot of safeguards to our agreements with them to prevent proliferation of reactor technology to making nuclear explosives."

"Oh," He says and closes his eyes again.

After some more heated discussion about the only topic on the agenda—the Chinese— the meeting is adjoined. It is unanimously decided to facilitate the advancement of India's nuclear know-how for defense purposes.

As the members are standing on the front lawn getting ready to depart, Swamiji approaches Cyril Dastur.

He says, "Cyril, I have a proposal for you. If you spend a week with me at the Haridwar Ashram, I will brief you on our findings pursuant to the visit by the Americans to the Ashram. It will help you in your work."

Cyril replies, "All right. I will get back to you."

In February 1965, as planned, Cyril Dastur arrives at the Ashram. Swamiji briefs Cyril Dastur about all the findings of the last five years since the Americans had visited the Ashram in 1959 and 1960. Swamiji shows him detailed logs of readings of the brains of a number of Americans and Indians who had been infused with a Mantra during their visits to the Ashram. After my graduation from the University of Roorkee, I have been working at the Ashram for three years now. I also participate in the briefings being given to Cyril Dastur, as some of the work has been carried out by me. What really impresses Cyril Dastur is the reading of his own brain that has been prepared by me. After he reads the log, he is absolutely flabbergasted by what he reads.

He says, "Oh my God. This technology is bigger than any invented so far in the history of the human race."

Swamiji says, "Calm down, Cyril. We did not invent this technique, we merely discovered it. It was there hidden somewhere in our scriptures for thousands of years."

Cyril still appears to be shaken up. He asks, "Have you given this technique to the Americans?"

"Yes, but only a part of it. Moreover, they have told us that they are not really having much success with it," Swamiji assures him.

Cyril says, "Swamiji, do not under estimate the Americans. They may be telling you that just to throw you off track."

"Don't worry about that. The key part of the technique is not known to them," Swamiji says.

"So, what are your plans for me?" Cyril Dastur asks.

Swamiji replies, "We will give you training in the technique of Celestial-vision, but it will take at least a month."

"A month? In that case, I will have to make up a story to tell my bosses back at Trombay."

In June, Cyril Dastur again visits the Ashram in Haridwar. This is usually the leanest month at the Ashram for visitors, and, also, due to Cyril's visit, Swamiji has not accepted any other guests. At the end of the four week training session, Cyril Dastur has acquired a fair degree of capability to read and influence the thoughts of people around him.

At the conclusion of his stay, Swamiji gives him a rather emotional speech.

"Cyril, you have to promise that you will use this unique celestial capability with a sense of responsibility. You shall not use it for personal gain and only use it for the benefit of our country. Do you agree to take an oath?"

Cyril raises his right hand and says, "I agree."

Over the next several years, Cyril Dastur visits many nuclear installations in America and Canada along with his colleagues. He meets numerous scientists and engineers in the field of nuclear science and technology, and, using his celestial capabilities, he acquires the missing links. He is able to 'visualize' classified information by just being in the vicinity of scientists who have the knowledge he is looking for. Swamiji is getting postcards from him with pictures of different landmarks of different cities he is visiting. Sometimes he is at the Chalk River Laboratories near Ottawa, Canada, and a few months later, he is in the Argonne National Laboratories near Chicago. There is always a line in his letters: Still lots of questions to be answered.

And, then, in one of his letters, there is a line: We have all the answers.

• •

Hari Nautiyal, Daddyji and I are sitting in Swamiji's office in the Ashram in Haridwar. We are pleading with him to accept the invitation from Jake Krieger to attend the Launch of Apollo 11 on July 16, 1969, the first manned mission to land on the Moon.

Hari Nautiyal says, "Swamiji, this is a once in a life-time opportunity; an historic event the type which Man has never seen before."

Swamiji is very calm about it. "You can go. As I have indicated earlier, I am not in favour of trespassing on God's domain."

I have been working at the Ashram alongside Swamiji for almost seven years now. I have become very close to Swamiji and consider myself his personal friend. On most matters I see eye to eye with Swamiji, but on this topic, I strongly disagree.

I am just not able to hold myself and start off by saying, "Swamiji, please forgive me." And then I say things that even I do not know that I knew.

"God has created this illusionary World, and in it all the creatures, for a purpose. The purpose of Man in this world is to find God. He wants us to explore and go beyond. Try new things, make new things, find new things and grow and use one step of discovery to build another step of discovery on top, and go higher and higher and one day... find Him. He has made Man, by nature, a discoverer and that is for a purpose. Discover, invent, innovate and improve the human condition. That is His wish and that is how we will find him... We must seek... the TRUTH."

There is silence. Daddyji looks at me with surprise and pride, as a father would to his son. Swamiji gets up and moves towards the opposite side of the table and stands behind me, holds me by the shoulders and makes me standup and says. "Gentlemen, I have found my successor.

• •

In the early 1970's, the CIA learns that India is getting close to testing a nuclear device. Intense pressure is brought upon India by the Administration of President Richard Nixon to sign the Nuclear Non-Proliferation Treaty. India suspects that American Spy Satellites are keeping an eye on the activities.

In January 1971, Cyril Dastur is visiting the Haridwar Ashram; Hari Nautiyal and Daddyji are also present.

Swamiji asks him, "Cyril, when is Buddha going to smile?"

Cyril appears taken aback by this question. The rest of us have no idea what Swamiji is talking about.

Finally, Cyril gets his wits together and asks, "What do you mean?

Swamiji says, "Come on Cyril; have you forgotten that I can read your thoughts? Everybody present here has taken an oath of confidentiality. You can tell us."

Cyril is still quiet for a while, and then he starts to speak with hesitation, "Smiling Buddha is the code name for the first peaceful nuclear experiment. We are looking for a test site. It will be all underground; we do not want any leakage of radiation."

Swamiji replies, "It should be at 99; you know... Celestial number 99."

Except me and Swamiji, the rest of them seem somewhat confused. Finally, I ask, "Swamiji, why 99?"

He replies, "According to Vedic scriptures, number 9 is considered a divine number. In Hindu astronomy we have nine planets, collectively known as the *Navagrahas.* If the nuclear experiment is conducted at a location where the addition of longitude and latitude is as close to 99 as possible, the experiment will be successful."

Hari Nautiyal, who has been sitting in a confused state trying to figure out what is being said, finally speaks, "What if we cannot find such a location in a suitable area?"

"In that case we will have to be content with what is available and take our chances," Swamiji replies. And then he goes around his desk to a map of India hanging on the wall and places the point of his pen at a location on the map and says, "This is it. Here you will not have to worry about the American satellites watching you prepare the site because it is so hot during the day that infrared imaging is difficult, and, usually, big sandstorms hide the activity on the ground."

We all get up from our chairs and walk to the map; all of us are crowding around the map and there is the tip of his pen sitting in the desert in the state of Rajasthan.

"This is 99," he says with confidence and a mysterious look.

In June, 1972, the Watergate scandal breaks out plunging the American Administration into chaos. In early 1974, the American President, Richard Nixon, is close to impeachment.

India sees this as an opportunity.

On May 18, 1974, in the morning, the meditation session at the Haridwar Ashram finishes at 8:30 A.M. Swamiji and I walk over to his office. As we enter the office, the Telex machine starts to type a message. The message: Buddha has smiled. Swamiji goes over to his desk, takes out the register of important religious dates, and, after turning a few pages, he says, "Do you know, Vikram, what day it is today?"

I reply, "It is *Buddha Purima*, the birthday of Gautama Buddha."

"I wonder why the test is code-named Smiling Buddha," Swamiji asks.

I reply, "I think, maybe, because it is supposed to be a peaceful nuclear experiment; you know Buddha is associated with peace ......Swamiji, I just remembered something interesting; the site where the first American nuclear test took place was named Trinity—the Christian doctrine of God as three divine persons. It seems that the American nuclear test was related to Christianity and the Indian test to Buddhism. I wonder why?"

Will there be an Islamic nuclear test? I do not say this aloud to Swamiji; just thinking.

Swamiji, who is still looking through the register while talking to me, looks up and says," Vikram, when did you acquire this knowledge about Christianity?"

"Swamiji, Saniya, my soul mate of seven lives, is a Christian. Have you forgotten?"

The next day, the newspapers are full of laudatory articles. The general public feels inches taller. A nation that has been colonized for centuries has found something to be proud of. Having missed the Industrial Revolution, India appears to have entered the Nuclear Age. This is the dawning of the age of technology in India. The Gods of Technology are smiling on *The Golden Sparrow.*

Over the next few days, newspaper and magazine articles place the location of the nuclear test near the village of Pokhran in the state of Rajasthan. I take out my books on astronomical survey and calculate the longitude and latitude of Pokhran as: Latitude 26.92 N and Longitude 71.92 E. The total of the two numbers is almost 99. It turns out that it is the same location that Swamiji had placed his pencil on in 1971. Did Cyril Dastur have anything to do with selecting the location, or was it just a coincidence; we will never know.

On August 15, 1974, Hari Nautiyal convenes a meeting of the *Shakti 9* group. The meeting is scheduled for 3:00 P.M., after the Independence Day ceremony at the Red Fort, Delhi. The occasion is to celebrate the 30th anniversary of the formation of *Shakti 9* and the successful completion of the peaceful nuclear experiment. The meeting is held at Hari Nautiyal's farmhouse at Chattarpur. Not all members are able to attend. As usual, Hari Nautiyal hands over the one page agenda. There are only two items on the agenda:

1. Vote of Thanks
2. New Blood

Hari Nautiyal starts to speak with pride, "Friends, with the grace of God and with our friends from America, Canada and England, we have achieved what we set out to do 30 years ago. I will send a letter of thanks to them on behalf of *Shakti 9*. We should look ahead 30 years and decide what is it that we want to accomplish. We are all in our sixties. We need to infuse some new blood."

After the brief speech, some discussion takes place about the future. Hari Nautiyal distributes another paper to all present. It contains the ten suggested names of the *new blood*.

Chandubhai runs his finger down the list and says, "Nautiyal sahib, we all want you to be with us forever. You have guided us for the last thirty years, and we all appreciate your time and financial commitment. But none of us are going to live for ever. I suggest that the third name on the list be considered as your successor."

The others nod their heads in agreement. Hari Nautiyal collects the two papers from everybody and sets them afire in the fireplace.

Swamiji is reciting hymns in Sanskrit as the flame is oscillating back and forth.

"Sire," the keyboard alphabets ask, "may we ask you a personal question?"

"You may ask," I say.

"What happened to your girl friend, Saniya, your soul mate of seven lives?"

"Well... there she is sitting by the window doing Sudoku," I reply.

The Alphabets are puzzled and say, "But she is your wife, Sheila."

"Yes. She changed her name from Saniya to Sheila. When the time came to get married, I asked my parents. Daddyji agreed, but Mummyji refused permission on the grounds that Saniya's mother is an untouchable.

Daddyji tries to convince her, "Look at the bright side of things, Kamla," he says one day, "Just imagine what beautiful children they will have: white like milk and red like apples."

There is a tug of war, and, finally, she agrees to grant permission, provided, Saniya changes her name to Sheila. But this was just an excuse. I am sure what really changed her mind were the two apple orchards in Simla and 500 acres of farmland, just south of Delhi, that Saniya's father had already transferred to Saniya's name. For I clearly remember the day Saniya and I got engaged; just after the engagement ceremony, Mummyji says to Devika Massi with a smile on her face, "Now we will not have to buy apples anymore. I am sure Saniya's father, Douglas ji, will send us a few crates every year."

The keyboard alphabets are a curious bunch. They ask, "Sire, can we ask another question?"

"No," I reply, "I now must end this story. Maybe, one day, I will tell you the rest."

"Oh, please, Sire. One more question."

I give in.

They ask, "Sire, where is your friend Suraj Rajpal nowadays?"

I reply, "You see that computer you are connected to; it is made by, Surajcom, the world famous computer company. Suraj is the CEO and the majority share-holder of the company. While we are on the subject of Suraj, and, before you ask me more questions about Suraj, let me tell you that he did make a movie starring Rani Roy, and, yes, he does own an airplane. And just to satisfy your curiosity about my sister, Suneeta, she is married to Suraj. And if you have anymore questions, I will answer them in my next life."

But the curiosity of the flbbertigibets knows no bound, and they ask.

"Sire, the 500 acres of land that your wife owns in the south of Delhi must be worth a fortune now."

I reply, "That is none of your business."

They ask, "Sire, these secret groups you talk about in your story, are they still around?"

"No comment," I reply.

"Sire, this is absolutely the last question."

"No," I say.

But the keyboard alphabets are an obstinate bunch. They ask, "Sire, now that you have got the speech recognition software, are you going to give us away for re-cycling?"

I reply, "Do not worry my friends. All who are born, one day, must merge with the universe. You will have no different fate. You will disintegrate into atoms, like the rest of us, and then be reconstituted as new."

And now my story ends.

49195370R00176

Made in the USA
Columbia, SC
17 January 2019